The Lumberjills

The Lumberjills

Stronger Together

Joanna Foat

Merrow Downs Press

First published by Merrow Downs Press, GB 2022
merrowdownspress.com

This novel is entirely a work of fiction. Names, places, events and incidents are either the products of the author's imagination or used fictitiously. Any resemblance to actual persons, living or dead, actual events or localities is entirely coincidental.

A CIP catalogue record for this book is available from the British Library.
ISBN 978-1-915702-05-0

Also available as an e-book.

For the original Lumberjills of World War II – the women who fought from the forests of Great Britain. To those courageous and strong women whom I was so blessed to meet – may you always be remembered for your fighting spirit, and forever remain within our hearts.

Prologue

West Firle, Sussex
18th January 1940

Dear Father,

I walked down to the beach at Peacehaven today because a man who lives there said I must go to see an extraordinary sight. Of course, Viola didn't want to come as she was wrestling with a disaster of a painting. With these arctic conditions the sea has frozen over. For about ten yards out, the once soft flowing waves have turned into solid ice with hard white snowy peaks. Shame you were not with me to see such a beautiful sight against the steel-blue sea and grey-washed sky.

People were skating on the ice too. Do you remember how, when I was five, I stood on your feet when you skated around the Firle village pond?

I hope you are keeping warmer than we are in this draughty house. We have completely run out of coal and are burning the last of the dead apple tree on the fires. I am often cold and hungry too; I hope the war does not last too long.

The butcher has not come for a week and so the villagers have been out shooting pigeons in the woods. I have tried to catch a rabbit for dinner and failed. And now, to make matters worse, Tiger has got worms and an insatiable appetite, so Viola says we must leave him to fend for himself like the other feral cats in the village. She knows how much I love Tiger and that he's never been a good mouser. I've told her if he starves to death, I'll throw her beloved books on the fire. So, help me, I will.

Viola has barely talked to me since, except to ask for a cup of tea or something to eat. She could help with the cooking at least, since she is my mother. But she refuses to do anything other than read or paint furiously. The other day I made her a cup of tea and by mistake I spilled the tea on her arm. She immediately threw the murky glass of water for her paintbrushes straight in my face. Father, you must do something.

Since you left, life in West Firle has been dreadful. Of course, no one comes to visit any more. You know how people have never liked us – now people cross the road when they see me coming. So, I've been wandering off along the lonely chalky tracks, through the icy fields and climbing trees all day just to get away.

When I get back home, Viola starts shouting at me, because she's been worried. Then she stomps to her bedroom and slams the door. You must find a way to come home, please. I know how disappointed Viola must be in me. She wanted another daughter, more like Dilly – a freshly picked apple from the orchard: round, smooth and sweet to taste. But I never asked to be like Dilly; I am a bad apple, wind-blown and bruised. I am not the miracle child of the gods, which Viola hoped me to be. She prefers to spend her time in the company of Roman philosophers and Egyptian mythology, rather than with me. And so, I have decided to leave.

You call me a wild creature and know I am happiest when I run with the wind, dance in the trees, flow down rivers and warm my body in the sun. I am happiest when I'm outside in nature all day. So, I have found myself a new home in a forest. I can't tell you where I am going or for how long. But please don't worry about me, I can look after myself. And don't worry about Viola, I am sure she will barely notice that I am gone, and when she does, she will probably slump down against the wall and cry for joy.

Goodbye, Keeva
P.S. I love you!

Chapter 1

Keeva

23rd January 1940, Parkend, Forest of Dean, Gloucestershire

'Gather round, girls!' The deep-throated bellow came from the pompous man in tweed, with his chest puffed out like a woodcock.

Thank goodness the training session in the awful jodhpurs was over. Keeva caught her breath as the blood-red sky brightened with dawn over the frosty forest. Her muscles screamed, exhausted by the endless sit-ups, push-ups, chin-ups and sprints she'd endured that morning.

Hadn't she signed up to do butter-making, digging, and carting manure in wheelbarrows in the Land Army, not this? Those were the only things she knew how to do. Oh, and taxidermy, of course. She mustn't tell anyone about that. A girl's education was a subject that well-behaved people didn't talk about, like copulation and lavatories, Viola had said.

'Toughen you up for a new life in the forest,' the man who called himself Captain Blunt said, sucking on his pipe.

Keeva didn't need toughening up. She'd lived in the woods her whole life. She imagined Captain Blunt, with his plus fours and whistle round his neck, going off into the woods with guns and dogs every Saturday morning. Like the men on the private estate at home, he would probably drag a deer carcass back and a dozen dead pheasants just for fun. Her heart ached; she couldn't think about home.

'You're not finished yet,' he said. 'There's a three-mile race back to camp, via Church Hill, with punishments for last man, err …

girl back.'

Maybe Blunt was trying to finish them off, she thought.

Other girls groaned, so she did the same. She'd always wanted to be more like other girls. Forestry camp was her chance to prove that she was just like one of them. But, how much more could she put herself through? Puffing so hard, she couldn't think. She would get to know every long dark path in the forest in time. Now, they all looked the same. Which way was the church?

'Stand by.' Blunt pointed, whistle in hand.

Uncomfortable cotton chafed between her legs, and her breeches had untucked from her coarse woollen socks, which stuck to the weeping blisters on her heels. A wing clapped above, and a goshawk released its cry, kreey-a. Her father had said the alarm call was to protect the chicks in the nest before they fledged.

'Go!' shouted Blunt.

Gravel crunching under their feet, the crowd of girls burst forwards to find their way through the frozen trees.

'Run,' a girl shouted, looking back. Confused, Keeva still stood at the start waiting for the whistle. Run, she told herself too late. The other girls were disappearing off up the path in their fawn socks, beige jodhpurs and bottle-green jumpers.

Overwhelmed by the cold, she wheezed for air as she started jogging. If only her legs weren't so skinny. Her foot slipped and she jolted her ankle. She hopped, in pain. The others leapt like deer, vanishing into the forest, and she lolloped behind.

'Come on.' She swung her arms to get going. Her father's favourite saying came to mind, and the soft feel of his pea-green cardigan against her cheek: 'Don't follow the common herd'.

The girl who'd shouted back at her to run now lumbered up the path just ahead, hair swinging left right, left right. Another girl she'd met last night, who'd got a telling-off from the cook, thrust out in front. She was the girl with the cockney accent, called Rosie, who had snuck round to the back door to pinch some bread and got caught red-handed.

She wouldn't like to get on the wrong side of Rosie. She had a mouth on her. The only girl wearing the PT kit – shorts and t-shirt – Rosie looked like a proper athlete. The other girls had insisted it was too cold for shorts and t-shirts, so Keeva had gone along with them because she'd wanted to blend into the group. She had worn stiff, new corduroy breeches and boots instead, like the rest.

The path was steep, winding and long. How could she run two miles to the top of Church Hill as Captain Blunt had commanded, and back again, when her feet were in agony and she hadn't slept a wink the night before? The girls from her dormitory ran ahead on the path through the forest, beneath the tall pines. Trying to ignore the aching in her chest and her sore ankle, Keeva struggled to catch up. She didn't want to get left behind. She could see Gladys, the blonde girl, ahead; the first girl she'd met on camp yesterday.

Keeva kicked a pine cone from the path as she overtook a group of four girls from the other dormitory. Her legs had come to life, and she longed to run through the forest as fast as the frost had coated the trees. Rosie was quick, still way out in front as she sped up the twisty path and ducked under a branch. Keeva passed two slower girls, one wearing glasses, the other puffing loudly, her breath like bursts of steam.

A flick of blonde hair caught her eye and she caught up with Gladys.

'Are you all right?' Gladys asked with a smile.

Why did she ask that? Didn't she look all right? Don't be nice, or I'll cry, thought Keeva.

'Oh, yes,' she croaked.

She'd be just fine if Gladys and her graceful, long legs kept running. They jogged on side by side. She had in fact first spotted Gladys at Paddington Station. She'd watched the parents hug Gladys goodbye for longer than Keeva could hold her breath. All Keeva had had to hug was her canvas bag and her father's tooth, wrapped in one of his old handkerchiefs after it had been knocked out. She'd sat on that freezing cold and draughty train for hours alone, with Gladys in another carriage. She hadn't known Gladys was joining up like her, until she'd arrived at Norchard Station.

They'd both thought they would be joining the land girls to do farming. Keeva knew about that. She'd turned over the earth before, weeded the vegetable patch and picked off the snails and cabbage white caterpillars in their dozens. She knew about growing mushrooms, digging up potatoes and picking strawberries. She remembered the boys from the village feasting on her family's berries like pigs, taking advantage, never offering anything in return for their pink lips, fingers, and full tummies.

Keeva didn't know much about working in a forest, she thought, as she ran. She certainly didn't expect it to be like this. She knew how to make a fire and light the stove. She always did that at home. She knew how to split kindling with an axe, stack the fire crossways with different layers of fuel. If they had any coal, it would make the fire burn white hot for longer.

Did Gladys know more than her, she wondered, glancing over to her? Gladys smiled. The only thing Keeva knew about the forests was that you could hide there, deep in the trees. Discover where the mistle thrush sang and treecreepers hopped along the branches. You could stay away all day, keep out of trouble in the forest. Just as paths became overgrown and disappeared, people could too. If she wanted to, she could vanish there. Who would know? Who would care, now her father had gone?

'I've got a stitch,' Gladys said, pulling to a halt. 'You go on.'

Keeva slowed with her.

'You carry on,' she insisted, 'you're doing really well.'

On her own again, Keeva felt dampness from her sweat coming through her Aertex and jumper. Discomfort crept up on her as the path climbed upwards more steeply. Beatrice, the girl in the bed opposite her with the posh accent, trotted just ahead and flashed a hostile glance her way. Keeva wished she could have stayed with Gladys. Looking back, she saw Gladys rubbing her ribs ruefully, waving Keeva on. She would have to keep going. Her legs carried her upwards towards the church, now in sight, on the hill.

Soon she was nearly at the top, Beatrice and her flappy elbows the only obstacles in her way. Keeva tried to pass her on the left edge of the path, but each time Beatrice stepped in front, so she pushed through the low hanging leaves on the right side of the path. Beatrice blocked her again and tutted.

Keeva had given Beatrice a wide berth since meeting her the evening before on the staircase. 'Frightful, darling,' Beatrice had said, complaining of the filthy steps. Then, patting her ringlets, she'd insisted Keeva carry her new blue Louis Vuitton overnight suitcase from Harrods up to her dormitory, as if she were her domestic servant. She wished she'd told her to carry the suitcase herself.

'Excuse me,' Keeva panted as she tried not to step on Beatrice's heels. 'Can I get past?'

'Do you mind? Don't try and push me out of the way. Let's play by the rules of the race, shall we? Don't want to turn people against you so soon, do you?' Beatrice replied, as she raised her elbows once again towards Keeva's face to prevent her from passing.

As Keeva dodged her elbow, heat burned in her chest. Her breath came as a growl. Spotting a path that tapered off the main track, she ducked under a low branch, heavy with glistening hoarfrost and took off.

Keeva wasn't going to follow behind or wait to be laughed at. She wasn't going to be told to calm down and stop making such a fuss. She wasn't going to be labelled the difficult one. She stamped her feet against the slope as dappled morning sunlight appeared across the path. She was starting to gain on Beatrice. Head down, she grit her teeth. She pushed down into the cold earth while her thighs burned. Lungs rasping, she beat Beatrice to the top of the hill.

'Rosie!' the cockney girl shouted as she reached the graveyard wall at the top. A bearded, male forester sat with a register, smoking his pipe. Not looking up, he noted down her name. Rosie turned for the final descent.

'Keeva.' Touching the frosty wall, a few moments behind Rosie, Keeva turned and began her descent at a sprint, throwing out her legs, every step so light as she leapt downhill through the fresh pine air. Beatrice's sour lips murmured something on the way past. Not caring, Keeva bounded forward, leaping like a giant. She danced over rocks, raced down the flat mossy earth and skipped over tree roots.

The furnace in her belly grew until she felt she could run forever. Sweat dripped from her temples, streamed down her cheeks. She was racing at full pelt, just like when the lads from the village had violently turned against her and her father. She could run as fast as them, as fast as a gust of wind rippling through the trees, when she wanted to. She wouldn't stop this time.

Rosie hawked phlegm on the path in front as Keeva twisted left and right. Ahead, a fallen tree blocked their path. Rosie slowed and crouched beneath. Keeva hurtled up behind, looked for another way round, a chance to get in front.

No one's going to call me a coward, she thought.

She scrambled over the fallen trunk, slipping down the other side, and landed right behind Rosie.

Arms pumping, knees flying, Keeva came neck and neck. Startled, Rosie gave a surge. The path sloped away, down the last straight, wide enough for the two of them side by side. What if Keeva won? She ran as if her life depended on it.

The path narrowed and Keeva, just ahead, pushed a branch out her way that whipped back.

'Oh, you bugger,' Rosie heaved.

Oh no! She hadn't meant to catch Rosie in the face. Keeva's neck and shoulders tensed; Rosie would really hate her now.

She could just about see the last turn on to the High Street. She ran like a speeding hawk, turned onto the final straight. The three-storey forestry school stood tall at the end of the road. Parkend, her new home, strong with its pillared entrance. Rosie was blowing at her shoulder.

'Get her,' she'd heard, that awful night with her father. Not this time. She would keep running. She was the hare that sprinted across the field, the fox that darted across the road. She was galloping with the wind behind her, determined that this time she would not get caught.

Fire took light in her chest, her legs like springs, her knees flying high, just as Rosie grabbed Keeva's arm and pulled. As Keeva tried to shake her off, she tripped and lost her footing. She flew forwards, legs still running, bracing herself with her hands and knees and skidding along the road. Dust smarting her eyes, grit tore her palms and dug into her knees as she crashed to the floor. Rosie sailed by, running through the gate and slamming into the forestry school doors. Boom.

Keeva's lungs burnt. Gravel stuck in her ribs, grazed her chin.

'She tried to push me before the gate, sir,' said Rosie, holding up her hands.

Keeva's mouth fell open. She couldn't believe this. 'What a liar,' she muttered.

Rosie walked back. Her plimsolls stopped beside Keeva's face. Flat on her stomach in the middle of the road, hands stinging, Keeva groaned in pain. Rosie reached her hands behind her head, bosom heaving. Victorious. She wiped her Aertex across her brow and looked down with a sneer.

Keeva barely had the strength to push herself up. Her muscles trembled as she climbed onto her throbbing knees. This couldn't get any worse, Keeva thought, as other footsteps slapped down the road behind her. She expected Beatrice the bully next; she closed her eyes and sighed.

'Oh, there's the cheat, who cut off the corners,' said Beatrice as she ran past Keeva to get clocked in. Captain Blunt's stocky fist obscured his stopwatch, as he pressed the button on top. Beatrice gulped for breath.

'Well done, well done!' he cried.

A trickle of blood dripped from Keeva's hand onto her corduroy jodhpurs. More feet approached down the road.

'Keeva, what happened?' called Gladys, panting and laying a hand on her back.

'Nothing! I'm fine,' Keeva said.

'Cheats never prosper. That's what happened,' Beatrice added, with a scowl, before she grabbed Gladys's arm and pulled her away. Together they disappeared inside the large double doors.

Keeva caught the whiff of toast and coffee escaping from the dining hall.

'Off you go, please, get changed and go help the cook serve breakfast,' said Blunt.

With a groan, Rosie strode towards the school, pulled open the door and let it slam behind her.

Shaking, Keeva stood up. Why had she even tried to beat Rosie and the other girls? What price would she have to pay? She, who never wanted to win anything, had already made a huge mistake on her first day. She was the oddball who was never going to fit in. The lump of lucky amber in her pocket that her father had given her was still there. She held the smooth egg shape safely in her hand to help her survive in the forest against these awful girls. In less than a day, she had made the girls in the forest hate her. Already it was just like home.

Chapter 2

Beatrice

After the race, Beatrice's thighs burned with every step and yet the old woman still had trouble keeping up on the stairs. She'd heard the south-west had a slower pace of life, but this was painful.

'Is this the dormitory for the forestry workers?' Beatrice asked Missus Potter, as she walked through the door into the miserable room that she'd slept in last night; it wasn't a difficult question.

'Aye. Is everything all reet?'

No, everything was not all right, Beatrice thought. The women recruiting for the Women's Land Army had said they wanted high-calibre applicants with an aptitude for mathematics. They'd said they were looking for university graduates for an elite army of timber measurers, not a gaggle of agricultural workers.

'Is there another room for the measurers?'

'What's yer name, dear.'

'Beatrice Oxley.'

It was obvious Beatrice was more well-educated than the rest. She daren't admit that Mama had been right when she'd warned Beatrice that she would be mixing with rough working-class girls who carried head lice and all sorts of infectious diseases. She still hoped there would be some other girls just like her. Missus Potter put on her half-moon spectacles, pulled out a notebook from her apron and leafed through the curled pages.

'Room two. That's it.' She pointed a wrinkly finger to her name, 'Beatrice Oxley … That is thee, isn't it?'

Beatrice quickly read the other names: Rosie Worsell, Edith Walker, Gladys Goodheart …

'Zee you're in 'ere, all together, love.'

Beatrice sighed. If she could just ignore the grey blankets, which made the dormitory look so awfully proletarian, it might help. She must maintain her good manners, however upset she might be.

'Did you not zleep too good, love?' She patted Beatrice on the arm. 'Don't worry. It was yer virst night in vorest. Aft' a few days you'll vlump into bed and zleep like you're jud.'

'I beg your pardon.' The woman was hard to understand with her strange accent, which everyone seemed to speak with in this remote and backward forest.

'I zaid you'll vlump into bed and zleep well …'

'Dismissed,' Beatrice said, briefly forgetting she wasn't speaking to the parlourmaid at home. With the cold, draught, and rattling window, she would hardly sleep well. The tears, nose-blowing and bed-creaking from the other girls last night was like a nightmare. She'd never had such a disturbed night as she'd had in the bed by the draughty window; one which she did not want to repeat.

'Oh well, one must make the best of it,' she muttered to herself as Missus Potter quickly left to return downstairs. Beatrice had to try out as a timber measurer, whether she wanted to stay here or not. Beatrice had fought long and hard to go to the University of Liverpool to study maths. Her mother didn't believe in wasting money on a girl's education, and at the first inkling of war, she had pulled her out of her course. Maybe here she could put her mathematical ability to good use.

Besides, Beatrice rather wanted to sport those daring and adventurous breeches. The curvaceous hips on the jodhpurs seemed made for her. So, she resigned herself to the fact that these coarse blankets, hollow floorboards, and off-colour walls would be her abode for the next two months. She hoped the fire would warm up her feet. But even that had a feeble glow from the dwindling logs in the grate. She was used to well-stacked fires at home, which the other girls would probably not have had.

'Everything all right?' the golden-haired girl asked.

'Fine, just fine.' Beatrice wondered whether she would catch on that everything was, of course, not fine.

The rest of the girls who had arrived on the same train as Beatrice were sitting on the beds chatting about the introduction of rationing in the last few weeks, which had barely affected her family. Her mother said she is in good favour with the fishmongers in Witley Bay and the local gamekeepers. If things got really bad, her mother said she'd go out and shoot the deer herself. But anyway, Beatrice didn't want to think about her irritable bowel, which was her euphemism for her mother. She was more interested in the empty bed opposite, next to the fire. She straightened up her suitcases and noticed Goldilocks admiring her stylish blue luggage.

'Beatrice,' she said to the girl, extending her hand.

'Gladys. Pleased to meet you.'

'How do you do?' Beatrice replied.

She couldn't help but notice over Gladys's shoulder that the wild red-haired girl, with the grubby hands, still hadn't returned to the dormitory. She hadn't been there after the classroom administration that morning, after lunch, or after the basics of forestry session in the afternoon. In fact, she hadn't seen much of her all day. No doubt the girl was ashamed of cheating on the final race back to camp.

'Where's that girl? Has she left already?' Beatrice asked, pointing towards the empty bed.

'Keeva. I think she was getting her cuts and grazes cleaned up by Missus Potter,' said Gladys.

'Oh yes, I did see her downstairs.'

Just a minute, Beatrice didn't remember seeing the name, Keeva, on the room list. She looked at the unattended bed by the fire and imagined herself in it – snuggling up in her silky pyjamas – instead of the one she'd been stuck with the previous night. She would have to take decisive action before Keeva returned to the room. If Keeva had minded where she slept, she would have made her bed properly. Between finger and thumb, she removed Keeva's grubby nightshirt and canvas bag from the bed and kicked them across the floor with the battered cardboard suitcase. Then Beatrice yanked her own floral eiderdown, and a blanket, from her old bed and claimed her new bed by the fire.

Beatrice rearranged her cases, three pairs of shoes and her slippers under the bed. The pyjamas slipped under her pillow; the art nouveau silver picture frame stood proudly with a photo of her parents on her bedside table. Once Beatrice had settled down on her new bed, she pulled out her decorative cake tin, which sparkled in the candlelight.

A quiet fell upon the room, and Keeva crept in with a large purple graze on her chin and white bandages on her hands. Beatrice watched Keeva hesitate, then slowly pick up her bag and case from the floor. She passed her old bed and made her way to a vacant bed in the dark corner at the far end of the dormitory. That's better, thought Beatrice.

As she watched, Beatrice grabbed a large slice of rich fruit cake from her tin and put it on her handkerchief on her lap. As she ate, she dabbed away the crumbs from her mouth. She could hear herself chewing in the silence of the room.

Keeva's hunched figure stood up and dragged the blankets, pillow, and sheet from the draughty bed where Beatrice had slept last night. Even her hands were trembling, Keeva was like a sorry soul.

When Beatrice had finished her cake, she dropped the metal

lid to the floor with a loud clang. The lid rolled like a hoop round and round before it stopped. She put the tin away in her suitcase, content that she was better prepared than the other girls, especially as she'd noticed the overweight one staring at her as she ate.

'I'm starving,' said the dumpling of a girl. 'The dinner didn't barely touch the sides.'

Beatrice gave her a conciliatory yet knowing smile. She wasn't going to share her cake.

'Oh flippin' 'ek, it's freezing in 'ere,' said the cockney girl with pouty lips, striding into the dormitory. The door slammed behind her on the wind, and someone screamed in fright: the poor girl with dark hair and an unsightly mole on her cheek had nearly knocked her glasses off, waving her arms around in alarm. How dreadful to be born with such a nervous disposition and atrocity to mark her face.

Pouty on the other hand was tall and apparently confident as she stood between her bed and Beatrice, warming herself by the fire. She had a shapely bust and was not afraid to stand up straight. The way she wore her hair short made her look boyish, but not unattractive. She was a curious-looking creature who had the frame to model a pair of riding boots, jodhpurs and jacket well. Shame about her dreadfully common accent.

'Well, it's a lot warmer since Keeva lit the fire earlier,' the blonde girl said to Pouty.

Beatrice wondered if Gladys's comment meant she had been pals with the red-haired girl and they'd purposely chosen beds side by side. Beatrice observed the girl they called Keeva, who was now in the furthest corner from Gladys, having made up her bed. She was rummaging inside her bag as though she'd lost something.

Beatrice noticed Rosie begin to undress for bed. She was in such close quarters that if Beatrice was not careful, she'd see more than she wanted to. Rosie pulled off her jumper and shirt, revealing her vested bosoms beneath. Beatrice diverted her gaze.

'Well, this is cosy by the fire, ain't it? We ought to get to know each other. I'll start. I'm Rosie and I come from Hackney in London, a rough part of town,' Pouty said, removing her skirt and revealing her knickers. Beatrice didn't know where to look and worried how she herself would manage to get changed demurely.

'Oh London,' Beatrice replied, 'Frederick, my brother, went to University College London. Do you know it? Wonderful facilities; offers world-class education. Frederick firmly believes it will help him to excel in his career and that is exactly what our family aspires to. Do you know it, Rosie?' Beatrice didn't think she would.

'I live in London, I'm not a university professor,' Rosie said.

'Oh, I'm surprised you haven't heard of its excellent reputation. And your father, Rosie, what does he do?' she asked loudly, keen to confirm her suspicions that Rosie was from a working-class family and would need putting in her place.

'He's a street cleaner and does boot mending,' she answered to Beatrice's horror.

'Oh, a tradesman,' she said, generously.

'My father already did his bit for this country, he fought in the first war. Can you say the same for your father, Beatrice, or is he too posh to fight?'

'My father is commanding officer in a mobile division in Egypt. One does worry, but not without feeling dreadfully proud. He is protecting our nation at war.'

Too late, Beatrice realised she had foolishly divulged her father's top-secret location. She looked to see who was listening and caught the eye of the girl with the mole on her cheek and the old-fashioned black-rimmed glasses at the end.

'My name is Gladys and I come from Cornwall,' said the blonde girl in the bed beside her, next to the door. 'I've got two brothers, and both have signed up with the army. I miss them terribly and they've only been gone a few months.'

'… And mother's doing her best to keep the two houses running,' said Beatrice, 'with all the staff she must manage. It's a dreadful worry to her, keeping those people employed during such difficult times.'

The pouty girl, Rosie, was listening with eyes on stalks.

'And you, Rosie, what did you do?' asked Beatrice, suspecting she was a domestic.

'I worked in a glass bottle factory, making baby bottles and poison bottles. I had to be careful they didn't get mixed up.' Rosie winked at her, as she got into bed and turned her back.

Goodness, Beatrice thought, how rude. She climbed into bed herself and pulled up the covers to her chest. She'd get changed safely under the covers, once the others were all settled in bed.

'Mother brought me home from university when the war started. I was studying mathematics. Dreadful shame, as I was rather enjoying it,' said Beatrice to the room. 'You three at the end, we haven't been introduced yet.'

'I'm Lily,' said the overweight girl.

'I'm Edith,' said the girl with the mole and glasses.

'I'm Hazel,' said the third, a bright-eyed girl with a strong Yorkshire accent.

'Hazel, how interesting, you do look like my parlourmaid Edna. What did you do?'

'I worked in t' woollen mills before.'

'And what jobs have you been recruited for?' Beatrice asked.

'Oi, do you mind? Some of us are trying to get some sleep here,' interrupted Rosie.

A minute ago, Rosie was keen get to know everyone, Beatrice

thought; now she's changed her tune, hasn't she? She realised the girl with the red hair, Keeva, still hadn't said a word. Had she lost her tongue?

Just then, Keeva crept over and picked up a log from the basket.

'I don't think that fire will last the night,' said Beatrice.

'I'm loading it up again,' she replied.

'Very good, thank you.' Beatrice was used to managing sulky domestics. But Keeva seemed a little more odd than usual, the way she walked barefoot, clearly never brushed her hair and stacked the fire with her bare hands, in an almost careless manner. Beatrice would never let Edna get away with that back at home.

When Keeva returned to her bed, she removed her clothes and stood bare-chested briefly, while she found her nightshirt. Goodness! Beatrice could see the girl had nothing much to show, unlike her own generous breasts, but at last the little imp covered herself. The curious creature climbed under the covers and pulled the blankets over her head. What on earth was she doing under those covers? Did she have something to hide?

Her attention moved to Edith, the girl with the glasses and mole, opposite Keeva. She had a pointy nose and thin lips and reminded her of a mouse. She was reading a letter by candlelight, so quietly that Beatrice barely noticed her presence in the shadows of the dormitory. She was quite pretty, despite the mark on her face, which didn't look so pronounced in the dark. She had a stubborn look about her, she thought, just as Edith looked up in her direction, as if she sensed she was being watched.

'Reading letters already,' Beatrice chortled. 'You've only just left home.'

Edith didn't smile and put her letter away. Beatrice felt snubbed. Would she ever feel that she belonged here with these rude, inarticulate, and ill-educated women? But, she reminded herself, she must remember the rules of etiquette and decorum, even if others didn't. Generosity, appreciation, respect for others, giving and receiving compliments. She'd ask one more question, just to show she was interested in others, even though she was tired. She knew sometimes she had to try to be charitable to others less fortunate than herself. Even though her mother said she was *très pénible*, she was a good sort, after all, wasn't she?

'And, and y … you, Edith, where is home for you?' Why had that blessed stammer come out now, Beatrice worried.

'Barnsley,' Edith said and pulled her blankets over her shoulders.

'Blow your candle out, Edith, we've all got to sleep,' Rosie said.

Chapter 3

Rosie

Blakeney Hill Woods, Forest of Dean

A torrent of dead leaves from beneath the trees flew at Rosie on the icy January wind the following day.

'Watch out!' yelled Rosie as a timber truck carrying enormous trees rumbled right behind her. Teeth chattering, she dashed across the road to catch up with the other twenty or so girls entering the woods. She caught up with the red head as she skulked up the path into the forest. Keeva, that was her name, she recalled, after a moment.

'It's flipping freezing,' Rosie said, licking her sore lips.

She wished she'd brought the tub of Vaseline with her. Her friend, Bets, from back home, had recommended it for all minor cases of cuts, burns, scalds, bruises, and sore places. They used to have a laugh about the miracle molecules in Vaseline. Bets said that's why Rosie had the biggest bosoms.

The wild-looking creature with freckles, and bandages on her hands, avoided her eye and walked ahead. Impulsively, the girl swung on a branch then shook her hands, as if they hurt.

'You need a bit of Vaseline for those 'ands,' Rosie said.

Keeva didn't even turn round.

Well, don't go swinging on trees then, Rosie thought. She'd met moody girls like her at the factory before. Whereas the plump girl, who'd eaten a bit too much give and take, but just about squeezed into the same brown woollen coat as the other girls, was much more friendly.

'Chilly, ain't it?' Rosie said, as she dashed up beside the girl.

'I'm called Lily, actually,' she replied.

Rosie smiled. 'I mean it's cold, chilly like.'

She turned round to see Keeva disappear from the path, like a lone wolf slinking into the woods.

'I'm Rosie.' Even with her old man's long johns cut down to size, all her jumpers, overcoat, and beret, she was frozen stiff.

'I'm lucky I don't feel the cold,' the big girl, Lily, replied. 'I'm used to working on a farm.'

She could obviously eat clotted cream until the cows came home, Rosie thought. They must look odd walking side by side, Lily so over-stuffed, while she was as thin as a rake.

'I guess you 'ad enough food living on a farm too,' asked Rosie, imagining chickens and pigs like she'd seen in a book once.

'It's a hard life on a farm but we've always had enough food,' Lily replied.

There was never enough bread to go round at home with her four brothers there; Rosie rarely had enough money to buy them one whole potato each.

Woodsmoke drifted on the air through the trees, as they went deeper into the forest. Rosie longed to be sitting by the hearth back at home. For a fleeting moment little Ben, her youngest brother, was sitting on her lap. Warm and toasty, soft pink skin, cuddled up to her, yelping as she combed his scrap of hair. Those were golden bedtimes, singing bedtime songs, except when her old man came home on a jug of wallop. He'd stalk round the kitchen, sucking the happiness out of the air, waiting for one of them to look at him like that.

Another girl from her room, the one with the round black glasses, called Edith, looked over at her. She looked bookish, not much fun. Rosie couldn't imagine being mates with her. She missed Bets and the other girls. She imagined them waiting for the factory gates on Chatsworth Road to open about now, as she had done since she was fourteen.

The bare silhouetted trees stood out against the washed-out grey sky, as she watched the girls disappear into the forest ahead. She imagined the smog-black factory buildings, Mr Paterson clanging the keys against the metal post and unlocking the gates. She'd never imagined she'd miss the factory, where she'd expected to go from making Allen and Hanbury baby bottles to using the banana-shaped Allenbury feeder for her own babies one day. She honestly had no idea she'd be out in the wilds of a Gloucestershire forest about to chop down trees for the war effort with a group of girls she barely knew.

At least in the factory Rosie would head straight indoors out of the cold, clock in with her friends and stand in line by her workstation. She'd pretend to be busy making sure everything was clean of bits of glass and stuff. And then every day Bets would nudge up beside her gently. All right, Rosie, she'd say. They were packed in close enough to each other that with the racket of the clinking bottles they could chat on without getting caught.

'Don't you love the smell of that woodsmoke?' said Lily to Rosie.

'Oh, yes, can't beat a good fire,' she replied.

'I hope that fire is for us,' Lily said. 'So, we can have a lovely cup of tea and w …'

The biting wind on the trees blew her words away.

Rosie pulled up her collar. 'It's wild out here,' she shouted to raise her voice above the wind.

'I've never been as far away from home before. The Forest of Dean is like the end of the world,' Lily said.

'Like the middle of flippin' nowhere,' Rosie agreed. 'Don't get lost, we'll never find you again.'

She'd heard there were a lot of trees on Hackney Marshes, but this was something else. Her elder brothers said the Marshes was a place where the lavender boys went to meet up at night. So, she'd never been herself. But now, here she was in the Forest of Dean, and it went on for miles; she'd never seen so many bleeding trees. The thought of being lost out in the forest at night terrified her. Every road looked the same, lined with tall dark trees, and not a signpost in sight.

Rosie climbed the steep meandering path up the hill to catch up with the rest of the girls. Fallen branches had left gaping wounds and splintered remains in the giant oaks above. The wind howled through the forest and sleet seeped past her collar and down her neck. There was no respite from the cold, even for the trees. They stood apart, exposed to the bitter winds, unable to wrap their limbs round each other for warmth or safety.

Three men in hobnail boots and khaki coats stood beneath a huge oak tree in the clearing and watched the girls arrive. The wooden shafts of axes and cross-cut saws were laid up against the trunk. Rosie hunched her shoulders and pulled her collar up. She'd never known Hackney to be this cold, even though her old man had said he'd seen people skating on the Thames this winter.

'Attention!' the older man in tweed shouted. He'd taken PT on their first morning.

A chill blew through the forest, as Rosie caught up with the huddle of girls under the oak.

'Come along, hurry up at the back,' the old Captain shouted as they approached. The girl with the strange name, Keeva, the one who'd fallen over, came and stood beside her. She hadn't meant Keeva to fall flat on her face and cut up her hands. She'd just wanted to get her back for flicking the branch in her face and not distracting the cook, like she'd asked, when she had nipped round the back to pinch some more bread. A gust caught Keeva's beret and her wavy red hair blew loose in the wind.

'I'm Captain Blunt, your officer in command.'

'My beret.' Keeva pointed at the small dark-green felt hat, which had been blown yards away beneath the tree and came to rest on a frozen stream that ran along the edge of the clearing.

'Are you paying attention?' he asked.

'Yes, sir!' replied Miss Goody Two-Shoes at once. Rosie could have guessed Beatrice would be sucking up to the captain already. She'd rather make a truce with Keeva, than Lady Eiderdown.

'You'll have to do better than that,' Blunt said. 'Attention!'

'Yes, sir,' the girls chorused.

'I ain't saying, "Yes, sir" to no one,' Rosie whispered to Keeva with a smile.

'When the Home Timber Production Department urgently requested more forestry workers, we weren't expecting a gaggle of girls. We wanted strong lads, dockers or firemen, to bring these trees down, but instead we have been sent you motley lot.'

What a flipping cheek; she was doing her bit for the war like her brothers, wasn't she?

'Excuse me, Captain Blunt, sir! I think you will find I have been recruited for my skills in mathematics,' said Beatrice.

'You think? Who asked you to think? Don't confuse your pretty little head with thinking,' he said.

That shut Beatrice up. Rosie nudged Keeva with her elbow.

'Life in the forest will be very different to life as a hairdresser, parlourmaid, shop assistant, typist or … ballet dancer.'

A chill passed through the densely packed tree trunks. Some twigs flew down to the ground around them and Rosie wondered whether she'd made a mistake joining up.

'Most of you are townsfolk and may not be tough enough for

life in the forest. So, I am expecting you to be redeployed to lighter forestry duties, such as tree nurseries, planting seeds and young saplings.'

'Not tough enough?' she repeated to Keeva. 'He's not met the Worsells before,' and she flexed her biceps. Not even a smile from Miss Scarlet Barnet; maybe she was scared of her. Instead, Keeva grabbed a long branch, squatted on the edge of the stream like a frog, and tried to hook up her beret.

'We have told the Ministry of Supply that life as a forestry worker in the great outdoors is men's work and quite unsuitable for young girls, who are more used to cooking and cleaning in service as domestics or at home.'

Blunt was droning on, and Rosie wondered whether she should have gone to work in the munitions factory after all, for her war work. She could at least have tried indoor jobs like the Wrens or the ATS. But they hadn't even suggested those at the labour exchange. Rosie's head felt itchy under the edge of her beret.

Beatrice pushed her way through to the front towards Captain Blunt, as the branches of the trees waved restlessly.

'I am B-B-Beatrice Oxley, sir. I joined because I have studied mathematics at the University of Liverpool … I was told I would be in training to be a measurer, sir.'

Beatrice was asking for trouble, Rosie thought.

'Do you want a tick and smiley face on your maths book? You need to listen to me and learn some discipline, girl. When I want you to speak, I will ask you,' Captain Blunt said.

Oh yes, Beatrice had been put in her place. Rosie smiled and jumped down the bank to the stream. She didn't want to lose her beret too, so she tucked it in her pocket, stepped onto the ice and reached out for Keeva's beret. Her foot broke through the ice and she slipped into the stream up to her ankle and squelched as she climbed out of the ditch.

'Oh no, I've got a flipping cold dog's stew in my boot now,' Rosie groaned.

'Thank you,' Keeva replied, as Rosie handed the wet beret to her.

'What on earth is going on at the back? There will be extra duties for all of you if you don't pay attention,' said Captain Blunt.

Grey clouds passed overhead, and hostile branches whipped around. Rosie's boots rubbed on her cold, wet feet as she rejoined the group.

'The pit props which support the roof of the mining gallery deep below the ground; the sleeper which holds firm the railway line for transporting cargo; the packaging case which carries the bombs from the factories safely; the telegraph poles which provide vital communication; the crosses for the soldiers, and the coffins for their bodies … they all begin life in the forest.'

'For someone who is called Blunt, it takes him a long time to get to the point,' said Rosie, for Lily to hear.

'Excuse me. But how do we find our way back to camp again?' Gladys asked. 'All the paths look the same to me.'

'Just don't wander off anywhere on your own,' Captain Blunt replied.

'When is lunch?' asked Lily.

'Pay attention, girls. You might appreciate how important the pit props were if you went down a mine to see for yourselves.'

'I ain't going down no mines. I'm afraid of the dark,' Rosie said.

'Me too,' said Lily.

'Girls.' Blunt sighed.

'I'm sure you'd scare the miners off if they met you in a dark tunnel,' Beatrice replied.

Flipping cheek. What did she mean by that? Rosie would give her a scare to teach her a lesson if she wasn't careful.

'Ssh, that's enough. On to business. The need for timber is urgent, and so today we are going to waste no time and give you a try with your hands on the tools. What you are about to do is very dangerous work, so you need to listen carefully. Local foresters Mr Williamson and Mr Harvey, Mr Hopkins and his … son are here to get you started,' he said, nodding to the three old men and looking around. They did look like werewolves, with those beards.

'Where's Arthur? Is he coming?' said Blunt.

''E'll be 'ere,' replied one of them.

'Right, girls, pair up, find an axe and saw, follow the men and we'll get you started on a tree.'

Where had that Miss Scarlet Barnet gone? She wanted to ask if she would …

'Do you want to pair up with me, Keeva?' Gladys asked before she got in there first.

'Oh, yes sure,' she replied, glancing over to Rosie.

Rosie realised she'd missed her chance: Lily was with Hazel; Edith with another girl. She wouldn't have minded pairing up with Keeva.

Watching Gladys link arms with Keeva made Rosie want to be back at home with Bets. The two girls held on to one another as they took an axe and cross-cut saw and squealed as they tripped over the handle.

The muddy ground was frozen hard, and it was dark and creepy away from the stream and clearing, under the dark canopy of pine trees.

'Aaargh!'

'Are you all right?' called Gladys.

'It's a snake. Look! There!' Rosie said, pointing at its several-yards-long body, the thickness of her arm, disappearing under the leaf litter.

'Where?' said Keeva, rushing over.

'By that tree,' Rosie said, pointing.

'That's a branch,' said Keeva, kicking it with her boot.

'I thought it looked alive, like it was moving,' said Rosie, rubbing the goosebumps on her arms. She wondered why she was so nervy. But anything could creep up on her as the wind picked up in the trees.

'Let's see what these girls can do,' Rosie heard Captain Blunt say, as he approached from behind.

'Berets on, please,' Captain Blunt said, poking Rosie with his stick.

She grabbed the stick. 'Get off me!' She remembered the first time her father had beaten her with a stick.

'It's not a question.' Blunt's eyes narrowed. 'Put your beret on that mop of hair.'

Rosie's neck twinged as she slowly let go of the stick and put the beret on. When he was gone, she pulled it off again. Just ignore the old bugger, she said to herself.

Behind her she heard the words, 'Are you paired up?'

She turned around and said, 'No.' Just her bleedin' luck.

'Shall we chum up together then?' asked Beatrice.

'Yes, sure. Give me a minute.' Rosie rushed off on her own to catch up with Keeva and Gladys. Not on your bloody nelly, she thought.

Reluctantly, Rosie followed Gladys, Keeva and two of the foresters into the dark pine trees.

'You come with me,' one of the men said to Rosie, and led her away from Gladys and Keeva towards a different tree, axe and cross-cut saw in hand. Rosie watched the others disappear into the woods.

'We'll start on this tree,' he said, patting a trunk and looking at

Rosie. 'I see what Jack means.'

'You what?' Rosie replied, watching him look her up and down, and waiting to be handed her tools and given instructions for felling the tree.

'About those breeches,' he said.

Rosie looked down at her beige, corduroy jodhpurs wondering what he meant, wishing the other girls were still with her.

'Look at those curves.' He smiled as he slid the axe shaft through his hand and walked behind her.

Rosie turned around quickly. 'Oi clear off. Ain't you seen a girl in breeches before?' she said.

'Not like you,' he said, eyes glazed.

'Give me the axe then. You're old enough to be m'old man, you know,' she said, holding her hand out.

She was used to attracting the men and having to fend them off. Her mother had said other girls would be jealous and she should feel lucky to be the object of male attention. But she'd seen that same look on the floor supervisor's face back at the factory, and didn't like it. The one all the girls said to keep away from. Never find yourself alone with Paterson, they used to say. At least here there were no walls or closed doors to escape. She could just walk away, she thought.

'Those legs, those hips,' he said, as she shivered and turned to go. 'Are you cold? Come here. I'll warm you up.'

Rosie felt his hands slide round her waist from behind her. Then he grabbed Rosie by the hips and pushed himself up against her. She could feel something hard in her behind.

'Get your bloody hands off me,' she said and stamped on his foot, turned, and gave him a sharp slap across the rough stubble on his face.

He grabbed her wrist and pulled her face to his. 'Thou

rasty cratur.'

She twisted her arm free and ran to find the rest of the girls again. Disorientated, she couldn't navigate her way back through the trees. Where were they? Never had she been so pleased to see those copper curls, as she reached out for Keeva's arm.

'Come on, let's get those trees down,' Rosie said, feeling out of breath.

'Where have you been?' Keeva asked.

'Never you mind.' She didn't want Keeva to know she had invited so much attention from the foresters already.

'What were you doing?' Keeva asked.

'We were just messing about. Nothing was meant by it,' said Rosie, hoping she hadn't seen what had happened. She knew that girls like her could get a bad name for themselves. She followed Keeva to where Gladys was standing by a tree the size of a telegraph pole.

'We need to cut a triangular wedge out of the bottom of the tree first, on the side we want it to fall,' said Keeva.

Rosie could hardly concentrate on what she said as she saw the man approach again.

'You all right, girls? Who is going to try dipping the butt of the tree with the axe first?' he said, as if nothing had happened.

'You go first, Keeva,' said Gladys.

'Oh! I don't know. Why don't you, Gladys?' Keeva replied.

'Please don't make me do it. I just can't do it,' said Gladys. 'You go, Rosie.'

'No.' Rosie edged away.

Keeva took the axe in her hands and raised it to her shoulders, then behind her, and swung. It stopped with a sudden jolt and hardly marked the tree. Rosie knew that feeling from when she'd tried to hit her older brother with a broom, and it had vibrated up her arms.

After five minutes or so, Blunt came over. 'Hmm! Resembles the work of a beaver, but keep trying. It should take a few minutes on these saplings. Watch Mr Harvey. A few clean swipes, that's all it needs, girls. Yes.'

Keeva passed the axe to Mr Harvey. Rosie watched him cut a wedge into the tree easily. He made the axe-work look like a hot knife going through butter. Each swipe peeled another layer of yellow pine clean off. With practice, Rosie could get the knack of dipping the tree with the axe like that. She'd show him. When the time came, every swing of the axe would be another stroke for victory.

Chapter 4

Keeva

Keeva didn't hold out much hope of Gladys cutting a wedge into the side of a tree the size of a telegraph pole. Gladys lacked determination, and the axe head needed sharpening. They had an almost impossible job on their hands when the forests were endless and the trunks were frozen solid like tombstones. The trees stood like gatekeepers to another world, and stubbornly they would not give way. Her wet beret hung upon a twig and Keeva was starting to feel the cold.

'Don't you feel like going home? I do,' said Gladys, passing Keeva the axe.

'Not really,' Keeva replied, lining up her feet and swinging the axe. The glancing blow made no mark, except for the blood blotting through the bandages on her grazed hands.

She offered the axe back to Gladys, not Rosie. Why was Rosie hanging around with Gladys and Keeva, she wondered, when she needed to find her own sawing partner? Rosie had made it clear she didn't like her, so why had she fished out her beret from the stream? Keeva wondered if Rosie was trying to get her into trouble. Be careful, she told herself.

'I'll 'ave a go when he's gone.' Rosie nodded to the forester and pushed up her sleeves as if she were getting ready to throw a punch.

'What about you, Rosie? How are you finding it here?' asked Gladys.

'I miss me mates. I'd go back home to see them,' said Rosie. 'But my old man would give me a good hiding if I went back now.'

Rosie spoke so matter-of-factly, like her father beating her seemed normal. Keeva's father wouldn't hurt any creature, let alone another human being. Last winter she'd found a family of slow-worms under an old hayrick. Keeva had thought they were dead. But her father had tucked their little torpid family up under the last of the hay that they really needed for their pony, Conker. A small sacrifice for a small family, he'd said.

Keeva ran her finger across the blade of the axe. There was no way she would go back home now. Viola would be livid; she was always so irritated by her daughter. Viola refused to be in service, cooking and cleaning for her children just because she'd given birth to them. She said it was reinforcing the gender inequalities in society, which didn't help Keeva when she was starving hungry. She hoped Viola was surviving without her though, feeding herself at least. Maybe her sister, Dilly, would return home from the Royal Ballet School. London would be more dangerous than Sussex, once the air raids started.

'Are you all right, Keeva?' asked Gladys, touching her arm.

'Yes.' She swallowed as her hands began to throb. The wooden handle pressing against her sore palms was becoming hot. She'd been taught to get air to wounds to let them breathe, so Keeva peeled back her bandages. Then she laid her palms on the cold grey metal of the axe head, which gave her some relief.

''Ows thee 'acker cuttin'?' came a voice from behind her.

'What?' Keeva turned.

'Oh sorry, I mean, is yer axe sharp?' A dark-haired young man about her age took the axe from her and ran his thumb along its blade.

'Not really,' Keeva said.

He checked his pockets. 'No matter. Watch how I swing the axe and then you copy me,' he said, as he stood feet apart, bent his knees and rolled his shoulders back. He gripped the wooden handle in both hands, swung it above his head and down through the air.

'Well, come on, have a go, or are you going to just stand there? I'm Arthur, by the way.'

He was handsome. His wedge of brown hair had grown out of a short back and sides, thick and long on top. His dimpled smile made Keeva giddy.

'You've got my axe,' said Keeva.

He laid the axe gently to the ground.

'No axe needed for the swing. Come on, follow me. You too,' he said to Gladys and Rosie.

The three of them mimed together. Feeling foolish, Keeva tried to follow his movements.

'Again,' he said, twice more. Keeva noticed Beatrice approach. She was still annoyed with Beatrice and the rest of the girls. No one had said anything about the beds being switched, so she hadn't either. But Gladys could've done something; she must have seen Beatrice take her bed. She'd seen fieldfare thrushes attack other birds entering their territory, after they'd flown thousands of miles to overwinter too. All the girls pretended it hadn't even happened, but she wouldn't forget.

To her surprise the boy, Arthur, picked up the axe and handed it to her, wrapping one arm around her. Now with an audience, he took hold of the axe in both his hands in front of her. Her heart thumped.

'You see how I'm holding the axe,' he said into her neck, keeping the wind from her back.

'Ooh, Keeva, you keeping warm?' teased Rosie.

Her hands slid up the wooden handle and touched his and together they slowly swung the axe up behind them. As she twisted, she felt her body press up against his. The axe became weightless as it took flight and swung through the air. Smoothly they struck the tree together and a slice of pine wood peeled from the tree and rolled to the floor.

'Good,' he said, as Keeva swept a spiral of hair back from her eye and smiled briefly.

'Again?' he said, his breath on her ear.

'Okay.'

They swung again.

'You've got it,' he said.

He released her from his arms, took her hands in his and turned up her palms. Then he looked up at her face and walked away. Keeva shivered.

'Oi, where you going? I want a go,' said Rosie.

He looked around at the trees nearby and kept walking away. Keeva caught her breath and thought of her Edward. The last night she'd seen him at home, before Christmas, when he had walked away. They were meant to be celebrating Christmas and he had left her standing in the middle of the road in the dark, all alone. He had laughed at her, asked her why she was always so difficult. He had said that Mary, her friend, had told him Keeva made the other girls feel awkward. He'd said, why don't you just fit in with the rest of the girls? She was trying.

The wind blew as Keeva watched the young forester stop underneath a silver birch tree and look up. He pulled out a knife from his pocket and flicked the blade open with his grubby hands. With a run, hop and a skip, he leapt up onto one foot on the side of the trunk and swiped a large bracket fungus from the tree with his blade, catching it as it fell. Then he turned back and walked towards her.

'Birch conk,' he said, showing her the coffee-coloured smooth surface of the fungus and fine white pores underneath.

'No good for the trees but good for sharpenin' axes, like a razor strop,' he added.

He slowly dragged the flat of the blade gently upwards against the fungus, turned the axe head over and repeated with a downward stroke. He continued stroking the blade back and forth, up and down. When he'd finished, he slipped up his sleeve and lay the sharpened blade on his wrist. For an instant, Keeva imagined him slitting his wrist, the blood appearing in a line along the blade. Slowly, he slid the flat axe up his arm and shaved the hairs from his skin.

'Zee. Put a strip from the fungus on them grazes too before you get an infection. It's medicinal and good for lighting the fire too. He passed her the large mushroom. ''Ere, 'ave another go now with thee 'acker,' he said, handing her the axe, now polished to a shine.

He turned to watch her try. Flustered and warmer than she'd felt all morning, Keeva tried again. The axe head sank into the trunk.

'That's good, much better!' he said, before he left.

'Oh, I bet that was nice, wasn't it?' said Gladys, once he'd gone.

'Ooh, he's lovely, isn't he?' said Rosie.

'Very handsome.' Gladys smiled. 'But do you already have a sweetheart, Keeva? Just checking for you, Rosie.'

'No. I mean, I did. But we ended before I left,' said Keeva.

'Oh no, why?' asked Gladys.

'He was signing up.'

'Is he not worth waiting for?'

'He was a liar.'

Keeva watched Arthur as he walked away at a comfortable stride. The wind blew fresh against her face. Lines of leaves chased across the ground, leaving drifts around trunks and bare earth exposed elsewhere. The constant rush of wind in the trees was enlivening, exciting. He looked back.

'Oh, better off without him then,' said Gladys.

'Yes. What about you?' asked Keeva.

'I'm engaged to a lovely man, called Bernie,' Gladys answered. 'He's in the Royal Engineers.'

Keeva swept her hair back and swung the axe into the tree.

Gladys continued, 'He proposed just before he left. We walked up to the clifftop at Porthcurno, overlooking the sandy beach and sparkling turquoise waters. It was so romantic, I'm sure I floated back down the hill afterwards.'

A dreamy look came over Gladys, as she smiled into the distance.

Keeva kicked the stump. 'Shall we give it a go with the cross-cut, Gladys?'

They got down on their knees, the way that they'd been shown, and took it in turns to pull the blade across the bark in line with the centre of the diamond. The teeth jerked and jumped across the bark and ripped into the wood inside. Sawdust trickled from the wound like tears. Within a short time, the saw was more than halfway through the thick trunk but stuck fast. Keeva wrestled with it, but it wouldn't budge.

'What about you, Rosie?' asked Gladys.

'Nah, I'm single. Mr Handsome would do very nicely.'

'Watch out! Here comes Blunt,' said Keeva under her breath. The large man shaped like a pheasant, with grey hair like a judge's wig, marched his way round the gnarled tree roots and rotten logs towards them.

'What do you call this then? he said, darkly. 'Up you get, girls! Up you get! And where's your felling partner?' Blunt asked Rosie.

Gladys scrambled on to her knees. Rosie wandered off. Keeva snatched the cross-cut and winced as she caught her graze against the metal blade.

'Oh, that hurt!'

'You'll need to toughen up if you think you're going to do

important men's work. Hands were made for blisters, you know; it's what toughens them up. There's no use crying over them like softies.'

Keeva rolled her eyes for Gladys's benefit, and they put their heads down to work again, while Blunt stood over them. The teeth of the blade slotted into the open cut of the tree and they pulled and pulled. Still the saw would not move.

'Dear oh dear! See how Sue saws. What a sight for sore peepers.'

'My name is not Sue.' Keeva yanked the saw free at last.

Gladys pulled the saw back towards her and this time it released the sawdust once more, as the blade cut further and further into the wound.

'There, you see. You girls just need a firm hand and a beady eye to keep you in check. Can't be trusted to get on with the job without it.'

'He'd be bloody lucky if this tree doesn't land on his head,' said Keeva, as he walked away.

Gladys giggled as she pushed the blade and it bent in the middle with a twang and stuck fast again.

'Oh Jesus, Gladys,' said Keeva.

'Stop messing around you two,' Captain Blunt shouted. 'Britain will lose the war if we don't chop down one hundred thousand cubic feet of timber this month to replace imports. If you can't even fell a pint-sized tree, we will have to send you back home.'

'Sorry, sir!'

'Sorry, sir!' she repeated after Gladys.

'That's enough from you two. Go and help some of the other pairs with the snedding – removing the branches.'

'What about the tree? Isn't it dangerous to leave it like this?' Keeva asked.

'I'll get the men to finish the job.'

Keeva worked the rest of the day with Gladys, trimming the branches with billhooks and cutting the pit props to length with bow saws. Their knees were sore from the cold hard ground and their heels formed blisters in their stiff boots. Keeva's arms ached; they felt pumped up like bicycle tyres and she could barely grip the saw any more. And her hands were a mess: filthy, dirty and painful. Blisters and grazes wept with pus and stung like mad.

She blew on her hands and tucked them into her pockets to try to protect them from the cold, when she remembered Arthur giving her the birch fungus. Warmed by her jodhpur pocket, under her coat, she pulled out the slab of rubbery fungus and sniffed. The girls were keen to get back to camp and were disappearing down the path into the trees.

The fungus had a familiar earthy mushroom smell, and she touched her tongue against the smooth white surface underneath. She immediately spat the bitter taste from her mouth. Cautiously she placed the mushroom between her palms. As if in prayer she brought her fingers to her lips and smiled. She wondered where Arthur had gone this afternoon, and drifted back to when he'd had his arms wrapped around her and she'd been so close to his strong body.

Keeva had admired how he'd leapt up the birch tree and landed so gracefully. She had cast her eyes over the curve of his neck touching his jacket collar and how he'd pushed up his sleeve on his muscular forearm. She replayed the intimate scene over and over, when the hairs from his arm blew from his skin into the wind. She shivered as it gave her a strange tingle inside. She took a deep breath as if to smell his sweet musky perspiration and followed the other girls back to camp.

Chapter 5

'Argh!' Keeva groaned as she dragged her heavy limbs upstairs, leaving a muddy trail behind her. She had never felt so exhausted and couldn't imagine felling again tomorrow. The upper landing within sight, Keeva pulled herself up the banisters and sat down on the top step, like she used to at home. She'd sit on the top step and chat to her mother at the bottom. She envisioned Viola in her orange full-length floral dress floating through the hallway. Keeva so loved the way the dress flapped round her ankles, swinging from her hips as she walked.

She wished Viola wore it more like a wildflower meadow, loose and free. But she didn't; she wore her dress, like motherhood, with impatience as if it were a tight two-piece suit. Was that Keeva's fault? Gladys appeared smiling from the foot of the staircase with Rosie, a tea in hand for Keeva.

'What are you doing?' Gladys asked.

'Resting.' Even though her house back home was like a building site in places – a few squeaky stairs, exposed brick, no skirting boards and floorboards rattling as she walked over them – it was still home, and Viola was still her mother.

'Come on, you can make it. Not much further.' Gladys handed her cup of tea to Rosie and reached out to pull Keeva up.

As they arrived at room two at the top of the stairs, Rosie stopped them on the top landing.

'New rules. No one is coming in the dorm until their boots are off. Look at the mud coming up the stairs. And Gladys, you can be on boot patrol,' she said.

'Why me?' Gladys replied.

'Because people will listen to you,' said Rosie. Everyone

liked Gladys.

'Oh, all right! What about yours?' asked Gladys, as Rosie rushed inside.

Keeva pulled her boots off carefully over her blisters and laid her woollen socked feet against the floorboards.

'Keeva … quick,' called Rosie.

As Keeva entered the room, Rosie had lifted the eiderdown, blankets and sponge mattress up off Beatrice's bed.

'Here, hold this,' she said.

'What are you doing?'

'Ssh!'

Keeva held up the sponge as Rosie slid the middle board to the end of Beatrice's bed.

'That'll teach her, won't it,' said Rosie.

Beatrice's loud voice came up the stairs and Keeva flinched, dropping the sponge.

'No, hold it up again,' said Rosie.

'Boots off before you come in, please,' said Gladys; other girls' voices echoed up the stairs.

Rosie laid the sponge mattress back down carefully leaving a gap beneath the mattress in the centre of the bed.

'Gladys, help me off with my boots. I've got blisters and I'm in dreadful agony,' complained Beatrice.

'Quick, she's outside,' said Keeva, grabbing her tea from Rosie's bedside table.

Rosie smoothed the blankets, pulled the eiderdown taut and jumped back on her own bed. Keeva didn't want to get involved, although it was too late now.

'Hang onto the doorframe then,' Gladys said.

Keeva tried not to spill her tea as she raced to the end of the dormitory and collapsed onto her bed.

'Oow, argh! Dear God, get me out of these wretched boots.'

Rosie's words, 'that'll teach her', repeated in Keeva's head and when her gaze met Rosie, she tried not to giggle. Beatrice limped out of her boots and into the room, followed by Edith. Keeva watched Beatrice, her heart thumping.

'Look at Beatrice,' Rosie whispered with a wink to Edith, Gladys and the others as they came into the dormitory.

Beatrice went to her suitcase, pulled out her cake tin and removed a slice of fruit cake. Keeva flushed with heat as Beatrice turned round slowly to sit down. The full width of her fawn corduroy jodhpurs hovered above her eiderdown. With a harrumph, Beatrice slumped down onto her bed. She squealed as her bottom sunk through the bed frame to the floor. At the same time her cake tin toppled off the edge of her bed and, as Beatrice tried to catch it, the tin flipped upside down and clanked onto the floor. Keeva could see her rich fruit cake tumbling across the wooden boards and disintegrating into pieces.

'Argh, what's happened? Is my bed broken?'

Knees squashed up under her chin, Beatrice peered over the top of the bed frame.

Rosie smirked. Gladys covered her open mouth with her hand. She tried not to giggle but she couldn't help herself. Edith turned to stare at Keeva and didn't seem to find it funny at all. But Keeva revelled in Beatrice's comeuppance briefly before her father's voice whispered in her mind: *seek revenge by digging two graves; one for yourself.* Why did she get involved? A pang of guilt crept up on her.

'Are you all going to just stare at me, or is anyone going to help me out?'

'Bloomin' awful these beds, ain't they?' Rosie gave Keeva a smile.

Don't look at me, don't incriminate me, Keeva thought.

Beatrice swivelled round like a large crab on her bed, arms like pincers, and shot a glance at Keeva. 'Grrr. Gladys, pull me out, at once. I can't move. I'm stuck.'

Gladys did as she was told. She reached one hand out to pull Beatrice up, but she didn't budge. Her bottom seemed to be wedged between the planks and the sponge mattress. Gladys gave her both hands and pulled harder, lifting Beatrice up off the ground a foot.

'Come on, you can pull harder than that,' said Beatrice, as Lily joined them, struggling to heave Beatrice up from under her arms.

'Don't pinch me,' Beatrice yelled.

'Sorry.'

Gladys and Lily gave one last groan as they finally lifted Beatrice out of the sunken mattress and Beatrice pushed herself out.

'It's obvious who has been tampering with my bed, and I shall be reporting you both.' Beatrice cast a glance towards Keeva.

Oh, bloody hell, Rosie, Keeva thought. Look what you've done now. She knew Rosie had meant it as a joke. But Beatrice didn't have a sense of humour. Hazel, one of the Yorkshire girls in their dorm, shook her head, and the others went to lie down on their beds to rest before dinner. Beatrice grunted.

'Was that you?' mouthed Gladys, as she pulled the curtains to. Beatrice wrestled under her mattress.

Keeva shrugged her shoulders. If only she'd stopped Rosie before it was too late.

Gladys came to sit on Keeva's bed. 'Oh, don't worry, it was just a joke,' she whispered.

Keeva rolled her smooth lucky amber stone in her hands and wouldn't look up. Gladys was kind. She couldn't remember the last time she'd felt the warmth of a friend by her side: someone she could confide in, someone who wouldn't judge her. She still felt wounded by the friends at home who'd turned against her. Keeva didn't know whether she could trust anyone ever again.

'Do you have good friends back at home?' Keeva asked.

'I realised who my real friends were after I suffered a loss in my family. The ones who stuck with me, who understood why I was so upset and kept on inviting me to play. There weren't many. Now I've left them at home, I've brought my teddy with me.'

She fetched a small brown teddy with a pointy nose from her bed, smiled and cuddled it.

'I've had Angus since … He's named after my brother. My nana bought it for me.'

Keeva said, 'I'm so sorry.'

'Oh, it was a long time ago. Not that I don't miss him. He would have been conscripted by now, part of the armed forces.'

'And your fiancé, Bernie.'

'Yes, he's just signed up. I do miss him so much. But none of us have a choice, do we?'

Her father had made a difficult choice. A nausea stirred in Keeva's stomach and her throat tightened.

'I made a choice,' said Hazel from the bed beside Keeva. 'I chose to leave home as soon as I could. I often thought my father would've made me work down coal pits on my belly, like 'im, if I'd been a son. I couldn't ever do that. I wanted to get away, so I left the woollen mills to work out in the forest. My mother was proud of me. She knew she was going to miss me. But my father, he wasn't best pleased at all.'

Keeva didn't want to know how Gladys's brother had died. She didn't want to hear about Hazel's mother being proud of her daughter either; Keeva might as well be dead for all Viola cared.

Keeva glanced at Beatrice covering herself with her silky dressing gown while awkwardly getting changed underneath. She slipped her jodhpurs onto the floor and removed her socks, hopping on one foot. As she squeezed her elbows out of her Aertex, her gown flapped open, briefly exposing her milky-white stomach. Realising she was attracting everyone's attention, she became red in the face. Keeva had never seen anyone make such a fuss about getting changed before.

Although food rationing had only been introduced this month, Keeva noticed Beatrice had a plumpness to her stomach like one of her father's well-risen banana bread loaves. Beatrice also had lots of fashionable outfits. Keeva had heard her parents talk about the wealthy aristocracy, and could hardly believe that here she was, sharing a room with someone who was part of it. She could see for herself the effect of all this wealth. 'The privileged and narrow-minded elite,' her father used to say.

'It's dinner time,' a girl shouted in the open door, and Gladys and Rosie rushed downstairs to join the queue. Keeva felt light-headed. She slowed down and reached out for the wall to steady herself, thinking she might pass out. She was so hungry and her whole body ached after a day of sawing and chopping.

Inside the dining hall, Keeva was hit by the steaming hot smell of a meaty stew, which she longed to taste. A ruddy-faced lady scraped noisily at square metal pans. Keeva joined the queue behind Gladys and Rosie. Beatrice pushed in front and held up her shiny white plate to receive a piece of meat, two potatoes, some carrots and wilted greens. Beatrice poked the meat curiously with her fork and rolled it around.

'Excuse me. This is … ?' asked Beatrice, shoving her plate under the woman's nose.

'Pig,' the hot-faced woman spat out.

'Is there any more?' Beatrice asked.

'No.'

The woman dumped a brown slab of meat on Keeva's plate.

'Really, mine is such a meagre portion. We may not be young

virile men, but this is certainly not enough to sustain a hard-working young woman. Is there at least any gravy?' Beatrice asked.

'No,' the woman shouted.

Keeva was so hungry she protected her tray with her arms while she found an empty table. Rosie followed behind and sat beside her. Keeva was used to eating mushrooms for a month, or beetroot when they were in season. They had little money to spend on meat and, besides, her parents were adamant they should be strictly vegetarian or fruitarian if they could. The orange ovals of carrot, fleshy pink thumbs of potato, silky green leaves and bark-like meat crust on her plate was like one of her mother's dreadful still-life paintings. But she was so hungry, the food disappeared from her plate and had slipped into her stomach before she remembered to savour the taste.

She noticed a noise coming from the plump girl, Lily, who had appeared opposite her. She must be even hungrier than she was, as Lily lapped her tongue around her lips like a fox on its final mouthful.

The hot-faced dinner lady clanged her ladle against the pan hard and fast. Keeva winced and Lily covered her ears.

'Right, my name is Redrum, Missus Redrum and it's my job to feed you ungrateful critters. I've been catering for the army since before you were born. I know how to do it and don't expect any of you to tell me how it is done. There is one thing I will not cater for and that is fussy eaters,' she said and jabbed her ladle in the air towards Beatrice.

There was murmuring and shuffling in the dining hall as a few more girls walked in.

'You will eat what you are given and, if you are late, you'll get nothing. We are not hanging around for no one.'

Rosie raised her eyebrows and Keeva pinched her smile shut.

'Now for the rules of the camp. Number one: any women's problems then see me, as I'm the only lady on camp.'

'That's debatable; she's more horse than 'uman with those teeth,' whispered Rosie.

'Shh.' Keeva raised her hand. 'What about Missus Potter?' she asked.

'Missus Potter is a spinster,' the cook whispered loudly, 'and as moral poison kills the soul, keep clear unless you want to be condemned like her.' Her chin shook as she nodded her head. 'And I don't regard washing hair in ice-cold water or whinging about period pain as women's problems,' she huffed and puffed.

Rosie's lips snarled up and Keeva felt a giggle rising from her stomach.

'Number two: doors shut, lights out, and in bed by ten o'clock.'

She squinted her eyes and pointed her finger across the room at Rosie and Keeva.

'Number three: if any girl goes out of the camp and is back late, after ten, they will be punished, severely. Strictly no boys and no hanky-panky. Got it?'

The dining room fell uncomfortably quiet, once Missus Redrum had finished speaking. Keeva didn't like that woman, and wondered whether Arthur wrapping his arms around her would count as hanky-panky. As chatter swept across the dining hall again, Keeva started to tremble. She must not cry, so she got up to fetch herself a glass of water.

While she stood by the tray of jugs, her back to the dining hall, Keeva overheard Beatrice whisper loudly, 'Did you see what happened?'

Keeva glanced over her shoulder to see her huddled around a table with Edith and Hazel.

'I thought it was her. Hardly surprising, after what I heard about her father,' Beatrice added.

Who was she talking about? What could she know about her father? Keeva thought, overfilling her glass of water.

'And have you seen her dreadful clothes? I'm sure she's the one that smells.'

Water ran across the table, as she tried to stop it from pouring onto the floor. She hated those girls, and wished she was back home.

Chapter 6

15th December 1939, West Firle, Sussex

'Mother, can I borrow a dress?' Keeva called downstairs. There was no reply, just a posh woman on the wireless who was making a wartime appeal on behalf of the YWCA. They wanted recreation centres and canteens to look after evacuated girls, female munition workers and so on. Keeva would be first in line for one of those canteens, because they'd been living on home-grown potatoes and Brussel sprouts for a month.

Keeva slumped down on her camp bed and looked at Dilly's ballet shoes hanging upon the wall by their pretty ribbons. Lined up in perfect ascending order of shoe size, the last pairs from when she'd progressed onto points. A reflection of Dilly's life, she had reached the point of life when she got into the Royal Ballet School. She was now a professional artiste and had achieved all their parents had ever wished for her.

She looked up, expecting her sister to leap into her bedroom at any moment and spin around the room on her toes. But the space was motionless and quiet. She crawled over to Dilly's bed and nuzzled her nose into her older sister's pillow, which still wore her sister's scent. Viola had hand embroidered the pillowcase with flowers and her name Dilys, which of course meant perfect in Welsh.

Surely it was her turn for some attention, now she was the only daughter left at home? Her parents had already spent their lives and savings on ballet lessons and getting her sister this far. Perhaps her parents could buy Keeva something she wanted for Christmas, like a football. But no, she would get nothing but a stingy stocking because they didn't believe in consumerism.

They used to go to The Ram, with their intellectual friends, sit in the snug and talk the night away about fruitarianism and feminism, any 'ism' that gave them a hope that society might change. Less than a month after war broke out, they'd been barred. But Keeva wasn't barred, was she?

Her parents, Stanley and Viola, even had dreadful names. But their views were worse and they were spoiling everything. Stanley had lost his regular plumbing customers because they didn't want him in their houses. Viola often quoted the Roman philosopher Tacitus; she said: '"The desire for safety stands against every great and noble enterprise", and that is why we must live a life of uncertainty on the edge of society and risk our freedom in the hope of a better world.' People thought their family was like a disease and would be contagious among the young people in the village.

Keeva knew she wasn't allowed to go to The Ram, which had a reputation for being frequented by magistrates, judges and lawyers from the Lewes Crown Court, which her parents rolled their eyes at. But that was exactly why she had arranged to go there with Edward. Stuck at home with her parents and no sister to annoy, Keeva needed some excitement and it would be guaranteed with Edward.

Keeva ran downstairs in her greyish vest and knickers and peered through the doorway, with goosebumps on her arms. The house was bitterly cold. Her parents sat in the Caravaggio glow of the oil lamp at the kitchen table and drank the last of the vile potato wine. They always ended up having intercourse around the house on home brew, so thank goodness she would be out tonight. She hoped Edward would soon be here so she wouldn't hear the groaning.

'Why are you lurking?' said Mother.

'I haven't got any clothes to wear.'

Keeva could only think of her mother's favourite orange dress. The new rayon crepe fabric dress, with high gathered collar, puff sleeves and broderie anglaise detail, which was not to be borrowed, however pretty it might look on Keeva.

'Don't talk nonsense. You got a bag of hand-me-downs quite recently,' said Mother.

'Recently? It was four months ago, in the summer, Mother.'

'You know the generosity of spirit has been abandoned now we are at war, Keeva,' her father replied.

'But I read in the paper that local people have given thirty pounds to the tobacco fund,' said Keeva as she watched her father nudge the last few strands of tobacco from the table into his Zig-Zag rolling paper.

'Oh, that's something,' he replied.

'Yes, you can get free cigarettes and tobacco in the New Year from the Mayoress of Lewes, if you sign up to fight, Father,' Keeva replied.

'Of course, how patronising to think young men could be lured into conscription by something as harmless as tobacco.'

Keeva sighed and swept back upstairs to her parents' room. The wooden drawer wedged tight in its chest before it slid out too far and dumped the contents on the floorboards. There, scrunched up on the floor in the pile of clothes, was the orange dress, the one Mother had worn to the Royal Ballet interview. She held the soft fabric to her nose; the musty smell would pass. The slippery orange dress fell over her head and felt damp against her skin. Keeva shivered and put the rest of the clothes back in the drawer. Edward would be here soon, she thought, as she buttoned up the collar and wrapped the ties around her waist twice.

She didn't want Edward to come into the house. She had

avoided it so far. Their house stood, where the path ended, at the snowy foot of the steep chalk ridge of the South Downs. Behind, to the north was a great patchwork of powder white farmers' fields and gardens, stitched together by trees and hedges. On the other side of the enormous chalk wave lay the sea.

'Chase me,' Keeva had called to Edward and he had run after her. She smiled to remember it again. Halfway up the slope, she'd stopped to catch her breath and fixed her gaze on the crest of the frozen hill. Keeva longed for the view of the distant blue from the top of the ridge, where her heart beat loudly and the edges of the earth and the sea met the sky. Up there, the sun dazzled her eyes; she leant against the breeze and her lips tasted of salt. Often she would roll back down the hill, giddy on fresh air and foolish hopes that she might even be in love with Edward.

Keeva didn't have much faith that the rickety barbed wire fence, stretching for miles along the top of the ridge, would offer any protection against an invasion by sea. And their little ramshackle flint-walled house would most likely be the first target as German bombers crossed the English Channel on their way to London. She joked her family would be Messerschmitted on the way.

She already knew her father would be so keen to show Edward his letter, which he'd got into the paper. She grabbed the paper from the top of the chest of drawers and headed back down to the living room, to hide it in the oak sideboard. The old fusty smell inside met her with the rattle of assorted glass bottles of home-made sloe wine and other dubious concoctions. She took a swig from one of them and returned the bottle to the back with the newspaper.

If her parents didn't keep the fire burning, the house would be freezing by the time she got back. She shivered, snapped some twigs and threw them on the charcoal embers. The apple tree wood crackled as it burst into flames and spat a smoking twig onto the hearth. She listened to her parents, still chatting in the kitchen about the man in the village stores, Mr Green, who had a habit of stirring up her parents.

'He said members of the community were being watched by the police and would be arrested for distributing certain leaflets and newspapers, which might introduce Hitlerism into the village,' said Mother.

'What poppycock,' Father replied

Keeva needed to dry the dress quickly anyway, so she grabbed the newspaper, with her father's letter in, from the cupboard and threw it on the fire. Immediately, she regretted her actions, tried to grab a twig and hook the paper out. But Gandhi's face curled up and disappeared in flames on the front page.

The chairs scraped across the kitchen floor and Keeva ran to the hallway to grab her coat. She threw it over her shoulders and buttoned up by the fire just before her mother emerged from the gloom of the kitchen. The fire blazed, she was too late to save the paper.

'Keeva. You going out now?' said Mother.

'When Edward arrives.'

Keeva had loved her wild, happy childhood; she'd climbed trees, picked armfuls of bluebells, crept through the deep swards of grass in summer meadows with her sister, gorged on sweet strawberries, and hid under piles of autumn leaves with friends. Like hedgehogs and dormice, Keeva called this place home, she flitted through the wildflowers like butterflies, sipped the nectar of life like bees and found music where the birds sang.

But with the declaration of war, Keeva's barefoot freedom of childhood had all too suddenly come to an end. Her urge to escape her parents had grown strong. So many times, she'd run up the steep slope to join the birds as they'd played on the breeze. Effortlessly they'd floated high, wings stretched out, black silhouettes of freedom above the barbed wire fence, which ran from Devil's Dyke near Brighton to Beachy Head and beyond.

Natural chalk or hedgerow borders were always just for play and having fun. Why were they so different to borders imposed by people: walls and rules created to divide, oppress and control, sharp fences erected to ensure no one crossed the line? With political conflict came bricked-up boundaries and violent revenge over an inch here or there in the wrong direction.

Her mother held her grandmother's silver brush in her hand before her, the one Keeva had hidden in the Romani caravan in the garden years ago after she'd died. To Keeva's irritation, her mother had found the brush, which in her grandmother's hand had stroked love and tenderness through her hair. In her mother's hand it bristled like a weapon.

'Oww, Mother.' Keeva clamped her hand against her head to stop her, as the brush scratched her scalp like a claw. 'What are you doing?'

'Your hair needs brushing; you can't go out looking like that.'

'Get off.' Keeva said, batting her mother away as her father appeared from the kitchen, drying his hands on a tea towel. Her father was more of a mother in the way he cooked and cared for Keeva; he even plaited her hair.

'Has anyone seen *Peace News?*' He checked down the sides of the sofa and on the floor. Keeva stood firmly in front of the fire.

'I'm sixteen, Mother. Why don't you brush Father's hair instead?'

Jesus, she didn't mind Father going out looking like a caveman. Now he was a conscientious objector he could do whatever he wanted, grow his hair long, become a threat to the British government and invite Germans round for tea if they should happen to crash land on his vegetable patch. Not that anybody else wanted to come over for tea.

'Why don't you stay in with us tonight, Kiki?' said her father.

She could not imagine anything worse, to be trapped in the draughty house her father had built, with its bare floorboards and unpapered walls, with Edward, her mother and father. She would brave the freezing weather, so she could escape for the evening.

'Stay in? To debate whether you ever knew who your real friends were?'

'Keeva.'

'I can read the newspapers. No, thank you, Edward is accompanying me to The Ram where we will tune into the Home Service on the wireless, sing "We Wish You A Merry Christmas" and other carols and even make a toast to the King.'

She knew that her parents would hate the idea of their daughter taking part in this patriotic ritual. Her parents glanced at each other.

'What?' said Keeva.

Mother unwrapped her paintbrushes and her father continued looking for his precious newspaper, without saying a word.

Chapter 7

6th February 1940, Parkend, Forest of Dean

While the others ate their sandwiches, Keeva waited on the brow of the hill. The Forest of Dean stretched out for miles into the distance in front of her. A million phthalo-green spires swayed on the breeze like an enormous city.

'Can't you sit down, Keeva? You will give me indigestion.' Beatrice was getting on her nerves. The chilly air crept through her coat to her damp skin, after she had worked hard felling trees all morning. She didn't want to sit down and get cold. Each tree that surged upwards from the deep brown earth, soon became another despatch of pit props in her mind. Each seemed so tall and strong, and yet their existence so fragile in wartime, when timber was needed so desperately.

One Scots pine tree stood out. Different from the others, this one had character, with boughs that twisted as if to protect itself from the harshest of storms. A giant contorted tree among a sea of smaller straighter trees. The magnificent veteran floated on the breeze, mesmerising, calling to her. She picked up an egg-shaped pine cone and tossed it down the hill.

'Do you want to share my sandwiches?' asked Gladys.

'No, thank you,' replied Keeva.

Although the porridge had barely touched the sides and she had eaten her stale Shippam's pink paste sandwiches mid-morning, she didn't want Gladys's lunch or her charity. A heady blast of oxygen filled her lungs as the wind blew and an idea formed. She'd go for a wander alone among the trees, while the others finished their lunch. She took her axe from the ground and slipped away into the trees.

Just over the hill, out of sight from the other girls, she looked around for that great gnarly twisted Scots pine tree. The broad, benign tree stood on the edge of the slope, where the rest of the trees had already been clear-felled weeks or months ago. Short stumps dotted the hillside among piles of browning brushwood.

From close up, the tree was bigger than she'd imagined, laced with lichen and mosses. She felt its deeply fissured trunk, glistening with frost in the shade, and peeled away a few crisp layers of purple-brown bark. It could be three foot in diameter at breast height; she checked her pockets for her tape measure, but she'd left it in her satchel back with the other girls. Thirty-six inches wide, which could make it over 150 feet tall. Just imagine how many pit props could be made from this mighty tree. Captain Blunt was always talking about timber production exceeding consumption to avoid the war effort grinding to a halt.

Keeva had never felled a tree this big before. She'd seen the men do it, of course. Obviously, they all knew that felling a tree like this was a man's job. The men were skilled fellers, while the girls were just forestry labourers, as they were frequently reminded. But maybe she could fell this tree?

Keeva imagined it might take a little longer. Maybe fifty blows of the axe. She only had to cut the wedge into a third of the tree, which would be sixteen inches wide. She would cut the wedge horizontally near to the ground on the downside of the slope and then the diagonal wedge above. This was the easiest way to bring a tree down she had discovered. The gravitational pull of the slope would help bring the tree toppling over.

However daunting it seemed, she knew she'd gain confidence once she had got stuck into the axe work. And Gladys, her felling partner, would be along soon with the cross-cut saw. This could be her chance to prove herself to Captain Blunt and the other men. And the girls would see for themselves that they are just as capable as the men. She could bring a big tree down too.

She tossed the seven-pounder between her hands, to and fro. Psyching herself up to make her first blow, she remembered when she was about five or six, some boys, twice her size, were daring each other to jump off a tree. Without hesitation, Keeva had marched over to them. She'd squeezed between the boys and climbed the tree. When she'd stood on top of the bough, the boys had fallen quiet and she'd leapt. Her favourite orange spot skirt had filled with air, like a parachute and she'd landed with a hard slap of her feet. When she'd marched away, her toes and sandals had been covered in dust. She hadn't said a word, and nor had they. But she'd shown them that she was the bravest.

Keeva checked which direction it would be best for the tree to fall. Directly down the hill would be easiest. But, if the tree landed on those stumps, the trunk might break into pieces, ruining the timber. Unsure, Keeva thought it safer to fell the tree at an angle across the slope.

Stepping over branches and bracken, she found a firm footing next to the roots of the great tree. Stood on the down slope, overlooking the valley of trees, Keeva held one hand either end of the axe shaft. She drew the axe back over her shoulder. You can do this, she whispered to herself. She took a deep breath and swung down with a grunt. Sliding her upper hand down the shaft to meet the other, the axe dug deep into the spongy layer of bark and through to the softwood. No different to any other tree, she thought.

Her hand lifted to screen her eyes from the sun, which broke through the clouds, as she sized up the conifer tree again. Later the faces of the girls would light up with awe to see this big brute felled. She could prove that the girls can fell any tree as well as the men. The enormous tree stood in dark silhouette against the dramatic Payne's grey-blue clouds and silver sky above. This tree would be a monument to their success.

The long, tall brown mast and great horizontal boughs were more than a hundred feet above, and the canopy sailed high above her head on the wind. Her arms lifted again and she sank the axe into the trunk. The softer flesh of this older tree was easier to work than the oaks. But the slope made felling more difficult, so her stance was crucial. A mis-swing or glancing blow off the wood could veer towards her front leg. A few scrapes and bruises had already scarred her shins in the short time she had been working in the forests.

The lesson that Arthur had given her that first time they met in the forest was imprinted on her mind. The way he'd taken her by the arms, stepped behind her, wrapped himself around her. His breath had lingered on her neck and his soft lilting voice had vibrated through his chest and into her back. Just the thought of him sucked her energy away.

She mustn't think of him when she needed to feel grounded and strong. Feet planted firmly on the earth – her hips square to the tree – just more than shoulder width apart, with her knees bent, provided her with strength and stability. Brute force as well as skill would be required for a tree this size.

She reached up to the sky with the axe and swung it down again, digging the blade into the trunk over and over.

'Laying in' or 'dipping' the trees, as the foresters called it, was getting easier. Her accuracy was improving with every tree she felled. But it had taken long and patient practice. Arthur had said she was getting very knacky with the axe. He'd reminded her that it wasn't something you wanted to be swinging around if you were losing focus, as that's when accidents happened.

She wondered what he'd be doing now. She remembered how he messed about with his friends, jumping from stump to stump on the hill below. They challenged each other to leap across gaps which were further and further apart. Keeva had tried it too when alone to see how far she could leap.

She checked the axe head, spitting on the wet stone, rubbing the blade back and forth to sharpen the edge. As her arms lifted, she felt her back and shoulders tire. The muscles in her shoulders and arms began to ache with every swing. She hoped the others would finish lunch soon.

Her mind replayed what Captain Blunt had said. I don't want you girls touching the big trees, he had warned them. We need the experienced men on the feature trees.

But surely felling this large tree would be just the same as any other tree. He had never warned them off this specific tree. She had brought down hundreds of smaller ones in the past fortnight. How could it be any different? She'd show Blunt that the girls could do it too.

The boughs of the tree creaked as they swayed in the wind. As the axe hacked away at the trunk, a hollow sound echoed back. She began to breathe more quickly. Another warning from her training darted to her mind. A tree that is hollow may not be safe to fell. Captain Blunt's words whispered on the breeze with every gust of wind. The axe slammed into the trunk again and again, the wedge sinking deeper. The strong smell of her armpits rose from her warm body each time the axe gave the hollow thud as it landed.

A niggling worry came to Keeva's mind that trees growing on slopes might not be as easy to fell as trees growing on the flat. Behind came the voices of the girls, chattering like peahens.

'There she is,' said Edith.

'Jesus, Keeva, have you gone bloomin' mad?' Rosie shouted.

Keeva hoped her hot flushed skin would disguise her blushing. She did not want them to make her doubt herself. Perhaps her confidence had been misplaced. As she paused for breath, she caught Beatrice giving Edith one of those condescending looks.

'That's a beast of a tree,' said Lily.

Aware of them all looking at her, Keeva continued laying into the trunk. She knew they were all meant to work in pairs, but now, as she swung the axe, she felt very alone. However, she trusted Gladys as her felling partner to help bring the tree down.

'Have you got the cross-cut, Gladys?' asked Keeva.

Gladys pushed her hands into her dungaree pockets and looked down at her toes.

'No! What are you doing?' Beatrice grabbed Gladys's arm and pulled her away. 'Captain Blunt explicitly said that the larger trees were for the men to fell.'

'Gladys? Won't you help?'

'I can't do it.'

Keeva turned away and rubbed her cheek. Now even Gladys was letting her down.

'You're on your own, Keeva,' said Rosie. 'I ain't cross-cutting that one with you neither.'

'You must stop. It must be over four foot wide,' Beatrice said, rushing forwards and trying to grab Keeva's arm as she swung again.

'Get off,' said Keeva. 'I need one of you to help me. Gladys?'

Gladys didn't look at Keeva. She didn't even say a word when Beatrice pushed her back. 'You're foolishly diving headlong into things without a care for the danger you might put yourself and others in,' added Beatrice.

The memories came flooding back of the girls in the playground calling her a coward. She couldn't win. She was being brave to show everyone that she could do the job really well. She was as good as the men. And Gladys's job was to fell trees with Keeva; she had to help her. Gladys was the coward. What was she frightened of? Couldn't she stand up to Rosie or Beatrice?

'Well, what do I do now?' said Keeva. 'I can't leave it like this.'

Keeva looked towards Lily. 'I don't know.' Lily muttered, looking awkward.

Edith took a deep breath and stepped forwards, as if to offer her help. But the other girls all stared at her. Seeing her chance, Keeva said, 'Edith, we'll need the six-foot cross-cut saw.'

'I don't know, Keeva, the lean on that tree looks dangerous,' said Rosie.

'I didn't ask for your opinion. I asked for your help.' Keeva wiped her brow with her forearm.

If Edith didn't hop to it, Keeva would lose her nerve. She looked up at Edith, as she leant on the axe.

'Please,' said Keeva.

Edith glanced at Beatrice, Rosie and Lily, and then walked off to get the cross-cut saw.

Thank God, Keeva thought, sighing.

'I'm not getting involved,' Beatrice said, linking arms with Gladys. 'Very sensible not to help. Come along, Gladys.' And together they walked away.

She was such a dimwit to have trusted Gladys.

'See you later, Beatrice,' Edith called.

'Huh. I wouldn't like to be in your boots when Captain Blunt comes up the hill,' Beatrice called back.

Beatrice and Gladys chatted as they made their way down the hill, like they were as thick as thieves.

Where were they going? She hoped they wouldn't go running straight to Captain Blunt.

However, Keeva breathed out as Beatrice and Gladys disappeared. Two less naysayers to deal with. She surveyed the tree as its aged muscular arms swayed on the wind. Up close, the vast 150-foot-tall specimen seemed to disappear into the sky and looked more daunting than before. Imposing and reminiscent of the pillars at the Roman Forum, that her mother had shown her in books, the broad, ridged trunk and pyramidal foliage was monumental in its grandeur. Standing firm against the wind, just its crown moving to and fro, its colossal size intimidated Keeva.

'Come on, Edith, let's get to it,' Keeva said, pulling up her dungarees with her leather belt.

'Are you sure?' asked Lily.

Keeva shivered, as she turned towards the sinewy bark at the base of the tree with a gaping wound in its side. What had she done? Doubt coursed through her body. But she couldn't leave the tree like this. Could she? Captain Blunt would never let the girls fell a tree again. They'd make the girls clean up after the men, just chopping and burning brushwood instead. She couldn't back out now.

'Don't just stand there watching. We're not a sideshow at the circus,' she said to Rosie and Lily.

'All right, calm yourself down,' said Rosie.

'We're trying to increase timber output, remember, not stand around wasting time,' said Keeva.

'We're off.'

Keeva hadn't meant that. She wanted them to be there to help. She still reeled over Gladys letting her down, as Rosie and Lily walked away. This morning had been so easy working with Gladys; the gentle wheeze of their saw had had such a calming rhythm. But now all she could hear in her head was the constant chomp, chomp of the saw munching its way through this giant beast.

Keeva wondered if something so large could be toppled by a thin strip of toothy metal, pulled to and fro by a pair of girls. Keeva eyed the monster that stood beside her, ready and awaiting its fate. A hundred or more years of growth and life, to be slain in an hour.

'Have you changed your mind?' said Edith, staring at Keeva.

What if the men used a different technique for the larger trees, which they had not been taught?

'No. No. Let's get it down,' said Keeva, flaking off some loose purple-brown bark from the tree. One girl either side of the trunk, dropping to their knees as if in prayer beside the tree, they looked across towards one another without saying a word.

As they pulled back and forth, Edith pushed her black-rimmed glasses up her nose more than necessary, as if she was worried. Keeva did not feel entirely comfortable with Edith and wouldn't have picked her to help. Aside from being a bit of a crybaby suffering from homesickness, she had latched on to Beatrice from the start. Keeva hadn't imagined Edith had a mind of her own, until this point.

'You all right?' asked Keeva.

'I don't want to talk right now.'

Of course, she was hardly the friendly type. Edith had a coldness to her.

'Did you have a better idea?'

'Yes, you should have waited for us before starting,' said Edith.

Keeva had been right to steer clear of Edith.

'None of you have ever waited for me.' Keeva's throat sounded hoarse.

'So, you want me to feel sad for you?'

'No.'

'We didn't think you would make a start without us. You're getting up my back.'

'You mean "getting my back up",' said Keeva.

 Edith looked round at her 'What?'

'Oh, nothing.' Edith had said her mother was a teacher, but they seemed to speak a different language in Yorkshire.

'You're not the only one here with problems,' Edith snapped at Keeva.

Keeva's fingers trembled as she grabbed the wooden handle and pulled hard. What problems did Edith think she had? Did she imagine that homesickness was all anyone had to worry about? She had no idea what Keeva had been through.

Keeva and Edith continued in silence. They worked their way sharply around the circumference of the trunk. With hardly a foot either side of the saw at the midpoint, there was barely enough room to move the tool back and forth. Keeva stopped and looked around. Was there someone she could ask for help? Where had Rosie and Lily gone if they needed them?

Was anyone else within earshot should they need to shout for help? She looked down towards the men and wondered if she could attract their attention. No, she would never live it down. They were too far away and she could not expect them to help. They already had no respect for Keeva or the girls.

'We'll need to cut a wedge into the sides of the tree,' said Keeva.

'No.'

'But we can't get the bite on the saw without more room to move.'

'We have not been told to do that, Keeva.'

'I've seen the men do it,' Keeva said.

'Why do you think that you know best?' protested Edith, sweat glistening on her forehead.

Keeva daren't mention the hollow sound she had heard before when she was thumping into the tree with the axe. She hadn't seen any evidence of hollowness in the trunk; but she had learnt to pay attention to the slightest change in sound on the axe or saw. She did not think the noise of the saw was consistent with a hollow trunk. The saw had a higher pitch, which could mean the grain was tight and straight. She hoped the lack of vibration in her hand meant there were few knots too.

Another worry came to mind – that the tree may be rotten. Her mind wound itself up, like her clockwork mouse, which her mother had thrown on the fire in a rage one day when she was a child. She had to look for bracket fungus, the most obvious sign of rot. Sweat dripped from her eyebrow, as she swayed from side to side. She should have considered this before. How could she have forgotten? She felt like such an idiot.

Keeva stopped and let go of the saw to look up at the trunk for any growths sticking out like elephant feet or big brown or white ears. If the tree had fungus growing out of it, the base of the tree would be rotten, and the tree would be more unpredictable as it went down. But she could only smell the citrus-fresh scent of pine needles on the air, not wood rot.

'What's the matter?' asked Edith.

'Nothing.'

Keeva stood up and stretched her back – left to right – then leant her back up against the tree. She looked up again at the dark-green seething mass of foliage agitated by the wind. Should she give up after all? She didn't want to fall out with Edith over this. She looked over to the stick men loading the trees onto the trucks at the bottom of the hill. They were using horses to winch the wood up off the ground and onto the flat bed of the trucks. She could just make out Beatrice with her jodhpurs in the distance and Captain Blunt in front of her. Oh Jesus, he'd probably be on his way over soon.

'Oh, no,' said Keeva, pointing.

'Come on then, quick,' said Edith, and pulled hard.

Keeva's thighs burned, and her palms were hot and red as the saw rasped and jumped against the trunk. Edith puffed and grunted as the saw caught fast in the crack. Her hands could barely keep their grip, as Keeva pulled back and forth. Edith was struggling now too, shaking with every exertion. Keeva felt a chill as the wind breathed across her skin and through the millions of trees watching in the forest.

She heard someone shouting. Was someone in trouble? Edith looked round, as a group of male fellers swarmed at the bottom of the hill, gesturing up towards Keeva and Edith. She couldn't make out their words, but she knew what their gestures meant: stand back and get out of the away. They knelt either side of the tree again, lowered their heads and lined up the saw.

'Come on, Edith. Let's get this brute down,' said Keeva, securing her grip on the sweaty cross-cut handle.

'What are you stupid girr … do … ?' an approaching man shouted from down below.

'Go,' Edith commanded. 'Pull. Pull. Pull.'

The vigour with which Edith pulled on the other end of the cross-cut surprised Keeva. She pulled the saw with all her might. With the saw taut between their hands, Edith's determination put fire in Keeva's muscles. They quickened the rhythm and Keeva's kneecaps ground into the sand as the blade cut almost through.

'Stop!' yelled Keeva.

'Stand back,' another man barked from afar.

'We must do this now,' said Edith, and, as the tree teetered on its hinge, Keeva got ready to run. Salty sweat stung Keeva's eye.

'No, don't stop. We're not there yet,' said Edith.

The men sieged up the hill, a seething mass of bodies. Angry men ready for battle.

'We've got to do it now,' said Keeva.

'Pull. Pull. Pull,' Edith growled.

An almighty cracking noise shuddered through the sinews of the tree. Birds took flight from the forest canopy around them. The enormous beast gave a deafening snapping, ripping yawn over Keeva, releasing a pine-scented liquor from its break.

'Timber!' Keeva yelled as loud as she could, springing from her knees.

She stood momentarily to admire the incredible monument tumble out of the sky, like a huge rolling wave about to come crashing down on the shores beneath. Below, the groups of men split in two and fled from the falling tree.

'Keeva!' Edith shouted.

The compost of pine needles and sand shifted beneath Keeva's feet as she turned to run up the hill away from the slain tree, which groaned across the valley and shunted forwards on its single cleft hoof. Excruciated ligaments of wood snapped, bursting apart at the ankle as the monster began to topple. Keeva fell over a branch and tried to get back to her feet. Sounds like gunshots ripped through the air, as the tree hinged forwards, slowly at first.

'Keeva!' Edith shouted.

She scrambled to get up but couldn't get a hold. Her feet shifted on the sand and she slipped onto her hands and knees. She had been warned that the base of a tree, like the hoof of an angry horse, could kick back behind the stump on forward-leaning trees. She knew she had to get out the way or the stump could kill her. But, instead, she fell to the ground, face in the sand and rolled over.

Immediately, the base of the tree opened towards her, sheered clean off its stump and thrust forwards. Just a few yards from the ground, the full weight of the hundred tonne tree snapped clean off and keeled towards the ground. Even in the panic of the moment, she hoped Arthur would be impressed with her. A gust of wind blew over Keeva's damp skin as the giant became airborne and gravity took hold of the falling beast.

Keeva felt herself being dragged across the sand by her dungarees, as Edith grabbed on to her. Holding Edith, she pulled herself further out of the way, as the Scots pine tumbled from the sky, downhill towards the men. Were they too close? Would it be her fault if they were crushed?

The huge trunk continued to hurtle down the hill, racing towards the men. Branches cracked, snapped and splintered as huge spears from the tree exploded across the hillside. The men fled, and she could still just see Captain Blunt shouting and waving frantically.

'No, no, no!' shouted Keeva.

Chapter 8

Lady Gertrude Denman

16th February 1940, Palace of Westminster, London

Trudie – Lady Denman – stood outside the subcommittee meeting in the Palace of Westminster. She was late. A cyclist had been knocked off her bike by a lorry and caused a hold-up on the road outside. She hesitated when her hand touched the brass Tudor rose door handle. She had an urge to make a refusal: like showjumping horses, she wanted to swerve out of this instead of jumping right into it.

'Nonsense, get in there, woman,' she said to herself.

She had noticed that men who came for meetings in the government offices were announced as they entered a room. She knew this was not the case for women. She took a deep breath, twisted the handle and felt the coil-sprung mechanism tighten as she pushed the heavy door open to the meeting room.

She looked over the bank of men, like undertakers in black suits, to see Mr Bevin sitting at the head of the table. She had hoped he wouldn't be present. He had a reputation for being a bulldozer in meetings. The light from the chandeliers shone on the bald heads of the other men, who looked like large flies that had landed on the table.

She was used to being ignored on entering a meeting or being asked for coffee, so she had several strategies and her first was to take charge. A high-risk strategy as Mr Ernest Bevin, the minister of labour in the coalition government, was in the room. But she was the expert in this meeting. She walked across the red and yellow zigzag carpet towards the red leather-topped table where he sat.

'Good afternoon, gentlemen, you may address me as Lady Gertrude Denman. We are here to discuss the Women's Land Army. Can we get started please?'

'The Women's Land Army?' asked the man to Bevin's right.

'We're discussing essential work orders and wartime labour needs, not flower arranging,' another man snorted to an avalanche of laughter from the committee.

'I have been invited by the office of Mr Ernest Bevin to address the committee.'

Almost bewildered, the men looked to Mr Bevin to grant permission.

'Yes, yes, that's right, take a seat, Missus Denman,' said Mr Bevin, pushing the bridge of his thick, black-rimmed glasses and leafing through his paperwork with his stalwart fingers. 'Ahh yes.' He pulled out a paper and looked at his wristwatch. 'Well, you'd better get on with it. You are already ten minutes late and we haven't got all day. Sit down.'

She walked to the empty seat at the other end of the table and remained on her feet.

'The Women's Land Army is vital to the war effort and desperately needed to increase home-grown food and timber production. Where the farmers and foresters are accepting their help, their contribution is increasing production beyond what we could achieve before. In short, their work is desperately important to the nation.'

'Yes, yes …' said Mr Bevin.

'But thousands will become tens of thousands and this group of workers need statutory working entitlements.'

Lady Denman looked at every member of the committee in turn. She drew a breath and then made eye contact with Mr Bevin.

'For their welfare, they need one day off a week, statutory holiday and sick pay entitlements.'

The men grunted in objection.

'No question of allowing this for farm workers. If you let that sort of thing go on, your bread and butter will be cut right out from under your feet,' said Mr Bevin.

'It would simply bring this group in line with entitlements for the other women's services.'

'A day off for farmers! Never heard anything so absurd.'

'There is a statutory forty-eight-hour working week across all industries,' she added, looking straight at Mr Bevin.

'Missus Denman, the first thing to decide before you walk into any negotiation is what to do if the other fellow says "no",' Mr Bevin said, shaking his jowls.

Several men laughed.

Trudie's body twitched and felt hot as she unbuttoned her emerald-green suit jacket. In the past, her determination to fight back was strong, like a fast-flowing river, but following acute appendicitis, she was concerned she had lost her edge. The stitches from several operations had distorted her stomach and caused discomfort as she walked towards Mr Bevin.

'Have you ever considered what it would be like if you were a woman, accustomed to wearing nothing but a dress and working in factories and shops?'

'Why would I need to do that?' Mr Bevin asked, leaning back in his chair towards the fireplace and cobalt-blue patterned walls.

'To enable you to understand the plight of the women who are required to work excessive hours out on farmland or in forests during the winter. Whether they are sick or exhausted, they will be expected to fell trees with an axe and saw, work in sawmills, deliver lambs and calves all through the night, or rake out the pig sties.'

The men reeked of sweat and cologne and an unpleasant feeling took hold of Trudie.

'Could we open a window, please?'

She pushed the stained-glass window open to feel a blast of fresh cold air on her face. The swirls of thorny rose stems on the window curled around the flowers like a boa constrictor.

'And what would you know about the needs of these workers?' asked another man.

'I am the director of the Westminster Press; we produce six million newspapers a week across the country, and I am in charge of editorial content. It is my business to know about the lives of my readers, many of whom live in rural communities and many of whom are women. They do not get the same rights as other groups of workers.'

'A newspaper has just three things to do: one is to amuse; another is to entertain; and the rest is to mislead,' said Mr Bevin.

Trudie leant on the table in front of Mr Bevin and spoke in her low, clear voice.

'But when you need women to register at labour exchanges for war work, your track record for misleading women into war work without fair workers' rights will guarantee you the headlines.'

Feeling her body tense up and become awkward, she returned to her seat for a glass of water. She had joked that she was a good advertisement for drinking and smoking too much when she nearly died after the operation to remove her appendix. But she could certainly do with a cigarette and a large brandy right now.

'Missus Denman—'

'Lady Denman.'

'The most conservative man in this world is the British trade unionist when you want to change him.'

'Is that because he is too old and set in his ways to learn?' She gained momentum and volume. 'Is he unable to do the kind of painful thinking about his own prejudices? And in the light of reason and facts, does he not realise his policy is based on an out-of-date conception of the world in which we live?'

'Dear oh dear!' he said, shaking his head. 'Unintelligent people always look for a scapegoat.'

'This winter, Mr Bevin, is one of the hardest in living memory, and the girls, many of whom are town-bred and wholly unused to outdoor work, refuse to be beaten by mud, snow and ice. But they must have one day off, sick pay and holiday pay, or they will be broken, and food and timber supply will stop.'

'If the workers, male or female, see themselves faced with defeat through starvation, they will prefer to go down fighting everyday out in the fields – whether or not we agree,' he said.

'Hear, hear, Mr Bevin!'

She stared at the men in disbelief and felt herself beginning to tremble.

'I will ask you again for a day off, sick pay and holiday entitlement for the Land Army in line with the other women's services.'

'No! Out of the question,' Mr Bevin replied.

'So, you think it is acceptable for the women to work seven days a week and be exposed to exploitation by the farmers and timber merchants?'

'Which "no" did you not understand?'

With the bit between her teeth she said, 'You cannot deny them these basic workers' rights.'

'I can do what I damn well please!' he shouted.

She felt the sting of the whip.

'You … have not … heard the last of this,' she stumbled over her words in front of the men.

She felt responsible for these women, whom she was recruiting by the thousands. They would not thank her if they were left out in the cold and wet, working for hours without any legal protection. She retreated towards the door.

'A word of advice, Missus Denman,' he said, as she looked over her shoulder at him. 'Taking your good conscience round from body to body to ask what you ought to do with it, is placing your directorship and the Women's Institute movement in absolutely the wrong position. The Ministry of Labour is quite geared up to recruit staff for agriculture and employ the best. Perhaps you should let us get on with it.'

'Thank you but that will not be necessary.'

She saw her brown envelope bag on the chair and returned to pick it up, bridling with anger.

'Good afternoon, gentlemen.'

She swept through the corridors and burst out into the bitter February air on Westminster Square. She found her Rolls-Royce among the orange lamps of twilight and climbed in, fumbling in her bag for her handkerchief and cigarette case.

'Balcombe please, John.'

She was annoyed she had forgotten to mention the great work the Women's Land Army and Women's Forestry Service had done in the first war, and that she was offering her home to the government free of charge for the Land Army HQ. Sniffing into her handkerchief, she watched the darkness descend upon a few shrinking drops of peach daylight as the sky pulled over its dark cloak.

She hated the government keeping her on such tight reins. In the last war she threatened riots in the countryside if the government tried to take control, but her threats today about the newspaper damaging Mr Bevin's reputation had not worked at all.

Chapter 9

Balcombe Place, East Sussex

A thick hoarfrost cloaked the canopy of trees on the narrow Sussex lanes, as Trudie returned from her meeting with Mr Bevin at the Ministry of Labour, which had been a disaster. Twilight had passed and she was running late. Hiding in the darkness of the back seat, she hoped her driver could not see her in the rear-view mirror. She didn't feel like talking. Suddenly burning hot, she wrestled to remove her jacket and her wretched feelings with it. Opening the window, she breathed away her tears on the frosty air.

She had a meeting with Inez at five, to compose a letter for the last post, and it was already a quarter to five. She couldn't be late for the post, or for dinner at six – and neither could she miss it; she needed to keep up her strength, while she was still recovering from her illness. Being punctual for mealtimes was her only rule in the house, and now all the new Land Army staff were adhering to her rules she couldn't flout them herself.

She wondered if the operations to resolve her acute appendicitis had affected her bladder control. By the time the car pulled into the gravel drive of Balcombe Estate, she was desperate. She entered the porch. She was getting used to the sight of the scores of young women in the main hall. Her butler took her jacket.

'Good afternoon, Lady Denman,'

'Afternoon, David.'

'How was your meeting, M'Lady?'

'Deplorable.'

'Oh dear! Are those Whitehall types trying to tell your ladyship how to run things again?'

'I'm afraid so.'

'And the rallies?'

'The cold stopped people from coming out. Excuse me, David.'

As swiftly as she could, she entered the main hall to hear the girls' accents from Manchester, Liverpool and London. She was concerned that the new staff might occupy every spare corner of the house, including the water closets. By the door, women huddled round a trestle table, creating a barrier to her passing through. Another young girl rushed towards her with a stack of paperwork piled up in her arms, and bumped into Trudie, launching a cascade of letters towards the floor.

'Flippin 'ek! Watch out why don't yer!' the girl yelled.

Trudie stepped aside.

'Careful,' she said sternly.

'Oh sorry, M'Lady,' she said, and started picking them up.

The huddle of girls looked up, suddenly more serious, and nudged one another.

'Afternoon, Lady Denman,' they chorused, and curtseyed.

'Afternoon, girls,' she replied as she walked through them, and disappeared into the corridor, heading for the staff WC. Relieved that she'd made it in time, she took several deep breaths and then checked her eyes for signs of redness in the mirror.

As she entered the main hall, the smell of the fires made her feel more comfortable. But she couldn't help noticing that her favourite landscape painting and antique chair gave her less pleasure now. They were pressed to the walls, hidden behind hordes of staff. She was even surprised that she missed her husband, Thomas, since he'd moved out to the hotel in Hove.

David, her butler, loitered around behind her. Now what was it, she thought.

'Have you got a minute, Lady Denman?' She checked her

pocket watch. It was five thirty-five and she was already late. 'It's rather urgent.'

She nodded and he bowed, indicating it was a private matter. Trudie left the hubbub of the main hall and entered her office, the business room. This room was out of bounds to staff, as a rule. A private space for Trudie. There were few of those left since the WLA had moved in.

'It's just that some of the new women here are testing the patience of cook and the rest of the household staff. I took it upon myself to have a quiet word with you.'

'What's the problem?'

'The girls don't seem to appreciate the food and it upsets the staff to serve people they feel are inferior to themselves. It is a very trying time for the staff. Some of them are threatening to leave.'

'I'm sorry to hear that, David. Has anything happened specifically to upset the cook and staff?'

'When the fresh fruit salad was served last night, one of the girls said, "What, no custard today?" There was mayhem in the kitchen at the mention of it. We've got nothing against them per se. They just need to learn some manners.'

'The women have been brought up on a different diet and have come to expect different food; it will take time to adjust. Is it possible to procure Bird's custard powder, say?'

'Well, yes, I suppose so.'

'Let's give that a try. In the meantime, I must say what a fantastic job you are doing. With the extra demands of an increased household, you are all really rising to the challenge. Please pass on my gratitude to the staff. I will speak to the cook myself.'

Inez entered the room with a waft of roast pheasant.

'Ah Inez, just the woman I wanted to see. Is that all, David?'

'Yes, M'Lady.'

David nodded and left the room, closing the door behind him. Trudie sighed and took a seat in her armchair.

'How are you?' asked Inez.

'Well, thank you. Take a seat,' she replied, glancing at her pocket watch. 'Have we heard back from the Forestry Commission yet? I hear the collieries are desperate for pit props.'

'A letter arrived this morning from Captain Blunt. Not with the response you were hoping for, I'm afraid,' said Inez.

'What did he say?' Trudie asked.

'He's rather confused and surprised he has been sent the girls for heavy felling work. He suggested that Timber Control only wanted girls at Parkend for measuring, which wasn't like … dressmaking.'

'Tussk! Forestry work is not a reserved occupation. We need more workers; it's urgent.'

For a moment, Trudie wondered if it really was too much to expect women to fell trees. She stood up to practice her golf swing, which was how she had mastered the art of axe work. Briefly, Trudie revelled in the fact that she was unbeaten on her golf course. She stoked the open fire and felt more confident.

'Where does Captain Blunt expect to find the thousands of forestry workers we need? Among the military?' Trudie tapped her fingers on the mantlepiece.

'I don't know, but he assumed it was a mistake,' Inez answered.

'I explained this in my previous letter. Was it sent?'

'Yes, of course.'

Inez had worked with Trudie for many years and rarely made a mistake. Inez had been Trudie's personal assistant at the National Federation of Women's Institutes briefly before becoming her assistant director in the Land Army. Inez knew how Trudie thought, which made her invaluable.

'Well, we haven't long before last post and we need to reply tonight,' said Trudie.

Inez moved to the typewriter as Trudie dictated.

'Thank you for your letter dated January thirtieth,' she said.

'I gather that at that time you had not received mine of January eleventh,' added Inez.

'I am afraid that, Captain Blunt, you could not have been aware that some twenty Land Army volunteers are to be employed as forestry workers.'

'They will be felling trees, trimming and lopping timber for pit props,' Inez suggested.

'Yes, then add: alongside a further twenty women who will be training to become forestry measurers,' added Trudie.

'And no previous training is required,' said Inez.

'Good.'

Inez pulled the return lever across to start a new paragraph.

'Something about the forestry measurers being drawn from a different type of girl altogether. They must, as Captain Blunt says, have a higher education, have attended university or had previous experience of mathematics.'

This level of detail was critical at this early stage when politics in the timber trade was hampering progress. Importers, merchants and the government were all vying for control. She felt the weight of the national timber crisis squarely on her shoulders, while the others squabbled between themselves.

Trudie continued, 'You will appreciate that for this special kind of work it isn't too easy to find the right volunteers. If you have any member of the force with you whom you think particularly suitable for attending the coming Timber Trade meeting in Yeovil, we should be glad to know. It is imperative that the Women's Land Army is represented at this meeting.'

The lessons of running the Women's Land Army in the first world war were still clear in Trudie's mind. There had been three thousand women working with an axe and they saw increasing home-grown timber production. Without the wave of power generated by the suffragette movement, this time round the organisation would have to face the same prejudices with even more determination, and increase their visibility across the timber industry.

'Still time for a glass of sherry before supper?' Trudie asked.

'I'll send this off,' Inez replied, pulling the paper from the typewriter and leaving Trudie to pour her sherry from the decanter.

With seconds to go until six o'clock, Trudie made her way to the high table in the window embrasure of the dining hall, where Inez was already seated. She walked past tables of six, where the girls sat chatting and laughing together.

'Is anything the matter? You look worried,' Trudie asked Inez.

'I was just thinking about the letter. It's just that the Forestry Commission want women to be university educated and physically strong enough to work in timber production. But they doubt whether women can be both?'

'Oh, the inconvenience of belonging to the wrong sex. We will prove them wrong, Inez,' Trudie replied. 'Don't worry.'

'And there's another thing. Who will look after the women out in the forest?'

The serving staff entered the room with trolleys of hot plates steaming and there was a hush as they began to serve the tables.

'Oh no, not roast pheasant again!' yelled the young cockney girl as her dinner was placed in front of her.

'I like that girl's spirit,' Trudie said with a smile.

Chapter 10

Keeva

22nd February 1940, Parkend, Forest of Dean, and Timber Trade Meeting, Yeovil, Somerset

Keeva made her way down the stairwell for breakfast. She was late on purpose to avoid the swarm of hungry girls in the dining hall and their gossip. She joined the back of the queue of girls in ill-fitting new uniforms, tucked in her jumper and bent over to make sure her jodhpurs were tucked into the tops of her socks.

The queue edged forward into the noisy dining hall, where every girl seemed to talk at the top of her voice. Missus Redrum stalked up and down the serving hatch like a bull ready to trample on them. When she reached the front of the queue, Redrum stared at her intently, the whites of her eyes enlarged. The cook slopped a lump of porridge into her bowl and threw a crust of bread onto her plate with such disdain, she reminded her of Viola.

'If you're late again, you'll get nothing,' Redrum warned.

'Sorry.'

'You will be, young lady. There's a fine line between bravery and stupidity.'

Keeva blushed as she walked away. Gladys jumped up to catch her attention.

'I've saved a place for you.'

'Thanks, Gladys.'

Gladys had been trying to make it up to her ever since she let her down when felling the big tree. Beatrice evacuated the wooden dining table as she arrived. Maybe she resented Edith, her own felling partner, swapping sides to work with Keeva.

'All right, how are you today, Cleaver?' said Rosie with a smile. 'Come over and steal a chair beside me. You had your little chat with Blunt yet?'

'No.'

Keeva knew the telling-off was coming. Blunt would probably take her outside and shoot her with his twelve bore. She wasn't feeling well at all. Her whole body ached. She was starving hungry and the dried-up porridge and crust of bread didn't look appealing. She had been in the place just over a month and hated it already: the strict mealtimes, all the questions and some of the girls. She'd never met anyone like Beatrice before and she hoped she wouldn't again.

'How are you?' Keeva asked with an awkward smile.

'Me muscles in m' legs, I could hardly get down the stairs, like a bow-legged old woman,' said Rosie.

'I didn't sleep well either. Did you?' said Gladys.

'No, not at all,' replied Keeva, 'I lay awake most of the night what with Edith sobbing again and beds squeaking all night. How was Edith this morning?'

'She seemed all right. It's not really what I expected here. But I guess it might not be for long, if what Blunt says is anything to go by,' said Gladys.

Keeva swallowed her porridge. 'What do you mean?'

'They won't keep us on after what happened.'

'Did he say that to you?' asked Keeva.

'One of the girls from the other dorm said so in the breakfast queue,' said Gladys.

'Here comes the old rusty saw himself,' warned Rosie.

'Attention girls, attention.'

The clatter of plates and clink of spoons in cups of tea on tables stopped and the room fell silent, except for the metallic scrape of Missus Redrum's ladle on the bottom of the porridge pan.

'As yesterday, the majority of you will be heading out to the forest. Except there is a slight change of plan for a few of you. The director of the Women's Land Army, Lady Gertrude Denman, has asked if three of you can go to the Timber Trade meeting in Yeovil to represent the women.'

'Sir, I should like to go,' said Beatrice.

'How dare you shout out! When I want your advice, I will ask for it. Rosie Worsell, Keeva O'Connor and …'

Keeva was surprised to hear her name being called out. Captain Blunt had said she was not to be trusted after felling the big tree on the hill weeks ago.

'Gladys, can Gladys come?' Rosie asked.

'Be quiet!' he barked.

'I am used to attending social meetings and public speaking,' Beatrice interrupted for a second time.

'This is not a mothers' meeting. It's about a very serious war matter. Rosie Worsell, Keeva O'Connor and Edith Walker, see me now.'

Blunt brought them into his office and closed the door.

'Sit down,' he said, as he stood looking down at them. He fastened the button that had pulled a hole in the tweed around his well-established stomach. A motor vehicle engine rattled outside as it pulled away and left the rasp of Blunt's breath in its wake.

'While there is enormous demand for pit props and we need all hands to the saw, Lady Denman, the director of the Women's Land Army, wants you girls represented at this meeting. The three of you came to mind. Meet me back here at zero eight hundred hours in full uniform with beret.'

Keeva sighed as she heaved herself upstairs to get her coat, wondering why they had been picked. Rosie was a good feller, stronger than a lot of the others. But why would Blunt choose her?

'Oh, I wish I was going with you,' said Gladys.

'So, you can stay out of the cold for a day?' said Rosie. 'Sounds boring.'

'Why did he pick on you then?' Gladys asked.

'Because he wanted us troublemakers out of the way, I reckon,' said Rosie.

The description bothered Keeva. She had tried to prove herself by bringing a big tree down. She wanted to impress the men. But really, she just needed to fit in. Gladys was so likeable, she would have made a good friend. But she couldn't rely upon her; she was just a fair-weather friend.

'We'd better get going, it's nearly seven already,' said Edith, looking worried.

Keeva hoped that Blunt had realised over the last few weeks that a tree that size had in fact contributed a huge quantity of pit props to the war effort, which were so desperately in demand. She hoped they wouldn't ask to see her identity card at the meeting. She didn't want them to find out she was only sixteen. It would be awful to be caught representing the Women's Land Army one year underage. If she was sent home, how could she face her mother, let alone all the other 'friends' she used to have? And where had her beret got to?

'Blunt said full uniform and he's already told me off for not wearing my beret several times,' Keeva moaned as she frantically searched her bag and under her bed.

'When did you last have it? I haven't seen you in it since the first day in the forest,' said Gladys.

'Oh no, maybe I left it in the forest. I'll never find it now.'

'Keeva, don't worry, borrow mine,' said Gladys.

'But what will you wear?'

'I can ask around for yours today and I've got a head scarf I can wear.'

'Oh Gladys, thank you.'

Maybe Gladys wasn't so bad. But she didn't want to make a fool of herself again. Gladys might not like her, if she knew the truth about her family anyway. Besides, Gladys might get in trouble for not wearing her beret, and then she would be annoyed with Keeva. Oh, she was glad she'd never had to wear a stupid uniform like this before. But here she was, dressed the same as all the others. Each one indistinguishable from the next, like a flock of chattering house sparrows. Maybe, over time, she'd wear in her new clothes. For now, she felt uncomfortable, every time she bent over to pick something up, the bottom of her breeches rode up over her knees and came untucked from her socks. She had to wiggle her legs to shake the blessed things down again.

'What if they ask us to say something at the meeting, Gladys?'

'You probably won't have to. But if you do, then just tell the truth. Say you've just started training at Parkend Forestry School, that's all.'

'But what if I say the wrong thing – will they send me home?'

'No, of course they won't. Go on, get down there. Oh, I wish I was going with you. I want to hear all about it when you get back,' said Gladys.

Keeva wondered why Captain Blunt would drive them to the meeting. Wasn't he too busy with important war work? Maybe the meeting was important? He had said so to Beatrice. But then why had she, Rosie and Edith been invited along? The three of them squeezed in the cabin of the lorry next to him. There wasn't much room for Rosie's long legs and their hips side by side on a seat made for two.

Rosie asked, 'How come you picked us then?'

'You'll see, girls, you'll see,' he replied with a smile on his face.

He just said they were representing the WLA at the meeting. When they had nearly arrived, he shouted, 'Damn and blast it!' where a tree had fallen across the road. They joined a queue of cars inching past the tree and, by the time they arrived, they were late.

The door creaked open slowly as Keeva pushed the handle and the girls entered the noisy hall, packed elbow to jowl with scores of men dressed in tweed and oilskin jackets. The three of them huddled nervously together at the back of the room, ushered forwards by Blunt.

On stage, a large man at the front, who wore a deerstalker hat, called the room to order with a sharp blow of the hammer to a block. 'Mr Frank Blackman, can you come to the front to tell us what you think of the impending and very grave situation we face as a nation at war please.'

The room fell quiet. Just the click of the man's heels could be heard as he took to the stage.

A tall thin man with a large nose and Adam's apple rushed towards Keeva. 'The WI meeting is not today,' he said and tried to push them out of the door.

'They are with me,' said Captain Blunt.

With a brush of eyebrows, thick moustache and bristles on his chin, Mr Frank Blackman stepped onto the stage. 'There is a swiftly developing crisis, which is breeding impatience. The crisis in timber shortages is a matter which will be the difference between winning or losing the war.'

Mr Adam's Apple raised his eyebrows. 'You might find some room at the back.'

'While timber production has increased,' the bristled man boomed from the stage, 'it's still nowhere near enough to meet the wartime demands.'

Keeva followed Edith and Rosie to the back. Hiding beneath her beret and overcoat, she avoided eye contact with anyone.

'Gentlemen,' said Mr Adam's Apple, to ask a row of men to allow them through.

'You go first,' whispered Edith, bumping into Rosie.

Keeva breathed in the smell of men's hair wax as she squeezed through. The men stood up one by one to let them shuffle past, pressed up against the men's stomachs.

'What's he on about?' whispered Rosie.

'Colliery owners have acute anxiety over the forward supply of pit props,' Bristles went on.

Keeva sat down between Rosie and a bearded man who stank of pipe tobacco.

'Something must be done to remedy the situation urgently,' the man on the stage finished and handed over to Harold McGinn, Forestry Commission HQ, who was the large, ruddy-faced man in a tweed suit and deerstalker hat.

'Look at that hat,' whispered Rosie. Keeva brought her finger to her lips.

An elbow pushed against her arm forcibly as the bearded man beside her folded his arms.

'Sorry, love.'

'The Royal Hotel, Bath,' Mr Deerstalker said, 'has become our new temporary HQ as we employ more staff. Mountains of paperwork to protect our forests created after the last war has had to be destroyed. Bathtubs became great lakes of wastepaper, which have rapidly overflowed. Bewildered hotel residents have found themselves retreating before a steadily mounting invasion of staff. And a fever of secret documents has rippled through the corridors laying the foundations for war.'

Keeva looked at Rosie and Edith, sat beside Captain Blunt. Silent and serious, Edith looked uneasy. Too hot, Keeva began to unbutton her coat as she wondered why they had been selected to attend the meeting, if not to demonstrate the good work the Women's Land Army could do. She and Edith must have felled a ten-tonne tree that day; she had felt it in her muscles for a week after. Crammed up so close to the man next to her, she felt his body belch. With little ventilation, she held her breath as a foul odour reached her nostrils.

'Edward Hopkins, private timber merchant, to speak from the floor,' said the chair.

''Ere what's 'e going to say?' whispered Rosie, nudging Keeva and Edith.

'Private timber merchants, like myself, don't want to be told what to do by the government as our commercial interests will be compromised. We need to ramp up production to meet demand. That's all.'

'That's Arthur's father, ain't it?' said Rosie.

'Shh,' whispered Keeva.

Mr Deerstalker leapt back up. 'We need to protect our forests while increasing timber production. Don't forget why the Forestry Commission was formed after the Great War in nineteen nineteen. We felled half of Britain's forests in the last war. The best half. There has been just twenty short years for new stocks of trees to grow. We need these trees to reach maturity.'

'Graham Minley, colliery owner,' said the chair. A broad-shouldered man wearing a brown cap slowly unfolded from his chair.

'Collieries are at risk of closure. We have just seven months of pit props in reserve. The situation is desperate. But what is more desperate is the lack of forestry workers to supply the pit props.'

Keeva wondered whether she, Rosie and Edith had been invited to be praised in front of the men. Maybe Blunt would tell the men that they had brought down a massive tree, to prove what could be achieved by women. She felt proud of herself for being invited to the meeting. They were good representatives of the WLA.

'We're here, ain't we?' said Rosie, frowning.

'Yes,' whispered Keeva to Rosie.

Keeva couldn't bear to wear her coat a moment longer. She pulled it off, revealing her green jumper and jodhpurs beneath and knocking the man next to her. She remembered Blunt's warning, 'Don't say a word.'

Bristles said, 'Schoolboys are welcome, before they are called up. Offering them work experience would be hugely valuable.'

'Hear, hear,' chorused a few men.

Edward Hopkins shouted out, 'We could use British prisoners or college boys.'

'Hear, hear.'

'Shall we say something?' asked Rosie.

'No, don't,' urged Edith.

Keeva's heart pounded. She felt the urge to shout, 'What about the Women's Land Army?'

Mr Deerstalker said, 'Still not enough – there's itinerant and Irish home rule workers.'

Another man shouted, 'And we need men to do this job.'

'Hear, hear!'

'What?' said Rosie, looking at Keeva.

Blunt had said to be seen but not heard – don't say a word.

'What about conscientious objectors?' asked another man to a chorus of groans.

'There is the Women's Land Army, of course,' Mr Deerstalker said.

Keeva immediately felt a shiver of pride.

'Oh dear! Don't mention it,' Bristles replied, and roars of laughter broke out in the hall.

Keeva looked towards Captain Blunt and saw Rosie's mouth fall open. He raised his stubby forefinger to his lips. While all around them the men guffawed.

'Flippin' cheek,' whispered Rosie.

'It's not the type of work for young women. We need strong men,' said Bristles.

'But we want to help,' Edith whispered across.

'We cannot help admiring the splendid spirit of the girls in offering their services.' Bristles winked. A few men huffed with amusement.

'I'm not having this,' said Rosie, 'I'm going to shut them up.'
Edith shook her head.

'The trouble is they are not home early enough in the morning to get on with the job,' Bristles added.

The huffing became a loud 'ha ha'. Laughter spread across the audience and devoured the oxygen in the hall. 'Get up, girls,' Captain Blunt said quietly.

They pushed up to their feet and a silence fell upon the hall. Rosie's face went red, Keeva's mouth was dry as all eyes turned on them.

'If I can come up with representatives of the Women's Land Army to say a few words?' Captain Blunt asked.

They were trapped by men on all sides. Keeva started sweating as her skin burned hot.

Bristles said, 'This is rather irregular. It is, of course, not intended the women should take the place of skilled men. But may this be permitted?'

Mr Deerstalker said: 'Yes, yes, of course.'

'Women may be of assistance to relieve the timber crisis,' a man called out from the front.

'They can relieve my hardwood anytime,' a man behind Keeva replied, to another outburst of coarse laughter.

'I can't breathe,' Edith whispered.

'Softwoods may rise in price if the Women's Land Army can give us a hand,' retorted another.

Rosie stood up and shouted, 'We work hard, we do.'

'Excuse me, excuse me,' Keeva said as she got up and they stumbled past the men.

'Get out of our way,' said Rosie loudly, tripping over a man's feet and falling on to his lap.

'Oh, you can sit on my wood anytime, love,' he said, smacking Rosie's bottom as she got up.

'Just a minute, just a minute,' said Bristles, 'Can we have some order?'

'Quite frankly, it's a crying shame there should be a Women's Land Army while men on the dole are idling on street corners,' said Mr Deerstalker.

Keeva, Rosie and Edith followed Captain Blunt up to the stage and stood in front of the sea of men. Every man stared at the girls. Some fanned themselves with hats and leaflets as the room grew hotter.

'I have been tasked with training the first cohort of Women's Land Army members,' Blunt said, 'at the Parkend Forestry Training School. These are three such members, who have been with me for a month so far.'

'Let's see the girls prove their strength then,' shouted a weasel of a man from the second row. 'Tell us why you should be able to fell trees with the men.'

Keeva moved her neck from side to side, with a click, as the sea of faces swayed from side to side in front of her. This was her moment when she had finally got something right, proved she was good at felling. She inched forwards forcing a smile, maybe for the first time she had found something she was really good at. She hoped this was her moment, when Captain Blunt would explain how she and Edith had brought down the massive tree that day. She pictured the great tree falling, its majesty and strength, the mighty trunk wrenched from its stump.

Captain Blunt began, 'You may have heard these young women managed to fell a fairly large Scots pine on the edge of a steep hillside.'

'Aye, we 'eard,' shouted the weasel in the second row. "Nearly killed 'emselves, my cousin said.'

'And while we may all appreciate their efforts, I regret to say that these women put the lives of myself and fellow lumberjacks at risk.'

A wave of disappointment came crashing down on Keeva. Edith and Rosie looked across at her like they hated her. Stunned, all Keeva could hear was a storm of groans from the men.

Blunt continued, 'Upon strict instruction not to do so, the tree they chose was directly above where the men were loading pit props onto trucks. In addition, the tree was gnarled and twisted at the roots and heavily forward-leaning down the slope.'

'Ooh,' groaned the audience.

'So, they can't follow simple instructions,' said weasel with a snigger. 'Felling in danger zones, without consideration for others, anyone would think they were acting on behalf of Hitler himself.'

Keeva wondered if she might pass out.

'I am afraid that, with flagrant violation of the rules and respect for my authority,' Captain Blunt said, 'I suggest these women are removed from heavy felling and put onto lighter forestry duties.'

'Hear, hear!' The room pealed with grunts and chatter.

Keeva tried to grab Edith to steady herself. Edith pulled her sleeve from Keeva's grasp and frowned.

Weasel laughed. 'The women have gone rogue.'

Why did Keeva ever think she could fell that tree? Why was she even doing this? She didn't believe in war anyway. Keeva fled from the stage followed by Rosie and Edith. Mens' eyes darted between each of them as they rushed out the hall. The urge to cry was overwhelming.

'Stuff you lot,' shouted Rosie, as she slammed the door behind them.

Why had Captain Blunt brought them all this way to humiliate them? Was this the worst punishment he could think of: humiliation, before a room of men? Did he hate them that much, that he wanted to shame and embarrass them in public? She'd only wanted to prove herself to Captain Blunt. How could they go back to Parkend after this?

There was a thud and the door flung open; Captain Blunt appeared puffing and red-faced behind them.

'That will show you, Miss Think You Know It All,' Captain Blunt said. 'Now, I hope you will do as you are told in future.'

Chapter 11

Beatrice

23rd February 1940, Parkend, Forest of Dean

Beatrice heard a noise as if someone were banging loudly on her bedroom door. In her half sleep she wondered if Edna, her parlourmaid, was coming in with the coal bucket to light the fire beside her bed. She snuggled into her warm floral eiderdown, which was so pretty with pink roses and green leaves decorating the corners and edges. Thank goodness she had insisted on the quality Egyptian cotton; it lifted her spirits on dark mornings. Then she realised she was in the drab dormitory, with creaking floorboards and those wretched grey blankets.

At this unearthly hour somebody was chirruping a song she'd heard on the wireless.

'You can only be an angel, from those beautiful skies,
And I see heaven, when I stare in those blue eyes.'

Gladys was definitely a morning person. She seemed to have such *joie de vivre*, which had abandoned Beatrice when she'd arrived at this awful place. In fact, she had never really had that same sense of vitality that Gladys wore so brightly every day.

The knocking on the door came again. Beatrice checked the bedside clock she was so fond of, with its elegant green surround and art deco-style numbering. Maybe it had stopped in the night. It said five o'clock but ticked onto one-minute past. The door banged again and was thrust open. Captain Blunt marched in with an oil lamp. Beatrice heard Gladys squeal as she pulled her Aertex shirt over her camisole.

'Good morning, girls!' Captain Blunt shouted.

Beatrice's pulse raced, as she watched that appalling man from the modest safety of her bed. Keeva scrambled into bed, wriggling back under her blankets.

'You shall be joining me for physical training again today. In five minutes, I want you outside on the lorry park,' Captain Blunt announced.

'How inconvenient,' Beatrice remarked.

She sat up to see Rosie put her pillow over her head as Captain Blunt marched past her bed. He lifted the pillow off Rosie's head and shouted, 'Wakey, wakey!'

'Oh, clear off,' Rosie shouted, pulling her blankets over her head.

Beatrice had never met anyone as gauche as Captain Blunt or as insolent as Rosie.

'And you have some explaining to do, you and your friends who went to the Timber Trade meeting yesterday.'

Beatrice felt gladdened to hear there had been a contretemps the day before, when she had already suggested she would have been a better representative of the Women's Land Army. She was the only one to have attended private school, and the Queen Elizabeth School for young ladies in Penrith had put her at ease amongst the social milieu of the petit bourgeoisie, wealthy industrialists and others of her own class.

'They were laughing at us. We didn't do nothin',' Rosie said, thrusting her head out from beneath the blankets.

'Well, then you must have done something. Outside in five minutes,' replied Blunt.

'Would you please leave?' said Beatrice, with her quilt wrapped around her. She didn't have time for their squabbling when she had to get dressed in five minutes.

'Not until you motley lot are out of bed.'

'If you ever enter this room again without permission, I'll see that you lose your job,' Beatrice bellowed. How dare he enter while the girls were getting changed. She had learnt how to put many a servant in their place for such a mistake and even Captain Blunt seemed to diminish in confidence before her.

'You may regret this,' he muttered as he left.

'Gladys, shut the door behind him,' Beatrice commanded.

'Jesus, I wouldn't want to get on the wrong side of you,' said Keeva, when the irritating man had gone.

Good, thought Beatrice. She was glad to hear it.

'Well, let's 'ope 'e doesn't kill us in the physical training after that,' said Rosie.

Gladys continued to sing, '*When I am with you, it feels just like paradise.*

There is no one else, an' nothing that feels just as nice.'

'It's a bleedin' miracle you can be so chirpy, Gladys,' said Rosie.

'But isn't it a wonder that some of the best days of our lives haven't even happened yet? Every morning I think it could be today,' Gladys replied.

Gladys was a simple soul and perhaps a little delusional, Beatrice thought. Hardly the best day of her life, unless she liked being shouted at by a lowly ex-army captain and forced to sit up, lie down, jump and run around in some chaotic fashion. Beatrice quickly pulled on her green lacy cami-knickers beneath her quilt. She wanted to have a little bit of glamour, if she was to wear those utilitarian navy PE shorts and off-white Aertex t-shirt.

Captain Blunt had prohibited her and the others from wearing jodhpurs during PT, even if the temperature was below freezing. What right did he have to tell the women what they could wear and couldn't wear? While jodhpurs were not the most feminine items of clothing, Beatrice liked the cinched waist and bell-shape bottom, which accentuated her generous hourglass figure. But, more importantly, the breeches covered her chubby knees.

Beatrice joined the herd of rough-and-ready women outside in the cold. It was still dark; the air froze on her breath and the gravel sparkled with frost.

'Get into line. Let's get some discipline into you,' said Blunt, standing in front of the women. He drew his whistle to his mouth and gave a short, shrill blast.

The girls jumped to get in line, and formed a queue. Beatrice shivered as she felt the bitter wind blow through her socks. Her feet hurt already.

'Side by side,' said Captain Blunt, as he walked past Beatrice and stared at her for a few moments. 'Heads up!' he shouted.

Rosie and Keeva were messing around again. What if they irritated Captain Blunt and he punished them with a longer, tougher PT session?

'Shoulders back!'

Beatrice caught a glimpse of Rosie as she thrust her breasts forward like some harlot.

'Stomachs in!'

With a stamp of his foot, he swivelled and squinted down the line.

'Bottoms in!'

Beatrice sucked her stomach in. With her hips forward and shoulders back, her back ached.

Blunt returned to the front and looked the women up and down. A few foresters stopped to stare on their way to their vehicles and it felt most unnatural being forced to stand like a statue. Meanwhile Blunt looked over the women with disappointment, as if their bodies with all the lumps and bumps were misshapen and broken without hope of being fixed.

'We have failed—' he said.

'Give us a chance, we haven't even started yet,' said Rosie.

'—to find dockyard workers, men on the dole, schoolboys or male students to take on the role of forestry workers. Nevertheless, we are hoping to be assisted by Italian and maybe even German prisoners of war to do the heavy felling work. One would not expect you girls to attempt this work.'

'You mean – they could be—' Edith paused '—National Socialists?'

She looked terrified, the poor girl. She was an interesting girl, more intelligent than the rest. But Edith lacked confidence and didn't always get things right, including her pronunciation. Beatrice assumed she was talking about the Nazi Party.

'We don't know at this stage. If they are Nazis, they will be under armed guard,' replied Blunt.

There … Beatrice had been right, of course. She suddenly remembered to breathe again, and relaxed.

'I did not say at ease. Attention!'

Beatrice stood tall and remembered her elocution lessons from when she was a child. They were meant to help address her stammer, but more importantly make sure that she did not adopt any hint of the local accent from the local children in Whitley Bay, near Newcastle. While they lived in a large house by the sea, her mother told her the village kids were common and was insistent that the 'Geordie' inflection should be banished from the house like insects.

Beatrice often got swatted when she was *sittin'* at the *din'in* table. She could hear the accent in her own voice, even though she was *tryin'* not to *tork* about *keek* and a *cop a tae* like her friend, whose father was a miner. She always had to make more *effart to be betta than 'er brotha at torkin' propa, becos 'eee was in the comfat of being the populaaa wan with 'er parents.* Sometimes, Beatrice put the accent on just to infuriate her mother.

She'd never forget the local girls picking on her for *torkin'* posh. They crowded around her and laughed at her when she pronounced her 'o' vowels. Then one day each one slapped her in turn, as they got off the bus. In tears, Beatrice told her mother, who ordered the parlourmaid scrub her forehead with soap. She worried Beatrice might be contaminated by the local girl's filthy hands. Beatrice didn't trust common girls like them anymore.

Blunt cast his eyes across the girls before he fixed upon Beatrice. Awkward. She became aware of her body underneath her clothes. The seconds seemed to last for minutes. She felt quite uncomfortable, imagining the curves of her bosoms and bottom that the men might find appealing. Her mother always said her fuller figure was attractive to men, both young and old, because it was a sign of wealth and a good diet. It was true – the other girls looked rather skinny and pale by comparison with her ample bosom, hips and rosy cheeks.

'So, until we can replace you with prisoners of war, we will have to repurpose your feminine disposition and make do and mend you into something more like young men.'

Sleet began to drive down.

'Left turn.'

Beatrice turned left, with Rosie in front and Keeva behind. Rosie was now at the front of the line. Blunt clicked his tongue against his cheek twice.

'And a ... left, right ... left, right ... Keep it going.'

Beatrice waited for Rosie to step forwards to march in time.

'Move at the front,' shouted Blunt.

Beatrice gave Rosie a push as she stepped forwards, while Keeva trod on Beatrice's heel.

'Oh Keeva, don't be so clumsy,' Beatrice said as she tripped and fell onto Rosie in front, grabbing onto Rosie's shorts.

'Get off me,' said Rosie, as she dodged out of the way and Beatrice slipped and fell to her knees on the ground, Keeva landing on top of her briefly.

'Whoa! Whoa! Whoa!'

As Beatrice stood up, cursing beneath her breath, Captain Blunt gestured, pulling the reins as if he'd never ridden a horse in his life. Beatrice noticed Rosie smiling and a snort of contempt escaped from Beatrice's nose. All the girls started laughing at her.

How was Beatrice ever going to rise above the rank and file of the common people? At least at home she mixed with families of equal status and intelligence. But this was just hopeless. She felt like she would be dragged down by the likes of Keeva and Rosie simply by association. Edith was marginally better, as she seemed more educated. But even Edith was only the best person in a bad situation.

'From now on physical training will take place every morning at zero five hundred hours.'

'What, every day?' protested Rosie.

'Yes.'

'Before breakfast?'

'Yes, no more backchat, please.'

The sleet turned to hail, pelting down on Beatrice's head and shoulders as Blunt continued to shout instructions.

'We hope PT will motivate you to improve your physical condition. Frequently women do not realise what poor physique they have. The tests have revealed your deficiencies across the board. So, I am sure you will be receptive to an intensive physical training programme, in order to remedy your shortcomings.'

Beatrice was sure she didn't have any shortcomings like the other women. You could see the way Keeva stood, for example, with her awkward posture and strangely shaped legs. It would be difficult for her to improve in physical condition when the shortcomings were bred into her bones.

The wind blew and forced Beatrice to close her eyes as her hair whipped across her face and she was pelted with hailstones. She already felt short of breath and wished she was at home in bed under her comfy eiderdown. She loved waking up to the sweet vanilla scent of cook's Victoria sponge rising up the stairs from the kitchen. What had she done in joining the WLA against her family's wishes and her mother's most of all?

'Right, jogging on the spot to warm you up.'

Beatrice began to march as she watched the other girls bouncing in an ungainly fashion with their knees flying up in all directions.

'I said jogging on the spot.'

Beatrice felt her lovely curves wobbling where they shouldn't. Rosie began to pant loudly as she made a fool of herself swinging her arms slowly and out of time with her knees.

'Drop and give me five sit-ups,' Captain Blunt shouted.

'But it's filthy on the floor and I'll get my uniform soiled,' Beatrice objected.

'Drop and give me five.'

She climbed down onto the frozen ground, wiped the grit off her hands and struggled to sit up.

She had only managed one sit-up before Blunt shouted, 'Five push-ups.'

Beatrice had never experienced anything so degrading. She lay face down and tried to push herself off the ground with her hands. But her arms would not move, however hard she pushed, after all the felling she'd done that week.

'Stomachs off the floor.'

If Beatrice went at her own pace, at least she could maintain some composure. She pained for the PT session to be over.

'As fast as you can, sprint to the end and back, three times.'

Beatrice was left behind as the other girls ran ahead of her. She was surprised how fast Rosie could run.

'What's wrong with you? A bit tired, are we?' Captain Blunt came up behind her. 'I said, sprint.'

Puffing and panting, Beatrice struggled to keep up as her legs seemed unwilling to carry her at a smooth pace.

'Oh dear! You don't look like you want it as much as the other girls,' Blunt said to Beatrice. She felt the humiliation as the rest, having finished running, watched her lumber back towards the group. Her heart was thumping so hard, she was concerned she might be having a heart attack.

'The last one goes again,' he said.

'Come on, Beatrice, you can do it,' shouted Gladys, much to Beatrice's embarrassment. How déclassé. She wished she hadn't put on her lacy green undergarment that morning. The lace had gathered and grated uncomfortably between her bottom cheeks, so she had to pull her knickers out. As she turned to make her last leg of the race, she saw the thirty girls' faces staring at her and she was sure she saw Rosie smirking.

'Next, five star jumps and then I want you to run up to the top of Church Hill, do five pull-ups on the tree in the graveyard and run back down again. Ready, set, go.'

*

After coming last on the PT test and a full day of felling trees in the forest, Beatrice was utterly exhausted. She felt certain that Captain Blunt disliked her more than the other girls. He ruthlessly criticised her work and had increased timber quotas for them all.

When she finally returned to the dormitory, Beatrice went to her suitcase to find her last broken piece of fruit cake she had salvaged from the floor. When she looked inside the tin, instead of finding her cake she found her alligator skin black purse instead. This was strange as she was sure she hadn't put her purse inside her cake tin. In addition, her last piece of cake had gone. Beatrice swallowed hard and looked again. Her cake was nowhere to be seen and, worse still, when she opened her purse, the forty-eight pounds she'd left inside was gone.

Frantically she flung open her suitcase and emptied out her clothes.

'What is it?' Edith asked.

'Oh, I don't believe it. Someone has stolen my money,' she said.

'Are you sure?'

'It's gone. It was here a few days ago. Look, my purse is empty.'

'Are you sure you haven't mislaid it?'

'No, I have not. It's Keeva or Rosie … I'm sure they have stolen it. They were the only ones here yesterday before we got back from the forest.'

'And me,' said Edith.

'Well, did you see them do anything?'

'No, no, I didn't.'

'Were you with them the entire time?'

'No, Beatrice.'

'Well, it was one of them then.'

'I don't think you can accuse them, Beatrice,' Edith said.

There was no need to convince Edith, Beatrice just knew she was right about Keeva and Rosie being thieves. Everything she had ever heard about the working class was being played out in front of her eyes. She was sure that Rosie, a factory worker, had never met anyone of Beatrice's upbringing before and would be jealous of her. Keeva, she expected, was behaving out of petty revenge, since Beatrice had swapped beds with her. From the condition of their clothes she could tell they had no respect for property, especially other people's. But she never imagined she would be sharing a room with criminals, or that girls of her age broke the law. Outraged, Beatrice stormed downstairs to the dining hall, Edith following her. She discovered Rosie, Gladys and Keeva sitting smugly at a table finishing their dinner. In a rage, she flew over to their table and shouted, 'Where's my money?'

'What do you mean?' asked Keeva.

'Don't be all innocent with me. One of you has stolen money from my purse.'

'No, we haven't,' said Rosie.

'Do you want me to help you look for it, Beatrice?' asked Gladys.

'We've already looked,' replied Edith.

'Let's get some dinner, Beatrice. You must be hungry,' said Edith.

She could see the guilt in their narrow eyes. They knew they had been caught. She was shaking with rage; she disapproved of their type and felt vindicated in her judgement now they had dared to steal her money.

In this horrible place where everyone dressed the same, one of the things that clearly set her apart was her good taste. If she ever got the chance to have a day off, Beatrice had been looking forward to shopping with the money from her trust fund. She wanted to purchase a heavy silk or velvet suit for elegant evening wear, to make a change from the robust common-sense utility day clothing, and make her feel better about this dreadful war. How dare they take that opportunity of a small, uplifting luxury away from her?

Chapter 12

15th December 1939, Harrods, Knightsbridge, London

'Isn't this the queerest Christmas ever, Mama?' Beatrice said.

She picked up a flower badge from the accessories display and pinned it to her black fur lapel, pouting her scarlet lips as she looked in the mirror. A luminous badge to prevent bumps in the dark was so very wartime. She'd rather imagine a luminous flower to aid a romantic encounter. Then she might buy one. Peering over her shoulder, she saw a soldier in uniform approach. She flicked her hair and followed him in the mirror, where he mulled over a frightful charm bracelet with an identification disk, probably for his sweetheart. He was not her type anyway.

'What a hideous brooch,' her mother said before walking off.

Beatrice flung the flower back on the display. People poured in through the main doors at Harrods and brushed snow off their coats and hats. Her glossy chestnut curls bounced as she followed her mother to the escalator. Without looking down, her mother stepped onto the moving woven leather conveyor belt and placed her hand upon the mahogany and silver plate-glass balustrade. The pair rose through the art deco halls and looked down upon the throng of Christmas shoppers below.

'What about a present for Papa?' Beatrice asked, feeling irritated.

'Whisky and cigars never seem to disappoint.'

'What about a new gramophone, Mama?' she said with a wry smile.

She knew her father didn't play the one her mother had bought him last year. He was never home long enough to enjoy the simple pleasure of listening to a record, let alone spending time with

Mama. He always had urgent matters arising and, now war had broken out, it was unlikely he would be home at all. She couldn't help provoking her mother, but she just ignored Beatrice.

The children's department was delightfully calm and unusually quiet. Occasional groups of children wandered through to shake hands with Father Christmas, before being chivvied along by anxious nannies to get home before a heavier snowfall. But with the prospect of staying a few nights at the Dorchester and no need to hurry home, Beatrice wasn't too concerned about the weather. After all, this was London not Newcastle and everyone knew it never snowed too much down south.

They spent some time browsing the aisles of military-themed toys, pilots, soldiers and naval officers sold for 5s 11d. Her mother held up two figures and said, 'Rather looks like your brother Frederick and Papa.' Beatrice just knew there was nothing that her mother would rather have more than statuettes of the men in their family to idolise forever. Even on a special mother-and-daughter shopping trip in the middle of Harrods she didn't have her mother's full attention.

Beatrice looked for a toy that might remind her mother of her. She saw some Red Cross nurse dolls, but Beatrice couldn't stand the sight of blood and didn't have the patience to listen to sick people moaning. She liked the mini-Maginot Lines; she had heard her father talk about the defence fortifications with weapon installations that had been so successful for the French. She could get these for Edna, the parlourmaid, who had asked for something for her son. But these would be more difficult for Edna to wrap and post to him. He had been evacuated out to the wilds of Durham. Sheep and cows might be more his thing, so she decided against buying anything for now.

'Let's go and order some hampers,' said her mother briskly.

They passed through the lingerie department, which was particularly busy with amorous husbands, wives and girlfriends buying special underwear for their long-awaited Christmas reunions. And the food hall was so bustling with ladies in fur coats and designer hats of all shapes and colours that they had to queue for a full fifteen minutes for the shop assistant.

'We must make sure plum sauce is in our hamper, Mama, and Christmas pudding. They are my favourites,' said Beatrice.

'Cook will make Chrissy pud, like she does every year, and they are far superior to Harrods'; otherwise, what are we paying her for?' replied her mother.

Eventually the shop assistant turned to her mother and asked how much she wanted to spend.

'No expense spared,' she said.

'Mama, you are indulgent. Shouldn't you be buying more modest hampers this year for everyone?'

'Nonsense, *Lady* magazine was adamant that rather than leaving the ghost of old Christmas past moping at the door, we should cut a bright square out of our winter of discontent. We must keep Christmas for the children's sake.'

Beatrice raised her eyebrows.

'You are my child, Beatrice, even if you'd rather you weren't, and you know how much I enjoy spoiling you and Fredders.'

Large snowflakes began to fall outside on the pavement as they waited inside Harrods for a taxi. The doorman asked where they were going and told them it was just a five-minute walk. So, they stepped out into the sparkly cold air.

On the way to Hyde Park, the snow fell more lightly. Beatrice saw a crimson-and-gold framed advert for Cinderella showing at the London Coliseum. She noticed how she had lost interest in this sort of thing. In the past she might have liked to see Cinderella.

But she felt too grown up for fairy tales since she had been to the University of Liverpool. Before the war she lived away from home for nearly a year. It had opened a whole new way of life to her, which did not include her mother and fairy tales.

Beatrice noticed some shops trying to entice people with early Christmas sales even with ten days still to go. Aquascutum was selling a cashmere coat reduced to just £10, which Beatrice rather liked the look of. She swept into the shop to try it on, and sashayed left and right in front of a large mirror to see how it hung at the sides and the back.

'This style of coat always looks better on taller women,' said the shop assistant.

Standing half a head taller than her mother, Beatrice felt she had a presence about her and a sartorial elegance in this fashionable coat, which others could not hope to achieve.

'Do you have this in any other colours?' Beatrice asked.

'Yes, madam, it comes in beaver brown, ebony and royal navy,' the shop assistant replied.

'I rather like beaver brown, Mama; it matches my hair.'

Her hourglass shape was complemented by the cut of the coat, which tucked in at her waist before curving round her large hips. The hemline covered her chunky knees, which she so detested. Her decision was made.

'I'll have it.'

'I want to go to Marshall and Snelgrove on Oxford Street to find a couple of evening and party dresses to welcome back Papa on his Christmas leave,' said Beatrice's mother.

'But I'm hungry, Mama. Can't we go for afternoon tea first?'

'Don't be selfish. You are always thinking of your stomach, Beatrice.'

'I beg your pardon,' said Beatrice.

'Perhaps I could do with a rest. I'm glad I reserved early as the hotel and restaurant are fully booked now,' said her mother as she paid for the coat.

They headed between the piles of ice along gritted pavements past Hyde Park towards the Dorchester Hotel, as the snow thickened.

What a shame the blackout regulations had killed off the traditional sight of lit-up Christmas trees in shop displays and people's front windows, thought Beatrice. The anti-bomb blast tape on the shop windows made the festive season rather less picturesque and feel just a little more sinister. Still, many shops had created a winter wonderland with bright-red baubles and tinsel on Norway spruce trees instead. But it rather lacked the twinkling lights, which normally added just a sprinkling of magic to the streets of Christmas shoppers.

'Oh look! A carol concert, Mama,' she said, pointing over the road to a crowd of people gathering on the bandstand at Hyde Park. To escape her mother for an interval was essential, if she were to survive the next few days.

'Come along now, Beatrice, don't be so vulgar,' her mother answered.

'It's hardly vulgar, Mama. I won't be long. You go ahead to the Dorchester and wait for me.'

'I'd rather you didn't join a public gathering for out-of-tune carolling. It is rather déclassé, darling.'

'Mother! I am not a child any more. I am a grown woman and can do what I choose.'

'I said no. Don't be petulant; we'll miss our afternoon tea reservation. If you behave like a child, I'll treat you like a child. After all I have spent on you, I would expect more gratitude and respect. University has changed you, dear, and not for the better.

Now let's go, you are getting on my nerves.'

'Now I know what to get you for Christmas.'

'You know I don't like surprises, Beatrice.'

'Some Sanatogen nerve tonic to win your war of nerves. Maybe if you'd drunk a whole bottle when war was declared I could've stayed at university too.'

'It's you that has ruined my nerves, you capricious *girouette*,' her mother hissed.

'In which case you won't mind me going to see the carol singers. It will provide you with some respite from my childish company. Didn't you say Christmas is for children after all?' And before Beatrice lost her nerve, she crossed the road towards the congregation of people, narrowly avoiding stepping in front of an approaching motor car. She dared not glance back; she felt like a caged beast at home, and even away she was trapped by her mother. Following the flow of people – free at last – she let out a sigh.

Heartily singing 'We Wish You a Merry Christmas' and other old favourites might help her relax. But, as she got closer, there seemed no sign of a choir, just a few women on stage. Beatrice pushed through the crowd to get to the front. There were mostly young women around her chatting, only a few men puffing on cigarettes, and some mothers rocking and baby-talking to small children on their hips. A tall handsome-looking woman stood on stage in a black hat and smart but conservative coat, tapping the microphone.

'Who is that speaking?' Beatrice asked a woman next to her.

'Director of the Women's Land Army, that's Lady Denman,' the woman whispered back.

Beatrice stepped closer as the crowd hushed.

'The Women's Land Army is in action,' Lady Denman said. 'Three thousand of its recruits are already at work out in the countryside, fighting from the fields and forests for our great nation.'

Beatrice listened intently as Lady Denman spoke of the excellent work being done by the pioneering women on the farms, many of whom had no previous experience but were doing such splendid work. Beatrice wondered if it was like going to university, joining up with the Land Army.

'One nineteen-year-old land girl was formerly a student of economics at London University. Her employer said of her, "She is doing vital work to support the armed forces and their families by providing food for the nation".'

A young actress joined Lady Denman on stage with a giggle and paraded across the stage as if on a catwalk.

Lady Denman said, 'These women are not only taking on vitally important war work but pioneering a new fashion. These jodhpurs are where fashion meets practicality and the challenge of war, and are not unlike the slacks you may have seen worn by Katharine Hepburn and Marlene Dietrich. We are fashioning these wonderfully designed breeches for stylish looks and comfort, in the finest quality corduroy.'

The curvaceous hips on the breeches seemed made for her. She strove to be just like the women in the highest tiers of society, who changed their attire several times a day. She had her afternoon, evening, about-town and dinner wardrobes, but little in the way of active sportswear. These breeches would be a perfect alternative and would begin her country wardrobe collection.

The glamorous model with scarlet lips said: 'I was brought up in the city. But I love my new life in the countryside, with the fresh air and beautiful views of rolling hills and fields. It's invaluable war work but I always keep my hands looking fabulous by rubbing plenty of cream in at night.'

Lady Denman continued: 'Actresses, students and typists are

among the Land Army recruits. Many of the girls who have been engaged on farms find their secretarial experience useful in helping fill in wartime forms.'

The Women's Land Army had a provocative and fashionable allure. Beatrice wanted to sport those daring and adventurous breeches, even though her mother would have a fit. But she'd be doing something for the war like her brother. She didn't have much time because her mother would be tapping her fingers with impatience at the restaurant. She joined the queue and was soon greeted by two ladies with fur hats and elegant wraps standing at the trestle table.

'Oh, what a beautiful coat,' one said to Beatrice.

'Oh, thank you,' she replied smiling.

'It suits your complexion. You look gorgeous, my dear.'

'The bottle-green jumpers would look good on her too, don't you think?' said the other.

'I find the j..j..jodhpurs rather daring; I'd like to wear the latest c.. c.. catwalk fashions,' Beatrice added, trying to ignore her stammer.

'Oh yes, with a figure like yours you'd look fabulous.'

Beatrice smiled. She felt as though these women understood her for who she really was, stammer or not, and it gave her a warm feeling inside.

'Were you considering putting your name down?'

'Yes, I have studied at university,' Beatrice added proudly.

'Oh really, how marvellous. And what did you study?'

'Mathematics.'

'Oh, my goodness. You are just perfect! Isn't she, Eleanora?'

'Yes, yes. You look very intelligent too,' the other woman agreed.

Beatrice didn't say she had only completed a year before her mother called her home before the war.

'How incredibly fortunate. You are just what we are looking for in an elite army where mathematical ability is the key. The perfect candidate for this vital war work.'

'There's a beauty in mathematics because there is always a right answer,' said Beatrice.

All her life, when she had been chastised for getting things wrong, mathematics had given her comfort.

'Will you sign up?'

She liked the sound of being part of the elite army. For a moment she wondered what her mother would say. But who cared what she thought? The women seemed so admiring of her. Here was an opportunity to use her mathematical equations and problem-solving skills. For the first time in a long while she felt important.

'Yes,' Beatrice replied as she signed her name on the form. She walked back to the Dorchester Hotel and smiled to herself for being so clever.

Chapter 13

Rosie

23rd February 1940, Forestry School, Parkend, Forest of Dean

Rosie hadn't expected a public confrontation in the dining room. Beatrice accusing the two of them of taking her money in front of the other girls and Missus bleedin' Redrum. Keeva had turned paler than Rosie's mother's sheets on laundry day and the girls on the next table were whispering.

'Rosie, what are we going to do?' asked Keeva.

'What do you mean? You've got nothing to hide, have you?' she replied.

'No, it's just I can't risk getting into any more trouble.'

'You finished your tea yet?' asked Rosie, wanting to get upstairs like the clappers, away from the other girls, and up to their dormitory.

Keeva nodded.

'Come on, let's go up,' said Rosie, hoping they'd be alone once up the apples and pears. Keeva pushed her chair under the table and hesitated.

'Come on.' Rosie grabbed her arm and pulled her from the dining hall. 'Jesus, you are in a right two and eight, aren't you, Keeva? Anybody would think you'd pinched the money or something?'

'No, I haven't. It's just, I'm not seventeen,' Keeva whispered, as they made their way upstairs together.

'How old are you, then? Twelve?' Rosie teased. 'Come on,' she shooed, to get a move on. Their room was empty. Thank goodness inside they were alone.

'Nearly seventeen, and if Captain Blunt finds out he might send me home. I can't go home,' said Keeva.

Why can't she go home? thought Rosie. She scanned Keeva's skin. There were no visible signs of bruises or scars like she had.

'Don't say anything, will you?' said Keeva, a shine of perspiration on her cheek.

So, Keeva had lied about her age by one year to get into the WLA. That was hardly anything to pipe your eye about.

'Oh, I don't know … You've broken the law,' replied Rosie. 'Maybe Blunt should know,' she added.

'Please,' Keeva begged.

'Only if you can keep a secret too, Keeva.'

'Of course.' Keeva lay down on her bed and rubbed her knuckles.

Rosie decided she could trust Keeva. If she couldn't, then Keeva lying about her age might come in handy. Rosie pulled out the envelope, 'Look, don't worry about nothing, I've got Beatrice's dough.'

Keeva looked startled when she spotted the notes tucked inside. 'Rosie!'

'Ssh,' Rosie whispered, 'Beatrice doesn't need it anyway. She's filthy rich. How much do they have if they can pay all those household staff? It makes me sick we have to beg for bread at the workhouse and people like her have got this much.'

The green notes purred like a pack of cards as Rosie flicked through them with her thumb. Every one of them read 'Bank of England promise to pay the bearer on demand one pound'. The paper was soft against her cheek and smelt of grubby fingers. She'd never laid her hands on so many pound notes before.

'We've got nothing, Keeva. It's why Mother had to send the little ones away. We couldn't feed 'em.'

Keeva screwed her face up, like she'd just got carbolic soap in her eye.

'I know what that's like, Rosie. But you still can't steal,' Keeva said.

'It's what me and my older brothers used to do, pinch stuff all the time. Nothing big, just little things from people who can afford it. It's fair then.'

'I'm not sure it's fair, Rosie. Jesus, what if you get caught and sent to prison?'

Rosie shrugged. 'It's my mother I'm worried about, now me and my brothers have left home. With this money she could leave my old man and look after herself. Honestly, he was beating me up good before I left; that's why I had to get away.'

'I'm sorry to hear that, Rosie,' said Keeva.

On impulse Rosie beckoned Keeva over to the window, where there was more light. She hadn't shown anyone else except Bets in the factory. Rosie closed her eyes, pulled her collar across her shoulder and leant forwards. Keeva wouldn't snitch now.

Rosie remembered that morning back at home, she'd gone out to buy the potatoes, only she couldn't help there was only enough money to buy five. The pavements had been wet as she'd approached their two-up/two-down terraced house on Homerton Road. She'd reached through the letterbox to pull out the key, which hung on a string, and opened the door. The whole family had been in the kitchen – her mum, dad and all four brothers bustling to get out the door for school, eating crusts of bread and jam. Her mother was sobbing while she dressed the little ones by the fire. Billy was scratching his head frantically, as he did when he was worried, and Johnny was scuffing his feet on the wooden floor. The tang of her elder brother, Bert's, body odour had filled the air.

'What is it, Mother?' Rosie had asked.

'It's your uncle, Alfie,' she'd said.

Her Uncle Alfie, who Rosie used to go birdwatching with on

Hackney Marshes?

'Suicide rate is so high,' her father had said. 'There's bodies in the canal every day.'

But Rosie hadn't understood.

Her brother Billy had stared at Rosie and shaken his head, then Bert had punched him on the shoulder. Father had huffed and puffed, as the kettle boiled on the hob.

'Tea, Rosie,' her father had demanded.

Rosie had crept towards her mother, coals ticking, as her father had tended the fire.

'Where are you going?' her father had asked.

'I want to speak to Mother,' Rosie had replied.

'Why?'

'I want to ask her a question.' Rosie had cowered.

'Don't ask her. Anything you want to know, ask me.'

She'd known better than to ask him. She'd made her father tea and given her mother the potatoes.

'Carve your initials into the skin, Rosie,' her mother had said.

'No point. They still get nicked from the school oven.'

'Do as I say, Rosie.'

'What's happened to Uncle Alfie, Mother?' Rosie had asked.

'What did I tell you, Rosie,' her father had whispered.

Rosie had heard the scrape of the hot poker being drawn from the fire against the metal grate. She couldn't remember what happened next. Her mother had said it was an accident. But in her older years Rosie knew what he was like.

Keeva's eyes looked like she'd just laid an egg. 'Your father did that?'

Oh, here we go again. Now, she wished she hadn't shown her the dark-pink scars across her back, as though her skin had been raked like the dirt in the back yard when they tried to grow potatoes themselves. If only she'd watered them, kept those plants alive.

Rosie heard some girls' voices coming up the stairs and crammed the notes in the envelope and slid them under her pillow again. She'd learnt over years of her brothers' thieving it was better to have an accomplice. Rosie could tell it was Edith and Beatrice approaching, so she sat down on her own bed, trying to look innocent. She didn't think Keeva would split on her now. But she had to find a better hiding place for the cash.

'Of course, I would expect you two to be up here,' said Beatrice.

'Well, it's our room, ain't it?' Rosie said.

Keeva lay upon her bed and buried her head in a letter, looking upset. She was better than Rosie at keeping her head down when she was in trouble.

Beatrice started looking under the beds in the room and then beneath her own mattress. Rosie needed to move the bees and honey quick, so she lay down too. Beatrice turned her back and she had a chance. But distracted by the rain rattling against the windowpane, Beatrice looked up at her.

'What?' asked Rosie.

Beatrice continued searching on the floor around her bed.

'You can't go around blaming people if you've lost your stuff,' said Rosie.

Edith stared at Rosie briefly and then looked out of the window. 'It's blowing a gale out there,' she said. 'There's a storm coming.'

Carefully Rosie tried to slide the envelope with the cash up her sleeve just as Beatrice stood up again.

'I have not lost my stuff, it's been stolen,' she said.

'Do you want me to help check your suitcases again with you, Beatrice?' Edith asked.

Edith was being too helpful, crawling about on her hands and knees peering underneath the bedside table, one eye on Rosie all the time – or so it seemed.

The flames of the fire were extinguished briefly by a gust of wind down the chimney.

'Jesus, I hope this building is safe,' said Rosie, looking beyond Beatrice as Keeva put her letter away in her bag.

Rosie watched Beatrice flip open the expensive leather suitcase lids and, together with Edith, she picked through the layers of expensive folded clothes. Who lined their bleedin' suitcase with tissue paper? Rosie wondered.

The wind howled around the eaves and a loud thunderclap overhead made Rosie jump. Edith screamed and ran to the window to look out and then pulled the curtains closed.

'No, it's just not here; I feel so violated,' Beatrice complained.

Beatrice started looking under pillows and blankets on Edith's bed, Lily's bed and then Mary's. Rosie's bed would be flung apart soon; she had moments left.

'Are you all right, Keeva?' asked Edith.

Rosie saw her opportunity and slipped the money up her sleeve. Keeva was sniffing and wiping her eyes. Rosie's heart pounded.

'Oh Keeva, what's the matter?' asked Gladys, as she arrived upstairs and rushed to put her arm around Keeva's shoulders. 'Was it the thunder?'

'I think she's homesick,' said Edith.

'She's guilty, that's what's upset her,' said Beatrice under her breath.

Rosie could tell Beatrice didn't know who had taken the money if she suspected Keeva. Anyone could tell, Keeva would never pinch anything.

Gladys frowned at Beatrice. 'Do you want a cup of tea, Keeva?' Keeva nodded.

'Come on.' Gladys took Keeva out of the room and Beatrice

continued to search around Rosie going from bed to bed.

'You can't start going through everyone's stuff,' said Rosie.

'And why not? Have you got something to hide?'

Hands shaking, Rosie stood up and before she could do anything the envelope slipped from her sleeve to the floor. She snatched it up again. She couldn't believe what she'd done.

'What's that? Beatrice asked.

'Just a letter.'

'Let me see,' Beatrice said, as she marched over and tried to take it from Rosie.

'Oi no! It's private,' Rosie was ready to punch Beatrice if she so much as touched her.

'Let me have it,' Beatrice said and tried to snatch it from Rosie, as the other girls, Lily and Hazel, ran upstairs into the room, squealed and jumped onto their beds.

In that moment, Rosie ducked out of Beatrice's way, hopped over Beatrice's bed and ran to Keeva's bedside table. Beatrice chased after her. Rosie scrambled over Keeva's bed and swapped the envelope with the letter in Keeva's bag with the sleight of hand she'd practiced picking pockets from her brothers. The exchange of envelopes was done in a flash so she was confident nobody could have seen. She then held Keeva's letter above her head out of reach.

'Give it to me,' Beatrice demanded.

'No.'

Beatrice snatched the letter from Rosie's grasp and slid her fingers inside the envelope, her face dropping when she discovered there was no money inside. With narrow eyes, she unfolded the paper and began to read the letter to herself. A smile met Beatrice's lips, followed by a look of horror.

'Listen to this, Edith.' Beatrice began to read out loud. 'Chichester Army Barracks, West Sussex. My dearest Viola, Dilly and Kiki—'

she read slowly and deliberately looking up to make sure she had Edith, Hazel and Lily's full attention '—how bittersweet to receive your letter. I miss you so much. I'm truly sorry if this is difficult for you. I am only allowed to send and receive one letter a month but there is no limit on drawings. Viola, I will send more drawings in February, like we used to in art school.'

'What is this?' asked Edith.

Beatrice continued, 'I only have a few minutes to write. I know you are concerned for me, but I can assure you I have been treated fairly well. After the arrest, I was taken by police to the army barracks. To begin with, the guards were amiable and left me alone, so I read books and drew pictures. Suddenly they hauled me out before the commander who was very threatening. He used verbal powers of persuasion.'

'Whose letter are you reading, Beatrice?' asked Edith.

'Ssh,' said Beatrice.

Rosie looked round at the other girls in the room, who all now sat listening to Keeva's letter. Lily's mouth was wide open. Beatrice's tone of voice changed from amusement to disgust as she continued, and the room fell silent.

'For days, they kept trying to persuade me to let go of my obstinate beliefs; as you may guess, their attempts were wasted. But I have certainly learned a lot of blue language in the guard house. To be honest, I expected worse. Then one night a soldier came back to my cell drunk. He threatened to beat me up, if I did not put on a uniform, and said he would get others to forcibly dress me. I was most scared at this point. But afterwards it just made me more determined,' continued Beatrice.

Bloody hell! She regretted grabbing the letter now. Rosie wished Beatrice would put the letter away, before Keeva came back in the room. Keeva was already upset and this wasn't going to help.

'Beatrice, you should stop,' said Edith.

Rosie knew it was wrong to read out a private letter.

Beatrice held the letter closer, squinting to read. 'The guard is back so I must go. It's my last day before twenty-eight days in solitary confinement in the glasshouse. They have played cat and mouse with others. But I will eat, so I will be fine.'

Rosie winced and looked down at her feet.

'Whose letter is that?' asked Lily.

Rosie heard footsteps approach. Gladys entered the room talking to Keeva, who clutched her tea in both hands as if for comfort.

'I love you, my darlings. Dilly and Kiki, take care of your mother. Your loving father and husband, Stanley.' Beatrice looked at Rosie. 'Your father is in prison?'

All the girls in the room turned towards Rosie.

'Not mine,' she said, acting as if she didn't know what Beatrice was talking about.

Keeva broke off from what she was saying, looked up and saw her father's letter in Beatrice's hands.

'Get off!' she screamed.

The tea slipped from her hands and fell to the wooden floorboards with a bang. The other girls screamed as the tea exploded upwards out of the mug like vomit. Gladys jumped back and the tea sprayed over Rosie's jodhpurs and jumper. Hot droplets of tea burned Rosie's hands as Keeva flew across the floorboards towards Beatrice, jumped over her camp bed and ripped the letter from her hands. Keeva was furious with Beatrice and she'd never guess that Rosie had been involved.

Lily's mouth was hanging open. In the past, Rosie had wished her father had been put in prison, just for a minor offence, at least then they would have some respite from him. She could see Edith and Hazel trying to work out what was happening.

'I don't think that's yoo'r letter to read out, Beatrice,' said Hazel.

'So, is your father in prison? Is he a conscientious objector?' asked Beatrice.

'It's not from my bleedin' father, is it?' Rosie said. At least Keeva's letter had taken Beatrice's mind off the money for now.

'That's my private letter,' Keeva yelled, scrunching the letter into her hands. She grabbed her bag and fled the room. Rosie heard her footsteps running downstairs and the front door slammed.

'What did you do that for?' asked Rosie. 'She's gone out into the storm. She could get killed out there because of you.'

With the money safely out of sight in Keeva's bag, Rosie returned to her bed.

'Her father is a criminal,' said Beatrice. 'I've heard it runs in the family. I'd urge all of you not to leave any valuables unattended. We don't know who we can trust.'

'One of us should go after her,' said Gladys.

'Leave her.' She'll be back soon, Rosie hoped.

Chapter 14

Keeva

Keeva ran down the road, over the railway line and entered the forest by the footpath, which led up to Church Hill. It was dark and her sobs were carried away on each gust of wind. Why did Beatrice take her letter out of her bag? Why was she reading it out loud? She growled as the wind beat against her chest and howled through the trees. The oaks waved wildly above her head as the rush of wind passed through. Rain pelted her face and she panted for breath. If only she had not got upset, not gone with Gladys. It was cold and the raindrops were heavy, and she had forgotten to put her coat on.

Just when she'd tried to put it all behind her, the awful memories from home came flooding back. It still hurt so much the way Edward humiliated her on that last night. One by one, each of her friends had dropped her. Janet, her closest friend, stopped inviting her round. She'd spent so much time at Janet's house before. She'd go around after school and stay for tea but that all stopped. And with girls like Mary, it was worse. She'd said to herself, 'Don't be stupid, you don't like them anyway.' But when they ignored Keeva, Mary and her friends seemed to represent the whole school community. She felt no one liked her. She wept after school each day as others began to call her father a Nazi or a coward.

'It's not fair,' Keeva cried.

Did they really think she stole the money? Only Gladys had assumed her innocence, even though she'd done nothing to deserve Gladys's trust. When Keeva had lied about her age, she'd lied about her father, and now she concealed Rosie's secret: the theft of Beatrice's money. Cold, wet and frightened, she headed to the church for shelter. When she arrived, she tried the door, but it was locked.

There was nowhere out of the wind or rain, so she crouched under the arched doorframe of the side door and pulled her crumpled letter back out. She tried not to worry about her father being beaten up in prison. Her memory of his damaged face upset her. Would he ever get out of prison? She knew he would never change his mind and that he could be bloody-minded. She wondered if he hadn't told them the worst. She folded his letter away again with her worries and looked inside her bag for the envelope addressed to her home in Sussex.

Instead, she found a thick envelope with no name or address, in expensive-looking cream paper. She slipped her finger inside the flap and pulled it open. Inside was a wadge of green one-pound notes. Each one the same – so many of them, they could have made up the leaves in an old notebook; soft and smooth with worn corners.

How could Rosie do this to her? Was she trying to set her up? Oh my God, she was trying to scapegoat her. Keeva felt sick; she'd wanted to trust Rosie. Her mind raced. She could barely breathe. She began to shiver uncontrollably as she felt the cold stone under her bottom and dampness soaking through her clothes.

Anger flared at Rosie, for trying to set her up. What should she do with the money? Should she give it back to Beatrice, or Rosie? It was Rosie's problem; she would need to sort it out. But she knew it was wrong to give it back to the thief that had stolen it. She was certain Beatrice would never see her notes again. Her heart raced. Was the money hers, to do with what she wanted, now that it was in her bag? She imagined what she could do with it. Buy some sweets, cola cubes, new cami-knickers, perhaps. She peeled through the notes, she'd never held so much money before. Rosie would take revenge if she gave the money in to Captain Blunt.

So, what would happen if she gave it back to Beatrice? Would she think Keeva had stolen it? She couldn't get in trouble for this; it would be so unjust. The colder she became the more impossible the situation seemed. She couldn't stay out here all night, she had to go back. But she didn't want to go back while everyone else was still awake. She shook uncontrollably with cold: her bottom numb and hands frozen too. Slowly she stood up. With her cold wet fingers, she pushed the envelope into one of the fawn woollen socks in her bag.

Desperate to be warm in her bed again, she turned back down the hill towards the forestry school. She hadn't asked to be in this situation, and she couldn't see any other way out. She decided it was best to keep the money and not mention it to anyone. The rain pelted on the road and through the shoulders of her jumper. She pushed slowly on the heavy door and crept in, hoping no one would see her.

As she opened the door, Missus Potter, who sat on a chair by the door, woke up.

'Oh, come yer, I am so pleased to see thee. We've all been worried. I sent the others to bed and said I'd wait up.'

She opened her arms and wrapped them round Keeva, pulling her into her soft cotton dress and plump, warm body. Tears welled up in Keeva's eyes.

'Ow bist thee? You're freezing, love. Would you like a warm cup of tea?'

'Yes, please.'

'Quat here,' Missus Potter patted the chair. 'I could never forgive myself if we lost one of thee girls 'ere. Away from home for the first time. 'Tis very difficult, I know, meeting people with different ideas and backgrounds from thine own. I know what 'tis like to be vilified. But we're all the same inside. I know 'tis hard but if thou can forgive people when they make mistakes, things'll get better. Don't go running away again, Keeva.'

She could barely stay awake while she drank her tea, so Missus Potter packed her off to bed with a hot water bottle.

*

She felt herself being shaken.

'Keeva, Keeva, wake up! Where did you go last night?' asked Gladys, crouching by her bed.

The vivid horror of what had happened last night came flooding back and made her feel sick. She looked around the room; the other girls had gone for breakfast already.

'We were worried about you.'

Why was Gladys being so kind to her?

Keeva had to protect herself. 'Oh yeah, right. Just get off me,' she said, shaking Gladys off her shoulder. 'You're better off leaving me alone, all right.'

'Oh, I just …'

Gladys stood up slowly and left her bedside. Keeva felt a pang of hurt. She wanted to take Gladys in her arms and say thank you. She wanted Gladys to be her friend. But she knew Gladys didn't understand how cruel people could be. She didn't want her to be caught up in the nightmare of being friends with a girl from a family of conscientious objectors. Gladys would soon see the vitriol and Keeva could not bear to lose another person she had considered to be a friend. She had to protect herself this time.

Gladys looked back at her with sad eyes. Keeva knew Gladys would be afraid like her school friends had been; if only she knew how quickly people would turn against her. It was like a disease that no one else wanted to catch, so they all kept away. Seeing Gladys walk away brought back all the heartbreak of school. Gladys was such a bright and chirpy girl. She seemed so loyal and true that Keeva wished with all her heart they could be friends. She watched Gladys brushing her hair in her pocket mirror as she sat on her bed. However much the two friends had liked each other didn't matter any more. She could not bear the people she cared for turning against her again.

Keeva remembered the day she had sat and waited on the stile for William, her neighbour, to come as usual. She always looked out for his crop of messy hair, as he jumped and skipped across the hayfield. But one day he didn't turn up; she waited for hours and he never came over again. She couldn't understand why, and it made her so mad when he refused to speak to her. She found out later he had been bullied and beaten by some boys at school for being friends with her.

Gladys got up, and as she stood in the doorway she turned. 'Are you coming to breakfast, Keeva?'

She couldn't face going; she felt so ashamed.

'No,' Keeva said and blushed, knowing she was being unkind to Gladys.

Keeva shook inside, her head ached, and she felt like she wanted to vomit. She supposed that if all the other girls hated her, including Gladys, she probably deserved it anyway. She squeezed her neck and wanted to rip her head off with all those damn thoughts. Keeva feared this horrible, trapped feeling would never go away.

'Come on, Keeva, it's better you come down with me. I'm not going without you. You didn't leave me behind at the station, no matter how awful I was feeling, and I'm not going to leave you. Come on; get dressed and let's go and have breakfast together.'

'No, go away, Gladys. Leave me alone.'

She was relieved to hear Gladys running down the stairs. There was no point Gladys being tainted by the same affliction; she had enough to deal with on her own. Keeva lay in bed turning over and over like a maimed animal struck with pain. Her stomach gurgled and ached. Was it her period due? Unable to lie in her bed of torment any longer, she flung her blankets off and got up. She had to escape, move, be free – but not without eating first. She was starving.

She got up, got dressed and went downstairs for breakfast. As she entered, a hush fell on the dining hall and she felt forty pairs of eyes sticking in her like pins. As she walked across to the serving table, goosebumps crept up her arms and her upper lip started to sweat. She collected the stale bread and scrambled egg and, just as she was about to go and sit down, Redrum appeared.

'What time do you call this? You're late again,' she said for all to hear.

Keeva's body burned with heat; her armpits wet. Shaking, she told herself to ignore her. As she turned to find a table, she saw Gladys giggling with Rosie.

'Keeva, come and join us,' Gladys called over, waving at her.

Keeva looked away quickly; she knew they were laughing at her. She wanted to tell Gladys to stop it, stop it!

Edith was sitting alone. She could sit at the other end of the table. She didn't talk much and had helped her fell the big tree. With nowhere else to go, Keeva headed towards her table. Maybe Edith wouldn't mind her sitting at the same table.

'Can I sit here?' Keeva asked.

'No,' Edith said. Her face seemed angry, as she rose to her feet. All the other tables were now full. Tearful and trembling, Keeva stood, not knowing what to do.

'I'm not going to eat at a table with someone who condones the Nazi regime. You disgust me.'

Keeva stood with her mouth open. Without warning, Edith pushed the table with a screeching noise across the floor towards Keeva. The table flipped upside down, Edith's tray and plate too, and landed with a crash. The whole room jumped. Edith ran out of the dining hall past Captain Blunt.

'What on earth is going on?' demanded Blunt.

Keeva tried to breathe. The aggression against her had started all over again. Captain Blunt stood in front of her waiting for an answer.

'I don't know.'

She had not been so violently abused before by the girls she knew. Maybe Edith was as bad as the shaven-headed lad who had beaten up her father on New Year's Eve. She huffed involuntarily and made a grunting noise she had heard a frightened hedgehog make once.

'What? Speak up, girl.'

'I don't know, sir.' Her mind went blank. She placed her breakfast tray on the floor, righted the table and sat down on the wooden chair.

'That is not good enough. You pathetic bunch of recruits. You call yourselves forestry workers? You don't deserve to be here at the finest forestry training school in the country, representing our nation in the war. It is humiliating enough to have women here complaining about washing their hair in cold water, or a twisted sock; but to have you squabbling at breakfast beggars belief.'

Rosie's eyes darted across at her, and Keeva looked down as Blunt continued his tirade. She tried to eat her breakfast, but the bread stuck in her throat and the eggs were disgusting.

'Today after work, you, young lady, and the other troublemaker will clean the ablution block from top to bottom, until it's so clean it shines. I want to see my face in the floor tiles. And I tell you, if the camp fails to increase timber production because of you motley lot, the repercussions will be far more serious.'

Keeva decided there and then she would get out of the Forest of Dean as soon as she could. She would take the money and go and get a job as a domestic. She couldn't face the abuse, the nasty comments and lies about her and her family again.

*

After breakfast, she followed the other girls out into the forest for their last day of felling for the week. Rosie tried to catch her eye, but Keeva looked away. How had she dared to put the stolen money in her bag? The traitor. There were branches strewn across the footpaths and some large boughs had fallen across the pathways in the storm. Nobody spoke to Keeva and, after the last group of girls climbed over the tree, they didn't stop to help her as they had the others.

When they arrived at the clearing, where they had worked all week, the foresters training them were already there with the tools and the horses. To her surprise, Arthur approached her, hands behind his back, smiling. She looked around. As she looked back, she found him standing right beside her, smiling and looking cheeky.

'I've got something for you,' he said.

'For me?'

For a second Keeva forgot her sadness as she looked at his dark-brown eyes and wide grin. Then she realised that he knew. Maybe he was going to give her a white feather or do the chicken wings, flapping his elbows forwards and back. She shook her head.

'Oh no, not you as well,' she said.

His smile dropped and he brought out from behind his back a green beret.

'It's yours, I believe.'

Keeva stared at him in disbelief.

'I found it by the tree trunk over there, soaking wet, and so I took it home to dry by the fire.'

Over his shoulder she could see Rosie staring at them. Stepping behind Arthur out of Rosie's sight, she took the beret.

'Thank you,' she said, thinking that she wouldn't be needing that much longer.

But he didn't let go.

'What's your name? Is it Keeva?'

She felt like crying; why wouldn't he leave her alone?

Blunt approached. 'Let's get down to work, Arthur.'

'Can I partner up with you?' Arthur asked.

'Me?'

'Just ignore Blunt. The way he goes on, anyone would think he wants you all to fail so he can get some men in to do the work.'

'For hell's sake, give me the axe,' she said, looking at him with curiosity. He smiled at her, stepped up close and handed her the axe. She felt him stare at her all the time. She looked across at Beatrice and noticed Edith looking too.

'You all right?' he asked.

'Yes.'

She took the axe, picked a tree and swung into the trunk and cut it cleanly. She drove her axe into that tree hard with anger and, within several swings, Arthur said, 'Come yer and grab the cross-cut zid. I 'eard what you did the other day.'

Keeva got down on her knees and took the wooden handle in her hands. What had he heard? She pulled the saw.

'That was one daddocky big tree thou flumped on the dipple.' He'd stopped pulling on the cross-cut saw.

'Daddocky on the dipple?' She couldn't help smiling at him.

'Big rotten tree on a steep incline. Impressive.' He raised his eyebrows and pulled on the blade again. 'You peeved Captain

Blunt though, my old butty.'

Less said the better. He seemed to approve. The wooden handle tingled in her hands as, alternately, she and Arthur pulled the blade across the trunk, back and forth. Where the end of each pull started and finished was a finely tuned dance. The teeth sunk into the bark and sliced right through to the softer wood inside, releasing the pine scent of sawdust. She dared not push the blade as it purred gently at its edges and made easy work. Within a short time the cut was nearly through.

Arthur stopped, stood back and shouted, 'It's going, Keeva, it's going. Run, run for it. Run.' Then he yelled, 'Timberrrrrrrrr!' and laughed as Keeva ran towards him and held onto his arm, squealing.

She looked up to see the cloudy shape of the treetop sway and shift away, slowly at first, and then it broke through the canopy. It creaked and whooshed to the ground and Keeva felt it thump beneath her feet as it hit the earth. The trunk bounced and branches waved vigorously before it came to rest.

'Oh Jesus, that was scary,' she said.

Arthur's eyes glistened as the sun broke through the clouds for the first time in days. Keeva felt cold damp perspiration on her cheeks and forehead.

'Come here,' said Arthur. He took her over to the foot of the tree and pointed at the rough toothy break. 'That's the hinge, which helps the tree fall in the right direction,' he said.

His warm musky odour was distinct from the sawdust.

'Not bad,' said Arthur, smiling at her.

'Thanks.' Keeva smiled too, and then, realising she was looking right into his eyes, looked away.

'I'd better go and help some others too,' he said and slowly walked towards them.

She watched him leave. She liked the way he walked. He looked back at her and he was still smiling. The sunburst was short-lived, as the grey clouds gathered in its place and the sky turned the forest a darker shade of brown. The gloss of achievement at felling a tree with Arthur turned dull, as Keeva remembered the turmoil of last night. Memories flooded back of breakfast, and she stood alone once more.

Chapter 15

Rosie

1st March 1940, Beechenhurst Sawmills, Forest of Dean

'This week we're helping out at Beechenhurst,' Captain Blunt shouted over the noise of the wind in the trees and juddering engine as they turned a corner.

Rosie held on tight to the seat as the lorry swerved and bounced along the dirt track through the forest. A glimpse of the timberyard appeared through the trees before the metal-framed sawmill buildings came into view on the road ahead.

'Would you look at that?' Her mouth hung open, as she stared.

The sawmill and timberyard were vast, stretching the length of the road. Enormous felled trees were stacked up beside the tramway tracks.

'This is the powerhouse of timber production for the war,' Blunt gestured grandly.

The biggest stack of logs Rosie had ever seen lay on one side of the road disappearing into the dark forest as far as the eye could see. The freshly felled trees were tightly packed like Player's Navy Cut cigarettes; but not ten or twenty in a pack, there was more like hundreds if not thousands of trees. The trunks dwarfed the men who stood on the roadside, towering over them more than thirty feet high.

A gust of wind rocked the lorry sideways. She scraped her fingers through her hair, holding her fringe back from her eyes. Fordson tractors and lorries charged back and forth, loading trees, logs and sawn timber from one place to another. She searched through a group of men, who stood around and kicked the ground like goats. She hoped Arthur was there; he was on the knocker and certainly got 'er attention.

'Look at that lovely red Maudslay, I never seen soo many tree trunks on top of a lorry,' said Hazel.

The trees lay lengthways on top and doubled the height of the cab, twenty or thirty trees piled high – each tree perhaps four foot in diameter. As the Maudslay thundered past, Rosie imagined buying her brothers a Tonka toy just like that one with Beatrice's money. They'd always wanted one to play with. Then she'd tell 'em how she'd driven a huge Maudsley out in the forest, tooting the horn at Beatrice to make her jump.

She'd look down on Beatrice from the cabin, while Miss Frilly Knickers loaded the logs up on the back, and she had her feet up puffing an oily rag. Come to think of it, how did they get those trees onto the lorries when each must weigh ten tons? Her own sweaty palms would never lift anything that heavy. They were enormous, not like the rolling-pin-sized trees she and the other girls had felled in the forest last week.

The sawmill blades screeched above the wind, ripping in the forest around them. A chill ran down her back. She'd give herself a piece of advice right now: don't you ever work on those sawmills. Something that could slice through the timber so easily would cut through her hands in a blink.

The driver dropped the tailgate and Rosie stayed put on the back of the lorry. She wasn't keen to leap to work. Hazel and Lily climbed down in front of her, to the sound of Lily's dungarees ripping. She'd be stitching those up again this evening. The wind blew the leaves down the path and goosebumps ran up her arms as Captain Blunt ordered them up the road towards the mills.

'Calm down, girls. You're like a herd of wild ponies!' said Blunt.

Rosie rubbed her warm arms, as the cold wind rippled through the wild forest. There were dark pathways that disappeared behind moss-green rocks and ancient trees criss-crossed in every direction. Rosie didn't fancy being on her own out here in this howling wind – unless Arthur was with her. She smiled as she spotted him standing in a ring of men with their legs astride.

Rosie hadn't really noticed Arthur before she saw his arms wrapped round Keeva. That had caught her interest. He looked like a cheeky bloke and Rosie fancied a bit of that. She had enjoyed the way he'd slid his hands slowly down the wooden shaft of the axe. Keeva might like Arthur, but Rosie had an advantage with boys because she understood how they ticked. With so many brothers, she knew how to mess around and have a laugh with them. Keeva, she could tell, was a bit of a wet blanket.

'If it's going to be windy like this all day, I'll be extra hungry,' said Lily. 'When will we stop for our sandwiches?'

'Lunchtime as usual. Come along, don't dilly-dally,' Blunt barked as he hurried them onwards.

The enormous, corrugated metal roofed huts, each the size of the Hackney Empire music hall, made her feel very small. These housed the sawmills where enormous trunks were laying on the skids, six foot in diameter – the same height as the men and the circular saws that sliced through them. One tree after another was shoved through. Those trees screeched through the saws, went in round and came out square. Head tilted back, Rosie watched the metal chimneys above puffing continuously with white smoke, which spun round in curls before disappearing into the grey sky, and forest beyond. She rolled her shoulders, to try to release the tension in her neck.

There was a massive timberyard behind. Stacks of freshly cut timber, now in planks, were piled high. They looked like all those matchsticks her father had pinched once and tried to sell when they had no money and no food. This was something else, Rosie thought; the factory she had worked at back in London was nothing compared to this. This timber yard was flippin' huge. She imagined the bees and honey her father could make selling these giant matchsticks.

That reminded her – she wanted to speak to Keeva about the money before Beatrice got to her first. She hadn't had a chance so far, wondering what to say. Rosie regretted swapping the envelopes. She'd never have read Keeva's letter out loud for everyone to hear, not on her honour. Keeping shtum was an oath never to be broken, her brothers would say, or they'll take something precious from you.

She couldn't stop thinking about Keeva's father being a conchie; a father who doesn't use physical violence, who won't fight. He must be a right coward. Rosie's old man said conscientious objectors were shot in the last war. Her father was angry because he'd risked his life for the conchies, and he'd had tough times as a prisoner of war in East Africa. But maybe conchies weren't so bad; she couldn't trust every weep and wail her own father told when he was on the drink.

Anyway, Keeva had to give the money back now she knew about Rosie's poor mum being knocked sideways. She'd better still have the money in her bag. If Keeva lied and said she didn't, Rosie knew how to make sure she got it back. She'd learnt the powers of persuasion from her big brothers. And if Keeva decided to grass her up, there would be trouble to pay.

'The sawmills are at full capacity,' Blunt bellowed, 'but our fellers are being called up to fight by the War Office.' The wind took his words from his crooked teeth.

Blunt waved the girls in and Rosie followed behind, slowly moving into the shelter of the sawmill. A large beech tree on a saw bench slid towards a circular blade spinning at full speed. Rosie covered her ears as the saw screamed and tore through the tree, pouring sawdust onto the floor. She shuddered as she imagined how easily an arm could be sliced off, like a pork leg at the butchers.

Captain Blunt waved them on and into the office at the end, where Rosie was pleased to find some respite from the noise and wind. Beatrice and Hazel stood at the front with Edith. Keeva stepped up alongside her and stood in the light of the paraffin lamp by the desk, leaning closer to hear what Blunt would say. It was a dull overcast day and the lamp made Keeva's hair glow like the copper fire extinguisher in the factory. It reminded Rosie of those days, which seemed so far away, standing waiting in line to clock in. She'd read the instructions on the Badger's water-filled fire extinguisher so many times, 'To play, pull over guard, turn bottom up, strike on floor.' It had always made her giggle and she'd wanted to be the one to set it off in an emergency or just to squirt it at the foreman. Those days seemed so far away.

'You need to pay attention,' Captain Blunt said as he looked at the girls crowded into the office. 'This is a dangerous place to work. Firstly, it is imperative to keep the floor around the saw bench clear. Ignore this at your peril; you could quite easily trip and fall, with fatal consequences.'

Rosie didn't want to think about that. She had felt sick as a dog the time her brother had chopped his finger half through with a knife.

'Secondly, you will need one of these,' he said, holding up a small plank with the corner cut out. 'It's a push stick, which is used for moving logs into the blade. Don't use your hands. You will be making these this morning and cutting the spacers this afternoon in the small sawmill. Any questions?'

'What are the spacers?' asked Beatrice.

'They are thin cuts of wood, which keep the gaps between the planks; they allow the air to circulate and the timber to dry. You will be cutting them on the small sawmill. Yes?'

'Yes, sir,' Hazel replied.

'Thirdly, if you have got any problems, ask Wilkie, the saw doctor, in the next hut. He sharpens the blades and fixes the saws. Dismissed to the small sawmill.'

They were taught how to use cant hooks to move large logs onto the skids, ready to be milled. Making the push sticks with a bow saw made Rosie's fingers sore with all the fiddly work, cutting small angles, and the wood catching on the saw. She then helped unload logs from the wagons, which had been brought in from the forest. After that she was put on stacking the timber in the yard.

'I swear the wood gets heavier.' Rosie laid one end of a freshly milled plank of wood on the spacers.

Gladys set her end of the plank down and lined it up with the others. 'It's back-breaking work.'

'I've been hungry all morning and Redrum has made sure there's no chance of getting any extra food. She's starving us,' said Lily, as Blunt approached.

'Let's make a start on the sawmills now. There are three sizes: small, medium and large. The small one is a twenty-eight-inch blade. Working in fours you'll start on the small one. The largest is sixty inches in diameter and is used to cut through these beech trunks,' said Captain Blunt.

Beatrice looked pale faced. 'I … I … c … c … could offer some help in the office on production quantities.'

'You, c … c … c … could follow orders,' he replied.

'It's the noise, it hurts my ears, and the sawdust, which is no good for my lungs. I have a history of suffering from asthma,' Beatrice added.

'Put something over your face – and twenty laps around the timber yard at lunch break should strengthen your lungs,' he replied, turning away.

The truth was even Rosie had a dodgy stomach that morning and didn't want to work the mills. The way the ferocious saws whizzed round was terrifying. In a second it would slice through a yard of the hard wood of a beech tree. Rosie could do with something to wet her whistle.

'Hazel, Lily, Keeva and Rosie – you four will start with cutting spacers for the timber and wood for the stoves, as shown earlier. Leave the men to cut the railway sleepers. The rest of you come with me,' he said.

'So, who's going first?' asked Hazel.

Now was Rosie's chance to have a chat with Keeva about the money and then she'd scarper.

'We'll fetch some logs first,' said Rosie, pointing at Keeva.

'I could do with some lunch to settle my stomach,' said Lily.

'We'll be back soon.' Rosie left Lily and Hazel in the sawmill, hoping Keeva would follow.

'Ain't it lunchtime yet? I'm starving,' Lily said behind her.

'I'll go first then,' said Hazel.

'You're brave.'

'We can't get started without a log anyway,' replied Keeva.

'Come on, Keeva.' Rosie and Keeva left the hut and crossed the road to fetch the timber from the other side of the track.

Coming up beside her, Rosie said: 'Keeva, I'm not going to beat about the bush – did you find the—'

'You—' Keeva pointed her finger towards Rosie's face '—have got a bloody cheek. Trying to set me up. Hiding the money you stole, in my bag, and taking my private letter. You're a snake.' Keeva bared her teeth.

She could see the fury pulsed deep in Keeva's veins, so why hadn't she lashed out at her. She wanted her to; come on, she was ready for a fight.

'It was Beatrice, not me. Anyway, it's not my fault if your father is a coward, is it?'

'How dare you speak about my father. You don't know what you're talking about.' Keeva stumbled over the logs and fell into the nettles. She stood up again and grabbed a log.

'If you don't give the money back—' Rosie pushed up her sleeves and drew her hands into fists '—I'll make you.'

Keeva lifted one end of the log higher and frowned at her. 'Are you helping at all?'

Rosie braced herself and hoisted the big log up at the other end. With the weight in her hands, she stepped backwards one step at a time. Slowly they carried the log across the road.

She wanted to finish their chat before they got back to the sawmill.

'Slow down.' It annoyed her the way Keeva kept pushing the log against her thighs. Then came a vicious shove – Rosie lost her balance and toppled backwards on to her bottom, dropping the log on the ground.

'Oi, watch out!' exclaimed Rosie, as she landed awkwardly on her elbows on the hard ground and her head jerked backwards.

'Oh, sorry, Rosie, I didn't mean to push you over,' said Keeva.

Dead-legged by the log, Rosie picked herself up again. She'd learnt to recover quickly, to avoid another blow. She'd taught herself never to retaliate. But still she had half a mind to knock the conchie's daughter sideways. She wrestled with the log once again, getting hot, and nearly losing her grip. Rosie backed into the shed a few more yards, where Hazel and Lily came over to help carry the tree. The four of them manoeuvred the trunk on to the skids, ready to be milled.

'Come on, we're breaking for lunch now,' Gladys called as she passed, lugging a billycan of water down the track. 'We're going to light the fire and put the kettle on.'

'Come 'ere.' A hand brushed down Rosie's back and she flinched. 'I'm just getting the leaves and dirt off you,' said Lily. 'Stand still.'

'That's better,' said Lily after a minute. 'Come on, Hazel.'

It was a good job the wind cooled Rosie's burning skin, as she stepped outside the hut and took a deep breath. She was relieved that lunch had delayed work on the sawmill. But now the stubborn pacifist was talking to Arthur over by the campfire. Keeva wasn't going to have all the fun.

'All right, Arthur,' she said, hand on hip.

'Hello, Rosie, how's the sawmill?'

Keeva turned away.

'Blunt said the men are being called up. Will you be signing up soon?'

'You trying to get rid of me, are you?' he replied.

'Now, why would I do that? I just wondered how old you were, Arthur?' She'd heard someone say he was eighteen already.

'And how old are you, Keeva?' She raised her eyebrows towards Keeva.

'How old do you think I am?' Arthur asked, staring at Keeva, and flexing his cheek muscles as the wind blew his mop of fringe away from his face. He was a handsome feller.

'I reckon you're eighteen. But because you've got a wooden leg you can't sign up.' Rosie gave him a cheeky wink.

He leant on his axe handle, bent one leg up and started limping. Rosie couldn't help herself; she was having too much fun at Keeva's expense.

'So, if it's not your leg, you must be a conscientious objector.'

'I'm going to sign up as soon as I can. Before I find myself in a reserved occupation for the war and stuck in the Forest of Dean forever. I'm already making plans to get out of here. I want to see the world.' He smiled at Keeva.

Keeva smiled briefly and then rolled her eyes at Rosie.

'So, what do you think about conscientious objectors?' she asked.

'It's up to them,' he said, looking warily at them both.

'Your father's an objector, isn't he?' said Rosie to Keeva.

Arthur turned and stared at Keeva, as she walked off abruptly to join the other girls. Rosie smiled to herself. She liked Arthur, with his cheeky sense of humour. And Keeva was so tetchy about her father; it was easy to wind her up.

'Let's get some grub,' Arthur said, going to stand by the fire. Her conversation with Keeva could wait, so she followed Arthur. He grabbed a Y-shaped twig.

'What's that for?' Rosie asked.

'A toasting fork for my bread,' he replied and found a log to sit on by the fire, poked his bread onto the stick and rolled a glass bottle with milky brown liquid gently into the edge of the fire to warm.

'Oh, what's that?' Lily asked.

'Cocoa,' he replied.

'Lovely,' said Lily. 'What I'd do for a taste.'

Lily was always cadging something for nothing.

'Budge up.' Rosie tried to squeeze in on the log between Hazel and Arthur, but Hazel didn't move.

'Don't push me off the end.' Hazel frowned.

Shuffling from side to side, Rosie held her hands up to the flames to warm them. Hazel was just being awkward; she only wanted to be up close with Arthur. She couldn't help smiling when she looked over at Keeva, eating her cheese sandwich on her own, through clouds of smoke pouring off the burning logs. Every now and again Keeva looked up at Arthur.

'That kettle boiled yet?' Rosie asked.

'It's taking ages to boil in this wind,' said Gladys.

'Pass us a cup, Arthur,' said Rosie, and Lily handed her an enamel mug as the girls chatted around the fire pit. The ashes and fresh woody smoke blew in gusts in different directions and the girls squealed and turned their heads away.

'Ow, that stings.' Rosie squeezed her eyes shut. A scrunched-up face wasn't the look she wanted when Arthur was by her side. Then she heard Beatrice heading their way, talking at the top of her voice, as usual.

'Integrating with all the hoi polloi one must be certain to keep up one's guard, don't you think, Edith. You never know who you can trust.'

Beatrice marched to stand in front of the fire.

'Will someone make room for me?' she said and looked around. Nobody said a word.

'Lily, you're normally a fast eater, let me sit there.'

'I'm just warming myself by the fire,' Lily replied.

'Don't be belligerent, Lily, it doesn't become you,' Beatrice demanded. 'I need to speak with the group on a matter of great importance.'

Reluctantly Lily got up and Beatrice took her place. Rosie had lost her chance to have a chat with Arthur again because of Beatrice, who loved the sound of her own voice.

Abruptly Beatrice said, 'I think it would be prudent to remind you all that we need to be vigilant for German spies.'

'What? You 'avin' a laugh?'

'German spies are a real threat to British security, Rosie.' Hazel shook her head.

'Thank you, Hazel. Father says, ordinary people are leaking

sensitive information back to the Nazis,' added Beatrice.

'Have you seen that advertisement?' asked Gladys. '"Wanted for Murder. Her careless talk costs lives." My brothers are away fighting, so I should be careful what I say.'

'I suppose you never know who might be a Nazi sympathiser an' all,' said Rosie with mischief. Maybe Keeva's father was one himself. She looked over at Keeva to see how she reacted to the conversation. Maybe she was German, with a name like Keeva. Her head was down; she did not make eye contact with anyone. Mind you, nobody wanted to talk to her right now.

Beatrice added, 'Hitler wants to know regiment names, where they are going and where they came from. Anything to do with ships, guns and shells is censored information and must not be divulged.'

'Why? Do you think there could be a spy among us?' Rosie asked dramatically, looking around and pointing at everyone, one by one. The wind changed direction and some girls jumped up, as smoke blew in their eyes.

Gladys smiled at Rosie.

'The men in the forest do have a funny accent, which sounds rather German, said Beatrice, 'How do we know that some of them aren't spies? They say vorest not forest.'

Arthur chuckled. 'Ze folk in zis vorest were born here, lived here and never been anywhere else. I don't zink you've got anything to worry about with zem. We can't help it if we talk vunny loike.'

Lily let out a little giggle.

'That don't sound German to me,' said Rosie.

'No, the Germans say, *"Warum ist der Wald so wild, wenn es windig ist?"'* said Gladys.

Edith looked up at Gladys, as if surprised, and Beatrice glared at her.

'That's good, Gladys,' Rosie giggled, 'What did you say?'

'Vy is ze forest so vild ven it iss vindy. I learnt German at school.'

'You girls are the strangers round 'ere. How do we know you aren't German?' said Arthur.

'Vy becoss ve need seese big logs to vin zee vor,' replied Gladys sternly to giggles all round.

'Look!' said Beatrice. 'This is not a laughing matter; it's actually very serious. It's important we know where we are from. I am from Whitley Bay near Newcastle Upon Tyne on the east coast, before we moved to our holiday home in the Lake District.'

'If you haven't worked it out by now, we're from Yorkshire,' said Lily, stuffing a cheese and pickle sandwich in her mouth. 'Me, Hazel and Edith too; isn't that right, Edie?'

Edith nodded.

'You don't sound the same as Lily and Hazel,' Rosie said to Edith warily, wondering what had triggered her furious outburst back in the dining hall.

'Different part of Yorkshire; it's a big place,' said Edith, curtly.

'All right,' said Rosie.

'Where's your name from, Keeva? Is it German?' asked Rosie.

'No, it's Irish.' Keeva poured herself a cup of tea.

Rosie enjoyed needling Keeva.

Captain Blunt came around the corner. 'Come on now, lunch break is over and it's time to get to work on the sawmills.'

'Vy are you ztill zitting there? Vee have vork to do,' said Arthur when Captain Blunt left. Rosie punched Arthur in the arm and laughed.

Rosie trooped into the sawmills followed by Keeva. She was still irritated by Hazel for backing Beatrice in front of Arthur and humiliating her. Maybe Beatrice was right: you couldn't trust any of the girls on camp, not because they were Nazis but because they couldn't take a joke.

'All right,' said Hazel, as she switched on the saw and lined up the timber on the sliders. 'Let's try this out.' Hazel rolled up her sleeves.

Rosie felt the wind on her back as she watched the twenty-eight-inch saw spin faster and faster. Rosie decided Hazel could do all the work on the saw bench that afternoon, while she took it easy. At full speed the sharp-toothed cutting edge of the blade became a blur, and the bench began vibrating under Hazel's arms as she leant on the platform edge. Rosie was glad it was not her turn.

Rosie watched Hazel as the steam engine that powered the blade whirred, gathering speed. Hazel picked up her push stick and positioned it on to the edge of the log. She bent forwards to look down the saw bench towards the blade and lined up the log with her hands to the width of the spacers. With the tips of her fingers, Hazel applied pressure to the push stick and the log slid slowly towards the blade.

As the blade touched the end of the log, Keeva came to watch too. The blade bit into the wood and ripped up the end of the log, causing splinters to leap from the saw. Suddenly the wood jerked, and Hazel's hands slipped.

'Oh my God.' Rosie drew her hand to her mouth.

'Hazel!' Keeva screeched.

Hazel's hands thrust forwards, fingers outstretched, as she fell towards the spinning blade. Rosie felt her skin go tight. There wasn't time to catch her, not if she didn't want to risk landing on the blade herself. She was too far away, too slow and too late.

Hazel's hand went into the blade. Red spots appeared on her face and beige coat. She howled as blood poured from her knuckles. Now it was too late. The mutilation horrified her. What could she do now? Her knees gave way. She tried desperately to hang on to consciousness, as her hand dragged down over Keeva's jumper.

'Help, someone help!' Keeva called.

Her fingers tried to hold on, sliding down corduroy jodhpurs. The metal blade shrieked and Hazel staggered backwards. Would Hazel die?

Chapter 16

15th December 1939, Glass Bottle Manufacturers, Hackney, London

Alongside hundreds of other bodies, Rosie waited for the factory gates on Chatsworth Road to open. The sky was a washed-out grey and the days were getting colder and darker. Rosie missed breakfast to get to work early to avoid her usual gang. She wore her mother's large blue hat to help cover her eyes on the way to work.

As the gates were unlocked, Mr Paterson clanged the keys against the metal post and opened the gate to the swarm of men and women. Rosie skimmed across the crowd for faces she knew. There were none. Good. She didn't want their pity or them nosing into her business today. She headed straight inside, removed her coat and hat quickly, clicked her card to clock in and stood in line by her workstation. She pretended to be busy making sure it was clean of bits of glass and waited for the others to assemble.

'All right, Rosie,' said one girl, yawning. She parked herself beside Rosie and nudged up against her gently.

'All right, Bets,' she replied keeping her head down.

A hundred other women nestled in, up and down the conveyor belts and moving trays. This week Rosie was to check for pieces of blown glass left inside the bottles and hook them out with a long-handled tool like a crochet hook. There were different coloured Glaxo medical bottles: blue for poison, green for pills and clear Cow & Gate baby feeding bottles. Thousands of these bottles, blown by the men just over the road, queued up to be checked by hundreds of hands and eyes. One by one she picked each bottle up, did the flick, and popped it back on the conveyor belt before it hurried on, to be topped and boxed by scores of other women along the factory line before the end-of-day whistle.

The engines started up and the conveyor belt started to move through, glass bottles clinking to the sound of grinding machinery and pistons pumping up and down to turn the belts. The cacophony of machines and bottles was some comfort to Rosie today. Although it was frowned upon to talk, she knew she could now chat to Bets without being overheard. The women were packed so tightly they could chat into each other's ears, while their hands moved automatically finding the next bottle by touch.

'Where was you this morning then?'

'Got up early, didn't I?'

'You never did?'

Suddenly Bets turned to look at Rosie and gasped.

'Oh, Rosie, look at your black eye! At it again, is he?'

'Shh, don't make a fuss. Mr Paterson will catch us talking.'

'Oh, darlin'.'

Before Mr Paterson arrived, they used to enjoy having a singalong to the radio. But he said it wasn't possible to hear the radio because of the noise of the machines. He did have a point, but when they had the opportunity, they could pick up a song and drown out the machines with their exuberant singing. The factory used to be more fun like that.

'You workin' overtime today?' Bets asked.

'I don't know.'

'There's a rush on for Christmas.'

'I got to get away, Bets. He'll bleedin' kill me if I'm not careful.'

'Oh, Rosie, you ain't going nowhere. You can't leave me 'ere.'

Rosie was looking for a way out of there today. She wanted Bets to clock in for her after breaktime, so she could escape just before lunch to go and sign up for war work. She didn't want to get her pay docked and there was a risk she might get caught. If she was going to do it, this was the best shift when Mr Paterson patrolled the labelling and packing areas and the lorries began rolling in and out of the courtyard. The packers had their breakfast later.

There were separate toilets for the men and women, and she was going to escape through the window above the men's urinals. But, if somebody came down from the offices she would be in trouble. The people who worked in the offices were stuffy, always dobbing on the assembly line workers when a few bottles went missing and messed up their accounts. Why did they care if a few workers got extras?

The only time the managers spoke to Rosie was when she was in trouble. She watched Mr Paterson walk past on his way to labelling. As the bottles clinked and rattled and pushed up against each other, sometimes shuffling out of line, Rosie counted down the minutes to 9.30am and the first break. Smoking wasn't allowed on the factory floor any more and Rosie was gasping for a puff. Eating on the factory floor wasn't allowed either and she was starving.

'You got any food, Bets?'

'No.'

Rosie had perfected thinking of nothing at the factory. She never saw the point in her job, save to keep her near home and her father in pocket. She'd wanted to go to secretarial school, but her mother had said it was too far away. Eventually the whistle blew at 9.30am and Rosie slung her arm over Bets' shoulder. Lolling on her, they wandered towards the green-walled dining hall.

'Will you cover for me after break?' Rosie whispered in Bets' ear.

'What if I get caught?'

'No, you won't. It's easy to put the two cards together.'

'Oh, I don't know.'

'I won't be gone long. It'll be all right, Bets.'

'Where you going?'

'Signing up for some war work.'

'Like that?'

Rosie felt her eye to see if the swelling had gone down yet. She sparked up and blew a puff of smoke above her head. A whistle blew sharply and she waved her cigarette in acknowledgement. She wasn't off the factory floor yet but wanted Paterson to remember seeing her today.

'Sorry, Paterson,' she said, smiling and working her charm on him.

'Why, Rosie?'

'I'm not going into a bomb factory from here just like Mother. I'll end up working in a factory my whole life.'

'But you don't need to sign up yet. Wait for me.'

'It's the boys; they are out of it having a lovely time in the countryside, living in a big house, and the others gone off to fight. What am I doing here?'

'You're doing something, making bottles for feeding all those babies.'

'And pills and poison bottles for all those old sick people. There's got to be more to life than this.'

'But we got Christmas on the way.'

Rosie remembered her first day at work. She'd left school feeling that she had no other option because when Mother said you've got to go, that was it. She hadn't liked the factory then. It was mostly older women, but eventually she made friends with the younger ones like Bets, who made her feel at home. Bets passed Rosie a mug of tea.

'Come on, let's have a bit of Judy Garland,' said Rosie, laughing.

' ...over the rainbow ...'

'All right, maestro that's enough from you two,' said Paterson.

'Don't forget, I'm in the toilet and not feeling well,' Rosie said, walking across towards the ladies cloakroom.

'Rosie … !'

She left the dining hall and noisy chatter of hundreds of women, passed a few people in the corridor, checked behind her and peeped her head round the door of the men's toilets. All clear, no one was around. She stepped inside the Gents to the foul stench and opened the window, kicked her leg up and rested her foot on the urinals. She jumped and pulled herself up, sliding her knee up the wall. Grabbing the window frame, she pulled herself through, one straight leg sticking out behind her. She heard a sound from the corridor, gave one last push, and fell out of the window, landing on the cold floor in a heap.

She jumped up, brushed herself off and walked down the red-brick alley, heart pumping. She saw the guard on the gate and the first of the lorries leaving, so she trotted up alongside it quickly. More easily than she had ever imagined, she left the factory confines. She knew she was taking a risk, but having her wages docked would be worse. She already skimmed off a few pence for cigarettes before handing it over to her old man for rent. He always said it was never enough.

Rosie had hoped that starting work would give her more freedom. But her parents just relied on her wages even more. Now the little toerags had gone, why should she do it any more? She knew they wanted to have a good Christmas, buy presents for the little 'uns, especially if they weren't coming home. But she just wanted to buy some scarlet lippy, flirt about, go to the cinema and have a bit of fun.

She held her head high and marched on towards the Ministry of Labour offices.

She breathed a sigh of relief. Now she could do whatever she wanted. She was going to do her bit for the war. Her black eye would help, when she asked to be sent away from home, she was sure.

Chapter 17

Keeva

1st March 1940, Beechenhurst Sawmills, Forest of Dean

Hazel screamed. Keeva rushed forward.

'It's all right, Hazel,' she said trembling.

'My 'and!' Hazel screamed.

Keeva watched deep-red blood pour out of Hazel's right hand. The colour of her mother's cadmium paint. She steadied herself on the workbench.

'Oh, my gawd,' Rosie said, her face a waxy white, reaching out.

Keeva ran to turn off the saw. The fresh smell of oil from a newly sharpened blade lingered and when she turned around Rosie had passed out on the floor in the sawdust.

'Jesus Christ, Rosie,' Keeva said, stepping over her.

Oh my God, she must help Hazel!

'You all right, Hazel?' she said loudly, looking away from her mutilated hand, tasting vomit in her throat.

'Ooh noo, ooeww, is it bad?' she replied, eyes tightly shut.

'You'll be fine. We just need to get some help. Can you walk?' Keeva asked, as calmly as she could.

'I think so.'

Captain Blunt would be furious after what he had said about push sticks. He'd warned them about this. Keeva preferred her chances with Mr Wilkinson, who was sharpening a large circular saw head in the next hut when they stepped inside.

'Mr Wilkie,' Keeva said, quivering, 'Hazel is hurt.'

'I think I've cut m' thumb off.'

'No, you haven't, you wouldn't be able to stand there if you had,' he said.

'I have, Mr Wilkinson,' she said.

He dropped his tools to the bench when he saw her bloodied face and hands.

'Where is it?' he asked.

'It's all shredded to pieces,' she replied, wincing.

'Apply pressure and hold it up for her, while I get transport for the doctor,' he said, 'We'll get you fixed up.'

'Rosie is passed out in the mill,' Keeva said, her stomach churning.

'Is she injured?'

'I don't think so.'

'Sit Hazel down here,' he said, patting the seat as he got up.

Keeva noticed the red Wesco oil can on the workbench, like her father's, as she helped Hazel onto the bench. She always liked the bubbling sound of it and petroleum aroma when you pumped the handle and oil dribbled out of the long spout. It looked like Hazel's hand, dribbling with blood.

'You are made of tough stuff,' said Wilkie; 'I've seen bigger men than you out cold.' He gently held her forearm and raised her hand. 'That's better.'

Hazel held her bleeding palm up, as he pushed a red first aid tin with a white cross into Keeva's hands.

'Bandage her up and keep her talking,' he said.

Keeva nodded and trembled, thinking how she might hurt Hazel by applying the bandage.

'I'll get the others and arrange for transport to the doctors. Pour the saline solution on the wound first.'

'Yes,' said Keeva as he walked out of the door. The wind outside the sawmill hut rushed through the trees, and sucked and sighed against the door, which swung loosely on its hinges.

'Father will be angry with me. He didn't want me here in the first place,' Hazel said as Keeva started to pour the saline solution onto her hand from the clear glass bottle, revealing the small jagged white end of her missing thumb and bone-deep lacerations across the knuckles of her fore and middle finger. They both took a deep breath and Hazel screwed up her face. The blood dripped more intensely forming a pool upon the table. The metallic scent of Hazel's blood mixed with the smell of petroleum oil. Quickly Keeva took the bandage and asked Hazel to hold the end. The soft cream gauze slipped through her fingers as she unravelled the roll and laid it across Hazel's palm carefully.

'Oough,' Hazel grimaced and turned away.

Hazel's butchered hand was so terrible Keeva wanted to cover it as quickly as possible. The burn of bile rose in her throat again. She softly laid the gauze over the splintered bone, took the roll underneath Hazel's wrist and swapped hands. Loosely, over and round again, she took the cream bandage. Swapping hands each time it went under her palm; she made sure the bandage laid flat.

'Nearly there.'

'The wind whipped t' sawdust up into m' eyes; I couldn't help it,' Hazel said, dropping her hand down towards the table as if it were too heavy to hold up. 'It's my right hand and all.'

'Keep your hand up and your head down,' said Keeva firmly.

Hazel slowly rested her head and pale face down onto the workbench, as Keeva continued to wrap the bandage. She was concerned that Hazel had passed out, but her eyes were still open. Her hand looked more like a bird's foot now, without the thumb. Keeva knew it was bad – blood seeped through the bandage with every fresh layer, so she pulled it tighter and kept wrapping until no blood appeared.

'You all right, Hazel?'

'It's my writing hand, my chopping hand. He told us not to work alone.' She shook her head.

'We were with you. You'll be able to write again.'

The door creaked open on the wind and Wilkie came back into the hut. 'Help is on its way.'

Gladys popped her head around the corner.

'You all right, Hazel?' she asked.

'Oh noo, I've lost my thumb,' said Hazel. 'Lucky it wasn't my arm.'

'She's going to be just fine. I've never seen courage like it in a girl before,' added Wilkie. 'Both of you. Some of the men look half dead with that same injury. What are your names?'

'This is Hazel,' Keeva said, smiling at her injured friend. 'I'm Keeva.'

'Keeva, I want you to go to the hospital with Hazel.'

'Why me?' Keeva asked, surprised.

'You are good in an emergency,' he replied.

The lorry, already on a trip to dispatch pit props to the station, was delayed two hours. At last, Keeva and Hazel arrived at the hospital emergency medical services department, which smelled of disinfectant. Keeva wished her father was there; he'd know what to do.

Young and old, patients waited to be seen by doctors. A young boy in a cable-knit brown sweater sat on his mother's lap just beside a green curtain. The boy had a large lump on his forehead and was crying as he had just vomited on the floor. The bruise reminded her of her father's beaten face on New Year's Eve.

'If that's because of his bump on the head, it's not a good sign,' said the nurse.

'He only fell off the wall. I was watching him, but it all happened so quickly. He just tripped and fell headfirst. There, there, Albert!'

Keeva's mother had gone to the community hospital with Keeva years ago, when she'd broken her arm. But when her mother had seen the bone sticking through her skin, she'd nearly passed out and had had to be taken to another cubicle for treatment, leaving Keeva alone while they'd set her arm. Why wasn't her mother stronger for her? Keeva went through that whole traumatic experience alone.

'My hand is throbbing now, Keeva. It really hurts.'

How could she comfort Hazel? She could see the blood had soaked through the bandages. She wondered what she would have liked her mother to say when her arm was broken.

'The doctors will see us soon,' she said, staring at Hazel's drooped shoulders. Keeva took her good hand and held it gently, rubbing her fingers. 'Don't worry, I'll stay right by your side.' In truth, she was relieved it wasn't her thumb. She admired Hazel's stoicism. But she couldn't help wonder, if she hadn't been arguing with Rosie, whether this would've happened at all. She swallowed and looked down at her muddy boots.

Hazel winced. 'Thanks, Keeva; I don't know what I'd do without you.'

A doctor approached hastily, his white coat flapping about his legs, and took another look at Hazel's thumb.

'Miss Hardy, I'm afraid we will need to amputate what remains of your thumb to avoid infection. You'll be out of action for at least eight weeks. No more felling trees or working in sawmills for you.'

'How will I write?' Hazel's face turned ashen.

'That's why it is a blessing we have two hands,' the doctor said, 'and people very easily learn to adapt. Unfortunately, we can't get through to your parents on the phone lines. So, without permission from your parents to give you a general anaesthetic, we need to get you sewn up using a local. We have asked the army doctors and nurses to assist. They are used to amputations, so you'll be in safe hands.'

The repetition of the word amputation sliced right through Keeva. 'This way, Miss Hardy. Your friend can wait for you.'

'Will you be here?' Hazel's lips trembled.

Keeva nodded as Hazel was led away up the corridor. While she waited, her mind drifted to somewhere new, where there was no shock, no upset or worry, and no amputation. She could make a fresh start where no one knew her father was a conchie, where she would not be judged and would be liked instead. She could work somewhere new – in a milk bar making shakes like Gladys – until the war was over, and then she would go home. People would forget about the war; her father would start plumbing again and everything would be happy, like before.

*

'We're all done now. If you'd like to come this way.' The nurse showed her down the corridor and into a ward. Hazel lay on a bed, her hand swaddled and face as pale as the sheets. It could have been me, Keeva thought. She was the lucky one. She imagined going home without a thumb, especially as her mother didn't even know she was working on the sawmills. What parents wouldn't be cross? She wiggled her fingers and thumbs and had a horrible feeling of dread, about things that go wrong. She'd had enough of that feeling since she ran away. She wished she could just wash it off with a jug of warm water to make her feel calm again.

'Here is a letter with instructions on how to recuperate at home, and recommending that Keeva accompany you home.'

The doctor gave a nod of his head towards Keeva. 'She needs looking after. Make sure she gets home safely. There's further information about how to care for your residual stump, Hazel, once you are home. Would you like us to arrange for a call to be made to the Forestry Training School to request you are collected.'

'Yes, of course,' Keeva replied.

She realised there and then that this was her chance to leave the Forest of Dean and never return.

*

While the girls made a fuss of Hazel in the dining hall the next day, after they got back from the hospital, Keeva readied herself for departure from the forestry school. She slipped upstairs and made sure she had all her belongings with her, including her gas mask. Time to go. She looked round at the ten empty beds with grey blankets, and Beatrice's eiderdown.

Keeva pulled out Beatrice's money, neatly placed inside the thick cream envelope. She had never stolen anything before, except for scrumping a few apples and plums. She wasn't sure she should. The money she had taken from her parents' savings tin when she left home was different because they were family. Taking money from Beatrice, someone she barely knew, was much more serious. She could leave it under Beatrice's pillow instead. But how could she run away without any money? She needed it to buy food or find somewhere to stay, until she found herself a job. The money was her ticket out of there and it was so easy to keep it. She stamped her foot and kicked the bed post several times as she agonised over her decision. She could always pay the money back when she got herself another job.

She took a deep breath and looked out of the window, which was rattling in the wind. She groaned as she caught sight of the church spire on the hill, knowing she didn't have much time. God would know what to do – take the money or not? Of course not. But if God didn't want her to take the money, why was the money hidden in her bag? No regrets, she told herself. The heels of her Land Army brown brogues sounded hollow on the wooden floorboards as she walked out of the room. She glanced back at the fire she had enjoyed lighting to keep the room warm. The lorry's horn tooted. She ran downstairs and arrived outside just as the girls assembled to wave goodbye to Hazel.

'Norchard Station,' called out Phil, with a grin.

'Ooh, there you are, Keeva. Stop faffin' around or we'll miss the train,' said Hazel.

'I can take her back, Keeva, if you'd rather stay here,' Edith offered.

'No,' Keeva replied abruptly, feeling all eyes on her.

She hoped she wasn't blushing. She got into the truck. Rosie passed her bag and Gladys helped Hazel climb up, using her one good arm – the other carried by a cotton sling.

'Ta-ra, pet,' Hazel said bravely.

The cabin door slammed shut, separating them from the song of 'goodbyes', 'take cares', and the crowd of pink faces. Hazel awkwardly adjusted her bandaged hand in the sling and waved the other hand until the girls disappeared out of sight. Then she slumped back in the seat.

'Thanks for taking me home, Keeva. I can't wait to see me mam. Although, I don't want Mam to worry and make a fuss over me. And I hope Dad won't be mad. No, he'll be all right,' Hazel said to herself.

Keeva smiled at Hazel nervously, worried how her parents would react to an amputated thumb. To take her mind off Hazel's parents and her injury, Keeva made plans to leave the Forest of Dean. She checked her bag contents and fastened it securely again. The money was safe. There must be the equivalent of three- or four-weeks' wages in that envelope. She knew the money would have been a chance for a new beginning for Rosie's mother. She could have found a new safe place to live, away from her father. But Keeva's family lived in poverty too; maybe she needed the same help.

Beatrice's privileged upbringing was almost repellent, when it was just pocket money to go shopping for clothes. Keeva justified her decision and imagined the money as her own. She could do exactly what she wanted now: get up whenever she liked, eat whatever she liked and do whatever she wanted, all day. She'd had enough of being shouted at by Blunt with his tufts of hair growing out of his ears and nose. She hated being scolded by Redrum for being late for breakfast and dinner. She was sick of all those girls who would be just as quick to befriend her as stab her in the back. There was nobody she could trust and she just wanted to be free.

'The train is already at the station,' said Keeva.

Keeva grabbed their bags and waited while Hazel eased her way out of the cab.

'Aye, quick, Phil, I need help.' Phil hopped down to her aid.

They just caught the Gloucester train, as the stationmaster blew his whistle and the engines accelerated. The heavy doors clunked shut, up and down the carriages, and Keeva and Hazel fell into the end compartment.

Hazel held her bandaged hand up in its sling, looking pained. The train sighed as the engine throttled away like a hammer on the track, sliding through the forest and trees that tunnelled the train.

Keeva watched the wizened trees and sturdy rocks disappear outside the windows. Seeing the views by day, Keeva couldn't take her eyes off the magnificent green forest. The train passed out above the canopy and she could see Symonds Yat, the rocky outcrop, and the miles of forest. which turned from green to blue in the distance. The trees gave way to large open fields, farmhouses and apple orchards – replaced by rows and rows of the same red-brick houses as they approached Gloucester. She caught a glimpse of the cathedral spire just above the town and looked at Hazel who was cosy on the seat opposite her. She had taken a painkiller and fallen asleep.

'Hazel, Hazel,' Keeva said, touching her knee gently to wake her. They climbed out and waited at the station for their next train, which did not come. Keeva thought of Beatrice's money in her bag. She suddenly felt ashamed. She reminded herself it was Rosie who'd originally stolen the money, not her. Did that make any difference? There were no fires in the waiting room, so it was freezing. The trains for Doncaster were delayed and the hours passed slowly. Keeva began to think about where she would go. Maybe she could stay in the town near to Hazel. She had never been up north before; some folks said the people are more friendly the further north you go. Maybe this kindly disposition would help her find a job. She'd decided, after all, she didn't want to work on a farm or go into domestic service. She'd try something different.

She'd had enough of being pushed around and told what to do. Now she wouldn't have Beatrice tutting and disapproving of her, or Rosie stirring things up about her father, and Gladys could be friends with Edith. She would be happier alone. She had her suspicions that even Missus Potter probably knew she was a troublemaker. She couldn't stand feeling so worried about her father any more. She was sick of listening to what other people thought of him. Was he a coward, a Nazi sympathiser, a German, a Quaker? No, he was none of those things.

'Do you think your father will be cross then, Hazel?' Keeva asked.

'Aye, he might.' Hazel said. 'He wanted me to stay at home, look after my younger brother. I didn't want to be a mother my whole life. So, the Land Army was one way of getting away from family and finding my own feet. He was not best pleased when I went against his wishes. Now this.'

'What are you going to say?' asked Keeva.

'The truth, I suppose. What else?'

Keeva considered the consequences of the accident and how a

single moment had changed the course of Hazel's life forever.

'Would your father be angry, if it were you?' asked Hazel.

'His temper flares up at times. I think he'd be upset, but he'd understand if I had an accident,' replied Keeva. 'He's a caring father.'

'Did he not mind you joining the Land Army?' Hazel asked.

Now Keeva wasn't going back to camp, she could tell Hazel the truth.

'He doesn't know and neither does my mother. I ran away from home after he was sent to prison.'

'By gum, Keeva, why did you not tell them?'

'I just had to get away from them. I wanted to do my bit for the war and you can guess their views on that. They always wanted to be different to everyone else and I just wanted to be the same. Joining up was a rebellion; I made a choice to take a different path in life. They'd never understand.'

'You should let them know you're safe,' said Hazel.

Keeva had never spoken to anyone about running away before. Her grand gesture of rebellion seemed to shrink in significance now she'd shared her reasons with Hazel. A pang of guilt twinged in her chest, when she imagined her father in prison, being beaten by the army guard, and her mother alone at home struggling to cope.

Why did she really run away? Viola was dreadful, always reading esoteric historical texts, like how the Egyptians ensured the transition into the afterlife through mummification. She had explained to Keeva that they had salted and oiled the body before tightly wrapping it in bandages and preserving their organs in jars. This was the most useful information Viola knew about mummies.

Where her elder sister had a creative passion and a drive for ballet, Keeva had been a disappointment. She was the black sheep of the family. Now she had all the freedom she'd ever wanted and just felt adrift in the world.

'Can I ask you something, Keeva? Why does your father not believe in war?'

'It's complicated. He said he never had faith in other people, not even as a small boy. First of all, he said his parents were in service and, as Irish immigrants, were badly treated. And after that, near his childhood house there was a hospital for first world war veterans. He called them the wretches in blue pyjamas and said he never wanted to get like that. So, he decided he would never go and fight in the war; he was adamant and that was that.'

'You all right, Keeva? You don't look well.'

Keeva worried she had said too much. She could tell Hazel didn't understand. Her father never liked talking about the horrors of what he had seen and heard at the lunatic asylum and how badly the veterans were treated. She just knew this had disturbed him so deeply as a boy. Even as an adult, her father said he could not forget the soldiers in wheelchairs, stammering disconnected words that dripped with murder.

'I feel a bit queasy.' Keeva felt bad. She knew she should be looking after Hazel, but all she could think about was running away.

'Maybe you're coming down with something. But it's been a shock, hasn't it?'

An hour had passed and there was still no sign of the train, which had been delayed further down the line. An ache gripped Keeva's stomach, which was so painful. She got up to walk up and down the platform to try to ease the pain. Her toes were numb, she stamped her feet and rubbed her arms. The pain could be wind or worry. She spotted a couple of jam jars left under the bench.

'Want a tea, Hazel?' Tea might help.

'Ooh, I'd love a cuppa.'

Keeva rinsed the jars in the hand basin in the ladies and took them to the station office. One in each hand, she tapped them against the door and a stationmaster appeared. 'Could I get a couple of teas, please?'

'What's wrong with the café down the road?'

'I don't want to miss the train; we've been waiting an hour already.'

'You in the Land Army?'

'Yes, it's just that my friend Hazel lost her thumb yesterday in the sawmills.'

'Now you're joking! Why need England tremble, when we've got the land girls,' he said, with a shake of his head. She wanted to say to him, have you never had an accident before? Have you still got all your fingers and thumbs? But she also wanted the tea for Hazel. She waited awkwardly outside the office in the cold, for what seemed like ages. Had he forgotten, while sitting in the comfort of his warm office? She peered round the door again.

'Excuse me,' she said, banging on the door. He stood up and poured the water and brought two teas over.

Keeva thanked him and carefully made her way down the platform to Hazel, trying not to spill a drop.

'Thank you, love,' said Hazel, taking it with her left hand.

'That wasn't easy,' said Keeva. 'He wasn't very helpful. The world doesn't seem to have much time for the Women's Land Army.'

Hazel and Keeva huddled side by side to try and keep warm on the platform bench, and sipped their tea.

'Oh, thank you, Keeva, I needed this. Thanks for taking care of me.'

'I haven't done much.'

'That's not what me or the girls on camp think,' Hazel replied.

'What do the girls think?' she asked defensively.

'They think you're brave felling that big tree, and after what happened in the sawmill, and Rosie said she and the other girls couldn't care less …'

'They couldn't care less about me.'

'What? Doon't be silly. Give them a chance, Keeva, you're very quick to judge them and what they might think about you and your father's letter. You're doing your bit for the war, aren't you?'

How dare Hazel suggest she was the one that was judging other people, when she had been bullied and picked on as soon as it became public knowledge her father was a conchie. Hazel didn't understand what it was like to be bullied and ostracised.

'The train!' Keeva jumped up.

'At last,' Hazel sighed with relief.

Keeva watched as the train crept into the station and slowed to a halt with a grinding vibration. Keeva and Hazel climbed on board and sat in the grey fading light of dusk. Could she really trust what Hazel had said?

A stopping train to Doncaster, people climbed on or off at every station. Keeva began to wonder if she had misjudged the girls. What if Hazel was right and they did think she was brave? Would they care if she didn't return?

The smell of the dust in the old seats filled every shadowy darkness as night closed in around them. Should she ask Hazel what else the girls had said? But Hazel was asleep. Keeva considered the lonely path ahead. Running away again, but without an address this time. Where would she go?

There were no lights on the trains in the blackout. Men fumbled across her knees as they climbed on board to find an empty seat. So dark, Keeva didn't even know who she sat next to as bodies came and went. She imagined being all alone, with no one to talk to after she left Hazel. She stayed wide awake as Hazel slept. The only light in the carriage came from the orange glow of a burning cigarette opposite her in the darkness. The light glared with more intensity on every inhalation and smoke filled every breath in the carriage.

Chapter 18

Clayton West, Yorkshire

When, at last, the train arrived in Wakefield Kirkgate Station in the dead of night, the clock tower said half past one, and it was bitterly cold.

'We'll have to walk from here,' said Hazel, as they stood on the empty platform in the dark.

'Can't we just sleep here? I'm too tired,' said Keeva. Her bottom had gone numb from sitting on the train for hours.

'I'm tired too. But the waiting room is all locked up at this time of night. We won't sleep in this cold – must be below freezing.

'How far is it to your house?' Keeva asked, her teeth chattering.

'It's a good walk, not too far mind.'

'But it's so cold.'

'Don't worry, I've done it before. You'll warm up once you get moving. I wish we had another of those Shippam's fish paste sandwiches.'

The apple from the barrow boys at the station was the last thing she'd had, but Keeva knew what it was like to go hungry. She'd endured worse.

Keeva couldn't keep warm; her hands and feet were chilly. Hazel was tough and didn't seem to feel the cold, even so soon after her operation. One foot in front of the other, one dark road or pathway led to another. Hazel hesitated before taking a new footpath and, after a long walk, they felt their way in the darkness beneath some trees. The path ended abruptly at a fence.

'Everything looks completely different at night,' Hazel said, turning round to retrace their steps. 'It's easy to miss pathways in the dark.'

'I thought you said you knew the way?'

'I do. I just got confused. They've taken the signposts down too.'

Keeva was sorry; she hadn't meant to sound so harsh. But she just wanted to get somewhere warm now, somewhere she could rest her aching head and body. Her blisters were rubbing again. She was panicking about everything: how dark it was, how late. She remembered the money she had taken. Leaving the Women's Land Army was likely to be a serious offence. Imprisonment might be the punishment for both her crimes.

She would have to hide for a while, maybe sleep out in the open, under a hedge. Once the money was gone, what would she do? Maybe she could try waitressing in a café like Gladys had done. But would that be doing her bit for the war? Oh Jesus, she just didn't want to go back and work with Beatrice, Rosie or those stupid men in the Timber Trade meeting.

Her eyes adjusted to the darkness of the night. The hours and footpaths went on and on with Hazel's stories of the place she grew up. Keeva tried not to think. Hazel pointed out where her father worked as a miner at Overton Colliery. She mentioned names of places of where she had been for a picnic once, with friends and how she'd got in trouble with her father for coming home late. Even the bones in Keeva's feet ached, so the stories passed the time with the road beneath her feet.

'I don't know what you think is a long walk, Hazel. This must be twenty miles.'

'Oh, I didn't want to tell you how far it was because I knew it would be hard. Not far now though, honestly.'

Somehow Keeva carried on, one step at a time, with Hazel's encouragement. The thump, thump, thump of their boots was all they could hear, as the clouds passed over in strange patterns above.

'I hope my father isn't cross with me,' said Hazel.

'Me too.'

Dead tired, Keeva was desperate to get to Hazel's house now.

'He won't be cross, will he, Hazel?' she asked.

'I don't know, depends how he's feeling.'

Fields blurred into one and Keeva felt as though the footpaths might take them back to the station; all sense of direction lost. A vehicle engine approached from behind and her memory of that awful night back at home before Christmas came back to her. She cowered by the hedgerow.

The car came towards them and a torch lit up their faces.

'Where are you lasses going to at this time of night?' a man asked.

'Who's asking?' replied Hazel.

'The home guard.'

'My parents' at Clayton West. I've been given sickness leave for an accident in the sawmills.' She held up her bandaged hand.

'Names and identity cards please.'

'Hazel Hardy'

'Keeva O'Connor.'

Keeva trembled as she got out her ID card and held it under the torch light.

'You shouldn't be out this late. Hurry on home,' the man said as the car changed gear and disappeared up the road.

'You could've given us a lift,' Keeva called after them, as they drove away.

Hazel began to giggle.

Darkness lifted and the birds began to sing, as they continued on their way. Keeva was exhausted and not comforted when Hazel said they were on the last few roads that led to her house. At last, in the grey light of dawn, they approached a row of a houses with a stone wall at the front.

'Is this it?' Keeva asked.

'Aye.'

'At last.'

Keeva followed Hazel as she approached the front door of the second house. Hazel smiled as she knocked. While they waited for the door to open, the next stage of her journey beckoned, when she would leave Hazel. She'd get work in a café, if she could, in the nearest large town or city. She stood on the doorstep and looked out into the dawn. But first they had to face Hazel's father.

Quick footsteps came down the stairs inside and the latch on the door opened. Keeva spied a little rosy-cheeked boy, with brown hair peering around the door.

'Hazel, Hazel, Hazel!' he yelled.

She took a step back, as the little boy in pyjamas jumped towards her, arms outstretched.

'You need to be careful; I've hurt my hand.' Keeva could see tears in Hazel's eyes.

'What have you done?' he asked, as Hazel wrapped her good arm around him tightly and lifted him onto his tiptoes.

'How I've missed you,' she said.

'Bless my soul! It's our Hazel.' Her mother hurried downstairs in her dressing gown towards them. 'What are you doing here? Oh no, what have you done, love?' asked her mother, seeing her sling and carefully wrapping her arms around Hazel.

'It's all right, Mam, I'm going to be fine,' she said, her voice breaking.

Hazel looked up towards the top of the stairs where her father appeared. He came down heavily on the treads, as Keeva waited outside. Hazel's father loomed behind Hazel in his long johns and nightshirt.

'I'm sorry to have woken you, Father.'

'What's all this?

He looked to her mother. 'Did you know about this?'

'No, dear, she just arrived.'

'At this time of the morning? How did you get home, Hazel?'

'We caught the train, Father. There were delays so we didn't arrive till late last night.'

'Last night? You've been out all night, till this time in the morning?'

'We had to walk through the night.'

Keeva didn't like the way this was going. She looked down and wriggled her numb toes inside her boots, wondering what to do. She could just walk away but she didn't want to draw attention to herself. She tried to blend into the street, the frosty bushes and cold air behind her.

'What have you done, girl?' asked her father, stood in the hallway, arms firmly crossed.

'Can we bring them in from the front doorstep, love, and not have this conversation 'ere for all the neighbours to hear?' Her mother reached out her arm to bring her daughter indoors. Her father put out his hand and stopped her.

'How did this come about?'

'I … I … I … had an accident, Father. I'm all right though.'

'Doesn't look all right to me. What's the bandage for then?'

'I lost my thumb in the sawmills, Father.' She hung her head.

'Dear love,' said her mother.

'Jesus H Christ, you've done what?'

Her brother squeezed her mother's leg.

'Go on upstairs, love,' she said as she shooed him away.

'It was badly damaged in the sawmills, so they had to amputate.'

'Who had to amputate? Without my permission,' he said, brows furrowed.

Keeva saw Hazel's brother disappear upstairs. She gulped, wanting to turn and run away as well.

'The army doctors at the hospital.'

'Who's she? Was she with you?' Keeva looked up abruptly to see him pointing at her.

'Her name's Keeva.'

Keeva nodded towards him.

'What the bloody hell were you doing in a sawmill? That's no place for any daughter of mine. You've been gone just over a month and you come back with your bleedin' thumb missing. Jesus Christ.'

'Let's bring them inside, dear, they look frozen.'

He turned and walked away down the hallway, running his hands through his hair, and disappeared through the kitchen door, slamming it behind him.

'You must have had a shock, love. Come in quickly and close the door behind you.' She hugged Hazel again. 'Are you all right, love?'

'I'm sorry, Mam. It was an accident.'

'I know, love. Your father's just upset, that's all. Does it hurt?'

Hazel grimaced and she nodded.

'Who's your friend, love? Come in, dear.'

'This is Keeva. She been looking after me, Mam.'

'Hello.' Keeva was suddenly desperate for the toilet.

'You two go into the dining room, while I speak to your father. I'll put the kettle on.'

'But Mam, it wasn't my fault.'

'I know. Your father just needs time to calm down. He's having a difficult time at work; there's strikes up at mines and he's worried about your brothers. This is unexpected.'

She took them into a cold uninhabited room with a dining table and six chairs, which was almost the same temperature as outside.

'Light the fire, love,' she said before she left and closed the door behind her. Hazel held up her bandaged hand to Keeva.

'I'm sorry, Keeva. Could you light the fire? The matches are on the mantlepiece. Father will be all right; I'll speak to him.'

Left alone, Keeva trembled as she took the Bryant and May box in her hand and tried to pick out a match with her numb fingers. As she struck the first, it snapped, she tried again and the draught from the chimney blew it out. With just a few matches left, she managed to catch the newspaper and watched the flames spread, as voices from the kitchen rose and fell. She wondered if Hazel would get a hiding; she hoped not, for her friend's sake. It seemed so unfair, as Hazel was trying to help the war effort.

'I said you were not to go, and you disobeyed me. Now look what's happened,' came Mr Hardy's voice through the wall. 'Your mother wanted you home to take care of the bairn. Now you won't even be able to do that.'

'It was just an accident, Father; the sawdust blew into my eyes and the wood caught on the blade.'

Keeva would have an accident if she didn't get to the privy soon. She couldn't wait a moment longer, she ran out of the room and burst into the kitchen.

'I need the privy,' she said as the three of them stared at her.

'I'll show you,' Hazel said as she led her out the kitchen door.

'I'm sorry, Keeva,' Hazel whispered.

Keeva bustled inside, undoing the button on the side of her jodhpurs while kicking the door shut, and squatted on the freezing cold seat just in time. She reached for the newspaper hanging on a rope as her stomach cramped. She worried about going back through the kitchen. She heard Hazel and her mother's voice murmuring amongst the noise of crockery and pans on the stove.

'Didn't they train you oop, before they let you on sawmill?'

'She's had a shock, love. Let her get a cuppa inside her first,' said

Hazel's mother.

When Keeva was ready, she walked cautiously back to the kitchen. Mr Hardy was seated at the head of the table and Hazel's mother was by the stove.

'Would you like a tea, love?' Hazel's mother asked Keeva.

'Yes please.' She stood awkwardly in the kitchen and noticed Hazel's father look down at her jodhpurs.

'You must be hungry too,' Mrs Hardy said, 'I'll put some eggs on.'

'Here, I'll help you, Mother,' said Hazel, knocking over a jug of milk.

'What do you think you're doing?' asked her father.

'It's all right, I'll clear it oop,' said her mother.

Keeva decided to keep out of the kitchen.

'And you are one of Hazel's friends, are you?' her father asked.

'Yes.'

'Were you looking after Hazel when she did this?' he said to Keeva.

'Yes. She took me to hospital and brought me home,' replied Hazel.

'Was she with you when this accident happened?'

'She looked after me, bandaged me up,' Hazel said.

'So did you join the Women's Land Army with your father's blessing?' Hazel's father asked Keeva.

What should she say? Keeva nodded.

'I was against my daughter working in agriculture, doing such a menial job. I didn't know she would be working in timber though. What does your father have to say about that?' he asked Keeva.

She felt so exhausted, she couldn't think straight. Keeva wanted to go back to the dining room to sit by the fire. She didn't want to talk about her father. She didn't want to accompany Hazel home anyway. Why hadn't she said no?

'They're tired,' said Hazel's mother.

'It doesn't matter, Father,' said Hazel.

He rose to his feet. 'You turn up here at the break of day, the pair of you, showing off your legs like that, wearing breeches. You will bring shame on our family. Not to mention what's happened to your thumb. And you tell me it doesn't matter. It damn well matters to me, my girl.'

Keeva couldn't understand what she should do for the best. She knew her own father would never treat her like this. He would look after her and be kind. He wouldn't blame her; he wouldn't make her feel worse. If Mr Hardy was really worried about Hazel, he would not raise his voice like that.

'What does your father do, now we are at war?' Mr Hardy asked Keeva.

'Jack, let them get some rest now,' Hazel's mother interrupted.

'I want to know who my daughter is mixing with, when she is not here for me to keep an eye on her. Well?'

Her father waited for an answer. Keeva shook her head and Hazel said, 'He's a conscientious objector.'

'A plumber,' Keeva said at once.

'A conchie!' Mr Hardy replied, with a jerk of his head and crack of his neck.

Oh no, Keeva's heart was beating loudly, as she took off back to the dining room. Taking her bag from the hallway, she cowered close by the fire. She tried to warm her hands but couldn't stop shivering. What was she going to do? Listening attentively to noises in the house, she heard the latch go on the kitchen door and then the handle on the dining room. She turned to see Hazel with a mug of tea, which spilled as she passed it over.

'Aren't you having one?'

'I'm sorry, Keeva.'

'Why did you tell him?'

'I didn't know what else to say.'

'He's a plumber.'

'I didn't know that,' Hazel said, before hurrying out of the room.

Keeva wanted her to stay. The fire crackled as she listened to their voices from the kitchen. She could hear Hazel pleading with her father. Keeva's legs ached from crouching by the fire, so she dropped onto the cold floorboards, holding her head in her hands. She had only tried to help Hazel. She had taken her home. She had walked through the night. She had tried to offer kindness to Hazel.

'I saw the way she looked down on us when she walked through the door,' said Mr Hardy's raised voice from the kitchen, 'as if we weren't good enough for her. What were you thinking? We would give her a slap-up breakfast on me?'

'She's just a young girl,' her mother said.

'While her father can have a clear conscience. I bet he's never done a hard day's work in his life. While I work my knuckles to the bone down there in the mine every day. It's disgusting.'

Keeva covered her ears. She wanted to leave as soon as possible. She willed the tea to cool down so she could drink quickly. How stupid she was not to realise this could happen. As if she hadn't experienced this before. She felt like a prisoner in their house, while they judged her. She checked inside her bag for the money. Hazel's voice became more emphatic as she protested.

'I'll not hear any more of it. Enough is enough. You are my daughter, and you won't speak to her any more. She's a bad influence on you. You will do as I say. I want her out of my house so we can deal with this matter properly as a family.'

The tea burnt her tongue. Off balance, she got up off the floor as she took her bag. Heat from the fire on her face soon went cold, as she quietly crossed the room and lifted the door latch. But now she could hear him more clearly than before.

'Who will marry you now? You'll be known as Jack Hardy's girl who went astray during the war.'

Holding her breath, Keeva tiptoed across the floorboards and reached the front door.

'A bloody conchie's daughter. The coward.'

The latch went on the door and Hazel burst out of the kitchen in floods of tears. They ran back outside to the street together as a man cycled past and called out 'Morning'. Hazel turned away.

How could Keeva be a bad influence? She could have abandoned Hazel, but she didn't. She'd bandaged her up, taken her to the hospital, brought her home. Rosie was the bad influence; she was always the one messing about. Keeva hadn't taken the money in the first place. But would the accident have happened had she and Rosie not been arguing? Was Mr Hardy right and was Keeva somehow to blame?

Hazel grabbed Keeva's arms. 'Listen, my father won't let me come back to the Forest of Dean,' she said quickly. 'Of course, I will write to you.'

'Don't worry, I'm not going back either.'

'What do you mean?' asked Hazel. 'I can't go back because I must do what my father says and stay and look after my little brother. But you must go back.'

'Live your own life, Hazel.'

'I've told him we've been working hard in the Women's Land Army, making pit props for his mines. He said they've got no right to call it an army and the pit props we make aren't straight.'

Anger burned inside Keeva; she'd heard the men talking at the Timber Trade meeting about how the collieries were desperate for pit props. She had understood they were doing important war work. But clearly, they were not appreciated by the miners or anyone for what they did.

'I better go.' Keeva turned to go back the way they'd arrived.

'I'm so sorry. I can't bear you leaving like this,' sobbed Hazel.

Hazel wiped her eyes with her sleeve and took a bundle from her pocket and put it into Keeva's hand, warm, wrapped up in paper.

'It's from Mother.'

She was starving and the gift was such a kind gesture. 'Thank you.'

Hazel breathed erratically in between her sobs, 'I'm so sorry.'

She hugged Keeva goodbye and said, 'Thank you so much for looking after me. I don't care at all 'bout your father, because you're doing your own bit for the war and that's all that matters.'

Keeva didn't ask for Hazel's opinion and didn't want anyone judging her or her family any more. She felt infuriated. She wasn't going to do her bit for the war, thank you very much. She jumped as Mr Hardy appeared at the door.

'What is he? One of those intellectual types? Too busy with his head in books to fight?'

'Both my parents read books,' Keeva shouted back at him. 'Maybe you should try it.'

'You can't learn about courage in a book, or how to fight.'

'I'm fighting from the forests, aren't I? We both are.'

'Not with those skellered pit props. They're useless. We don't use your warped pit props down the mines, we chop 'em up and bring 'em 'ome for firewood.'

'You've insulted me and my family. You're a disgusting bully and a coward!' she yelled.

'I've heard enough from you. Who the hell do you think you are?' he said as he loosened his belt, his eyes never leaving Keeva.

'Keeva, go! Now!' Hazel urged.

'If you don't get out of here, I will come over there myself. Your father has likely never benselled you in his life.'

Keeva started to run.

'Coward,' he shouted after her, which took her straight back to that awful night before Christmas.

Chapter 19

15th December 1939, West Firle, Sussex

Where was Edward? Maybe the first air raid of the war had already happened, and it would be just her luck that their ramshackle house on the hill, first in the line of attack on the south coast, had somehow been missed by the German bombers. Keeva knew it was her parents' dream to build a house on a smallholding in the country, but they would never finish the job. Maybe Hitler could drop a bomb on the house to finish it for them. Keeva had always wanted to live in a normal house, in a terraced street in the village, like everyone else.

But after four months and still no raids, the arrival of German bombers looked unlikely. Her father insisted Hitler still hoped to persuade Britain to agree to peace. In truth, war was the biggest event not to happen in Keeva's life after not having a boyfriend. Until Edward had asked her out for a drink, that is. If it wasn't for Edward, her life would be utterly dreadful. She could hardly believe he liked her, despite her oddball family.

Mother laid her brittle gouache paints out on the table, next to the black and earthy mustard tones left in the mixing palette. Keeva expected to see another tortured modernist portrait of her older sister when she got home. Keeva always knew Dilly was her parents' favourite and resented that her father worked all hours plumbing and thatching to pay her school fees.

She had only just realised how poor they were. Since the war started, it was even worse. Father said he wasn't bothered about the abusive letters – most of them anonymous – calling him a skunk or scum. Father said being called a lily-livered curr, which was a line from Shakespeare's *Macbeth*, just gave him pleasure. Keeva couldn't bear to think about it any more. Where was Edward?

'It's getting late, Kiki darling, stay home with us. We can paint a snowy scene together to remember this extraordinary winter,' her father said.

'I'd rather not.'

A pang of guilt rushed through her; Christmas was meant to be a quiet family affair this year because of the blackout and noise restrictions. Her parents said they wanted them to be together this evening. But the rest of the year they had no time for her and never listened to her.

They treated her like a child who still wanted red-, yellow- and blue-patterned spinner discs in her stocking. She picked up last year's brightly coloured disc and watched the colours merge as it spun on the table next to her mother's paints. Mother returned with a glass of water and stopped the disc spinner abruptly as it jumped across her paint palette.

'Keeva, have you seen my letter in *Peace News* on page eleven?' said her father.

Keeva worried about her fathers' views as a conscientious objector and that he might be taken by the army against his wishes. If that should happen, she really didn't know what he would do. He reassured her that only men under twenty-five were really wanted. Where was Edward? It had been dark for hours; was he really coming?

'Keeva?'

'What?' she replied.

'You look beautiful,' her father said, touching her cheek. 'Just like your mother.'

'Father.'

Why couldn't she be beautiful in her own right? She hated

being compared to her mother or her sister.

'Have you eaten?' he asked.

'I had the bubble and squeak left from lunch.'

'I'm not cooking anything else for you. If you're hungry, make it yourself,' said her mother, positioning her stretched canvas on the easel.

'Anything else? Sorry, did I miss your hearty home-cooked meal today, Mother?'

'I'm cooking on Christmas Day,' her mother said.

'Oh yes! Thank goodness I only need to eat once a year,' said Keeva.

'Have some water,' her father said, lifting the glass to Keeva.

'That's to wash my brushes.' Her mother grabbed the glass and replaced it on the table.

Keeva wondered if the snow had delayed Edward or prevented him from getting up the hill. Before it was too late, she decided to walk down to meet him. At least the moonlight reflecting on the powdered white hedgerows and fields made it easier to see, now the twinkling lights from the village were heavily veiled.

'That's him now,' Keeva lied.

'I didn't hear anything,' said her mother.

'I heard him on the path outside. See you later,' she said as she kissed her father on the cheek.

'I'll close the living room door to keep the warmth in.'

'Don't be too late,' said her father.

'I won't.'

The Arctic air stung her lips and face, as she slammed the door behind her. Shoulders hunched, she stomped past the Romani caravan in the garden, where they used to sleep at night as little children. Now a sorry state, with icicles hanging from the roof and rotten wooden wheels frozen solid on its rusty frame. She crunched through frozen puddles down the long road where she would surely see Edward on his way.

The shock of the cold air made her breathe in sharply, so she pulled up her scarf over her mouth. As she turned away from the house, she could barely make out the road ahead.

This was the coldest winter in twenty-five years, and these were the most miserable months of Keeva's life. But she always remembered the beautiful moment when she first met Edward, the new boy. She used to watch the boys kick about on the village pitch and longed to play, although she had not told a soul. Afterwards, Edward had rolled a football towards her and smiled. Permission for her to play was like a burst of oxygen; she felt high on the freedom of running and kicking the ball. Then one day it was decided, no girls.

The freezing air crept inside her duffle coat and the icy cold fabric of her mother's dress clung to her bare thighs. She lost her footing a few times on the ice in her oversized leather German army boots. Her thick woolly socks were warm but kept falling down as she walked down the country lane towards the pub.

The trees and hedgerows, familiar by day, now seemed sinister under the jet-black sky, as they lurked by the side of the road. She hurried to the end of the road, past the church, the village stores, the row of terraced cottages but there was no sign of Edward. By the time she neared The Ram Inn, he was still nowhere to be seen. She lingered outside, wondering what to do and remembered Aunty Margaret, who always seemed to care more about her than her own mother, saying, 'Nice girls don't go to pubs.' She walked back and forth looking up and down the road.

Just as she had decided to go in through the back door by the stables to look for Edward, two older lads, one stocky and the other tall came around the corner. Side by side, the lads emerged from the snug and stood in Keeva's way.

'Sorry,' she said, stepping aside.

The stocky one stuck out his arm and blocked the corridor by the water closets.

'What are you doing in here?' He looked her up and down with a sneer on his face.

Then the tall one in the Fair Isle jumper leaned over her. 'We've heard about you. You're the conchie scum's daughter.'

She recoiled from them, out of arm's reach.

'You can tell your father …' said the stocky one, as he pulled his tweed cap down over his eyes.

A chilly wind blew about her legs.

'Excuse me,' she said and pushed past, shoving the taller one with her elbow. He tried to grab her arm as she burst through the door into the snug and she shook him off. She ducked through the throng of farmworkers shrouded in tobacco smoke, drinking pints, and made her way through a gap to the main bar. She hid behind a local lorry driver she recognised until he caught her eye and stared at her with a look of disgust.

Under the dim light of the burning oil lamps, she looked around desperately for a friendly face, while chilblains stung her fingers, and smoke her eyes. She hoped Mr Fielding, the landlord, would turn a blind eye if he spotted her; she only wanted to find Edward. She saw another group of lads by the bar from her sister's year who looked over at her. But Edward wasn't there either.

She kept her coat buttoned up and stood by the mantlepiece. The fire glared at her, but she could feel none of its warmth, just the damp chill of her mother's dress. Alone in the middle of the bar – a novel experience – she watched while mostly boys and men talked and laughed merrily with friends. She glanced into the Court Room bar upstairs, where judges and barristers argued in loud pompous voices. A man looked down his nose at her as he passed wearing a tweed cap and cape, like something Sherlock Holmes would fashion with a shiny black paisley scarf.

If only she could start a conversation with one of the lads she recognised. Surely, she could say something. She tried to go over to them, but her heart thumped loudly. She couldn't do it. Edward was her way into this group and, without him, who would want to talk to her? She was a nobody to them.

Just as she decided to leave, Edward stumbled in through the front door. Mary, a girl from the year above, was right behind him. Keeva's breath quickened; he was drunk. She could tell by the way he staggered. The excited mob of lads met him from the bar, the stocky one grabbing Edward's neck and rubbing his knuckles against his head, the smaller one laughing, slapping his back and a third pushing a tankard of beer into his hand. She could see how people lit up when he entered the room.

She saw him look round, but he didn't see her through the smog of smoke; he found Mary instead. Mary smiled at Edward and began talking at him like a typewriter trying to leave its mark. Mary liked Edward and he knew it. Mary, who had been the first to find out about her father. Mary, who had taken satisfaction in telling everyone, breaking the news at school. It was Mary who had been the first to publicly ignore Keeva, starting a chain reaction amongst the other local girls. Now Mary, whose fleece was white as snow, had all her little lambs following behind. Keeva went up to Edward as if on rails.

'Where have you been?' Keeva asked.

Edward spun round, leaving Mary agape.

'Keeva, what are you doing here?' asked Edward.

'And where were you?' Keeva became very hot.

'What are you talking about?'

'You were coming to pick me up.'

'No,' he said as he looked towards his mates and laughed.

'I've been waiting ages for you at home,' Keeva replied, unbuttoning her coat, flushed with heat.

'Calm down, will you?'

'Don't tell me to calm down.' She shook her coat off.

'Are you going to a dance with your parents in that dress, Keeva?' asked Mary, smiling and linking arms with Edward.

'You're talking to me now, are you?' said Keeva.

Full of festive stupidity and beer, the lads rounded on Keeva.

'She needs taming, this one,' said the stocky one, stepping towards her from behind. She spun round and he blew smoke in her face.

'Aren't you going to say something?' she said to Edward.

'What do you want me to say, Keeva?'

She turned and pushed past people to find her way out of the pub into the darkness and slammed the door behind her. She held her breath and her face burned. How could Edward humiliate her like that. She heard the latch go behind her and laughter came from inside the pub.

'Keeva,' Edward called after her.

Chapter 20

2nd March 1940, Clayton West, Yorkshire

Keeva ran and ran until her chest burned for breath. The tarmac slapped against her feet as hard as Mr Hardy's words had whacked her. How could he say they chopped up the girls pit props for firewood, Keeva thought. Their props weren't warped. They weren't useless. How dare he say that. Her bag flailed, she looked behind her and the road was empty. Should she turn left or right at the end of the road? She saw a familiar gate and just kept running, breaking into a sweat. She passed the enormous Oak Mills building where Hazel had said she'd worked as a woollen spinner before she left home. Licked with anger, her body was hot as she ran towards the open fields and back the way they'd come. She could smell the fear in her armpits, like she had the day she left home. At last, she bent double and gasped for breath.

Poor Hazel, with a father like that. He reminded her of the way her friends, teachers and Edward at home had judged her and her family. Their cruel words had lain like sleeping dragons inside her mind, hidden among her own thoughts. She had come to understand why people had started avoiding her. She had felt ashamed of herself. She had come to agree with Hazel's father. She had begun to think she deserved their scorn.

Everything went round in her head, as she stomped up the road and discovered the parcel in her pocket from Hazel's mother. Inside was a bread roll and scrambled egg; she shoved the roll in her mouth and took a bite. Maybe she was like her father and didn't believe in war. The abuse her family received was like war itself – so unnecessary. But she and her father had never done anything to harm Hazel or her family. She'd done nothing wrong. But maybe she was a coward if she kept running away? She devoured her roll and, before she realised, the last mouthful had gone and she wiped her mouth with her sleeve. She was still thirsty.

She reached a crossroads, took the right-hand turn and began the long walk back along the road toward Wakefield Kirkgate Station and the bus stop Hazel had pointed out to her. The grey tarmac divided the sodden fields from the unwelcome dark forest. Keeva breathed slowly and deeply. She was so insulted; she had never expected that to happen. But with the intensity of her anger, she could see the injustice. She could see more clearly than ever before that she had done nothing wrong.

Nearing the bus stop at last she noticed a figure slumped against a tree. As she approached, she wondered if he might be dead. Tentatively she got closer; his arms jolted to life and he began talking to himself. This was all she needed right now, a beggar, but she couldn't ignore him.

'Are you in need of help?' asked Keeva.

He appeared to be an old man in a ripped woollen coat, brown with filth.

'Is that you, Hilda?' he asked.

Keeva looked about her, trying to see if there was anyone else nearby.

'Hilda, it's me, your brother,' he said.

'No, you are mistaken,' she replied. What on earth was happening today? She was worried to wait about at the bus stop with this drunken tramp so close by.

He stretched his arms out towards her and she caught a waft of something unpleasant. Had he lost his mind? Was he harmless, or dangerous?

'You're not Hilda.'

She looked into the blue eyes of the dishevelled man. 'No.'

'What's your uniform, love?' he asked.

'Women's Land Army,' she said, taking a gulp of fresh air.

'I was in the Armed Forces once,' he said.

'Were you?' Keeva did not want to get into a conversation with him. She looked over her shoulder hoping the bus would come.

'After two and a half years or so, I went absent without leave in the first war.' His words punctured the air.

So, you're a deserter. The words did not leave her lips.

'They all think I'm dead, so I never went home.'

'Why don't you go back now?' Keeva's bag strap pulled against her neck.

He climbed to his feet, straining and shaking as he stood. The stench of his body odour and urine filled the air. He looked around wildly, as if pained. 'I'd have been shot. They would have killed me.'

He raised his hands as if pleading with Keeva, then wobbled and fell over, landing on his hands and knees.

'Are you all right?'

Keeva watched him struggle. He couldn't get up. She took a deep breath and held it, reaching under his armpits and pulling him upwards. Once he seemed steadier, she let him stand alone again.

'I can't feel my feet. Frostbite.'

'Oh dear! What about your family?' asked Keeva, backing away.

'I made a mistake and I've been living with this shame for twenty years. I've been on the road that long. I can never go back to my family. I am a nobody now.'

She couldn't bear to stay any longer, she could barely breathe. *What have I become? Would she ever see her family again?*

'Hilda, forgive me. I'm sorry, I didn't mean to hurt you, Hilda.'

His guilt weighed down upon her, smothering her like a black cloak. She wanted to leave but the bus was due. Where was it? She couldn't shake off his shame, as though she herself was responsible. Was Keeva a nobody now? It was true nobody knew where Keeva was, not even her family. She could fall down a ditch, die, and nobody would know she had left the Women's Land Army.

So wrapped up in her plan to leave, she hadn't properly taken care of Hazel on her journey home. She'd been so selfish. Keeva's fuse was burning so short she might blow up if even a fly landed on her. Thank goodness a bus approached, and the engine growled up alongside her.

Unsteadily she walked towards the bus with her arm out, leaving the dishevelled man, Clayton West and Hazel's father behind her. Her hands trembled as she fumbled in her pocket for her purse and climbed on. The man at the wheel of the bus smiled at her as she paid her few pennies. The bus went quiet when she turned to find a seat, and a crowd of men's faces stared back at her. They were a rough assortment of men in flat caps with old worn jackets and loose collared shirts. Anxiously, she looked down at the floor to avoid their gaze and made her way to an empty seat.

A more friendly, cleaner man at the front smiled and moved the newspaper from the seat beside him.

'Thank you.' Keeva flopped down. The bus pulled away and exhaled.

'Aye oop, love,' he said.

She watched the tramp disappear as the bus moved off. How did she not notice the bus was full of men, as they started chatting once again?

'Women's forestry?' the man next to her asked.

'How did you know?'

'The size of your feet.'

She looked down at her boots, where screwed up newspapers and black dirt lay in the footwell. Her blisters were sore again and even the soles of her feet hurt from walking through the night with Hazel.

He chuckled. 'You can't swing an axe without 'em or you'll fall over.'

Keeva tried to smile but her face was stiff.

'I know a girl in a pair of jodhpurs when I see one,' he said with a wink.

A chill crept up her back. What did he mean by that? How did he really know she was in forestry? Did he work for the Ministry of Supply? Was he a spy? She wanted to ask but she was conscious of her accent and that she was a stranger to this area. But the men behind were all chatting loudly, so she could not be overheard.

'Really, how did you know I was in forestry?'

'The beret, love.' She'd forgotten she was wearing the beret for warmth. 'What brings you to Wakefield?'

'To Wakefield … ?' she stuttered, remembering what Gladys had said: 'Careless talk costs lives'. He was waiting for an answer and so she blurted out, 'I was visiting a friend.'

'Okay, and where did you say you were from?'

She remembered what Beatrice had said: 'Hitler wants to know regiment names, where they are going and where they came from …'

She told herself not to answer.

'The Forest of Dean.' Keeva's bag strap snapped in her hands.

'Well, you are a long way from home, aren't you?'

Now she was really worried. Her cheeks burned. His eyes had a keenness as they darted towards her. Keeva shrank into her seat. Out of the corner of her eye, she watched the hedgerows and trees flash by.

Miles passed. Suddenly startled, she felt the nod of her head and herself being pulled awake. She must have nodded off; she hadn't slept for days. The warmth and motion of the bus had rocked her gently to sleep, however hard she'd tried to fasten her eyes, like hooks, on the road in front. She'd barely eaten or had much to drink and drifted off again. She pinched her arm and tried to watch the driver as he steered the big wheel.

She awoke again to the sound of a man's voice, and felt her mouth open and tongue dry. She became aware of her head leaning back – so uncomfortable, but she'd been asleep.

'You'll have to change here, love. There's another bus for the station.'

Suddenly she sat up straight, felt her sore neck and looked around her at the empty seats of the bus. The men from the bus walked in a group up the road.

'Where are we?' she asked the driver.

'Overton Colliery.'

'Thanks,' she said.

She stood up, grabbed her bag and made her way off the bus, jumping to the ground. Overton! Fear lurched inside her as Hazel's father came to mind. This was where he worked.

The bus door was pulled shut and the bus drove away. She was left on the grass verge, feeling dazed. Her mouth was dry; she needed a drink. Where was the other bus stop? Shaking and feeling nauseous, she didn't know what to do. She walked down the road one way and then back the other. Damn it! What should she do? She looked for another bus stop. She didn't want to miss the next bus and be stranded by the colliery, when Hazel's father could turn up for work on the next bus. She started to panic.

Her bloody father, his stupid pacifism. Her mother's feminist nonsense. Her sister, always in first position at home, literally, feet slapped outwards like a penguin with her *port de bras* irritating the hell out of her. She was mad with herself too. How did she get herself into this situation? The middle of nowhere, nowhere to go.

Some coal trucks passed, one tooted its horn, the next passed with a gust of wind and the driver shouted out of his window at her. She decided to follow in the same direction. After a short while she saw a young woman come out of a cottage ahead.

'Excuse me,' Keeva said, catching her up.

'You all right, duck?' she said with her red lipstick and lovely smile, as if she knew Keeva.

'Which way is the bus stop for the station?' said Keeva.

'Wakefield Station?'

Keeva nodded.

'Down by Overton pits,' she said, pointing. 'But the next bus is not till this afternoon,'

What was she going to do now?

'I like your uniform, love; what do you do?'

'I'm in the Land Army,' she answered.

'Oh aye! Just to warn you, they're striking there.'

'I heard.'

'So, don't thee darenst go wait by there right now.'

What should she do then? The woman was kind, maybe she would know. But how would she begin to explain? She wanted to sob on the woman's shoulder and stay with her. She looked so friendly, good company, like she'd be a laugh. But what could Keeva say? She'd look crazy, if she said help me, look after me. Keeva said nothing but pleaded with the woman with her eyes.

'All right, then. Well, I'm sorry, love, it's back way you came and turn right. Follow road straight on after.'

The lady turned her back and walked in the opposite direction. The only friendly face she'd seen since she left Hazel, was gone. She coughed to clear the lump in her throat.

Part of her just wanted to go back to camp now – even Blunt didn't seem so bad. The road was so lonely. With each step another tear rolled down her cheek. The colliery seemed miles away because she had gone the wrong way. Soon, however, she heard men shouting from farther up the road. She tried to be brave, tried not to cry.

Black-faced men, with white eyes, rounded the corner towards her. Please don't notice the tears. Oh no, don't wink and don't wolf whistle with those grey lips; she tried hard not to look up at them. The corrugated iron buildings, against the grey sky, lurked behind the colliery gates. Would the men notice that her eyes were red?

Where was this stupid bus stop? There the woman had been right. She could just make out the metal post with the black and white West Yorkshire bus stop sign not far from the colliery gates. The woman with the red lipstick said the bus was not for at least three hours. But how long was it now? What would she do till it arrived? Her tongue was as dry as sawdust. She hadn't finished her tea earlier, before she had been thrown out. She touched her throat and swallowed. Her head ached; she desperately needed a drink of water. She could walk back to those houses she had come to, find that woman or knock on someone else's door. But what if the bus came sooner and she missed it? She couldn't walk back now.

Oh Jesus, what if she waited around at the bus stop and Mr Hardy pitched up to work? He would easily see her there, waiting alone. He might even threaten her again. She looked at the colliery gates and the swarm of angry miners. She wiped her cheeks and took a deep breath; she wasn't scared. She would bloody well go and ask for a drink of water and double check when the next bus arrived. She took a deep breath and headed towards the colliery gates. She might even find out if their pit props were being burnt for firewood too.

Chapter 21

Overton Colliery, Wakefield, Yorkshire

The red-brick wall was dwarfed by the monstrosity of strange dark warehouses behind. Keeva had never seen a colliery up close before. Two giant chimneys squatted over buildings, blackened with coal dust and belching smoke. The air was acrid. Three metal work towers dominated the sky, their giant wheels winding.

Then she noticed the crowd of men – miners – entering the gates, and more behind. Sweat pricked on Keeva's upper lip as she stood in the middle of the road for them all to see. She'd got this far, she couldn't go back. All she wanted was a drink of water; she could do this, she told herself. She wasn't going to wait around for three hours at the bus stop with a thirst and a thumping headache just because of Mr Hardy.

''Ush, there's a lady 'ere,' a miner said.

'Aye up.'

'It's come to something when land girls come down the mines.'

'There's no cows here, love, just a few pigs,' one snorted.

Keeva walked through the miners towards the main gate. Their clothes were ripped to shreds and a drab grey, apart from coloured mufflers wrapped round their necks. One wore bright red, another orange; they looked more like of a crowd of rag-and-bone men.

'Can I get a drink of water, please?' she asked the man behind the gate.

'You've forgotten something, love,' one man said.

'Your pit props,' another sniggered.

'Come in, duck,' he replied.

Keys clanked against the lock. The latch hurt Keeva's ears as it screeched across the metal gate.

'Maybe she's come to do some strippin' for us.'

'Aye, that's enough,' the guard said.

'Strippin' the bark from the pit props in the yard,' he replied.

Keeva had heard forestry girls were employed to do that at mines, to help the pit props dry out quicker. She slipped through.

'Speak to Big Joe at the office in the large shed, next to the boiler room.'

She made her way across the pit yard, where coal wagons and lorries were constantly in and out with the passing waft of diesel. Piles of pit props were stacked, some men shovelled coal into the railway wagons on the colliery sidings, while others pushed waste to slag heaps, smouldering like small volcanoes. She stepped behind a wagon loaded with coal and leant against it out of sight to catch her breath. What would she do now? She hid herself from those staring eyes, then made her way towards the building with the tall chimney. A huge man, more than six foot tall, appeared from behind the large metal cages in the yard.

'Aye up!' he said.

She lifted a sweaty palm up in salute towards the man, with his large ears and stomach.

'Keeva O'Connor, sir, from the Women's Land Army, sir.'

Chest height to him, she looked up timidly and tried to moisten her dry mouth.

'By gum! What you strutting in 'ere for like tha' all posh? Don't go around calling me sir. You call me Big Joe.'

She blushed. Was he annoyed with her or being friendly?

'I 'ope you're delivering that there pit props be'ind.'

'Yes. I mean, no. Could I have a glass of water, please?'

He fetched her a glass and she drew in her breath and stood up straight. 'Thank you.' She glugged the cold water down. Sweet to taste, like water with honey. Cooling her mouth, the water washed down inside her throat and chest. She asked for another.

'What you doing 'ere, love?'

'Waiting for the bus.'

'Oop 'ere! Don't be daft. Next one ain't for three hour.' He looked at the clock on the wall.

'I thought so.'

'You in forestry section? Make us them pit props?'

Keeva nodded.

'Do you use the pit props from the Women's Land Army?'

'Aye, of course.'

'Can I see? Where our pit props go, down the mines?' she asked.

The man, Big Joe, scratched beneath his flat cap.

'There's 'undreds of miners a' work. It's no place for a bairn like you.'

'I just want to see. Please?'

'No, I don't know love, I don't think so,' Big Joe replied.

'No, no, you see I have to. I'd be in trouble if I don't; Captain Blunt ordered me to find out how the mines work before I go back to the forestry section. So, we can learn exactly what you need,' she lied. Surely Blunt would be impressed. He'd often said they should go down a mine to see how important pit props are to the war effort.

'Clearly, we need them nice and straight, cut to proper size,' Big Joe said.

'Well, if I could see how they are used, I'd tell the girls to make sure they're straight. You would be helping me out and I would be helping you. Please!'

'Sorry, love,' he said, walking her out.

'I work with Mr Hardy's daughter.'

'Oh, do you now?'

'And we've been felling hundreds of trees for the mines,' she said. 'I've just been to his house, he lives in Clayton West.'

'I never, Hardy's girl, you say?'

Keeva nodded, wondering what she'd done.

'All right, don't dilly-dally,' Big Joe said as he beckoned Keeva to follow.

'A need to go and make sure they're workin' again after t' snap. I'll take you down. Follow me.'

'Thank you.' Keeva followed him into the metal building and down a corridor.

'Better put this on yer 'ead,' he said, handing Keeva a helmet. 'Stand 'ere, there's miners ready to go underground.'

The scent of hair oil came from inside the safety helmet as she placed it on her head awkwardly. Too large, the helmet slipped to the side, hard against her head, and left greasy dirt on her fingers. What was she doing here?

She waited alone in the corridor at the end of the queue. A shiver wormed its way up her spine. She shuffled with the queue, moved down into the cold, grey corridor, which led into the narrow mineshaft entrance. A brass lamp was thrust into her hand before she was herded across a narrow metal bridge that shook under her feet. Below was a vast empty black space. On a firm platform again, the mineshaft entrance narrowed, and she was pushed between the men's coal-black clothes. The cold damp air crept up from below with the taste of coal dust on her tongue. A metal gate clattered as it opened.

'Move down inside,' Big Joe shouted.

The cage shook as she stepped inside and her legs began to tremble. Where's Big Joe? She'd heard some pits drop for almost a mile. The cage empty at first, the miners kept a distance from her, and she listened, baffled by their conversation.

'Whist they bin?'

Another replied, 'Pony putting.'

'Artowrate, don't be playin' silly buggers.'

Keeva stood against the side bars near the gate, so as not to lose Big Joe.

'Where's tha' shovel then?' Men sniggered.

'Doug found it, didn't he?' Now they were laughing.

As the cage filled up, more and more men ducked under the chain curtain and shuffled inside with their sour meaty breath.

'This is a bastard place.'

'Hush, there's a girl present.'

Uncomfortably the men could no longer keep from pressing up closer to Keeva. Her chest rose and fell sucking in the air with deep breaths as if they might be her last. How many more men could squeeze in? They crammed, like herrings in a tin, into the cage. She counted another five. Jostled in all directions, a miner stood heavily on her toe, pinning her to the spot. He didn't notice, but her toe hurt.

Now tightly packed like pit props in a wagon, Keeva breathed erratically, elbows braced. That must be all there was room for now. Two more large men squeezed in, then two more. She could hardly breathe; her chest was so squashed by the cram of men. The air was thick with foul breath and something stank like a decaying carcass from below. The door was released and slid down, slamming against the metal platform. Keeva blinked. What on earth was she doing here? When she could be at home or on camp, back in the forest?

A man looked down at her over his stubbled chin. 'By gum, where did you come from?'

'Sussex,' she replied, politely.

'Oh, she's from Sussex,' he said, mimicking her. 'How very posh.'

Men sniggered around her. Keeva couldn't hide her accent;

she couldn't help that it was so different from theirs. Next to the guttural chorus of men's voices from Yorkshire, her voice cut through like the song of a thrush in the forest.

'How now is your brown cow in the Land Army,' another piped up, to a peal of laughter.

'I'm in the forestry service, actually,' she replied, trying to deepen her voice.

'She's in the airborne Land Army. Thinks she's above the rest,' the first man said.

Keeva's nerves got the better of her and she began to tremble.

'Don't you worry, we're only teasing you,' he said. 'What you doing coming down here?'

Besides the clanking chains, shuffle of feet, everyone seemed to be listening.

'Leave the young girl alone, Robin, and move down,' the big man called again.

Someone broke wind and Keeva braced herself as the smell of something worse than a stinkhorn fungus found its way to her nostrils.

'Argh, ta arse on fire, Bob?' a man jibed.

'Make some space for the lass,' the man next to her said.

'Below!' Big Joe yelled.

'One 'undred and fifty yards in less than ten seconds, 'old on, love,' said the man next to her.

'No worries 'cos mad Harry is in control of the winding gear, so the cage drops at the rate of gravity.'

She held her breath as she felt the platform release. She lost her stomach at the top as they plummeted down into the dark chasm beneath. The wall of the recess smeared past in an instant, the rope snatching and looping, before the weight pushed down through her feet with a hefty jolt at the bottom.

As the crush of miners left and space appeared, the hair on her arms prickled with goosebumps. A mix of odours penetrated the air and crept around her: coal tar, the stench of human faeces, urine and sweat lingered in the air. She panicked and wanted to escape but told herself to stay calm. She knew what fear could do, if unleashed. She waited to escape the cage, breathing steadily to calm herself.

Keeva shuffled forwards and stepped out of the mineshaft looking for Big Joe. Under the dim electric lighting, the mine looked like an unfinished underground railway station with two set of rails.

'Up, up, we're drawing coal again!' Big Joe shouted as he hammered against the steel tracks. The engines started up with a high-pitched whine, which became a shriek. Coal crashed down chutes into tubs and the rattle of wheels on rails began. Men began to shovel coal and shout.

Keeva found her way to Big Joe for safety.

'Deepest mineshaft in Yorkshire 'tis,' he said to her.

She felt her hand lifted with the lamp. With a click, Big Joe lit her wick and a dull orange light glowed around their faces. Keeva had to trust him.

'Them tunnels,' Big Joe said, 'are what we call the roads, and those are the tubs or wagons for collecting the coal – empties on the inbye and fully loaded on the outbye.'

The light dimmed as the miners disappeared and the tunnels got smaller and narrower.

'Some got a mile to walk to call face,' he said.

A mile; she hoped they wouldn't go that far.

'This way.'

She could just see some men at work by the flicker of light further along the tunnel. In the places where no one worked it was pitch black and she could see nothing, as if she were blind. She did not want to think how deep underground she stood.

'We got to keep these coal seams going,' Big Joe said. 'The government is desperate for coal to go to all the factories, making munitions and army supplies. But we can't keep workin' without them pit props, you see, love.'

As the bodies moved away down the tunnels, under the dim light she saw the pit props in place for the first time. Twenty or thirty were wedged in, upright, holding up a whole ceiling of coal. She could not imagine the weight of that coal seam bearing down on those pieces of wood. When she had sawn those trunks to length, she had never imagined them being used down the coal mines.

These were the short ones she'd cut to size so many times, without a thought for the strength or their shape. The gap was just six foot high; Big Joe crouched underneath, so small in comparison to the tonnes of rock above their heads. All that rock, colossal in weight, bearing down on those pit props. Further down, the props were smaller.

'Head,' Big Joe called and ducked down.

These must be just four foot four, as she had to stoop as she walked down the tunnel. She'd chopped many of those props to size. Goodness knows how the men coped with the cramped conditions, sat beneath the seam, chipping away with their pickaxes. The full importance of the pit props struck her. She shuddered. One crooked pit prop could give way. Water dripped from pipes and down walls, glistening in the dim light of the miners' lamps. As the men made their way down tunnels with their lamps, they cast long dark shadows behind them. Keeva looked for Big Joe. Where was he? She didn't want to lose him.

'We need pit props urgently, we're running low. You see them all? There are hundreds of them down here and we need thousands more for the war. You see, love, nice and straight and no knobby branches sticking out. That's a rough one there and its only good for hanging the bait tin up.'

'I'm feeling a bit queasy,' she said.

'Feel that air, can you? It prevents build-up of methane. Poison us in no time. So, I check it every mornin' with m' canary, Hughie. Ain't nothing you can do 'bout the lads on the shovel though, they forgot to build bog down t' mines.'

'Urgh!'

'If Hughie misses any sign of gas, I use me lamp. If the flame burns blue we've had it,' he said, adjusting his lamp flame to low.

'There's the pit props, love. If they creak and groan, you know they' is goin' to break and it gives us time to get out.'

'What's that noise?' Keeva called out with terror.

'No, that's roof cracking o'er our heads, not the pit props; everything is shifting down here all the time. No, that's all right love.'

The tunnels were so long and black and Keeva didn't feel safe with the coal seams cracking above their heads. She followed Big Joe closely, further into the darkness down the tunnels underground. The surface underfoot softened and Keeva shone her lamp towards the ground. The coal dust that lined the passage was as soft as black velvet.

'Woud'st tha' like a little brush and pan to sweep up dust and put on t'belt?' Big Joe asked.

Keeva hurried on. They approached men at work; Keeva heard the chip and clang of pickaxes. At first, she had been cold; now she was getting hot. Another wave of panic swelled inside her. The darkness consumed her. So dark and black, the absence of lamp light disorientated her, stole her sight at every corner.

She could just make out some men working by their lamps,

rivers of sweat running down their bare backs; others laid on their bellies in the deepest cracks of the coal seam. The pit props were all they had to protect them. The trees the girls had felled were urgently needed, as Captain Blunt had said. As tempting as it had been to ignore him, she could see the quality of the pit props meant the difference between life and death. The whole country depended on those trees to keep the coal mines open to fuel the industries of war. She needed to get back, to tell the other girls.

She could not imagine what it would be like for these miners working in the darkness all year round. In the heart of winter, they wouldn't see daylight at all. She remembered the happy times out in the forest, with the girls all singing along together, stopping for a tea break, the wind on her face. She remembered the beautiful play of light through the canopy of trees on the forest floor, the changing patterns and colours, even in the rain and frost. But here, down here, it was so dark, the air heavy, rock dust in your lungs. You would never know whether the sun shone or the birds sang. The noisy chains along the conveyor belts. That was the only similarity, the noise of the chains above and below the earth.

'Ready, set,' a miner shouted from further down the tunnel ahead of them.

'Hold your fire,' Big Joe shouted back.

'Let's go back now,' he said as he pushed Keeva's shoulder back along the tunnel from where they'd come.

The blast of the explosion left her ears ringing. Hundreds of feet below the surface of the ground, Keeva was disorientated and didn't know which way to go. Ahead she heard some scuffling and scraping and, crouching down to look, she saw colliers lying down in the dark on their stomachs, using short-handed pickaxes and shovels. They threw the coal behind them. Her eyes strained when a figure crawled out of the coal seam backwards. As he turned, his lamp swung lighting his naked body. Goodness. Keeva stared.

'You taking a photo?' Big Joe said, when the lamp lit up the man's crotch.

Keeva looked away.

'Eee, by gum Joe, what yer doin' bringin' a lady down 'ere,' the man said, covering himself with his bucket.

'You seen enough, love?' Big Joe asked.

'Yes. It's getting hot down here.'

'Aye it's maftin' and we better get you back for that bus,' he said.

Keeva was relieved to be on her way back up the mineshaft, as the chain gate clanked shut.

Just the two of them, Big Joe smiled at her. 'You're brave. I've got a daughter your age and she wouldn't come down 'ere.'

'Well, Hazel, Mr Hardy's daughter, she lost her thumb in the mills making sawn timber props for the pits.'

'By gum, she must be a brave lass working on sawmills. You too, Keeva, did y'say yer name was?'

Keeva nodded. 'I'd give it a go.'

'Not many men would do a job like that. You should be proud of the work you're doing.'

Keeva said, 'Do you need the pit props us girls are making?'

'Are you joking? We couldn't do without them. We'd be nearly out of props without you lasses. What makes you say that, pet?' Big Joe replied.

'Someone said our pit props aren't straight enough – is it true?' she asked.

'Now, where d'you hear that?'

'One of the miners.'

'Don't take no notice. Any pit props that aren't perfect they say come from the land girls. We all know it's an excuse, so the men can chop 'em up for firewood and take 'em home. Mr Hardy, he's a fine one for that.'

A welcome breeze reached Keeva's face as the cage slowed towards the surface. She knew that she must go back to the forest. She had made up her mind; no matter what waited for her, she would return to camp. Gladys had been so kind to Keeva when they had first met at the station, and arrived together at forestry camp. She was looking forward to seeing her again; she had been a good friend. The lift sprung to a halt at the top and rattled.

Relieved to surface from the dingy mineshaft, the bright light of day brought a blast of oxygen to Keeva's lungs. Big Joe took the hard hat and lamp from Keeva. He walked her down the corridor to a new sense of freedom and life waiting for her outside, back in the forest. She wanted to do her bit for the war and for these miners – to keep felling those trees for pit props.

'Now, if it isn't Mr Jack Hardy 'imself coming this way.'

Keeva held her breath as she looked up to see Hazel's father approaching. As he got closer, he stared at Keeva with a menace. She was scared about what he would say, seeing her there.

'All right, Jack,' said Big Joe.

'Hello, Mr Hardy,' Keeva said nervously.

'Who thee think t'ar, coming in 'ere?' he said.

'She's 'ere on business,' replied Big Joe.

Keeva kept her distance, safely behind Big Joe.

'By gum, Jack, I'm sorry to hear about your Hazel losing her thumb.'

'What?' he said, spinning round to look at Keeva.

'You must have been worried sick about yer daughter. Is she all right?'

'Aye, she is.'

'You must be proud of her, mind,' said Big Joe.

'I'm not sure about that,' Mr Hardy replied.

'I'd be proud if she were my daughter. And having met this brave girl here, Jack, I'd say we owe them a great deal of thanks.'

'And to you, Big Joe. Thank you,' said Keeva, with a smile.

'W'emgo, as yer late, Hardy,' Big Joe said with a wink to Keeva, as he led her out towards the pit yard.

'Can you tell Hazel, Mr Hardy, we'll miss her, and hope to see her back in the forest soon,' Keeva called back.

'Over my dead body.'

I hope so, Keeva thought.

Chapter 22

Rosie

3rd March 1940, Beechenhurst, Forest of Dean

Rosie looked for the next tree to bring down. Perspiration under her arms and damp beneath her camisole, she hooked her warm brown coat over a nearby branch carefully. She didn't want her coat to end up on the floor again covered in leaf litter and burs. That conchie girl had dropped Rosie's coat – the only one she'd ever owned, ruined after being picked and pulled to get the flippin' bits off.

The weight of the axe head counterbalanced on her shoulder; she grabbed the end of the wooden handle firmly. She couldn't work out Keeva; she thought she was so clever with all her high and mighty ideas. How could she judge Rosie for taking the money from Beatrice, and then keep it for herself? She didn't have a lot of money either, just like Rosie's family. What was her problem?

The cheek of her to call Rosie a coward for stealing the money and trying to blame it on Keeva, when she bleedin' hadn't. Rosie was sick of everyone else saying, 'Isn't Keeva brave for felling that big tree; isn't she brave for looking after Hazel in the sawmills?' Rosie had never been able to stand the sight of blood, but that didn't make her a coward. Dungarees pinched in at her waist, the cool breeze against her biceps – she'd show her. Her back ached, but seeing one tree after another brought down to the ground made her realise she could do this job. She could do anything if she wanted to.

Like a salute, she swung the axe up in the air behind her. Then gravity, and a twist of her hips, helped the axe furrow straight down into the tree. She reckoned Keeva's family acted like they were intellectually superior to others; to Rosie. Who did Keeva think she was when she didn't have the wealth or education, like Beatrice, to prove it? Rosie raised the axe and with a grunt the blade disappeared into the tree. She was felling that tree to provide timber for the war effort, doing her bit, wasn't she? She flicked her head over to one shoulder and heard a crack; her shoulders ached.

A twig snapped. She flinched and looked behind her, worried that it was that Mr Harvey creeping up on her again. She'd never felt entirely relaxed since he'd grabbed her from behind and rubbed himself up against her. She had the jitters. There again was the sound of someone's feet in the leaves.

'Gladys, is that you?' Rosie called.

'Rosie,' replied a deeper, male voice.

'Oh, you made me jump.' Rosie said, as she looked over her shoulder to see Arthur behind her. 'Sorry, I didn't see you there.'

She'd been so lost in thought; she'd had no idea he was that close. He must have heard her. She wondered if he'd been watching her getting hot and sweaty all along.

'Don't you know better than creeping up on someone?' she said.

She stood up and leant her back against the tree behind her and smiled. He was a lovely looking lad – a bit like Tyrone Power in that western she'd seen at the cinema. She wondered if he was a bad boy, like that Jesse James too. She wouldn't half mind if he put his arms around her, like he'd done with Keeva.

That girl gets right up my nose, she thought. She gets asked to take Hazel home; well, she's not going to get the boy too. Here was one way that Rosie could get her own back, take something that she knew Keeva wanted. She'd seen the way Keeva looked at Arthur, all misty-eyed and smiles. She'd taken her money, but she wouldn't stop Rosie having the lad she wanted to spoon.

'Oi, Arthur, can you give us some advice on my axe swing?'

She flicked a piece of ivy off the end of her axe head. Then she gripped the wooden handle firmly and swung the axe up in the air and accentuated her twist, so she could show off her curves fully as she spun round and whacked the tree. The sun was out, and it felt good on her face. She leant against the tree again and slid her hands down the axe handle. For a moment he said nothing and just looked at her.

'So, what do you think then?' she asked.

There weren't many people nearby; Captain Blunt was busy up at the sawmills. Rosie and the other girls had been sent back into the wood for felling, after Hazel's horrendous accident. They were only allowed to work on the saws as tailsmen, helping to bring the wood in and out of the mills. They weren't allowed to operate the sawmills for now, thank goodness.

'All reet.'

Rosie was relieved as she had been thinking how useful her fingers were for all sorts of things, least of all felling trees. Funny how you take things for granted until something like Hazel's accident, and then you appreciate your hands even more. She ran her fingers down her other hand and touched the axe head. What did he mean 'all reet'?'

What happened with Hazel showed anything could happen in wartime. Live every day like your last, Rosie's mother used to say. Who knew what would happen tomorrow, but for her, today, she had her eye on Arthur.

'All reet! What does that mean?'

'No wuss than when thee started.'

'Oh, thanks.' Was he flirting with her?

He walked across the forest glade, where a few trees had been freshly felled, sawdust on the air. He put his hand on a trunk as though sizing it up for felling.

'Oi,' she called out to him.

He looked up and she smiled as he raised the axe above his head and swung it down into the tree trunk. Rosie hoped he'd look back at her again and he did. This time she gave him a wink. He looked around the tree, as if checking where it should fall, and back at Rosie. Slowly she walked towards the holly bushes, smiling at him. He stopped chopping and watched her. With her finger, she gestured for him to follow.

He looked around and wandered over towards her, with his axe in hand. Nobody could see them behind the holly bush further down the path. Not unless anyone came wandering by. Rosie stepped into the bushes and waited for him; she breathed on her hand and sniffed. Then she saw his brown boots appear a few feet away as he stepped into the holly bush, ducking down out the way of some low branches.

'All right,' she said.

Rosie stepped backwards to take a good look at him. She liked what she saw. The way he stood with his legs slightly apart, shirt collar loose and sleeves pushed up showing his muscular forearms. The way he looked at her, she could tell he liked her. He had an intense gaze with those chocolate-brown eyes that made her feel hungry for him.

'What are you doing?' he asked.

He smiled at her in a mischievous way, which made her feel giddy. She looked down at the leaves on the floor and drew the toe of her boot through them. She couldn't think straight, and now she didn't know what to do with her hands. She rested her chin on one knuckle and felt herself blush.

'Nothing, I just wanted you to come over here.'

He was staring at her still, as she stepped backwards slowly till she bumped up against the tree trunk behind her.

'Why was that?'

'I wanted you to show me that action again, with your axe,' she said and giggled.

'Oh yeah?' he said, sliding his hands up the axe shaft as he picked up his axe. She could feel her heart beating, and became aware of her nipples against her Aertex shirt as the wind blew. She shivered.

'You cold?' he asked.

'Maybe. Maybe I need warming up?'

She rubbed her hands up and down her arms and could barely breathe as he walked slowly towards her. She stroked her hands down her own chest as he slipped his jacket off. The tension was flippin' thrilling. Now was her moment; she reached out slowly towards him and puckered her lips. He stood still and stared at her, eyes widening.

''Ere, me old friend, don't get cold in the drizzle,' he said, stiffly handing her his coat.

Rosie leant towards him, delighting in the prospect of his warm lips against hers.

'What yer doing?' he asked, stepping back, pulling his jacket with him.

She wanted to feel Arthur's warm body beside her. But as he recoiled, the wind blew through her clothes and the vast forest around her. No kiss, no fluttering heartbeat, no breathless embrace. He shook his head.

'Rosie, I thought you were better than that,' he said, as he jerked his arm back inside his jacket.

He was bloody lucky to have any attention from her at all. Her mother always said she was bloomin' gorgeous. Why didn't he like her? No slap, punch or kick could ever hurt more. His words ripped through her chest. Face scarlet. Now she was stiff, cold, and her fists were curled ready to hurt him back. He might as well have said she was a tart.

'You'll get yourself into trouble like that, round 'ere.'

Of course, back at home she'd heard other girls get called Gypsy Rose Lee, after the American stripper – a mort and a whore. How dare he judge her. Her head whirled. Rosie could barely breathe; she was so angry. One minute he was all flirty … I'll keep you warm. The next minute, he's calling her a bleedin' bicycle. He's got no right to say those things about her, call her loose.

'Sod off then,' she said to him.

'Arthur, Arthur, where are you?' timbred a deep voice from across the forest, through the branches.

'It's Blunt,' he said. 'I've got to go.'

Rosie ducked down and hid behind a tree, Blunt's footsteps coming closer, as if she had something to hide. She wrapped her arms around her knees and watched the goosebumps stand up on her arms like chicken skin. What was wrong with Arthur? She didn't understand him. Most men would take advantage of an opportunity to have a cuddle, if she behaved like this. There were different rules here in the countryside that she didn't understand. What did she know about love? If her parent's marriage was anything to go by, it was her father beating her mother. What did she care? She was a Worsell, and the Worsells were tough.

'Blunt,' he called back with a deeper voice, like when her brother's voice had broken. Rocking forward and back on her heels, Rosie toppled over and got stung by a nettle on her hand.

'Ah, there you are, Arthur.'

'Haven't seen that Irish girl, have you, today?' Blunt asked.

'Irish girl?'

'The girl with the peculiar name?'

'What, Keeva?' he asked.

'Yes, that's it,' Blunt replied.

'She's not Irish. But anyway, no. She's taken Hazel home, hasn't she?'

Why were they talking about that flippin' conchie girl? Arthur disappeared with Blunt back up the forest path towards the sawmills. Why did he like Keeva more than Rosie? She stood up, took a deep breath, the forest flippin' pen and inked. Foxes maybe. Keeva had said foxes marked their territory with urine. She wished that conniving Keeva would get out of her flippin' head. If she never saw Keeva again, she'd be quite happy. She brushed down her dungarees and picked up her axe again. The forest was so different to the city, damp and cold. People were different here, unfriendly.

The city was warm. Rosie remembered faces peering out of warm steamy windows down her street. She lived in a community; neighbours looked out for you … friends too, like Bets and the other girls up at the factory. Her feelings drifted to her mother. How she missed her and wished she was back at home. She wanted to give her a hug. She hoped her mum was safe. She hugged the nearest tree instead.

'I miss you, Mum,' she said.

Chapter 23

Keeva

Forestry School, Parkend, Forest of Dean

Keeva's body trembled with exhaustion as she arrived back at the forestry school at Parkend. She was thirsty and her tongue felt like sandpaper. She'd missed dinner, so, weak with hunger, she climbed the forestry school stairs, apprehensive about seeing the girls again. Having had barely any sleep in the last two days, her head was throbbing. She hung onto the banisters, determined not to be pushed around by Rosie or Beatrice or anyone else now. She hoped that at least one person would be pleased to see her after her eventful journey to Yorkshire.

As she arrived at the top of the landing the door to her dormitory was closed and she could hear gentle voices talking within. The five girls, like an assortment of Gustav Klimt paintings with colourful clothes, were peacefully getting ready for bed together. Rosie and Lily in a state of undress, pulling on nighties and chatting. Beatrice stood boldly brushing her glossy locks. Gladys and Edith were snuggled up on a bed together chatting. They looked cosy; Gladys had her back to Keeva and arm draped around Edith, who was still knitting that scarf.

Keeva caught Edith's eye first, but Edith did not smile at her. Instead, she ignored Keeva and carried on chatting. What was up with her? Edith blew hot and cold; one minute she was nice, the other she was barbed. You never knew what to expect. Keeva's cautious entrance seemed to have escaped the notice of the others, so Keeva just walked past their beds, put her bag down and wearily climbed onto her bed.

Rosie turned round, 'Where the bloody 'ell 'ave you been, eh?'

'How is Hazel? Is she all right?' asked Beatrice.

'She's home with her family now.' Keeva sprawled across her bed, the weight of her body on her mattress at last.

'Well then, what have you been up to?' asked Rosie, standing over her.

Keeva was relieved to be back; the dormitory was warm, but she didn't know what to say about Yorkshire. The firelight formed sinister shadows across the ceiling as the girls approached her bed. Edith walked over slowly, with her knitting needles in hand as she cast off her knitting, one stitch with each step.

'The visit to Hazel's didn't go well; her father practically chased me out of the house.' Keeva shuddered.

'What do you mean?' asked Rosie.

'Jesus, he was so angry. He said she couldn't come back.'

'No. Why?' asked Edith.

'You're not going to believe what I'm going to tell you.' Keeva caught her breath, and held back the tears.

'What happened, Keeva?' asked Gladys.

'I think he was most upset about Hazel's thumb. Hazel's mother said as much. But after that he looked down at my jodhpurs and said he didn't like women wearing breeches.'

'No,' said Rosie. 'How rude.'

'He's not the only father to say that,' said Lily. 'My father said I could wear them in the back garden, out of sight, but forbade me to leave the house in them.'

'I just can't believe everything he said. He was getting more and more angry. He said he didn't want any daughter of his chopping trees, even though he works down a mine.'

'Did you not explain to him that without our work, he wouldn't have a job,' said Beatrice.

'We tried. He said our pit props weren't straight and they chopped them up and burnt them for firewood.' Keeva's voice became tight.

'Flippin' cheek,' said Rosie.

'That's not true, is it?' asked Edith.

'No. Not at all. I went to his colliery and asked,' she replied.

'Did you?' asked Lily.

Keeva nodded. But she didn't say that he'd called her a disgusting conchie's daughter and had insulted her father, called her a coward and the rest. She had been so shocked by his torrent of verbal abuse.

'Anyway, he won't let her come back here.'

'Poor Hazel,' said Gladys. 'We'll miss her.'

'Let's write to her,' said Lily.

'Yes!' said Beatrice, joining Rosie. 'We expected you back yesterday.'

She was tired of Beatrice's disdain for her. 'It's a long way to Yorkshire and there were delays on the railways,' she explained calmly.

'By gum, that's true enough – almost the other end of the world.' Lily gazed kindly at Keeva.

Keeva realised Lily had only ever been an honest and straightforward girl.

'We thought you'd gone absent without leave,' Beatrice persisted, pulling her jumper over her nightgown.

'Not all of us,' replied Edith.

'Well, Captain Blunt has been asking where you are.' Beatrice turned and swept out of the room.

'Aw gawd, there she goes again,' said Rosie loudly. 'Don't you want to know what you've missed?' asked Rosie, with a cheeky smile, always ready to stir up trouble. 'Can you Adam and Eve it? She only asked for a transfer to another dorm.'

Keeva fully expected Rosie to ask about the money again and whether she had spent it. Well, too bad – Keeva had decided she was going to give it back to Beatrice somehow. Rosie wouldn't get the money, that was for sure.

'Beatrice was refused, of course,' said Rosie laughing. 'She'll have to put up with us for a few more weeks.'

'We don't want to lose anyone else from our room,' said Gladys.

'One is enough,' added Edith.

Gladys sat beside Keeva on her bed. 'I'm so glad you're back, Keeva, I missed you.'

Gladys reached out her arms and gave Keeva a hug. Moved by her kindness, Keeva began to weep and hugged Gladys back. Her chest rose and fell in Gladys's warm embrace. The last hug she'd had was with her father before Christmas, when he was hauled away by the police.

'Are you going to tell us all about your travels?' Gladys asked.

'Tomorrow,' said Keeva. 'I'm exhausted.'

'Of course.' Gladys smiled. 'You get some sleep.'

As she watched Edith, Rosie, Lily and Gladys getting into bed, she enjoyed the sound of their bright voices like the birds twittering in the trees at dusk. She wanted to tell them all about the mines, but wondered if it would be of little consequence to them. She felt like she had missed out, while their friendships had blossomed.

'You look dog-tired, Keeva,' said Lily.

'I am,' she said, trying to free her blanket trapped underneath her heavy body.

Keeva lay down and closed her eyes. She needed to sleep but her mind spiralled with visiting Hazel's house, her horrible father, risking the visit to the colliery, going down the underground shaft in the darkness. She was shocked by the injustice of Hazel's father, disturbed by the naked miner. She screwed up her eyes so she couldn't see the candlelight, and covered her eyes.

'There's a glass of water for you, Keeva,' said Edith. Keeva leant on her elbow and sipped the water as Edith walked away. Maybe she wasn't so bad after all. She stood apart from the other girls at times with a different opinion. Maybe Edith was more of an independent thinker than Keeva had given her credit for. Perhaps Keeva hadn't made much effort to get to know her, because she'd tagged alongside Beatrice ever since they'd arrived.

Exhausted and hungry, she lay back down, relieved at last to be safely back on camp. On the way home she'd been afraid to sleep, as a young woman travelling alone. She'd heard stories at camp from other girls about men groping women in the dark, and worse, while travelling at night. She already knew that some men thought that women who wore jodhpurs were asking for it. So, she'd tried to stay awake all night. Curled up in a doorway, trying to keep warm on a station platform was something she never wanted to experience again. She began to drift off at last.

She awakened to Beatrice's voice. 'Here she is, sir!'

Where was she? Keeva heard footsteps approach and she startled awake, her heart pounding. Intense woody pipe smoke breathed down upon her and she opened her eyes to see a pair of men's tweed trousers.

'Oh Jesus, you scared the life out of me.'

Captain Blunt stood over her bed in the candlelight.

'About time you appeared, Miss O'Connor. Follow me to my office, immediately.'

Disorientated, she lurched forwards and nearly lost her balance, so sat back on the edge of her bed. Then he made that annoying click, click noise, inside his cheek, like she was an animal that would bend to his will.

'Is it the morning … ?' Keeva blinked and rubbed her face to try to wake herself.

'I said, immediately,' he repeated.

Couldn't this wait till the morning when she had slept? There was no point in talking to Captain Blunt now, she was far too exhausted. But Blunt waited by the door, so she had no choice. She dragged herself up from her bed, shaking, and grabbed her bag.

Keen to be part of the action, Rosie jumped out of bed. 'You're in trouble now. Remember what Redrum told us about staying out.'

'If I'm in trouble, then so are you,' Keeva whispered.

And when she passed Beatrice, who was lingering by the door, she gave her a withering look, that she'd learnt from her mother.

'Wait in the dormitory, Beatrice,' Blunt ordered. 'And Rosie, back into bed.'

Keeva was glad to be back, but was in no mood for any tripe from Blunt. Keeva's shoulders tensed as stocky Missus Redrum came into view across the hallway inside Blunt's office, pink-faced even when not serving dinner from a hot pan.

'About time,' said Redrum, hand on hip as Keeva walked through the door. 'I'd be home by now if it weren't for you, miss.'

Captain Blunt pulled up a chair for Redrum.

'Some people like to come and go as they please, Captain. But us forester folk have more common sense.' With a wobble of her head, Redrum showed Keeva her double chin of disapproval.

Captain Blunt patted the table gently. 'I will speak to her. Where have you been, Keeva?'

Unable to speak, she collapsed into the chair and spluttered a few unintelligible 'ums' and 'errs'. Still drowsy from sleep, her mind swirled and her stomach ached with hunger. She almost nodded off as she focused on the oil lamp that burned dimly in the corner.

'Miss?' Redrum's tight lips opened and closed quickly.

Keeva shook her head and focused hard on Redrum's squinting

eyes. Alcohol fumes emanated from her and Keeva noticed two glasses on the desk. Strange, this short chubby woman, who normally wore a frilly floral pinny over a plain shirt, was wearing a blue dress and deep-red lipstick tonight.

'Well,' said Blunt, puffing and standing abruptly.

'Oh sorry … Yorkshire, with Hazel,' Keeva replied, rubbing her eyes.

'A bit tired, are you?' Captain Blunt said. 'Oh dear! Want me to tuck you in bed and read you a bedtime story, do you? Well, if you hadn't come back to camp so late, you might not be so tired. So, I repeat: where have you been? Yorkshire and back should take no more than twenty-four hours. You were gone an extra day. Account for your time.'

'The trains were delayed, and we had to walk through the night to get to Hazel's house.' Keeva gritted her teeth.

She'd done nothing wrong. She had visited the colliery, but she would only have been waiting for the bus instead.

'You need to keep your nose clean, young lady,' Redrum snapped.

'I took Hazel home to her parents, like you asked.'

'Keeva, this is to be taken very seriously. You know the discipline expected in camp. You have missed a day,' Blunt explained.

'That makes two in total,' said Redrum.

'You should have left Hazel yesterday and we expected you back late the same evening,' added Blunt.

'Where have you been?' Redrum demanded, raising her eyebrows. Keeva wanted to get out of there as soon as possible.

'The trains were delayed … cancelled … in both directions.' She could hardly put a sentence together.

'The trains were delayed or cancelled – which was it?' asked Blunt.

'Do you expect us to believe that? I've met girls like you before. Off with some farmer's son, more like. Think you can take us for fools,' Redrum said loudly and adjusted her skirt under the table.

'Let her explain,' said Captain Blunt.

'You don't know what you are talking about,' said Keeva.

'Don't be impertinent.' Blunt cut in.

'After we arrived at Wakefield Kirkgate, we had to walk through the night to get to Hazel's house, which was miles away.'

'So, you admit you stayed out all night,' Redrum jumped in. 'I've heard it all before, Gerald, girls sent to me straight from home with all their disgusting habits, from bed-wetting and stealing to staying out all night.' Redrum crossed her plump arms.

Why didn't Redrum listen? Her words were being twisted.

She turned to Blunt. 'I've told you. We didn't get back to Hazel's till first light and then I left first thing this morning. But I had to wait hours for one of the buses. The bus stop was beside a colliery. So, while I waited for the bus, I went inside to get a glass of water and went down the mine.'

'You did what? Who told you to do that?' Blunt demanded.

'Nobody. But I was there anyway.' She swallowed hard.

'Why did you do it then?'

'I was thirsty and I wanted to find out why our pit props are so important.'

'Good God! That's the last thing I need, you girls wandering off willy-nilly and showing your incompetence to the people we most need to impress. We'll be a laughing stock,' he said, shaking his head.

'But Hazel's father worked there, so I thought—' She blushed.

'You have undermined my authority,' he said, pressing his fingers into the desk.

Keeva thought he'd be pleased.

'She's lying, Captain, I can tell,' Redrum interrupted. 'What was the name of the coal mine then?'

None of your business, Keeva thought. 'Overton Colliery near

Wakefield,' she said at last.

'Poppycock – you expect us to believe that? That's one of the largest collieries in Yorkshire. You'd never be allowed to cross a picket line with all the trouble there at the moment,' said Blunt.

'Never heard such nonsense in all my life. That won't wash with me, my girl,' said Redrum.

After everything she had been through, Keeva was furious with herself for coming back to camp when she should have gone home. But then things were no better there. Her life couldn't get any worse. What was the point when no one believed her? When was she going to learn how to stand up for herself? She didn't want to be pushed around any more.

'I may as well come out with it, Captain,' Redrum blurted out. 'Rumours have it she spent the night with a local boy.'

'What? No, I didn't.'

'No good will come of strangers in the forest, Gerald, leading our young folk astray,' said Redrum.

'How could I, when I haven't even been here?' protested Keeva.

Captain Blunt shook his head.

She was furious with that stupid woman.

'I know your sort. Look for the dirty nails, that's what I say. Where there's dirt, there's trouble.'

'The girls work in a forest, Doreen.'

'No, it's their education that's the problem. A good brain is a weakness for women; domestic service is the only cure.'

She wanted to run out and slam the door behind her. But then Redrum would win, and she wouldn't be there to defend herself. She wanted to stay in the forest, and she wasn't going to let Redrum ruin it for her.

Captain Blunt got up and, as he loosened his tie, disgusting sweat patches flashed under his arms. He stood, legs apart, hands on hips and said, 'We'll deal with her, don't worry.'

Redrum looked up at him admiringly, as if he represented an all-powerful being.

'Can I go now?' asked Keeva, beginning to stand.

'Sit down,' said Blunt. 'We haven't finished with you yet. There's one more thing, Keeva. You may remember, Beatrice reported her money had gone missing.'

Keeva looked down at her bag nervously.

'Do you know anything about it?'

'No,' she said and shook her head.

As he walked out, he turned back. 'Nothing at all?'

'No,' she replied.

Her heart was racing. She hoped he would not ask to check her bag. Keeva felt a sinking regret; what had she done?

'Charge her,' said Blunt as he left.

Now she was alone with Missus Redrum.

'Don't look all innocent with me. You take a day and an evening away from me and the captain, and I'll take away your privileges. You'll have extra domestic duties for a week. You'll start by mopping the floors, cleaning the toilets and sweeping up leaves outside in the yard. You'll be up early at five o'clock to make the bread and porridge, and you can stay late to wash the dishes after dinner. The discipline will cleanse your mind and body and keep your thoughts away from temptation. Dismissed.'

When Keeva returned to the room, the girls huddled round her bed.

'What did he say, Keeva?' asked Rosie.

'I've got to do extra duties for Redrum for a week.'

'Why, Keeva? Where were you?' Gladys asked.

'Someone said you went with a soldier,' Rosie said.

'What?' the girls chorused.

'No, no I didn't,' Keeva said.

Keeva couldn't believe it. Her mother always said people must have such boring lives themselves if they gossiped about other people. She said her daughter should feel flattered to be the subject of conversation when she wasn't present. But Keeva hated it. Other people would lie and say hurtful things behind her back for their own entertainment.

'Of course, you would say that,' added Rosie.

'Well, I hope he was worth it,' said Lily.

'Was it any good?' asked Rosie, smiling.

'Were you safe?' asked Gladys.

'Does it hurt?' asked Lily.

'Spare us all the revolting detail. I'd rather not be sullied by talk of this nature,' said Beatrice.

'Look, nothing happened. I have got to report to Redrum at five o'clock tomorrow morning for my punishment, I need some sleep,' Keeva said, turning to leave with her wash bag and towel.

'Wait, Keeva, you know what her name – Redrum – spells backwards, don't you?' said Rosie.

'What?'

'Murder.'

'Ooh,' the girls purred.

'She'll give you murder all right,' smirked Rosie.

Chapter 24

Rosie

5th March 1940, Beechenhurst, Forest of Dean

The pit prop weighed down on Rosie's shoulder and she caught its end on the flat bed of the lorry.

'Edith, don't get too close,' Rosie warned.

'I wasn't, Rosie,' said Edith, waiting behind her to load up onto the lorry.

Instead of sliding straight on top, Rosie's pit prop fell to the ground and she left it there.

'This is more like flippin' weightlifting with barbells,' Rosie said, not that she'd ever done that before. Her muscles ached in places where she never knew she had muscles. With a groan, she kicked her foot up onto one of the big tyres and pushed herself up onto the lorry.

'Edith, pass us my pit prop,' she said.

Edith wiped her brow and hoisted the log up against the side of the lorry. Rosie grabbed and dragged it up and over the side.

'One down, another three hundred to go,' she said.

She sat down for a breather, pumping her hands open and closed to relieve the soreness in her muscles.

Edith grabbed her knee and said, 'Come on.'

'Get off,' Rosie snapped.

'How bist me old butty?'

Rosie knew that voice. It was Arthur's.

'Keeva, you're back,' he said with a big smile, as if pleased to see her.

Keeva! Who was he calling Keeva? Not her, surely?

'I'm back,' she replied from the other side of the lorry.

Rosie had seen a different side of Arthur that she didn't like. Here was Keeva, all smiles, falling for his charms, when he'd completely humiliated Rosie.

'How's Hazel?' he asked Keeva.

Keeva loved all the attention she was getting for taking Hazel home, Rosie thought. Talking about Hazel's angry father threatening her, like it was so awful, turning on the waterworks. Rosie had seen the back of her own father's hand many a time. That's just what fathers did; just because her father wasn't normal, she didn't have to make a big fuss of it.

'She was tired and slept a lot on the way home. But she's safely home,' replied Keeva.

'Unlike you, eh, Keeva?' Rosie couldn't stop herself from saying. 'Up to all sorts of fun with that soldier you met on the train.'

'What? No, I wasn't.'

Arthur looked from Keeva to Rosie and back.

'Come on, we've got work to do.' His father loomed behind him, tugging at Arthur's sleeve.

Rosie watched him walk away under the shadow of the big oak, noticing how he looked back at Keeva.

'What did you say that for?' asked Keeva, grunting as she gave her pit prop a push up and over the edge of the flat bed.

'I'm only saying, it's what I heard,' said Rosie, raising her hands.

'But I told you it was just a rumour, and it wasn't true,' said Keeva.

Rosie had started the rumour herself, in case Arthur started telling people what she had done. She leapt off the lorry and went to collect another log.

'It's not true,' said Keeva, catching up with Rosie.

'There's no smoke without fire,' Rosie said.

'You shouldn't go around believing everything you hear. And don't go around spreading rumours about me, all right.'

Rosie stopped and squatted down to pick up another log, leant it upon her shoulder and pushed up. 'Why do you care what Arthur thinks of you anyway? He was coming on strong with me while you were away. Couldn't keep his hands off me.'

'I don't care,' Keeva replied.

That was fine because Rosie didn't care about him either.

Keeva walked off, but Rosie hadn't finished with her yet. Why couldn't she just stay, have a chat or a laugh? Keeva thought she could just ignore her if it suited her. Like Rosie was beneath her or something. Rosie tripped on a tree stump and the log fell from her shoulder to the ground again. She kicked the earth and a sour peaty odour filled the air. Keeva wasn't like the girls at the factory, who'd made an effort with Rosie to become friends.

Legs astride, she bent down and grabbed the log; a piece of bark jabbed underneath her nail.

'Ow, flippin' 'ek!' She'd pulled her nail backwards and, with a sharp pain, a red lining of blood had appeared. Ouch, it really hurt. She clutched her hand and squeezed it, as if to protect her wounded finger. She felt sick and wondered if she might pass out. Light-headed, she sat down upon the nearest tree trunk until the pain eased. Hand on thigh, she watched the blood fill her cuticle and seep underneath her nail. She had to be careful, what with Hazel losing her thumb. Then she hoisted the pit prop onto her shoulder and headed for the lorry.

Rosie had felt really homesick after that accident in the sawmills. For a few days, she'd just wanted to see her mother. She missed her and hoped her mother was all right. Now Keeva was back, she would get the money back, so she could send it home. Nothing more mattered than her family. She hoped Keeva hadn't spent the money already.

Another pit prop loaded. Each one seemed heavier than the last. Her shoulder felt sore, where she was carrying them. On the way to fetch another, she passed Keeva, who ignored her. Rosie slid her hand inside her Aertex shirt to rub her shoulder muscles and her collarbone felt bruised. She hoisted another pit prop up onto her other shoulder.

Back at the lorry, Keeva guzzled water from a flask.

'Oi, let's have some before you finish it,' Rosie called.

'Drink your own,' said Keeva.

'I forgot to fill mine up today.'

'So? There's a jerry can. Use that.'

'But that's right over there.' Rosie pointed towards Blunt and the fellers on the far side of the clearing. A dark cloud loomed over the forest and was heading their way. She didn't like people who didn't share. In her house, if you didn't share you got walloped. There was never enough to go around, and Rosie had been taught the hard way.

'Not my problem,' said Keeva, screwing the lid back on her flask.

Rosie couldn't bloody believe it. She wanted to fly at her, take that bottle out of her hands and empty all the water on the floor to teach her a lesson. The flippin' selfish cow. Rosie was gasping for a drink, and it was no hardship to Keeva. She was as bloody self-entitled as Beatrice.

'Oi, you got that money still?' Rosie whispered.

'Yes, but you're not having it.'

'Oh, I don't believe it. My mother needs it.'

'No, I'm going to give it back to Beatrice. That money isn't yours, so get off my back.'

'What? You're joking.'

'You stole it and put it in my bag, if you remember. So, I can do what I want with it.'

'You've heard her talk about her holiday home in the lakes. She don't need it. Don't bloody give it back.'

'I will,' Keeva said, marching off.

'Can't you think about anyone else? You only care about yourself, just like your dad.'

As the sky darkened, rain started to fall. Raindrops exploded like bombs as they hit the dust, spreading in dark-brown patches, vegetation shaking. Rosie heard Gladys shriek and saw her and the other girls run for cover under the nearest trees – the broadleaves, Blunt called them. She felt the rain on her head and shoulders, dripping onto her face.

'What you going to say to Beatrice?' Rosie called out to Keeva.

'That you took the money.'

'Don't you bloody dare.'

Keeva was shorter than Rosie, but strong and wiry. Rosie wondered if she could have her. She'd seen Keeva fell big trees and Keeva was looking strong today, after a few days off work with Hazel, while Rosie had been working hard all week.

'Or what?'

Even if Keeva could beat her, Rosie was sure Keeva didn't know how to fight. She'd probably never had proper fisticuffs in her life. Whereas Rosie had been in a dozen brawls, at least.

'I'll bloody wallop you.'

'Don't be so pathetic. We're not on the school playground.'

'I will. I'll punch you in the face.'

'Get stuffed.'

Rosie had just about had enough of that girl. Rosie watched Keeva walk off, with her nose in the air. Nobody called Rosie pathetic and walked away.

'Jesus! You've already made it bad enough for me, Rosie,' Keeva called back.

'Me?'

She couldn't believe Keeva as she watched her run across towards the other girls sheltering under the tree. Soon there was a small gathering by the foot of the oak. Rosie walked the other way, over towards the main felling site, to fill her flask with water. She was livid; she might not be able to help herself. On the way, she bumped into Blunt, who was putting up his large green umbrella and brushing down his tweed jacket.

'Rosie!' he shouted.

'What?'

'Where have all the girls gone?'

'Under the tree, governor. I mean, sir!'

'We don't stop for a drop of rain. We keep going. You don't think the war stops when it rains, do you? We fight on, come rain or shine.'

He jogged over to where the girls stood huddled together. She could hear him shouting at them, waving his arms and repeating what he had just told her. The girls left the cover of the trees and carried on out into the field.

Once she had filled up her flask and taken a good long drink, Rosie looked up at the sky. There was no sign the rain would stop anytime soon. So, she found her beret in her pocket and pulled it on, turned up her collar and stepped out into the heavy rain. The heavens opened and mist sprayed up from the earth. Everything was a blur behind the pencil-grey deluge of water. Rain pelted down and stung her face.

Rosie set to work, alongside the other girls. She was tough; she wasn't going to let any toffy-nosed snobs or intellectuals look down on her. Rosie clenched her fists and looked at her muscles in her forearms. They were definitely bigger than when she'd arrived.

She could have Keeva, anytime she wanted.

Blunt marched over. 'Come on, girls, chop, chop. There's already doubts about your work. Questions are being asked of me by the Ministry of Supply. As you are the first women in the country to be given the chance to work in forestry, it's not looking good for others, based on your performance. We are down on pit props and under pressure from collieries. Get moving!' he shouted.

Head down, Rosie tramped across to the far side of the clear fell. The mud was getting worse, making it slippery under foot. Rain was running into her eyes. Her boots were more like cardboard as they got wetter and wetter; her woollen socks were soaked through. She bent down to pick up another log, which seemed so much heavier when wet. She had mud on her hands, on her shoulder and up her legs. The ground was churned up by their feet as they tramped forwards and back, to and from the lorry. Her pace was slow. With the weight of the pit props, she'd easily slip over.

Log after log, the hours passed. Rosie walked more slowly with each pit prop as they felt heavier and heavier towards the end of the day. On Rosie's last journey to the lorry, she came side by side with Keeva. The muddy puddle had become more of a lake, which they had to wade across to the lorry. The water was up round Rosie's ankles now and she could hear it squelching in her boots.

'Talk about a dog's stew in my boots,' said Rosie, breathing heavily.

'There are only four pit props left. We're nearly there,' said Gladys.

'Well, I'm not going. I've done my fair share.' Rosie looked over at Keeva.

'I'll get one,' said Gladys, walking off to fetch it.

'Go on, Keeva, pull your weight,' said Rosie.

'Jesus! Why don't you just bugger off?' Keeva replied.

'Oh yes, that's right, I forgot you are an objector,' said Rosie.

Keeva slammed the pit prop down in the puddle, which splashed

Rosie up to her waist. Her dungarees dripped with brown muck.

'That's it. I've had enough of you. Will you just leave me alone?' said Keeva.

Here she goes, Rosie wanted her to bite. She wanted Keeva to fly into a rage. Rosie wanted a fight.

'Go on then,' said Rosie, lifting her fists up.

'Do what?'

'Go on, hit me.'

'I'm not going to hit you. I was taught to walk away and to defend myself with my mind, not through physical violence,' Keeva replied.

'Your father wouldn't even defend you, would he? Bloody coward. How about you? Want a fist sandwich?' Rosie pushed her. 'Go on then, defend yourself now with your mind.'

Keeva stumbled. 'Get off me, Rosie. I am not interested in fighting.'

'I'd fight to the death for my mum,' Rosie said, circling around Keeva.

'If everyone believed in pacifism, there would be no war. It's acts of aggression that kill people,' said Keeva, looking frightened.

'So, let's see how your pacifist values help you now,' Rosie said, and pushed her again. 'Go on, defend yourself.'

Keeva turned her back.

'Go on, walk away, like a coward. You're just like your father,' said Rosie.

'Don't push me any further. You really don't want to be getting in any trouble,' said Keeva.

'You're like a basin of gravy. You can't even stand up for yourself,' said Rosie.

'Not with violence,' said Keeva, walking away.

'Go on then, just run away again,' said Rosie, giving Keeva a sharp punch in the middle of the back. Keeva fell to her knees in the puddle, coughing.

Then she leapt up and flew at Rosie, pushing her over backwards. On top of Rosie in the puddle, she punched her in the stomach. Rosie's chest heaved but she couldn't breathe.

'Keeva!' shouted Beatrice from somewhere behind her.

Someone else, perhaps it was Edith, tried to pull Keeva off.

Rosie groaned, could barely move, as her breath had been knocked out of her. As if in slow motion, cold water seeped up through her dungarees under the arches to her crutch and armpits. Like a beast, Rosie moaned in pain as her lungs drew breath once again. She pushed on her heels, arched her back and shoved Keeva off. On all fours, Rosie pressed Keeva to the ground, grabbed a handful of mud and wiped it across Keeva's face. Staring at Rosie, Keeva's posture stiffened and her lips curled.

'Quick, fetch Captain Blunt. Dreadful upbringing, they're as common as muck,' said Beatrice.

'Don't you dare say anything about my family, Beatrice,' Keeva shouted.

Rosie watched Keeva scoop up a handful of sludge and throw it at Beatrice. Beatrice screamed as it splattered across her coat. Slugs of thick brown soil sprayed all over her.

'How dare you!'

Rosie clambered up, grabbed some more mud and threw it at Beatrice too.

'And that's from me, you stuck-up cow,' she said.

This time the muck caught Beatrice across her head and shoulders. 'My scarf,' she cried, and made a throaty growl. 'Oh no you don't.' Grabbing a handful of sludge, Beatrice threw it back. Then Rosie slung a handful back at Keeva. There were screams as the splatter covered other girls who had gathered to watch.

Rosie gasped as a wedge of mud hit her face, entering her mouth. Grit between her teeth, she spat and wiped her tongue, noticing over her sleeve Edith kicking mud up from the puddle. Spray filled the air and went all over her. She flinched and turned away as a heavy body landed on her back with a grunt; she knew it must be Beatrice. Off balance, Rosie stumbled forwards under her weight. She couldn't keep upright. As she fell, she twisted, and Beatrice rolled off her back onto the ground. Rosie toppled down beside her, cold water seeping through her coat and down her neck.

Then a knee, elbow, or something hard jabbed Rosie in the ribs. She tried to lift her head out of the foul water, pushed up on her elbow. Arm submerged in mud, cold water surged up her sleeve. Keeva hurtled towards her, and then Rosie was wrenched from behind. She rolled over and, with an arch of her back, flipped onto Beatrice. A lighter body, now Keeva knocked her sideways, pushed her on her back. Bodies scrambled over her as if in a street brawl. They tossed to and fro; she tried to push them off, Keeva and then Beatrice.

'Get off me,' she groaned.

Arms weak, body wrestled to the ground, feet wrapped round her ankles. Keeva on top of her, Beatrice or someone else panting, screaming. Rosie's jumper soaked through, pinned to the ground. Trying to breathe, but not inhale mud and water. With a grunt and hip thrust, Rosie threw Keeva off. In a scrum, she writhed on top, kneeing Keeva in the thigh, punching her in the stomach.

A tug on her collar, Beatrice loomed above. 'Get off her, Rosie.'

Rosie swiped a handful of mud towards Beatrice and down she went again. Splashing, thumping, coughing, kicking. Chaos around her. Girls fought and screamed. Mud flew from all sides and whacked against Rosie's ear. The world went silent as cold wet sludge slipped into her ear. An elbow landed in her face. Ouch.

Rosie wiped her eye, thrashed her limbs around, grabbed hair, as she writhed and wrestled. Over and over, they turned each other; she saw the sky, the mud, and sky again. A knee landed in Rosie's stomach. Mud pushed down her neck. Disorientated, Rosie turned to see Keeva's fist fly at her. Ringing in her ears, her vision went black, she could hardly breathe momentarily. Her arm yanked backwards, twisted and her face forced into a puddle.

'Keeva … Keeva … stop!' someone yelled, as the grip on Rosie's arm released. Rosie slumped into the mud and pushed back up slowly, coughing, wheezing for breath.

'What the blazes is going on?' Rosie recognised the deep voice of Captain Blunt shouting.

Blunt waded into the mud towards Rosie. She cowered, covered her head instinctively, in case she got punched, like her father had done so often.

'What the bloody hell do you think you are doing?' he spat and yanked them apart, pulling Keeva up off the floor.

'Get up!'

Rosie's neck jolted as Blunt pulled on her coat.

'Beggars belief.'

Rosie got up from her knees. Keeva staggered beside her.

'The fighting is not done here; it's done out there,' Blunt shouted, pointing, 'with an axe and saw in the forests.'

Rosie wiped the mud from her ear; Captain Blunt's voice cut though like a hammer on steel.

'You should be using that fighting spirit for our nation!' he yelled, and gave Keeva a shake.

He was right, Rosie thought.

'If you have the breath and strength to fight each other, what are you doing on this training camp? Why don't you show some of that spirit in your work? You have the cheek to call yourselves the fairer sex when you behave like animals.'

He shook his head. 'To see young girls behaving like mongrels. It's disgusting.'

Keeva stared at Rosie.

'I tried to stop them,' Beatrice said, plastered in thick black mud, across her face and hair.

'I can see that, all right,' he said. 'I saw you in the thick of it.'

'The three of you are to finish loading the pit props. The others, you're dismissed. You three will walk back to the forestry school and the others will get a ride back on the truck.'

'What? You're joking, aren't you?' Rosie stamped her foot.

'And this evening at eight o'clock, I want to see you in my office. You three will be charged and may be expelled from the Women's Land Army. Let this be a lesson to the rest.'

Chapter 25

Keeva

Keeva wove her fingers together to offer a foot up onto the lorry. 'Here, Gladys.' Gladys hopped up and squeezed her shoulder. She hoicked Gladys up onto the tailgate with a heave. Gladys carefully switched hands and reached up for Edith who pulled her up on top of the pit props.

'Thank you, Keeva.' Gladys smiled from above.

'We'll save you some dinner,' Lily called down from beside her on top.

'Don't let the old nag leave us the dregs!' Rosie yelled from behind Keeva, washing her hands in a puddle beside Beatrice.

'I'll try,' Lily replied.

'Hurry back, won't you, before dark?' Gladys added, looking down from ten foot above the ground, perched on the stacked wood. The engine shook and the lorry growled to a start, and the other girls left. If only she could be bouncing down the forest track with Gladys by her side. They'd be back on camp, warm and dry soon. Gladys waved as they disappeared up the road and turned the corner.

Alone with Beatrice and Rosie, she felt a chill in the air. She paused a while, wondering who would be most angry, and then her homing pigeon instincts kicked in. She might as well get started on the long walk home.

'I'm setting off.' She turned and left Beatrice and Rosie behind.

Dark puddles reflected the vast grey sky and the gentle mist that descended through the upper canopy of the forest. Feet already sodden, she stomped through the cold water.

''Old up, Keeva,' said Rosie.

Keeva ignored her; she wanted to walk home alone. She could hardly believe Rosie had yanked her head back with a tug of her hair. She walked more quickly, wiping the mud from her face.

'Oi,' Rosie added. Rosie had punched her in the back, winded her and it really hurt.

'I need to get moving to keep warm.' That was her excuse; she didn't want another fight to explode between them.

'Oi, don't blame me when it's all your fault.'

'My fault?' Keeva turned abruptly. Don't rise to Rosie, she told herself.

'If Blunt hadn't come up when he did, I bet you would have drowned me, an' all. Wouldn't ya?' said Rosie.

'Ach, hould yer whisht,' said Keeva, her cheek throbbing. An Irish saying her father used to say, which meant be quiet. More than ever, Keeva wished she could see her father again. She longed to be home and safe, relaxing by the fire, together as a family.

'Yer what?'

She didn't want to be outdoors, exposed to the open sky in the dwindling light, in a forest with no trees. Keeva longed to be home, just as she longed for the blue layers of the forest as they faded towards the horizon. So distant and out of reach. Beatrice's footsteps crunched, gaining on her as the track turned into a stand of trees. Darker and closer among the upright conifers. She wiped her eyes. Rain dripped from branches, pine needles, and ran down trunks.

'You two will not be forgiven for your disgraceful and vulgar behaviour,' Beatrice said as she caught up with them.

Rosie replied, 'Who d'you think you are? A bottle and stopper?'

Rosie couldn't help herself from winding up Beatrice, thought Keeva.

'When you are sent home, I for one shall be glad to see the back of you both.'

Beatrice always had to have the last word. She could only see this walk home with them both being fraught with tensions. She wanted some space to lose herself in the forest, spend time alone in the trees.

'Hold on, let me check my diary. Nope, going home is not in there,' said Rosie.

'You have never demonstrated any responsibility to your job, or duty to your nation,' Beatrice continued. 'You are intent on behaving like dogs – no, mongrels – biting and scratching each other. I have never witnessed anything so degrading and, by the sounds of it, nor has Captain Blunt. I am sure you will both be sent home on the first train in the morning.' Beatrice marched off ahead.

Keeva noticed a path running along the edge of the stream leading into the forest. She could follow the route of the water and find a shortcut back to camp.

'Oi, where are you going now, the bleedin' cliffs of Dover?' said Rosie.

'Back to camp.'

'What about us?' asked Rosie.

'You two go on. I'm not asking you to come with me.'

'Beatrice is only going to stir it up with Blunt when she gets back, ain't she? We better go back with her,' said Rosie.

'You better catch her up then, Rosie.'

In a rage, Beatrice had already disappeared around the corner.

'Come on, it's safer if we all go together – and you might get lost.'

'Lost?' Rosie had no idea that she'd spent years rambling through the woods back at home. She could find her way back with her eyes closed; she never got lost.

'Aren't you scared to go back through the forest?' asked Rosie.

Keeva the coward, Keeva the conchie scum, the other kids in the village had called her. Mary and her friends said they'd always thought she was weird and had never liked her. Perhaps Rosie was just the same.

'You're a bully,' said Keeva.

'What, me? And you only ever think about yourself,' Rosie said.

'I do not.'

She stomped off along the gurgling and gushing stream, which drowned out Rosie's voice. The rainwaters had flooded the banks, covering tree roots and brambles along the path. Rosie flitted between the trees, as she ran after Beatrice up the road. The cool water refreshed her aching feet; she was relieved to be away from Beatrice and Rosie's bickering. So tired, she went on, stepping over tree roots and weaving round trees. The path had become a stream and she had to wade through the flowing waters, her feet icy cold.

The pathway gradually became a mud slide and Keeva struggled not to slip over. The path ahead was unclear, seemed to disappear over rocks and piles of leaves. She looked for signs of a well-worn pathway alongside the stream. Her whole body ached, her limbs were heavy and breath laboured. She loosened the mud that caked around her neck, a handful fell to the ground. Her underwear, wet and soggy, had started to chafe. She must keep warm, so she carried on.

Decaying wind-fallen trees sprawled across the forest ahead of her, ivy-covered trunks criss-crossed the descent. 'You sure this is the right way?' Keeva asked herself aloud. She wanted to make it back for dinner; she was starving. What time was it? The lorry must have left around half past five. On foot, she wouldn't get back until six thirty or seven and it would be dark by then, even with the daylight-saving hours early that year.

The trail went deeper into the forest. Step by step, she hurried on as the light dwindled under the shade of the pine trees. Torrential downpours had brought down sticks and debris from the trees, the newly formed stream had eroded the path. The spongy layer of leaf litter turned to sludge. Keeva wondered if this was the right direction or whether she should go back to the road.

The shadows filled every hole and crack along the bank. But she was sure Cannock Brook flowed back to Cannop Ponds. She'd seen it on the Ordnance Survey map on the wall back on camp, but as she surveyed the terrain there was no sign. The flattened light made it harder to judge each step. Keeva tried to navigate a route down over some rocks, but that route veered away from the stream. She returned to the stream, where the deer had crossed and continued following the water flow. As she descended into the valley, the tree canopy grew dense, and she lost her foot in a hole, fell over and wrenched her ankle.

Sharp pain shot up her shin bone. Keeva stumbled to get up and every time she tried to put weight on her foot she winced in pain. A tree had come down nearby and so she hopped and hobbled towards it to rest. What could she do now? She started to panic, imagining spending a night in the forest, unable to walk home.

A branch cracked from somewhere behind her. She scanned through the foliage, searching for something – a deer or a person moving between the trees. When she looked, there was nothing there. Then she heard a twig snap again, crunching; someone walking through the leaf litter, perhaps. She held her breath, and slid off the trunk to the floor. The sound came closer. She couldn't escape if she tried. Heart thumping … Could it be a forester or a vagrant? What if someone was living out in the forest, cast out from society, a murderer or lunatic? Keeva grasped the trunk and peered over. Who was it?

She thought she spotted a green beret and a beige shoulder

disappear through the trees. 'Rosie,' she croaked. But she'd seen her go after Beatrice. She cleared her throat and called, 'Rosie.'

'Keeva,' came a voice in reply.

'I'm here.'

'There you bleedin' are. I was getting worried,' said Rosie. 'It's getting dark, Keeva. We better get back.'

'Don't you think I know that?'

'All right, I'm relying on you to get us home you know. I don't have a clue where we are,' Rosie whispered.

'I'll get us back.' Keeva started to tremble with cold. 'I've hurt my ankle. I don't think I can walk on it,' she said.

'Flamin' Nora. Why the hell did you go off on your own?' Rosie's tone changed then. 'Come on, let's get you up.' She tapped her arm.

Keeva hopped up to her side and put her arm around Rosie.

'Come 'ere.' Rosie grabbed her round the waist. 'Put your weight on m' shoulder.'

Keeva could still feel the knee in the thigh, the punch in the back. She hurt all over. What would her father think of her brawling? Keeva had never questioned pacifism before. You had to help people, not hurt them; she understood that and felt guilty as she relived how she'd attacked Rosie. She knew she could've walked away.

'Why did you come back?' asked Keeva, leaning on Rosie as she touched her injured foot down.

'I'm not a demon. I wouldn't leave yer, would I?' replied Rosie.

'You did hit me,' Keeva reminded her.

'What's that got to do with it?' said Rosie.

'And you pulled me over on the first day of camp,' said Keeva.

'Yeah, but that was an accident. And you whipped me in the eye with that branch,' said Rosie.

'I didn't mean to,' said Keeva, hopping on her good leg.

'Anyway, are you going to stand up for yourself or are you always going to be a wet blanket like your father?' said Rosie.

'What do you mean? It's not my fault my father is a pacifist; it was acceptable once, wasn't it? People saw what damage the first world war did to people, their livelihoods and their minds.'

'It's not my fault,' Rosie mimicked. 'It's not my fault my father first knocked me off my feet with a sideways swipe when I was five years old, is it? But I don't say 'poor me'. Do you hear me saying I don't believe in violence? Even when the soles of your feet are so bruised you can't walk for two weeks because he's beaten them black and blue with the back of a brush.'

'I'm sorry,' said Keeva.

'Yeah, well, you need to toughen up.'

'The girls in the village back home either used to ignore me or pick on me, call me names, laugh at my hair and say I was Hitler's daughter.'

Rosie giggled. 'There's nothing wrong with a bit of banter. You know what it's like to tease others; it's funny.'

'I'm glad you find it funny,' said Keeva.

'It is funny, calling you Hitler's daughter – a little bit of banter never hurt.'

'Oh, right, I knew I shouldn't have told you.'

'We used to say the more nicknames you got, the more people liked you.'

Keeva frowned. 'Not in this case.'

'So, you were picked on at home. Boo hoo. So, what are you going to do about it?' asked Rosie.

'I can't do anything about it now,' Keeva said.

'Nothing?'

What could she do? She'd left home now. There was no point in trying to change people's minds when you know they won't listen.

As they came closer alongside the stream again, they could hear it bubbling and, in places, gushing like a waterfall from the heavy rain.

'You know, you were right about what you said,' said Rosie. 'The damage the first world war did to people, to their livelihoods and their minds. My father is living proof. He was a prisoner of war in the Great War. He never talks about it now. Sometimes, I think it's why he turns to violence. I can only imagine how they must have hurt him. He is a tortured soul, can't keep down a job.'

'That's what my father said. He saw the wretches in the blue pyjamas at a care home when he was a teenager. He said they were yelling and screaming, didn't know their own names let alone their minds. He said he never wanted to end up like one of them. I think it really frightened him. That's why he became a pacifist. He said he could never kill anyone.'

They descended into the valley towards the ponds.

'It's getting dark, Keeva. How much further have we got?' Rosie asked.

'Not far now.' She had no idea what 'not far' meant. Maybe another hour?

'All right, I'm relying on you to get us home. I don't have a clue where we are,' Rosie whispered.

'I'm relying on you to get me back too.' Keeva was beginning to tremble with the cold.

'You're getting quite a shiner,' Rosie said. 'I know what that feels like. Best get something cold on it.'

The lump on her cheek was sore, and she imagined she had a few more bruises elsewhere. She ached all over and wanted to feel the cool water against her skin. Dams had built up behind fallen branches and twigs, forming deep pools of water. The water was dark but clear. Rosie helped Keeva kneel beside a pool. She unscrewed her water bottle and let the water glug inside. When full, she passed it to Rosie.

'Oh, thanks, I'm gasping for a drink.'

Rosie scratched beneath her Aertex shirt.

Keeva caught sight again of the scars on her back. 'Sorry about earlier."

'Yeah, me too.'

'I've been wondering how you got those scars on your back?' asked Keeva. 'You mentioned potatoes … but you don't have to tell me.'

'No, it's all right. He took the hot poker to me. He was angry with us.'

Keeva's chest rose quickly as she wondered whether Rosie's father was really a monster.

'What's the matter?' asked Rosie.

'Nothing.'

'You shuddered,' said Rosie, sipping on the water again.

Keeva hadn't realised. 'Sorry, it's just awful.'

Plump tussocks on the rocks drew Keeva to touch them. She sunk her hand into the soft wet moss and felt the rock beneath.

'Yeah, well, I don't have to worry about that now, do I? I'd forgotten about it. That's why I like it here.'

'What do you mean?' asked Keeva.

'There's no need to put on a brave face. You can be just the way you are here.'

Could Keeva just be herself? Accept who she was? Accept how she was different to the other girls? She gazed into the pool of water at her own upside-down reflection and bedraggled hair amongst the wet tree trunks and last light of day. The lemon scent of pine drifted on the air, the damp moss, fresh rain on peaty ground. The forest air smelt good.

'So, is that what you are? Someone like your dad, a person who uses violence to get what they want?'

'No, I'd fight to protect myself and I was just testing you. You need to be tougher; stand up for yourself more.'

'I did.'

'Yeah, you did. Maybe I can rely on you now, when push comes to shove,' said Rosie, giving her a prod.

'Jesus, what time is it?' asked Keeva.

She'd whiled away whole days in the forest before, lost in insects, pine cones, leaves, foraging for fungi. She'd lose her sense of time letting the forest soothe her teeming mind.

'What is Blunt going to say?' said Rosie. 'I don't want to get sent home now.'

'Me neither.'

'Did you hear what Beatrice said?' asked Rosie.

'Don't worry.'

'I'm not going to let him throw a grenade into my life,' said Rosie.

'He can't throw us out. What grounds has he got?' added Keeva, her stomach rumbling. She got up and they crossed the stream.

'All right, let's back each other up. No more playing the victim though.'

Rosie spat on her hand and held it out.

With a moment of pause, Keeva wondered what she was expected to do. She'd been told spitting was a dirty habit, but she loved doing it anyway. So, she spat on her palm and took Rosie's hand in hers and squeezed them together, wondering what she had agreed to.

Chapter 26

Keeva waited in Captain Blunt's office. A pair of black binoculars lay upon the windowsill like rifle barrels pointing. The wood-rimmed clock on the wall ticked. Keeva itched her neck and found some mud she'd missed behind her ear. She'd had less than twenty minutes to get cleaned up and gobble down her meatloaf and boiled potatoes. Where were the others?

Blunt did not blink as he stared at her, waiting for Rosie and Beatrice to arrive. Oh God, what was he going to do? She caught her breath. She could see the whites of his eyes around his grey-blue irises. Jesus, he looked angry. This was her second time in his office in a week. The minute hand reached the roman numeral twelve; it was eight o'clock.

The other girls should be there by now. She'd been terrified of being late, but now she regretted being early. The brown leather strap of the binocular case hung over the window ledge. She should have gone to the lavatory, after guzzling down all that tea when she got back.

'Make yourself useful and fetch me a whisky,' he said, pointing to the decanter on the sideboard.

She blinked. What? Fetch him a whisky? Who did he think she was? A parlourmaid? Reluctantly, she went over and poured him a glass from the Bell's Scotch Whisky bottle, hands trembling.

'Steady on,' he said, as she returned, sliding the glass upon the desk.

The moss-green walls gave Blunt a jaundiced look under the dim lights. She sat back down and looked to the pair of compasses on top of the huge red leather-topped desk, their sharp points stabbed in her direction.

She heard his rasping breath as he glugged the whisky and,

unable to bear to look at him again, stared at the large map of the forest on the wall.

Where were Beatrice and Rosie? Why didn't they hurry up? If they were late, it would only make him angrier. Footsteps echoed down the stairwell. Finally! But the sound slowly dissipated as they clicked away. She could smell the tobacco from his old brown pipe, which rested in the square gun-metal ashtray. The dark-brown wooden in tray was filled with cream papers, held together with a bulldog clip.

Then there was a knock at the door. Thank God!

'Enter,' said Blunt.

The door opened slowly. Beatrice entered, wide-eyed, with her hair still damp. Her nostrils flickered slightly as she spotted Keeva.

'Glad to see you looking more respectable. Sit down.'

'I'd like to explain,' Beatrice said, standing in front of him.

'Did I ask you to speak? Sit down,' he instructed, grabbing his glass and sinking the remains of his whisky.

Beatrice blushed and tapped the arm of the chair nervously. Keeva looked down, her heart beating: boom, boom, boom. Could they hear it? Would Rosie and Beatrice both attempt to blame her, even though Keeva had been provoked? Her father's disapproval sounded in her head. People who fought were no better than animals, he'd always said. Blunt had called them dogs as well.

Blunt's tweed jacket with brown suede elbows was hung up to dry on a picture hook above the fireplace. The fire was unlit, filled with ashes and a half-burnt log.

Keeva sighed; tick tock, another minute had passed. At last, another knock at the door and Rosie bustled in. She dropped down into the chair next to Beatrice, lent back on her elbows nonchalantly and stretched her long legs out in front of her.

'What?' Rosie said, turning to them both.

'Good,' Captain Blunt said as he rested his fingertips together and flexed them slowly. 'Sit up straight.' Rising from his chair, he strode across the room towards them.

The three of them sat upright.

'In the months preceding war, I was involved in lengthy discussions to restructure Britain's timber industry. There was chaos and confusion hampering the urgent need to increase the supply of timber and I was called in to avert the crisis.'

He marched back and forth, pointing at them.

'Under my command, civil servants, in consultation with the timber trade, worked out a blueprint for the production of timber. I named it "The Bible" because it answered essential questions. Top secret work, I ordered all divisional officers to be sent heavily sealed packages marked "Secret: Not to be opened until the outbreak of war". Yes! I know what you are thinking: that I am a man who sorts things out. I am. But the last thing that I want is for my reputation, my command, to be compromised. Do you understand?'

'Yes, sir,' Beatrice replied.

'I said, "Do you understand?"'

'Yes, sir,' Keeva and Rosie chimed together.

'I will be frank with you; amidst these chaotic wartime preparations, the final straw was the suggestion that women like you should work in forestry. This ridiculous idea was conceived of by that Lady Gertrude Denman. She should stick to running the Federation of Women's Institutes, rather than meddling in important war work.'

Keeva curled her fingers around the arm of the chair and squeezed it.

'I understand there is a fundamental problem, which can't be helped. The shape and size of women's bodies prevents them from doing the job competently, while men's bodies are well-suited to forestry work.'

Upon the desk stood a black inkpot and writing pen poised in its holder. He slid a black book with a blood-red spine across the table and opened it.

'Names, please?' he said, turning to each.

'Beatrice Oxley.'

'Rosie Worsell.'

'Keeva O'Connor.'

'You leave me with no choice but to expel you from the Land Army and to send you back to wherever you miserable … incompetent … and undisciplined girls came from. I don't know how you were brought up, but your parents should be ashamed of you. Fighting? Women don't fight; their job is to look pretty.'

Rosie cleared her throat and Keeva thought she coughed the words 'clap trap' into her hand. Wasn't Blunt even going to give them a chance to speak? What should she say? She couldn't say Rosie had attacked her. No; she bit her tongue. But this was her only chance to stand up for herself. If she didn't, he would send them home.

'Please let me stay,' she pleaded when she could contain herself no longer.

Captain Blunt shook his head.

'Your work was to carry out haulage today, not fight each other,' he said. 'Your behaviour is totally unacceptable. You have proved you are not suitable for work and, besides, I know that none of the timber merchants are prepared to give you work once you leave here. I will see to it myself that your work stops here.'

'C … c … c … can I just explain?' asked Beatrice.

'I haven't finished. And if I don't give you work, no one will. I oversee buying. I know all the major estate owners in the south-west of England, and what I say goes. An army is only as good as its weakest recruits, and I will not have you make a fool out of me.'

'I saw Keeva throw the first punch,' said Beatrice.

'That's not true,' said Keeva, holding back the urge to lay the blame on Rosie. Keeva caught Rosie's glare and remembered their agreement.

Beatrice continued, 'As an innocent bystander, I was appalled by their behaviour. Naturally, I tried to stop their common brawling. But they were determined to continue, despite my pleading them to stop. The working classes probably know no better.'

Rosie screeched her chair leg across the floor, 'You snooty cow. You've done nothing but cause trouble since we arrived.'

Beatrice winced. 'There must have been an error in the recruitment process. I was told that I was needed for my knowledge in mathematics, having studied at university. But that is obviously not the case. The rest of the girls lack even a basic education. I was told I'd be needed as a measurer, not a common feller and haulier.'

'Thank you, Beatrice,' said Blunt. 'This is exactly what I am talking about. I've seen you leaving the hard work to the others. You seem more worried about a broken nail than getting the pit props onto the lorry. You'd rather put down your colleagues than support them, breaking the very trust you need to build a team. You need to help lighten the load for the rest by working together, not fighting against one other. None of you are fit to serve in the forestry service.'

Beatrice gulped and shook her head. Captain Blunt was right; she was divisive and she didn't pull her weight.

'None of you are the calibre of forestry worker, even unskilled, that we need. I have no option other than to charge you and send you home,' said Captain Blunt.

'Oh, sir, you can't, I ain't going home yet,' said Rosie staring at Keeva. 'Can't we just finish the training?' She kicked Keeva's chair and made her jump.

'I'm afraid it's too late for that,' he said.

'Have you got a quarrel with our work?' Keeva asked.

'What?' Blunt replied.

'Did we load up the pit props like you wanted today?'

'Not with any speed, efficiency or without disgraceful misbehaviour.'

'Five of us worked for eight hours today,' Keeva went on. 'We loaded up more than three hundred pit props onto two lorries. We must have carried at least sixty pit props each and worked non-stop, except for a half-hour lunch break, and most of the afternoon we carried on in the rain. We completed the task, didn't we?'

'Well … yes,' he said.

'Then stop picking on us.' Keeva felt her biceps twitch. She had learnt the skills of felling and lifting, was getting into the rhythm of the work, and surprised herself how strong she had become.

'Yeah, we did what you asked today,' said Rosie. 'Didn't we? We got it all done and we walked home.'

'But we are not here to talk about haulage, are we? Your conduct is in question.'

'I ain't going home, sir. We've learned our lesson and it won't happen again,' said Rosie.

Keeva lit up inside as Rosie gave her a nod. She wasn't going to be sent away like her father; she would stand up for herself. No more playing the victim.

'I want to stay too,' Keeva added.

'And you?' Blunt asked Beatrice.

'Well, I am only too happy to go back home, of course,' she sniffed. 'I was told that I was needed for my knowledge in mathematics but that is obviously not the case.'

'Well, that is a shame as we will be needing mathematicians

next week for measuring,' he said. 'Not that you girls would be useful. I'm sure you'd be far too emotional to do simple sums.'

'What? But …' hesitated Beatrice.

'Let me speak,' he said.

Beatrice twitched. The irony. She'd been going on about being a measurer since they arrived, how she was suited to more intellectual work.

'It's all right, I can do that measuring stuff. I can use a ruler,' said Rosie.

'What experience of figures do you have?' Blunt asked.

'I have experience of figures,' she said, running her hands up her long thighs and over her shapely hips before resting them on the arms of her chair.

Captain Blunt didn't know where to look. His eyes wandered from his leather-top desk to the map on the wall.

'And I used to 'elp the foreman in the factory with the tallying up of bottles off the production line.'

Rosie looked across at Keeva and gave her a little wink.

'I can do it too,' said Keeva. 'I'm good at maths.'

'Can you read an Ordnance Survey map?' he asked.

'Yes,' said Rosie, 'of course.'

'Well, prove yourself then. Show me New Fancy on the map.' He pointed to the large wooden-framed wall map – a network of faded green, orange and blue shapes and lines.

Rosie jumped up to look more closely at the map.

'Where is my New Fancy?' she said, running her fingers across the map provocatively.

'Keeva, what about you? Can you find New Fancy?' he said.

She stood up and scanned the map so closely her vision blurred. She felt herself get hot and wiped her brow. Trying to read the tiny letters and feeling the three of them all staring at her. She could not find New Fancy either.

'I'll show you,' said Beatrice, flicking her hair, and the three of them scoured the map together. Eventually they turned to see Blunt smiling.

'Dear, oh dear, is it much too difficult for you girls? There will be no great loss to the team of measurers without you three,' he said with a chortle.

'You find it then,' said Keeva.

'What?' he replied.

Keeva pointed. 'Where is it on the map?'

'Of course,' he said, swaggering over towards them. 'It's right … uum … Now, where is it? It should be somewhere round here … in between … Parkend and Ruspidge. Now where is it? Well, I'll be damned; it's not even on this map. It must be an old map. No New Fancy! Ahem!'

She wouldn't let one man decide her entire future. She would do everything she could to stay.

'Ahh yes, the problem is there are lots of smaller privately owned woods. Perhaps no one knew who New Fancy belonged to,' he added.

Rosie started to snigger.

'Think it's funny, do you?' he said.

'No, no I don't, sir,' she replied.

'Can I ask, Captain Blunt,' asked Keeva, 'who are you going to get to replace us, when all the young men are signing up to fight?' Even Arthur was going to sign up soon.

'I've changed my mind. I'd like to stay,' said Beatrice.

'If you let us stay, we can prove ourselves.' Keeva had listened to what Rosie had said. She needed to stand up for herself. She looked for Rosie's acknowledgement. Rosie nodded.

'Pull yourself together, girls. Don't start snivelling.' Blunt returned to his desk. Resting his chin upon his hand, he pondered for some time, turning the pair of compasses with his index finger. 'It is unlikely the Ministry of Supply would allow rejections so soon, when you have not completed your training, and especially when there is such an urgent need for measurers.'

'You won't know what I am capable of,' added Beatrice, 'if you don't allow us to complete the training.'

'Hmm,' Blunt grunted. 'Short-term loss to yield long-term gains, perhaps. Seeing as you are all suddenly so keen, I'll make use of your enthusiasm.'

'You won't regret it,' said Rosie, with a smile.

'Let's put that incident behind us. Shall we?' Blunt walked towards the door. 'No more fights.' He grabbed the door handle. 'No more staying out late.' He pulled the door open. 'No more chances.' And with a flick of his finger, he growled, 'Dismissed.'

Chapter 27

Beatrice

12th March 1940, Forestry School, Parkend, Forest of Dean

Beatrice smiled to herself as she sat upon a sunny tree stump in the forest and slid her hand inside her cool coat pocket. Perfectly sized for her hand, she pulled out her special cherry-red notebook. Fond memories of her time at the University of Liverpool came flooding back, when she had mixed with intelligent men and women of her own class. Beatrice had kept her expensive red leather notebook since then, in the hope she might find a use for her skills in mathematics once again.

Out in the forest, Beatrice was about to prove herself as a timber measurer at last. She would become a valued member of the elite army. In the early morning sun, she ran her finger up the spine and over the embossed gold swirl-leaf corner details. She opened the book to marvel at the beautiful, marbled orange, gold and green endpapers, then, book pressed to her nose, inhaled the fresh new paper. The crisp edge of the cream lined paper had a good tension against her fingertips.

She hoped Gladys would be some time fetching the pots of paint to mark the trees as she turned over the first page on which she had written, 'Beatrice Oxley, BSc. Mathematics, University of Liverpool, 23rd September 1938', in her best calligraphy writing. Each page was filled with lecture notes, maths formulae and numbers. The tails of delicate red ribbons lay over her little fingers and marked the last page she had written on.

A page of notation, a calculus question –

Evaluate, using trigonometric and / or hyperbolic substitutions:

$$\int \frac{dx}{x2+1} \quad \int_1^2 \frac{dx}{\sqrt{x2-1}} \quad \int \frac{dx}{\sqrt{4-x2}} \quad \int_2^\infty \frac{dx}{(x2-1)3/2}$$

- was presented and remained unanswered. Beatrice fumbled in the pocket of her beige overcoat for a pencil. Her heart leapt; she had loved the challenge and satisfaction of integration to find out the answers. There was always a correct answer. She pressed the lead to paper to jot down some workings, searching through her memories for the tricks and techniques. But the blank page stared back at her. She could hear Captain Blunt on his way over to the meeting place, where she waited. Then she heard something nearby, scuffling, and looked up to see a black and white badger trundling by.

Her enthusiasm for studying and hopes for a future had been snatched from her by her parents. And now she feared she couldn't remember where to start with calculus and found herself sitting on a dirty log in the middle of a forest. She had done everything in her power to persuade her parents to let her continue at university. Their decision pained her to this day: to deny her the opportunity when she was bright enough.

She had told her mother that every equation was filled with the hope of meeting other like-minded people, who felt the same way as her about numbers. Her mother had mocked her: 'So you can solve complex numbers and have little baby multiple equations of your own.' Her father had questioned her desire to earn a decent wage: 'But who would pay the bills once you are married?' Beatrice had said, what if she didn't want to get married, and they had laughed. She knew her parents resented investing in a career for their daughter. They said marriage was a fait accompli for a woman of her breeding, and now there was a war on that was the end of the matter.

Take Gladys, for instance, whom she'd partnered with for measuring; she had worked in a milk bar making milkshakes and clotted cream before the war. She was uneducated, much like the other girls. Surely Beatrice had more to offer than Gladys, who at that moment approached her carrying two pots of paint and wearing a broad smile. Beatrice closed her notebook and put it away in her pocket.

Maybe her hopes for a future had not been snatched from her by this dreadful war as her mother had said. Behind Gladys the yellow primroses were blooming across the open glades, and the forest seemed a more welcoming place in the sunshine. Kindness and a cheery disposition made up for Gladys's lack of mathematical ability, and was at least some consolation for having her as a partner. Beatrice looked forward to putting all her learning about cubic quantities of wood into practice, while Gladys held the end of the tape measure for her.

Now, perhaps Beatrice was being given a chance to shine in her new role as a measurer. The other girls started arriving in the glade, and took their places in pairs, awaiting instructions. The twittering voices behind her belonged to the antics of Keeva and Rosie. She wondered how, so soon after pulling each other's hair and wrestling one another, they appeared to be the best of friends. How Keeva suddenly seemed so popular with the other girls simply baffled her. What had she done to win over their friendship? She'd hardly been given the best upbringing with such a dysfunctional family. Beatrice could not help herself: she huffed and turned away as Keeva flashed a cheeky smile at Rosie. The two were getting on better than ever now, after their brawl.

A tall slim man with dark hair and olive skin approached with a tan satchel slung over his right shoulder. He stood a few yards in front of Beatrice and cleared his throat. 'Welcome ladies, I am Rupert Studman, chief measurer for the south-west of England, and I'm going to teach you about measuring today. Does anyone know what we are measuring?'

'Trees,' said Rosie.

Beatrice didn't want him thinking they were all that asinine.

'Very good,' he said.

'How tall a tree is?' suggested Gladys, from beside Beatrice.

'And the width,' said Edith, who was doing up her laces.

'Yes, that's right, we measure the length and the girth of a felled tree. Does anyone know why we are collecting these measurements?'

'The length and girth measurements,' Beatrice answered, 'are required to calculate the cubic quantity of wood in any tree. Thus, giving us the volume of timber.'

'Excellent, that's right.'

The birds sang up in the boughs and the gentle breeze touched Beatrice's glowing cheeks.

He folded open his satchel. 'To begin with, I'm going to show you the tools we will be using,' said Mr Studman, and Beatrice stepped closer.

'You have probably seen one of these before,' he said, rubbing his thumb across the blade.

'A bark scraper,' said Edith.

'Come over and gather round,' he said.

The other girls huddled around Beatrice. The antiseptic smell of carbolic soap wafted over her, which reminded her so much of blistered and smelly feet. She nursed her nose with the delicate rose scent of Pond's Cold Cream from the back of her hand. She looked up at Rupert once more. Handsome and elegant, she admired how he held each object up for everyone to see and then placed them carefully back in his satchel. His voice suggested he was of Beatrice's class. Here at last was someone she could relate to, on the same level, and she wondered what else he would conjure from his bag.

'A one-hundred-foot-long tape in a wind-up leather case, a six-foot girth tape, chalk, a thick blue wax crayon, a paintbrush and a scribe knife.'

Mr Studman passed each item around. Beatrice didn't want to touch them when all the other girls had rubbed their filthy hands all over them. But then he handed the last item directly to Beatrice: 'A Hoppus Ready Reckoner book for calculating cubic content of wood.'

How could he have known how much that meant to her. She sighed as she studied the tall, slim blue book. 'Decimal Hoppus Table, Wilson' was written in small navy letters on the front, and inside she noted that S. E. Wilson had MSc., PhD. and DIC attributed to his name. The Hoppus system of measuring timber was named after Edward Hoppus and had been in use for more than a hundred years. Her applied mathematics course might have covered this system if she had continued at university.

Inside the book was page after page of numbers, each giving the exact answers to the solid contents of a tree trunk. It started with a one-foot-long log with two foot girth, which equalled 0.03 cubic feet and ended with a twenty-foot-long log with a sixty foot girth which was 500 cubic feet. With a turn of a page, the cubic volume of any size log could be found. Beatrice found it curiously soothing as she looked down at the numbers, each an increment on the one before.

"Ere, let's 'ave a look then, Beatrice,' said Rosie as she leant across and tried to snatch the all-important blue book. Rosie yanked on the book, but Beatrice would not let go. She pinched the book more tightly and tried to gently prize Rosie's fingers from its spine. A minor tussle, which reminded her of the many fights she'd had with her brother Frederick. Beatrice pulled harder and Rosie tugged back, a mini tug of war ensued until Beatrice ripped the book from Rosie's grasp.

'Each pair or three will be getting their own satchel filled with these items, so please don't fight over them. You will all have your chance to familiarise yourself with the tools.'

A mature man, perhaps in his thirties, Beatrice guessed, as she admired Mr Studman. The way he engaged with the other girls, paid close attention when they spoke and seemed to listen to what they had to say, was charming; thoughtful and yet confident at the same time. His physique was as robust and manly as his voice, accentuated by the gentle movement of his Adam's apple when he spoke. She caught a look of James Mason as he smiled at her.

'It's a modern calculator,' he said, holding out his hand.

She reached out and touched his hand impulsively, no longer aware of what he had said. When their hands met, she wondered if her fingers might ignite.

'The book,' he said.

Beatrice wondered if her brain had nearly all but fallen out of her head, as she passed him the book. Giddy, she remembered to breathe, as she gazed at his cleanly shaven face. He seemed so relaxed around women, not like Captain Blunt who just now was bustling up towards them. She wondered if Rupert had sisters and adored his mother too.

'Not only will you be calculating wages for the fellers,' Mr Studman said, 'but they will also be used for Income Tax records for the timber merchants and timber supply for the whole country.'

He would be a good catch for any young woman, she thought. She imagined promenading with him in the forest together, holding hands.

'The country depends on your figures,' Captain Blunt butted in. 'They are of utmost importance. 'They will be essential to all industries of war: military aircraft construction, ship building, pit prop production for coal mines, railway sleepers for transport, telegraph poles for essential wartime communications, and the list goes on. These figures are essential to crucial decision-making in the War Office.'

Goodness! Beatrice was dizzy with the importance of what she was being asked to do; she could barely think straight. It had been nearly a year since she'd studied at university and she was worried that everything she had learned had been replaced with fondant fancies, frilly underwear, and creams to keep her complexion free from blemishes and spots. What if she couldn't remember a thing? What if, now her chance had come to prove herself, she would discover she was as hopeless as her mother had always said?

Her mother and father always said Frederick, her brother, had been blessed with the brains. While she knew he was cleverer than her, of course, he was rather cavalier with his studies. He freely admitted he had drunk his way through university and barely studied at all. He'd still managed to get a degree in geography from University College London. He hadn't fought the same battles as she had to go to university and there was no question that it was a waste of time for him. He was congratulated for his intellectual prowess by her father and had received countless pats on the back. The only patting Beatrice got from her father was on her head.

'Beatrice,' Gladys said.

'What? I mean, yes.'

Mr Studman walked away and Beatrice wondered what on earth had just happened.

'Captain Blunt said he's going to be keeping an eye on us.'

'R … Rupert, erm, Mr Studman?'

'Sorry, no. Blunt.'

'Okay.' Beatrice nodded her head, as she remembered the instructions they'd been given the day before. 'So, we need to calculate the amount of timber between here and the next footpath,' said Beatrice. She wasn't sure Gladys would have understood what was required. Beatrice couldn't afford to make any mistakes with Blunt and Mr Studman watching. She imagined herself promoted to work alongside Rupert, if she could show her potential. She might even be given more responsibility and a higher rank than the rest.

'Yes, that's right. Have you got your notebook?' asked Gladys.

'Yes, of course, and we need to mark the trees to fell with a white dot at five foot up the trunk, and the ones to leave with a red L,' Beatrice said, glancing at Captain Blunt, who was looking at his watch and flicking the back of his hand impatiently towards them.

'Get on with it. Chop, chop,' he said.

'Yes, I've got it. Shall we get started?' asked Gladys. 'I've got the pots of paint.'

She mustn't let Gladys be too laissez-faire, thinking she knew what to do, when in fact she didn't. How they proceeded from the beginning was important with Captain Blunt's beady eye upon them, after the awkward scenes in his office.

'Right, shall we start on the opposite side of the glade?' asked Beatrice. This could give her some time to make sure Gladys didn't make any silly mistakes.

'Looks like as good a place as any,' Gladys answered.

Beatrice was determined to create a good impression in front of Captain Blunt. She had listened carefully to the instructions. Gladys was armed with her measuring tape, scribe knife, chalk, crayon, billhook, paintbrush and white paint pot, and set off. Beatrice had the all-important Hoppus Measuring Book securely in her hand. But realising Gladys had left the red paint behind, Beatrice grasped the handle and rushed to catch her up. Beatrice was a natural leader and preferred walking ahead. She strode out across the forest and looked down to check she still had her notebook to hand when she caught her toe.

Just a simple tap of her toe on the root of tree and she tripped. Still moving forwards with the paint pot in one hand and notebooks in the other, she had no way to break her fall. She couldn't right herself as she began to topple forwards, turning in the air. 'Timber!' cried out in her head, as Beatrice felt herself keel over. Foot trapped, her right knee landed first with a thud upon the hard earth. Then her body landed heavily in a heap on the ground. With the paint pot already open, a slop of paint shot up her arm and flew up into the air. Splatters of cold, wet paint covered her coat and speckled her face.

'Aargh!' Beatrice screamed, wondering if Rupert might have seen her fall.

'Oh my God, Beatrice!'

'My clothes!' she sobbed. 'Get off me.'

'What on earth are you doing?' shouted Captain Blunt from across the forest.

Her hair and clothes were ruined. She still had mud ingrained in the corduroy stripes of her jodhpurs, from the mud fight; and now she was covered in red paint. She had never seen a can of paint explode like that before. She couldn't bear it if Rupert saw her with what looked like blood splattered from head to toe. How could she continue today, looking like such a mess? She had no dignity left any more. Sniffing, she sat on the floor, hoping no one else would see her.

'My notebook, it's covered too,' she cried.

'Don't worry, it will clean off.'

'But it's my university notebook.'

'Beatrice, have you hurt yourself?'

'What do you think? Of course, I have,' she replied.

'Up you get. Let me clean you up,' said Gladys. She took the paint pot and settled it on an old tree stump.

Oil-based paint would never come off her clothes, Beatrice thought; she wished Gladys was Rupert as she opened her water bottle and dowsed the paint of her hand.

'Now give me your coat,' she said.

Beatrice groaned as she carefully took her coat off.

'Here, let me pull your sleeves, so they don't pull inside-out,' said Gladys.

If only Rupert's handkerchief was being unfolded instead. Beatrice whimpered as Gladys began to wipe her face. She dabbed her nose so tenderly; Beatrice already felt a little better. Gladys was so close, she could feel her breath against her damp cheeks, where the tears had fallen. There was no scolding or familiar 'you stupid girl', which she could hear her mother shouting in her head. Gladys was pretty.

'You have got such a beautiful face, Beatrice. No amount of paint could ruin your looks. Honestly, I am so jealous of how gorgeous you look in your uniform. You make it look so glamorous, with your red lipstick.'

Beatrice felt quite overwhelmed by her affection; she went to look away, but could not help but gaze into Gladys's big blue eyes.

'Is Captain Blunt watching?' Beatrice asked.

Gladys looked over Beatrice's shoulder, 'Oh, who cares?' With her pink tongue against her top lip, she wiped paint from Beatrice's nose.

'Why are you being so kind to me?' asked Beatrice.

'Why? Because we all deserve some kindness. I've never lived away from home before and I miss the comfort of my family. You probably do too, I expect. It's nothing at all, Beatrice.'

'I do. I feel like such a fool. This is the last straw,' she said.

'No, no, it's just an accident. It could happen to anyone,' Gladys replied.

'Why does it always seem to happen to me though?' Beatrice sobbed.

'Ssh now, come here. I haven't finished yet.'

Gladys looked for paint under her chin and inspected her cheeks closely. She dabbed under her nose and then found a new clean section of handkerchief for Beatrice's ear, which caused a tingling sensation down Beatrice's back.

'There, you're nearly done. The cold cream is helping it to come off. Back to your usual beautiful self,' Gladys said and smiled warmly at Beatrice.

Beatrice took a long deep breath and exhaled slowly. She was not used to such kindness from anyone. She looked down at her notebooks, which lay on the floor. Gladys picked them up and gave them to her.

Gladys smiled. 'Not a spot of paint.'

To her horror, Beatrice looked up and saw Captain Blunt marching across the forest towards them.

'For Christ's sake, this is no time for a hair and make-up session. This is urgent. We need more pit props before the mines run out. I've got the Ministry of Supply breathing down my neck. Get on with it!' he yelled.

Chapter 28

Keeva

20th March 1940, Symonds Yat, Forest of Dean

The room was in darkness when Keeva awoke before the alarm clock rang. She wiped the sleep from the corner of her eyes. She couldn't believe it was her last day of training at Parkend. She had lain awake for hours in the night thinking about the girls: Gladys, Rosie, Beatrice, Lily and Edith, and everything they had been through together.

In the early hours, she had ruminated about leaving the girls and moving onto a new billet on her own. Her mind fretful, she remembered Rosie tripping her up, Beatrice reclaiming her bed and reading out her private letter. She'd recalled how awful it had been when Hazel had lost her thumb, seeing the splintered bone and how much pain she'd suffered. But everything always seemed better in the morning.

Now she felt a fondness for the girls after their eight weeks on training camp. The bitter cold, dreadful food, chilblains and tough work had been exhausting. They had laughed at eating solid porridge loaf for breakfast and cried over septic blisters, endured Redrum's rage and Blunt's humiliation. But they'd also discovered her parents were pacifists and didn't seem to mind. At last, she could be herself; maybe that's what friendship was all about?

And today was their last day together on camp; she wasn't ready to say goodbye. What was going to happen next? Where would she be sent and with whom? There was talk of Scotland, which really was the other end of the earth. Beds began to creak as the girls got up. She remembered the lorries were leaving at six today. She needed to get up, but she was fagged out after such a sleepless night.

She heard Gladys begin to hum a cheerful tune, as she tried to recall where they were going today. This week was measuring, which was meant to be easier. Blunt kept referring to lighter forestry work, which was more suited to the girls. However, her lower back was aching, either from looking up at the tops of the trees all day to count them or because she was about to get her period. She must remember to take some cotton rags in her satchel, just in case.

Captain Blunt's goal was to measure a vast area of forest on their last day, over the border in Herefordshire. Keeva had looked at the map – it was past Symonds Yat rock, over ten miles away in the north of the forest. At least they had been given the luxury of transport. Nonetheless, it seemed like an impossible task to achieve in a day. She'd prefer to spend a day with the girls, because she might never see them again. They hadn't been given a single day off since they'd arrived on training camp.

The other girls chatted as they got dressed, but Keeva couldn't move.

'Come on, Keeva, up you get,' Gladys said kindly, as she crouched beside her bed.

'No! I can't today. My bed is too warm and cosy.'

'Come on, get up, sleepyhead,' said Rosie, rocking Keeva's shoulder.

A soft warm hand slipped under the covers and squeezed her arm.

'Keeva. First day together, last day together,' said Gladys.

'Ssh, I'm coming,' Keeva said and pulled the covers over her head again and snuggled down once more.

When the other girls left for breakfast and all was quiet, she peered out from under her blanket and saw Edith still sitting on her bed, pulling on her boots.

'It's late. You'll miss breakfast and your boyfriend,' Edith said.

'What?'

'Arthur.'

'He's not my boyfriend.'

'But you like him, and he likes you.'

'I thought he was more interested in Rosie.'

'No, he doesn't look at her the way he looks at you.'

'How do you know?'

'I've seen him.' Edith stood up.

'Hmm, I don't think so,'

She wondered if Edith was right. Maybe she was. She'd caught Arthur's eye three times this week and he'd smiled at her twice. She hadn't seen him chatting to Rosie at all. Her eyes closed as she imagined him in front of her, close enough to touch.

'You're smiling, Keeva. Why don't you speak to him?'

Keeva had nothing to lose. On her last day in the forest … maybe she would, she thought, as she caught her breath. She jumped out of bed and started getting dressed, making sure to wear her favourite underwear and cleanest dungarees.

'I don't want to leave yet. Do you?' asked Edith.

'Not really.'

'But I suppose there are many things I don't want to do. It's worse to be stuck somewhere you don't want to be,' said Edith.

'I agree with that.'

'However much you don't like a situation, it's better to keep moving forwards,' said Edith.

'What do you mean?'

'We all have to change, don't we? Adapt to our new lives, however much we hate the war.'

Edith had been so mercurial at times; one minute she blew hot, the next she was cold. Keeva had been convinced it was because Edith didn't like her. But now she wondered if maybe Edith had her own problems to worry about. She remembered how tearful she had been when they arrived. In the past, she'd ignored Keeva and yet now she'd waited for her and wanted to talk.

'You haven't spoken much about home. Will you try to visit your parents soon?'

She nodded and stood up. 'We must go for breakfast now,' said Edith, putting on her glasses.

There was a tightness to the way she spoke, which was unfamiliar. And even though Edith seemed distant, she realised the beautiful girl with glasses and a mole on her cheek had been a good friend after all. She'd been the only one to offer help in felling the enormous tree, and never blamed Keeva when they got in trouble. Not only was she beautiful on the outside, but she had an inner beauty too. Not easily influenced by the whims of others, she had an inner strength. Her father had often quoted Shakespeare: 'to thine own self be true'. Beneath her mystery, Edith was a true and loyal friend.

On the way downstairs to the dining hall, Keeva saw a lorry already leaving with the girls from room one. Phil, the driver, leant on the horn – toot toot – Blunt in the passenger seat next to him.

'It's all right; the second lorry is leaving in ten minutes. We're waiting for you,' said Lily.

'Thank you.'

'Here's your cheese sandwich, Keeva,' Rosie said.

'Only one? Have you eaten my other one?' She grabbed Rosie's hand.

Rosie revealed another two rolls from behind her back. 'I'll share my second one with you.' She smiled.

'There's one consolation to life in forestry,' Gladys said, 'it will make us lean and fit.'

'Lily is on six cheese sandwiches a day,' said Rosie. 'I don't think that will make her any leaner.'

'It's the only way to survive the war,' said Lily.

'Yeah, let's erect a monument to the said "cheese sandwich".' Keeva saluted to her cheese sandwich.

Rosie poked her in the ribs. 'You better get in there, before Redrum cleans breakfast away.'

She slipped into the dining hall behind Redrum and fetched her tea and porridge. Edith joined her.

'In two days we might be sent away across the country and …' Edith said.

'We might not see each other again?'

'I hope we do,' Edith replied.

'Me too. I'd like to get to know you better.'

Edith jerked her head back. 'Who do you want to be paired with after here?' she asked cautiously.

The idea of choosing who to work with had not entered Keeva's mind; she'd spent so long looking for an excuse to escape these girls. But if she could pick only one person, she'd choose Gladys. She was the first person she'd met here and was always so kind.

'I don't know.'

Edith looked at her, waiting for an answer.

'Well, if I had to choose only one person, Gladys maybe,' replied Keeva.

'Well, I would pick you,' said Edith immediately, looking down at her bowl.

'Why would you pick me?' asked Keeva. 'I thought you didn't like me or my conchie father.'

'We all have our own axe to bear, don't we?' said Edith.

Keeva smiled. 'Yes, we do.'

'Oh, I mean cross!' Edith's eyes sparkled.

Keeva would never have chosen Edith before. But now, maybe she would.

'I hope we all stay together,' Keeva quickly added, squeezing Edith's arm.

'Is there any more porridge?' Lily asked Redrum behind them.

'Too late, it's in the pig bin,' snapped Redrum.

'Come along, it's time to go.' She downed her lukewarm tea and jumped up from the table.

She linked arms with Edith and pulled Lily up from her chair. Stepping outside, she took a deep breath in the cool early morning breeze. Then, spotting Gladys, she skipped across the yard, climbed up on to the lorry tyre and pulled herself up and over the side behind her.

'Budge over.' She sat by Gladys who was singing, 'You are my sunshine …' as she often did. Yes, she'd pick Gladys to be her partner. Lily climbed up and Keeva heard the familiar rip of the cotton under her crutch.

'Oh no, not again,' she said, blushing.

'Oh, Lily, we're going to miss that sound,' said Keeva.

'What do you mean? I'm not going anywhere,' said Lily. 'We'll stay together after training, won't we?' Carefully she sat down on the lorry and crossed her legs on the side bench opposite. Keeva wondered what would happen when they'd finished their training.

'Captain Blunt said we'll be sent wherever he can find us work,' said Edith.

'What?' said Rosie.

'No guarantees we'll be working together,' Edith added.

'But we have grown so close,' Gladys said, 'I admire you all. Rosie, you are so strong.'

Sleeves pulled up, Rosie flexed her biceps.

Keeva swayed over to Rosie. 'She's a bully.'

Rosie grabbed her round the neck and nuzzled her knuckles into her ear. 'I bet you love me for teaching you how to fight, don't you?'

'Get off,' she giggled.

'Keeva, you are so determined,' said Gladys.

'Determined to bring a tree down on Captain Blunt's head.' Edith's remark was met with sniggers.

'Lily, so brave.'

Lily blushed. 'Who, me?'

'You are,' said Gladys.

'No one else would dare ask Redrum for seconds,' said Keeva.

Rosie laughed. 'Please, ma'am, can I have some more?'

'What about Beatrice then?' asked Edith.

'She's got the mathematical brain of a genius. And Edith, I've never had a more loyal friend than you.'

'Aaaw.' Lily nodded.

'I think of you all more like sisters now,' said Gladys.

'Well, I hope the girls I get billeted with won't be as touchy as you, Keeva,' added Rosie.

She pouted, remembering how her own sister, Dilly, got on her nerves at times.

'We're all very fond of you, Keeva,' said Lily.

She tingled inside and put her hand over her mouth. Today was going to be a good day.

'Speak for yourself,' added Rosie, with a broad grin.

'No, don't say that, Rosie. I can't bear to be split up from any of you,' added Edith.

Gladys was an incredible friend. She was gentle, kind and generous to others. She spoke to people with an open heart and had a knack of giving such a warm feeling inside. She wished she'd not been so suspicious of her to begin with.

The thud, thud, thud of the engine sped up. There was comfort to being on the lorry, sitting side by side, while enjoying the views. Now the lorry passed through Coleford and they rose out of the forest on the ascent towards Symonds Yat rock. The road narrowed in places and, with a toot of the horn, their lorry squeezed past another lorry in descent.

'Oh my God! Look down there,' Rosie said, hanging over the edge.

Keeva looked down at the precipitous drop, some hundred yards of sheer rock face. At the bottom lay the deep-green bed of forest and the long sweeping, blue bend of the River Severn, reflecting the cerulean sky as it curled around the valley. Keeva marvelled at the immense landscape of ancient forest and craggy outcrops.

The far-reaching views were like nothing she had ever seen before. Up high above the Symonds Yat rock, a large bird of prey shot across the sky. Banking abruptly, it dived with incredible speed down into the valley. The sun peeped over the top of the forest on the horizon and dazzled her eyes.

'Look.' She pointed at the sunrise.

'Ain't it lovely?' said Rosie. 'Blimey, girls, looks like we've arrived in heaven.'

A chilly wind rushed through the canvas tilt and through Keeva's coat, as she drew it in more tightly around her.

The lorry passed over the Severn and took a left turn along the edge of the riverbank. After five minutes, the lorry took another left turn and entered a muddy track with huge ruts. The lorry mounted the siding and lifted to a forty-five-degree angle to avoid a great hole.

'Flippin'' ek! Hang on!' cried Rosie.

The lorry lurched and the suspension creaked as they drove around huge bowls of mud.

'It's like being at the fairground,' she added.

The lorry drove beneath the trees, up a steep hill, and Keeva saw a handwritten sign: 'Ashes Lane leading to Sawpits Lane'.

As soon as they pulled up, Captain Blunt hurried the girls off the lorry and dispatched them in pairs with groups of men, laden with cross-cut saws and axes, into the forest. They were to measure felled timber as the men worked through the stands of trees. Keeva watched the number of girls dwindle. In physical exercise at school, she didn't like being left till last. Some girls were being sent to work alone, so she stepped closer to Gladys.

'Gladys, I want you and … urm, Keeva to measure standing timber in this triangle of Sawpits Lane,' Blunt said, handing her a map and stabbing the location with his chubby forefinger.

Gladys's cold hands grabbed onto her arm and she jumped up and down. 'I'm so glad I'm with you.'

They gained their bearings and followed the footpath on the map, crossed into the forest, over the stile and found the triangle area for measuring.

'Do you want to measure the trees to begin with and I'll make notes and then we can swap?' asked Gladys.

'Of course,' Keeva replied.

Gladys got out her old worn notebook and pencil from her coat pocket, as Keeva looked down for her satchel.

'Oh Jesus, what was that?' The noise came from behind her.

'What?'

'I thought I heard a whining sound,' she looked up.

'Trees creaking on the wind probably,' said Gladys.

'Damn—' she slapped her hips '—I didn't bring the satchel and measuring tape. I left it on the lorry.'

'Oh no! Will the lorry still be there?' asked Gladys.

'I don't know. I'll go back.'

'Here, take the map. I don't want you getting lost,' said Gladys.

'Are you sure? No, come with me.'

'It's not like anything is going to happen,' said Gladys.

'OK. I'll be quick. I'll be back soon.'

She grabbed the map and, as she ran back down the forest path, she could still hear Gladys singing. She was always happy, even when skies were gloomy. She jumped over the stile and checked the map to see which way they had come. The noise came again. This time more loudly, like a plane with a rattling engine. All she could see were trees and blue sky above. She turned back down the path to the lorries. Catching her breath with relief, she saw her khaki satchel was there on the floor under her seat. She flipped it open to check her quarter girth measure was inside with the paint and other things she needed.

The eerie wailing sound was now above her. She looked up to see the black silhouette of a plane as it passed low overhead. She heard a metal clunk, and a screeching noise as the plane disappeared. An ear-wrenching cracking sound followed, like trees being ripped apart. Keeva lost her balance, looking up desperately to the treetops swaying on the breeze. Next, the thunder of a jet engine nearby grew louder and louder. A flash of yellow through the trees and Keeva felt herself dragged by a powerful wind. Everything stopped. There was silence before a huge blast shook the woods and the windscreen exploded with a bang.

As if weightless, in slow motion she lifted off her feet, her breath sucked from her lungs through her eardrums. The explosion pummelled her back and she landed on her stomach against the hard flat bed of the lorry. Winded. A severe pain gripped Keeva's chest. The boom echoed through the valley and shook the lorry. Was she going to die? Woodsmoke met her nostrils. A blanket of smoke came across the road and engulfed her where she lay.

Stunned, Keeva lay still, as a black vignette closed in. Her view of the world disappeared to darkness. She told herself to lay dead in a place where there was no sensory stimulus to stir her. Then there was nothing.

A moment later, Keeva involuntarily rasped for breath, jolting back to life, her ears ringing. She tried to make sense of the situation but couldn't see what was happening. Adrenalin rushed through her body as she groaned for air. She wriggled her fingers and toes. Quick, shallow breath. She looked down at her body and saw she was all right. Everything was going to be all right, she repeated over and over.

Pulse racing, her body vibrating with energy. She became aware that a heat-haze consumed the forest and lorries around her. There was a fire. What on earth had happened? She saw the male fellers with bodies hunched, running for cover. She hung on to the side of the lorry. Were they under attack? Had the Germans come for them? Her heart pounded against her breastbone and in her head.

Dense black smoke billowed from the forest and blew on the wind towards her. She looked about her, but it was like a jigsaw falling apart. She couldn't make sense of what she saw as fire flickered through the trees, leaping and jumping. Her skin prickled all over.

Had a plane crashed, or had it been a bomb? She couldn't breathe as the terror leapt into her throat. Were more planes coming? Pushing herself up. Where were the men? She dragged herself over the side of the lorry, thinking she could hide beneath, but her legs were like jelly, as she crawled underneath the flatbed. She lodged herself in a ball behind the wheel arch. Mud, thick grease and oil scraped across her coat and the metal edge cut into her back. She stayed there shaking uncontrollably, biting her collar.

What if the Germans had landed and were about to rush in with rifles? Keeva could not bear to stay, waiting to be captured.

She wanted to run, run far away. But what about the girls? Gladys, Rosie, Edith or Lily … What if they were hurt? What about Arthur? Where was he and all the rest?

The smoke and explosion seemed to come from Sawpits Lane, where she and Gladys had been starting work. She had almost forgotten their task to measure the woods. Gladys was still there, she remembered with a shiver. Would she be all right? She saw Captain Blunt approach.

'Daylight raid?' someone shouted.

'Are we being attacked?' asked another feller as he ran and dived for cover under a lorry.

Keeva ducked down again and heard Blunt say: 'It's where two of the girls were working.'

At once men ran down the path where she had come from. Gladys! What about Gladys? Keeva wriggled out from under the lorry, stumbling. She brushed past Blunt, legs shaking with adrenalin, and started running after the men, down the path towards the smoke.

Another explosion and Keeva fell to the ground, splintered branches landing round her. A huge blast rippled through the forest, shaking the trees close to her. Keeva fell to the path as a large tree came hurtling towards her. The ground shook as it crashed down to the ground a few feet from her; one of the big beech trees, floored. Great limbs snapped and cracked apart as they crumpled into the ground. So close to her, she could have been impaled. She tossed her head wildly to take in the swaying trees and destruction around her. She was in terrible danger; she could have been killed. How could she escape? Each deafening crash slowed down as if everything was stretched in time. Shattered images crawled through her mind, her sister Dilly and her mother. Winded by the fall, a strange, depleted noise ran through her lungs like she was dying. It hurt.

Someone shouted. Her ears deafened by the explosion, she could not make out what they said. Would the blast happen again? Was a bomb or an ammunition dump about to explode? Had the blast come from where she'd left Gladys?

Plumes of dark grey smoke billowed up around her. Keeva heard her name. Some men emerged on the path in front of her. They held up their hands and one grabbed Keeva's arm as she tried to run through them.

'Get your hands off me,' she said.

He pulled her back and Keeva pushed back against him.

'Gladys, I've got to find Gladys. She's waiting for me,' she shouted, wrestling him off her. He wouldn't let her go. She felt her wrist burning as the man tightened his grip. She looked up and saw that it was Arthur. Eyes red from smoke, a shine of sweat across his brow and dirt smeared across his cheek.

'It's too dangerous,' he said.

She wrenched her arms free and tried to push past another man, but Arthur caught her again.

'Get off me.'

'It's Gladys,' she rushed.

'Come on, love. There's nothing you can do,' an older man with a beard said.

'We need to find her!' Keeva screamed.

Chapter 29

'Get off me!' Keeva yelled.

She fought free of Arthur's grasp and ran past the other men towards the place where she had last seen Gladys. Only she knew where Gladys was, and she would be quickest to find her. The map. She fumbled for it in her pocket but, as she pulled it out, she felt time running on and didn't want to waste any by stopping to look.

'Gladys!' Smoke in her eyes, burning her throat, clogging up her lungs. 'Gladys!'

Shouting. Girls' voices shouting from somewhere. The heat-haze scorched Keeva's face, and her throat strained to pull in air. She had to find her, get her out, help her through the smoke to safety. They would laugh after all of this. She would find her with streaks of black ash upon her face. They'd look at each other, laugh and hug; that's what they would do.

The smoke was acrid. She tried to spit to get rid of the taste, her tongue dry. She coughed to stop it from going into her lungs. She could barely see. A dreadful groaning and cracking sounded. Wildly she flung her arms over her head and ducked down. A tree falling … she knew that sound. A dull thud followed, close by.

'Gladys!'

She covered her mouth with her hand. Her eyes began to water and sting. She imagined Gladys, as if trying to conjure her up from the smoke. Heart pounding. Unable to see, she lost all sense of direction. She didn't remember where she had left Gladys. No pathway now, only bracken and rough ground beneath her feet. The searing heat of the flames and destruction all around her. She must find her.

'Gladys, Gladys, where are you?'

'Keeva. Come back.'

Was that Arthur?

Barely able to speak. Nauseous. Nothing looked the same as when Gladys had been sitting on a log, tying her laces and singing. A firestorm burned the trees and consumed bushes, an intense heat, as she inched her way forwards. She must be near her.

'Gladys.'

Her voice barely sounded. Perhaps she could not hear after the explosion. The fire devoured fence posts, engulfed hedgerows, rushed towards her. The infernal beast breathed on the forest wind, one second it sucked air back, the next it torched forwards. Clouds of smoke formed a thick smog.

'Gladys, where are …' Keeva tried to shout.

The glare was so intense it pricked her eyes. Flames twenty foot high perished the thought that they could be extinguished. Petrol or diesel hung in the air. Ashes were falling like tiny white fairies around her. Was Gladys nearer to the explosion? Keeva wheezed, covering her mouth with her sleeve to mask the fumes.

Overwhelmed by heat, she turned and tripped. Falling forwards, she hit her knee and cheek on something hard, jerking her neck. In pain, she crawled along. She imagined the fire engulfing her and looked over her shoulder. The blaze wasn't far behind, she would be burnt to death.

'Get up,' she told herself.

The wetness on her cheek covered her fingers with blood. From far away she heard a voice call her name. Where did it come from? Was it Gladys? Legs trembling, she tried to stand. She felt so weak, her energy sapped.

'Keeva,' she heard again.

'Help me,' cried Keeva.

Maybe Gladys had found the others and Keeva was the only

one left out in this blaze. She would suffocate if she didn't get out of here soon. The inferno seemed to be getting closer still. She no longer knew which way was out. There was shouting all around her. All she could think of was Gladys. She was singing. She tried to move towards the soft, clear voice, but all she could hear was crackling and hissing as branches burst alight.

In the smoke, Keeva smelt something horrible, the unmistakable fetid smell of sizzling hair, as bad as rotten eggs.

'Help,' she whispered, 'Gladys where are you?'

She tasted vomit in her throat.

'My dearest friend, where are you?' whispered Keeva.

The smell was gut-wrenching, disgusting. It hurt. Keeva crawled across the bracken and found the hard earth and stones of the path. Her breath came shallow. The faint word 'help' barely left her lips. She dug deeper inside herself, pushed herself to keep going. Slowly she crawled through the mud. Fresh air reached her lips.

She found a puddle and scooped water into her mouth. Gritty, but moisture for her tongue once more. Cool water against her face as she lay down. The water seeped into her clothes and she imagined the cool refreshing feeling of going swimming. Plunging down into pools of deep water, her skin soaking in the water like a sponge.

'Keeva!'

She felt herself being dragged up off the ground, lifted up and away from the smoke. She was carried as if in a dream, flying down forest pathways. Her chest heaved as she tried to breathe again. An arm around her back, holding her up as her legs gave way. She collapsed down by the side of the lorry and vomited on some boots. Someone would find Gladys. They would find her and they would all be back together again soon.

She awoke on the lorry, laid across the benches. Uncomfortable, the rocking motion made her retch and she was sick once again. She felt a hand on her shoulder, looked up and saw Rosie's dirty face, not smiling. Rosie rubbed her back. Edith passed her water and she took a sip. No one spoke. She looked around for Gladys. Where was she? Maybe she was on the other lorry with Captain Blunt.

'Where's Gladys?' she asked Edith.

Edith shook her head.

Keeva tried to sit up but her stomach muscles were too sore against the motion of the lorry. Exhausted, she lay back down. She could barely move, her body a dead weight. She thought of happy Gladys, always smiling. Her truest friend here, Gladys who loved her life in the forest. She couldn't wait to see her back at the forestry school. Safe in the bed next to her. Why had this had to happen on their last day?

She looked around. Edith started to cry and Lily lay her arm over her shoulders. Beatrice looked haunted. The smell, the raging fire, the explosion …

*

Arm in arm with Rosie when they got back to the camp, Keeva pulled herself up the stairs to their room. Every bone in her body ached. Keeva crawled onto her bed, curled up under the blanket and rocked herself back and forth. So cold, she couldn't stop shivering. Her cheek hurt when she touched it and her knee too. Every part of her, even the top of her head, felt scalded by the searing heat. But inside she was cold, so cold.

'Keeva, dear,' she heard a voice say by her bed. Missus Potter peered under her blanket.

'I've brought you up some tea with sugar and some biscuits, to help with the shock. You must drink and eat,' she said.

A while later, as if she had only just heard the instruction, she sat up on her bed and drank the tea, ate the biscuits, drank more tea, lay down again and fell asleep.

She did not know how many hours had passed when she woke up to the comforting sound of the girls' voices whispering. The cotton pillowcase peeled the congealed blood from her cheek. She lay back down and closed her eyes again, feeling sore. Lying in bed, semi-conscious, she stayed under her covers and listened, not wanting the world to carry on. She wanted the world to stand still so she didn't have to relive what had happened in the forest.

'It was only yesterday Gladys and I were out in the woods together,' came a voice. 'We made such a great team with our notebooks and measuring tapes. She said how much she loved the citrus smell of the pine woods and, and … she told me I was beautiful.' Beatrice began to sob.

Within her mind, Gladys smiled at Keeva and squeezed her hand. She could see the red golden glow of the sunset between the trees behind Gladys out in the forest. The end of another day in the forest gave a soft golden glow to her face and lit up her aqua-blue eyes.

'Shh. Let's try not to wake her. I'm not sure that she knows,' whispered Edith.

She turned over, escaping into dreams.

Chapter 30

Forestry School, Parkend, Forest of Dean

Keeva lay in bed still in her jodhpurs and jumper under the blanket, getting hot. Her cheese roll, which had been packed for lunch in her bag, was unwrapped and sat on a plate on the table beside her bed. She wasn't hungry. She had a faint recollection of a doctor asking her questions, prodding her and looking in her ears and eyes with a light.

The light of the fire surged towards her and her body convulsed as she drew her breath. Her heart started racing. Her body ached so much, her stomach muscles felt like splinters inside, she couldn't sit up or attempt to speak, her tongue was so dry. The other girls whispered and she listened intently.

'She's dreaming again,' a voice said.

She worried she was in trouble for leaving Gladys alone in the forest.

'When I was so homesick just after we arrived, she came and sat with me downstairs like she knew,' Edith said in a hushed tone. 'We were in the dining hall and Gladys held my hand and said, "It's normal to miss those you love." Honestly, I'll never forget her.'

Gladys was the first person she had met at the Forest of Dean, the day she'd run away from home. Gladys had stood in the snow in twilight at Norchard Station. Seeing Gladys in her large duffle coat and beige jodhpurs, another person in the WLA uniform for the first time, had been such a relief. Her smiling face had made Keeva feel like everything was going to be all right that day. She'd needed Gladys then.

'We had such a laugh yesterday measuring the trees,' Rosie said, but her voice conveyed no laughter, only sadness. 'We threw our arms around the trees, with the girth tape in hand and caught it behind. I threw my leg around it an' all and gave that tree a good smooch. She laughed so much when Captain Blunt popped up.'

Somebody sniffed and blew their nose. Keeva touched her cheek again; it was swollen. She smelled smoke on her jumper and her knee was sore to touch. She heard Beatrice's voice again, different, whimpering.

'I stood in the middle of the forest and wrote down the measurements Gladys called out, sixteen and a quarter, seventeen and a half. She said, "It sounds like I know just what I'm doing." Every word so precious now,' added Beatrice.

Keeva heard the sound of paper, as though the leaves of a book were being turned. Keeva remembered that second evening when she chatted with Gladys about her fiancé, Bernie, and how she was waiting till the end of the war, when they could marry. She spoke of how much she loved him. Keeva hoped she was not hurt like Hazel. She imagined having tea with her downstairs.

'How many times she saved an extra bit of bread and cheese for me,' Lily said. 'It really helped me to get through the afternoon hunger when I was dog-tired. I'm going to miss her.'

'It's so very sad. Why would they drop a bomb there?' asked Edith.

'Maybe the Germans know what we are doing here and how important it is to the war. They could put a stop to timber production,' said Beatrice.

Keeva couldn't bear to listen any longer. What bomb? Why were they talking about Gladys like that? Had she gone home or was she injured and in hospital? She pulled back her blanket and pushed unsteadily up on her elbow, muscles tearing inside. She winced. The girls were sitting on the end of Edith and Lily's beds in a huddle.

'What on earth are you talking about? What bomb?' she said, with a creeping dread.

They stared at her.

'Oh my God, Keeva, are you all right?' asked Rosie.

'Where's Gladys?' asked Keeva.

The girls all looked at each other awkwardly. She'd seen girls do this to her before when they talked behind her back. But she wasn't being excluded this time, or being picked on. They were protecting her. She could trust them.

'Do you know what has happened?' Beatrice asked quietly.

'What … ?' replied Keeva. 'To Gladys?'

Beatrice fidgeted uncomfortably; she swallowed hard and her brow wrinkled as if she were about to cry. Rosie swept over to sit on Keeva's bed.

'Keeva,' said Rosie gently.

'Did they find Gladys?' Keeva asked, panicking.

She tried to fill the gaping hole of foreboding. She couldn't bear to imagine the worst. The others crept over to her bedside. A fog of pain ached inside her head. Rosie looked up to Edith, who took Keeva's hand. Edith gently stroked her.

'Keeva, Gladys was caught in the explosion,' said Edith.

Keeva knew.

'I'm sorry, Keeva. It's true,' said Rosie, wrapping her arms around her.

'But I was with her. We were meant to be together.' Keeva breathed heavily.

A tear rolled from Rosie's cheek.

'Is she … ?' said Keeva.

'Someone said she's died, Keeva,' said Edith quietly.

'No, no, I should have stayed with her!' Keeva pulled at her shirt, and started shaking.

'You would have died too,' said Lily.

'She can't be dead. It's my fault. I left her. If only she'd come with me.'

'No, Keeva, it wasn't your fault,' said Beatrice. 'She died in the fire.'

'How could it be your fault?' said Edith.

'I had a bad feeling when I went back to get the satchel. I'd left it on the lorry,' she said, each moment vivid in her mind.

'Thank the Lord you did, otherwise it could have been you too,' said Lily.

'If only Gladys had come back with me.'

Waves of fear burnt through Keeva. If only she'd done this or said that. Edith squeezed her hand. Lily sat at her feet looking up with her large brown eyes. Beatrice fetched a glass of water and held it out to her.

'If only I had insisted that she came with me.' She sipped the water. 'She was singing, and I left her there. Tell me, it's not true.'

She remembered how kind Gladys had been; it made hot tears swell in her eyes. She was the first friend she'd had since everyone turned against her back at home. She had felt the warmth of a friend by her side, someone she could confide in and someone who wouldn't judge her. A true friend who she had only just begun to appreciate and trust.

'No, she can't be gone.' She rubbed her arms absently.

'It was an inferno,' said Rosie. 'There was nothing anyone could do.'

'A huge area of the forest has been destroyed,' added Beatrice.

'Do you think it was a bomb that started it?' Edith sat forwards on the bed and reached for Keeva's hand.

'Do you think it could have been a German raid? What if it happens again? I don't feel safe here any more, I'm frightened.' Lily hugged herself.

'It must have been a German attack, what else could it have been?' asked Rosie.

'But I haven't heard of bombing in Britain yet. And why here?' added Edith.

Beatrice frowned. 'Maybe they were given the wrong intelligence, it was a mistake, or they were aiming for that ammunition dump.'

Keeva remembered hearing the whining noise. Now she remembered seeing a plane low above the trees. The black underside of a double engine plane was familiar to her.

'But it was a British plane,' she said.

'Could you be mistaken?' quizzed Beatrice.

Didn't they believe her? They all exchanged glances, like she was confused. Maybe they were right.

'No, it couldn't be,' said Lily.

'What makes you think it was a British plane?' Rosie asked gently.

'I heard someone say. One of the fellers. But I heard this noise and saw the plane too, flying so low and making an awful noise. I looked up and saw twin engines, black underneath.'

'That could be any aircraft,' said Beatrice.

'No, because it had that red, white and blue target insignia on the body,' said Keeva.

'Are you sure?' asked Beatrice.

'Yes, I think so. Do you think I'll be in trouble, for saying so?' asked Keeva.

'No, of course not. I'm just trying to work out what happened,' mused Beatrice.

'I heard the wailing sound. But I didn't see a plane,' said Lily.

'But if it was British, it couldn't be a bomb. Did it crash?' asked Edith.

'If a whole plane crashed in the forest, we'll soon find out,'

Rosie said.

Lily was still hugging herself. 'What about Gladys? Did they find her … her body?'

Keeva felt sick again. 'Oh no, oh no! Such a useless waste of life.' She could hardly breathe as she remembered Gladys was going to be married to her fiancé Bernie.

'She said she was going to wait for her fiancé until after the war. You know how they were so in love? They'd already spoken about where they'd marry. A church near the top of a hill with a beautiful view of the sunsets. She said she loved it up there,' Keeva said softly.

'Maybe she will always be looking over us,' Lily said. 'Her spirit will always be here. She might visit Church Hill here or just enjoy the view from Symonds Yat.'

'I can't think of a better place to be,' added Keeva.

'I can. Alive. That's where I'd prefer to be,' said Rosie.

'What will they tell Gladys's parents? Oh Jesus,' said Keeva as her thoughts ran on.

'What is it?' Beatrice asked.

'Gladys had already lost her younger brother in a road accident when he was eleven. He was run over,' said Keeva.

'It's wretched!' said Beatrice.

'Oh gawd,' said Rosie.

'Her elder brothers have been conscripted too. Her mother was fraught with worry about her sons, but not about Gladys. She thought she'd be safe out in the forests, under the trees out in the countryside. She thought that she'd be safe.'

Keeva could smell the smoke from the fire again on her hair and clothes. She could not bear the memory of the disgusting burning smell in the forest. She ripped her jumper off as the other girls looked confused.

'Help me get this off. I can't stand the smell. I need to change out of these clothes. I can't bear it.'

Missus Potter appeared at the door. 'Captain Blunt would like to see you all in the dining hall, girls.'

'Gawd, sorry, Keeva, you'll have to wait,' said Rosie.

Beatrice rushed to her bed, returning with a silk scarf, which was scented with lavender perfume, and gave it to her.

She descended the stairs, with the scarf around her shoulders, and the other girls forming a protecting flank around her. 'This is not the way I expected it to end here in the Forest of Dean,' she said.

In the dining hall, she could see that girls had been crying. She tried not to stare but it was as though, by searching their faces, she was trying to find an answer. She could not cry. An intolerable time passed before all the girls squeezed into the dining hall.

Captain Blunt tapped a spoon against a glass and waited for them to quieten. He seemed no longer the same woodcock-shaped man they were used to seeing. His shoulders slumped, his size diminished, and he clenched his hands over and over again.

'Good afternoon, girls. It is a very sombre occasion for which we find ourselves gathered today.'

He paused and stroked his chin with his hand, covering his mouth briefly. The silence was frightening and Keeva held her breath, waiting for him to speak.

'I imagine you must have all heard the very sad news about Gladys. I'm very sorry to confirm she passed away today.'

The room bustled with fractious movements, gasps and groans. Distracted from Blunt, Keeva looked aghast at the collective reaction unfolding around her. Girls sobbed, hysteria bubbling below the surface. She gripped the table in front of her to steady herself.

'There will be a full investigation forthwith and we will let you know more when we are informed. We regret that sometimes accidents are unavoidable during wartime.'

Beatrice raised her hand. 'But do we know whether it was a bomb, sir? Whether it was a German raid, which means we are under attack?'

Captain Blunt raised his hand: 'We must not speculate. We do not have any further information at this point. We are at a very sensitive stage of the war; it would be wholly inappropriate to say what might have passed, when we do not have conclusive evidence.'

'What do we say to our families?' asked Lily. 'I want to write to Mother. But what should I tell her?'

Blunt held up his hand for quiet. 'The authorities would not want this incident talked about if it could affect the morale of the nation. For security reasons, you must say nothing about it. Do you understand?'

'Oh flippin''ell,' said Rosie, 'I ain't going to tell my parents; they'd make me come home. Anyway, what's the point in worrying them? They won't understand.'

'Quite so. This must be something we bear with a heavy heart and keep to ourselves,' added Blunt hoarsely.

Feet shuffled. Keeva curled her fingers into fists. Keep it to themselves? First Hazel, now Gladys … Foreboding filled the air in the dining hall. Bad luck comes in threes … could things get any worse?

Beatrice raised her hand again and Blunt shook his head.

'But some girls said they saw a British plane,' she said, her voice trailing off.

Keeva felt stupid for saying it was British. She must have been mistaken. What good would it do to suggest such a thing at a time like this? Rosie's eyes were full of tears. Lily hung on to Edith, who was sobbing. Keeva still could not believe anything she'd seen. Surely at any moment Gladys would walk into the dining hall and ask what they were doing.

Chairs scraped across the floor as everyone stood up. Keeva closed her eyes but couldn't keep her balance. She grabbed on to the table, then felt an arm around her shoulders. She opened her eyes to see Beatrice next to her. They stood together, all except for Gladys. God rest her soul, dear sweet Gladys. May she rest in peace.

Captain Blunt continued, 'Thank the Lord that the rest of you were spared. Her parents have been informed. Now we will hold a minute of silence for Gladys.'

Chapter 31

15th December 1939, The Ram Inn, West Firle, Sussex

The night was intensely black outside, after the lights of the pub. The frosty grass of the pub garden and the tarmac of the village road helped her find her way. Edward was close behind.

'Keeva, wait.'

'Leave me alone.'

She stomped past the cold black houses.

'It's my parents, they don't want me to see you any more.'

Keeva spun around. 'Why not?'

'You know why, Keeva.'

'I can't believe you!' shouted Keeva. 'When were you going to tell me?'

'I'm telling you now, aren't I?'

'And that's all right? To ditch me and then spend the evening with your friends? Letting me look like a fool in front of them?'

'I forgot.'

Keeva heard an engine start up by the pub; dazzled by the head lamps, she couldn't see a thing. The car turned past her and slunk away.

'There's another thing, something you won't like,' he slurred.

'I don't want to know.'

'I'm—'

'No, I'm not listening.' She put her fingers in her ears and sang, 'La, la, la, la.'

'—signing up.'

'You what?'

'It's what all the lads are doing.' He caught her arm. 'Keeva.'

His breath hung on the freezing air and she saw the face she had so adored in the moonlight: his long lashes, shining eyes, sprinkle of freckles and the way his dimpled chin and angular nose both drew her eyes to gaze upon his full lips.

'All the lads are signing up? Can't you think for yourself?'

'I want to fight for my country. I can't have a girlfriend that doesn't understand that, whose father is a conchie. Keeva, I don't need all this drama. My mind's made up.'

'I thought you liked me.'

'Mary told me you'd try to make a scene. Why are you always so difficult? You make the girls feel awkward. Why don't you just fit in? Look, I'm going now. Keeva, look after yourself. Think about what I said.'

Edward took one last look at her before meandering back down the street to the pub. Keeva clung to the cold, hard wall. First the local farmhands had turned on her, then the schoolteachers and her friends; the thoughts screamed inside her head. And now Edward. She'd thought she could rely on him. He said he might join the Peace Pledge Union; that's why she liked him, she thought he was different. But he was just like everyone else. She had no one left, no one who cared enough to stick by her and her family. She searched in the darkness for Edward, but he had gone.

She stood alone, chilled, with a pain in her throat, suddenly aware of the graveyard at the end of the long, dark hedge. Shakily she began her walk home, a numbness stealing over her. She was such an idiot! Wearing this stupid dress. Believing Edward was different.

Her eyes began to prickle with tears; she groaned, the pain channelling through her. She and Ed used to play a game together, where they could see how long they could walk down the road with their eyes shut. They used to laugh and hold onto each other's hands, walk the other into hedges, trip each other up, and once he'd stopped her suddenly and kissed her on the lips. It had been so sweet. Now it made her stomach churn.

The gravel track crunched under her boots as she paced along the mile of dark road. She knew that there were fields that rose steeply to the Downs behind the tall hedgerows. She reached out, trailing her hand along the hedgerow. The leaves and twigs and branches whipping against her hand was strangely comforting. She had first reached her hand out like this when she was four years old, facing her walk to school alone, teased once she'd got there.

And the teasing hadn't stopped. They had given her white feathers and surrounded her, clucking and flapping their elbows. Chicken! Keeva is a chicken. Once they'd pushed her over. Her father had always taught her to walk away and to defend herself with words. So, instead of fighting, she'd called them silly buggers. When the teachers had heard, it was she who'd got in trouble for swearing, not them. The teachers had had it in for her, had always picked on her, disapproving of her parents and saying they were ridiculous for sending her sister, Dilly, to dance school.

She saw a light flicker ahead; a figure walked towards her, quickly closing the gap between them. She knew this sight. Her father holding a small candle: coming to find her again when she least expected him to.

'What are you doing? I've told you not to come,' she said, swallowing down how pleased she was to see him, as the tears rolled like hot coals over her cheeks and blurred her view.

'I was worried about you.'

'Da? You know I can walk home alone,' she said, desperate to give him a hug.

'It's nearly Christmas and I wanted to make sure you were safe.'

'Yes, but a bit late to look out for me now, conchie,' she said.

His brow furrowed and he turned away.

'I'm still your father, or doesn't that mean anything to you anymore? You are sixteen, Kiki, and too young for pubs, seventeen-year-old boyfriends and staying out all night. You know I want you to have a normal life, go out like your friends. But I worry.'

'Normal! We've never had a normal life and thanks to you I don't have any friends. And you don't have to worry about the boyfriend. Thanks to you, he's called things off between us.'

'I'm so sorry, Kiki.'

'It's all your fault. I hate you!'

She saw tears in her father's eyes in the light of the candle, before he blew it out and tried to put his arm around her shoulders. She pushed him away. In the distance, a car engine throttled through the village. She glanced back to see dipped headlamps round the bend in the road; vehicles often used the track as a turning circle.

The car continued up the track behind them. As it approached, her and her father's long leggy shadows fled across the road as they stepped to the side. They flattened themselves into the hedge, as the car passed by quickly and stopped abruptly in front of them.

'Oh no, Da!' Keeva grabbed onto her father's sleeve.

The doors opened and four shadowy figures burst into the darkness like a pack of dogs full of limbs and anger.

'Come on, lads!'

Not again! Keeva's head was thumping, but this time her father didn't stop to reason with them.

'Quickly, Keeva,' her father whispered, grabbed her hand tightly and pulled her sharply towards the gap in the hedge by the trees where an overgrown footpath led to their back garden. She held on tightly to her father's hand.

'If something happens to me, run home and bolt the door,' he said, breaking into a run.

'Coward! That's him,' the lads barked.

She looked back and saw them eat up the road between them.

'Don't stop,' he panted.

She felt a shock of sharp pain on her back, couldn't stop herself and screamed. A stone had hit her. She spun around in terror, to see the dark chasing figures through the hedge, just behind them. Her breathing erratic, heart pounding in her ears, she ran as fast as she could.

'Nazi lover!'

They ran down the scrubby pathway, the one they had walked a thousand times, weaving between trees, stumbling and tripping, struggling for breath. Keeva could hear the lads were gaining on them. She knew her Da was behind and as she looked back, she saw the stockiest lad hurl himself on her father's back, tackling him to the ground. The house was just yards away. Keeva froze, horrified as the other lads landed kicks and punches. Her father was grunting and groaning. They swore at him, calling him a bastard.

Sensing Keeva, the stocky lad looked up. 'Get her!'

With a jolt, she fled to the house, fumbling with the latch, which seemed so awkward and slow in her panic. The lads raced towards her as she burst through the door, slamming it behind her and pulling the bolt across.

'Mother, Mother!' Keeva screamed, and unusually her mother came running.

'Da! They've got him. You've got to stop them; they're going to kill him!'

Every second lasted too long. Her mother went to the sideboard, which she had painted long ago with blue and orange ellipses and diagonals, and pulled out the drawer and a notebook. Keeva watched her mother write down 'time – it was late'. They didn't own a clock as her parents preferred to follow the natural rhythms of the sun rather than being a slave to the hours and minutes of the clock face.

Keeva ran to the window and watched as the four lads beat her father. She glanced back at her mother, who stood clutching her pencil and notebook.

'Mother, what are you doing?'

'What can I do?' Her mother shrugged.

'Stop them!'

She crouched beneath the window to watch, while being well-hidden. The blows subsided and she counted three of the lads as they swaggered off down the path to where the car awaited. Where was the stocky one? She heard a scraping noise on the front door that seemed to fill the room. Then she let out her breath as she watched the last lad walk away from the house, tugging at his belt. The car doors slammed shut and she listened as the engine accelerated away. Silence. Then the soft moaning of the wind. Keeva ran to the door, slid the bolt, lifted the too-slow latch and opened the door to a foul, meaty smell of shit smeared across the doorstep.

Jumping over, she ran to her father, who lay curled on his side, motionless, arms covering his head. She knelt by his side.

'Oh my God. Da, Da, it's Keeva, Da, everything is going to be all right. They're gone.'

He tried to push himself up slowly, feeling his ribs. He groaned as he knelt, rose to his feet and then lurched towards the house. She pulled gently under his arm to help him to walk, thinking how often she had relied on him for comfort. Mother was waiting silently by the door, looking deathly white.

Keeva helped her father to the kitchen and sat him down. Oh my God, Da. She couldn't look at his grazed and bleeding face. One eye was swelling, and half-closed. A muddy footprint showed on his cheek and blood dripped from an open wound on his eyebrow, studded with grit and small stones. His mouth was lopsided with lips already twice their normal size. His hair was matted and wet-looking. He barely moved.

She glanced at her mother angrily. Why couldn't she even look after her husband in a crisis? All she cared about was reading Roman history and Greek tragedy. She had read so much she had become a tragedy herself.

'Go and make some tea, Keeva.' There was an edge to her mother's voice. 'With lots of sugar.'

Keeva poured water from the kettle into a bowl and laid it on the table in front of her father with the cleanest cloth she could find. With the dirty dish cloth, she wiped a hawk of saliva off his arm.

Sweet tea brewed in the large brown teapot as she put the green and fawn crochet tea cosy on top. Her hands started shaking as she placed the tea strainer on the table and fetched the milk from the windowsill, watching her parents. Her mother sat and poured the tea silently, her eyes like dark splinters in the light of the oil lamps.

Her father held the cloth to his face. Few words passed between them as Keeva shivered and started to feel bitterly cold. She wondered whether she recognised the lads outside as the ones in the pub, the same ones that were outside the toilets – Edward's friends. He had mentioned one of their fathers owned a motorcar for a taxi business. Her stomach churned and her head ached.

'Your father and I are going to bed now, Keeva; I suggest you do the same.'

Her father lumbered awkwardly out of the kitchen door, with her mother, and crossed the hallway to their bedroom; Keeva was left alone. The fire was dead now.

She ached with cold as she climbed on to her camp bed, still in her mother's stupid dress. She pulled it off and tugged on her nightshirt. She reached for an old, grey army coat and blanket and lifted it over her as she lay down and pulled up her knees and feet under it. The bedding felt dank and heavy. Her teeth began to chatter.

She lay awake, running through everything over and over: Edward being late, the lads in the pub, how she herself had reacted, Edward walking away from her. Was it all her fault for going out to The Ram Inn? Why would anyone attack her father so viciously? He was a good man.

Did she make her friends feel awkward? Some friends they turned out to be. And were Edward's any better? Did he know that his friends had followed her? Beaten up her Da? She couldn't trust anyone. She pictured her father's beaten and swollen face and felt afraid. She could trust her father. He had protected her by taking the beating. She heard a noise outside and jumped. What if they were back? She lay still, listened to her heart beating against the mattress as she tried not to make a sound.

Eyes heavy and gritty, Keeva realised that it was light. How had she managed to fall asleep? And there it was again, the sinking dread as she remembered the night before. She tried to crowd out her feelings by moving, getting up, slipping her arms into the great coat and knocking on her parents' bedroom door.

'Da.' She needed to say sorry, to tell him she didn't hate him. She needed him to be all right, to know she loved him.

'Don't come in!' Her mother's voice was harsh. 'Your father needs to sleep. Go away!'

Keeva stumbled back from the door. Keep busy she told herself. Da just needs more sleep. She made herself breakfast. Mushrooms again, from the never-ending crop. She mopped up the brown liquor with a crusty piece of bread, suddenly ravenous, and sipped thirstily at a cup of tea. The hot sweetness of the steaming tea was comforting. She looked around the kitchen. Ice on the inside of the window, blood-stained cloths across the back of the chair. Bracing herself, Keeva opened the door, saw the brown smeared step and went to fetch a bucket of water. She swilled and loosened the muck with the broom and washed it down again, several times over, until it was clean once more. Outside in the cold morning air, Keeva walked down the pathway to clear her nostrils from the smell of shit.

She could not forget seeing her father's battered face and matted hair, eyes swollen shut. There on the pathway was a dark-red patch of his blood, soaked into the earth. She saw a shiny white stone and, reaching down to pick it up, realised it was his tooth. As she turned to go back to the house, tooth in hand, she saw a police car go by, through the trees, to the front of their house. They might want to take down a statement. But it had been dark. How could she have recognised the lads, except for the stocky one? She ran through the house with anticipation and opened the front door.

'Is your father in, Keeva?'

'Yes, of course. Are you here about the assault?' she asked.

'Assault?' the officer repeated and looked at his colleague.

'We're sorry, Keeva, it's not about that. Could you get your father please?'

If it's not about that, why are they here? She went to her parents' room and knocked again.

'Keeva, I've told you it's too early. Go away.'

'Mother, the police are here. They want to talk to Father.'

She heard movement from behind the door.

'Tell them we're coming.'

Keeva stood awkwardly by the door.

'How have you been, Keeva?' the first officer asked. 'Keeping out of trouble?'

She pressed her lips together and clenched her fists so tightly her nails cut into her palms. Eventually her father appeared. Bent over, he limped towards the front door. Her heart was crushed seeing him like that.

'Mr O'Connor … Stanley,' the policeman greeted her father, his face registering shock at her father's appearance.

'Are you here about the assault?' he asked, barely able to move his lips.

'We're sorry, Stanley … Mr O'Connor, anything you say may be taken down and used in evidence against you. You are under arrest. We have been given orders to take you down to the station.'

Keeva's father hobbled inside to fetch his coat.

'What about his face? Aren't you going to ask what happened to him?'

'That's enough, Keeva,' interrupted her mother's sharp voice from the bedroom door. 'Tell them we are coming.'

Keeva ran into the house. 'Father!' She felt desperate. 'Please change your mind,' she pleaded. Even though she knew he wouldn't put up a fight.

'You know I can't, Kiki.' He turned to kiss her mother goodbye at the bedroom door.

'I'll be back soon,' he said, and gave Keeva a long hug. She wrapped her arms around his rough woollen jacket.

'Ooh, don't squeeze too tight, Kiki.'

She looked up at his wild-looking hair and bruised and swollen, but still handsome, face.

He held her face in his hands and said, 'I love you, Kiki, you remember that.'

'Da, I'm sorry for everything I said last night! I didn't mean it.'

'It's all right, I know.'

Tenderly he kissed her on the forehead with his swollen lips and turned to leave with the policemen either side of him.

Her heart pounding, she watched as the black Wolseley police car flickered away through the trees until it was lost from sight. Keeva felt hollowed-out and exhausted. She knew he would come back soon. They were just trying to scare him.

Chapter 32

20th March 1940, Forestry School, Parkend, Forest of Dean

Keeva sat on her little wooden chair in the dining hall after dinner, staring at the puke-green wall, where the paint was flaking off. She hadn't moved since the other girls had gone upstairs. She would never have chosen that colour. It made her feel like she wanted to vomit all over the wall. Then she noticed the fire extinguisher standing in the corner of the room, waiting for when it was needed. Little use now.

Her time at the Forest of Dean was near an end. What would happen now? She did not want to be alone any more. Dark clouds of smoke tortured her, tumbling trees ripped and cracked through every corner of her mind. What if she had remembered her satchel, or Gladys had come back with her or she had died instead? Maybe that would have been better.

'You all right, Keeva?' asked Rosie.

Keeva stared at the fire extinguisher, absorbed by its futility. The fire extinguisher would never be enough in a proper fire like the one in the forest.

'Come on, let's go up.' Rosie took her by the arm.

'Thank you, Rosie.'

But dread and nausea crushed Keeva's chest like a tree crashing down upon her. Like the moment she spun the handle on the fire alarm at school and knew there would be trouble. The overwhelming state of panic returned. Make it go away, she screamed inside.

Rosie held her more tightly. 'Come on, we're all in this together now.'

The stairs were steep and made her breathless on the way up to their room.

'We'll be all right.' Rosie smiled at Keeva and lay down on her bed by the fire.

Keeva walked slowly on to her bed in the corner and considered whether to go back home. She had lied to her family and run away and now she had to face the consequences of her actions alone. Then she looked around at Rosie, Edith, Lily and Beatrice and realised, perhaps for the first time, that she didn't feel alone. She wasn't a lone wolf any more; she was a lumberjill. Where there were once only lumberjacks, now there were lumberjills.

'Keeva,' whispered Edith.

She raised her chin.

'Have you seen Arthur yet?'

Oh Jesus, Edith. She shook her head and frowned.

Edith took a short intake of breath. 'You have to speak to him before we leave.'

She remembered her conversation with Edith that morning. But now was not the time to talk about Arthur.

'Oh yes,' said Rosie, sitting up on her bed. 'Keeva, he found you.'

What was Rosie talking about? Keeva's heart started beating quickly. He found me. Where?

'Nobody found me,' she coughed.

Lily bit her lip. 'We were worried we were going to lose you both.'

Rosie jumped out of bed and rushed over. 'You were hanging in his arms.'

'You might not be alive if he hadn't saved you, Keeva,' Beatrice added. 'Don't you remember?'

Her chest tightened with a sharp pain as she searched in her mind for something about Arthur. She remembered the view of Symonds Yat, arriving at the forest, leaving Gladys, her satchel, the plane, the explosion and then nothing.

'No,' she said breathlessly.

Rosie stared at her. 'But Keeva, do you not remember being in his arms? I wouldn't have minded being rescued like that.'

She knew that Rosie was trying to distract her but how could she say such things when Gladys had died? She couldn't talk, or think, about Arthur now. She started chewing on her knuckle. She remembered telling Edith she was going to speak to him and how much she liked him.

'I didn't ask to be rescued.'

'You would have died,' said Edith.

'Why didn't he save Gladys instead?'

'I don't think anybody could have saved Gladys,' said Beatrice.

'How do you know? How does anyone know?' Keeva couldn't remember anything. 'Why will nobody explain what happened?'

'Because the devil's favourite piece of furniture is the long bench.' Edith covered her lips quickly.

'Jesus, what does that mean?' Keeva rubbed her neck.

'Ssh, ssh. It's all right, Keeva. We all need to get some rest,' said Lily.

Keeva remembered that plane. She didn't have any doubts that it was British.

'Why don't they want anyone to know Gladys was killed by a British bomber?' she demanded.

'Keeva, listen to me.' Edith took her by the hands and looked into her eyes. 'What you don't know can't hurt you. But, if you are right about this British plane, it won't bring Gladys back. You understand that, don't you? We must all accept what has happened, so we can move forwards. We are at war and some of our loved ones have died.'

Keeva buried her head under her arm. She thought of her own father away in prison. Now Gladys's precious life was gone in an instant. None of it made any sense to her.

'It was just a dreadful accident,' said Lily.

A stiffness in her neck and shoulders made her look round at Lily awkwardly.

'Just an accident? She died doing war work for our country,' said Keeva.

'It could have been any one of us,' said Beatrice.

Edith stood up. 'This is not the time to be so emotional.'

'What?' Keeva yelled. 'Don't be so emotional? Our friend has been killed.'

'Killed?' said Edith.

Keeva wanted to run away as tears stung her eyes. Her mouth went dry and she remembered again the terrible pain of when her father went to prison. This memory now joined hands like a paper chain of people with Gladys and Hazel too. It was all too much. The shocked faces swirled round her like a nightmare.

Lily began to weep. 'Stop it, stop it,' she wailed, wrapping her blanket around herself. 'There's nothing we can say that will bring her back. Can't we have some calm? We are grieving the loss of the beautiful and happy girl we all knew Gladys to be.'

Overwhelmed with grief, Keeva wanted to leap out of her bed and run downstairs, lurch against the banisters, and push the door open to the forest air – to escape reality, the accident and Gladys's death.

Instead, she lay down on her bed. In her head, she ran out into the forest up towards Church Hill. She imagined it was getting dark outside, with the fog like a purply white blanket hanging in the sky, and soft-edged black twigs emerging from the mist as she ran along the path.

'Keeva,' said a voice.

She ignored it and imagined the noise of the camp left behind.

Her chest burned as she ran like an animal through a spider's web of trees, ascending towards the church. A shaft of light appeared on the path ahead of her and the moon shone through. How bright it seemed on this dark night. A figure appeared from the trees before her.

'Keeva,' Edith said.

Breathless, she jumped.

Edith sat on the side of her bed, took her in her arms and squeezed her tight.

'I'm so very sorry.'

Over Edith's shoulder, the girls she had lived with for the last two months were still there. Gladys had been right when she'd said Beatrice was so clever, Rosie was strong, Edith a loyal friend, and Lily brave; each one different, but stronger together. Feeling her panic subside, her eyes lingered on Gladys's empty bed at the other end of the room. The picture of her sweetheart Bernie smiled by her bed. When would he find out the love of his life was gone?

She got up and walked slowly over towards Gladys's bed. A lump showed under her covers and a pointy nose peeped out when she lifted the blanket. A small brown teddy bear with a tartan waistcoat lay beneath. Keeva had left her little Pippy, the puppy dog, behind because she was too grown-up for cuddly toys. But Gladys had brought Angus; he belonged to her nana and was from Scotland. Keeva hugged Angus in her arms. As she did, she could smell Gladys.

'What you got there?' asked Lily.

'Angus.'

'Let's have a butcher's,' said Rosie.

One by one the girls gathered round and took turns to stroke this little teddy's face and soft fur, as though it was Gladys herself.

'I wish I could hear her sing again,' said Keeva.

'We'll meet again,' sang Rosie, putting an arm around Keeva's shoulders, and Beatrice joined in.

Keeva felt the warmth of bodies huddle around her.

Lily sighed, 'God bless your happy soul, Gladys.'

The girls joined in.

'You were our dear friend.'

The sweet song drifted around them, as their voices came together in harmony, chests rising and falling. More girls from the other dormitory entered their room and sang along. Keeva longed for Gladys to hear, losing herself in the words, happy knowing Gladys had been singing as she'd taken her last breath.

Keeva sighed deeply as she looked up at all the girls gathered in the room, breathing and singing together in time. Dozens of them, standing around Gladys's bed. Keeva felt a real sense of belonging – something she had never felt before. All the girls standing together, in sisterhood, giving their last loving wishes to Gladys. The other girls began to drift out, back to their own rooms.

Every day was a sunny day with Gladys in the world. She made everyone believe they mattered, that Keeva mattered. Even on the hardest days, Gladys had said, 'Isn't it a wonder that some of the best days of our lives haven't even happened yet? Every morning I think it could be today.' Maybe she was right, and every day had been the best day of her life.

Rosie linked arms with Keeva. 'Do you think she heard?'

'She was singing too,' said Edith.

Beatrice was quiet. 'If only I'd appreciated Gladys more,' she said, 'like she seemed to appreciate me. I'm not sure I deserved her kindness.'

'Me neither,' said Edith. 'I wish I'd done something more for her, listened to her more. I've been so wrapped up in myself; it's all too late now.'

Rosie dropped onto her bed. 'She 'ad an 'eart of gold. There wasn't a more good-natured girl among us. She puts me to shame. You don't realise 'ow much you appreciate someone till they're gone.'

Lily came to stand at the end of her bed and crossed her heart. 'Like name, like nature; she had a good heart and she never judged me.'

The group seemed to settle into their own memories. Keeva realised with absolute clarity that Gladys had been there for them all and asked for nothing in return.

'She was like a sister I never 'ad,' said Rosie.

Keeva nodded, 'In sisterhood, Gladys.'

The five girls left in the room hugged each other. 'In sisterhood,' they repeated.

She needed something that would connect her to Gladys. The tape measure! If she hadn't returned to the lorry to fetch it when she did, she would have died. The tape measure had saved her. An effervescent energy coursed through Keeva, as she realised how glad she felt to be alive. She knew what she had to do next: she needed to speak to Arthur.

Chapter 33

22nd March 1940, Mallards Pike, Forest of Dean

Keeva stepped over the tree roots that pushed up through the path as she approached Mallards Pike lake. The morning sun dazzled her eyes through the branches. Every step closer made her more nervous. Today was her last chance to see Arthur, before she found out her next billet at midday. Then she would be sent to a new forest.

The stone-walled garden and cottage appeared through a gap in the trees, as a robin flashed across the lawn and disappeared into the forest. What would she say? Nothing came to mind, except that she noticed the trees rotting into the damp earth. There was fungus everywhere and the forest stank of death.

Her last-minute jitters as she approached the door tripped her up on a paving stone. A large tree stump, scarred by an axe, lay beside a pile of chopped wood by the door. She took a deep breath, knocked and waited. Inside, a chair scraped across the floor, and the cold air chilled her lungs as footsteps approached.

'He … llo, is Arthur in?' She clasped her sweaty hands together.

'Oh, he's not up yet.' The blonde-haired woman, who had a likeness to her son, smiled tenderly.

Keeva pulled back her hair, as wisps escaped on the wind. She was ready to turn and flee.

'But it's time he woke,' the woman added. 'Why don't you come in?'

The opened door breathed Keeva into the kitchen and in a moment she was inside Arthur's house. His mother was welcoming.

'Just a minute.' His mother brushed together her floury hands. 'He'll be right down.' She turned and hurried out of the room.

Keeva was left alone. Bread dough his mother had been kneading lay upon the kitchen table. There were oily rags on the floor, with a whetstone, and axes lined up against the wall. They were not like the blunt and damaged blades that the girls had to use. Without thinking, she picked up an axe and ran her finger across the smooth sharp blade.

'Arthur, there's someone here to see you,' his mother called out.

Keeva jumped, put the axe down quickly, and stroked her hair. She heard softly trodden footsteps meet up the stairs.

'You might want to get dressed.'

Her breath quickened as he came down the stairs wearing a beige nightshirt, open at the neck with some khaki long johns. Barefooted, like he'd just climbed out of bed, he seemed unaware that she was there. Noticing his sleepy eyes and puffy hair, she covered her mouth and giggled. Startled, his face lit up when he saw her. He smiled. How she loved that smile; he was so handsome, and her whole body tingled with joy.

'Oh, Mother! Just a minute.' His back, made broad by axe work, disappeared as he rushed back upstairs two steps at a time.

His mother returned with a smile and loitered in the kitchen. She looked pretty, with silver strands of hair sparkling in the light.

'How are you, love? Keeva, is it? I'm Nancy.'

How did she know? If she were honest, she'd say terrified. But if his mother, Nancy, was too kind, Keeva would cry.

'I'm fine.'

'I'm so sorry about Gladys. Can I give you a hug?' She opened her arms wide and pulled Keeva in gently towards her. The warmth of her soft bosom and hands firmly on her back made her feel safe. She remembered her father's final hug; she'd squeezed him too tight and it had hurt him. Arthur's mother gave her a squeeze now and said, 'It must be very hard for you.'

Keeva nodded. This warm reception was so different; Edward's parents had loathed her. Maybe she was good enough for Arthur's mother. Come to think of it, even her own mother had rarely hugged her. After a short time, Arthur was back in his brown slacks and cinnamon-coloured shirt. He grabbed an apple from the bowl, hopped his feet into his boots and beckoned to her.

'Are you coming?'

'Goodbye,' she said politely to his mother. She bumped into a chair, then steadied herself on the table before she stepped outside.

He hurried her out of the garden and into the forest, tucking his shirt into his trousers as he went.

'Wait!' Keeva rushed after him following the sweet smell of his cologne. Once they were out of sight of the cottage, with the apple between his teeth, he stopped to do up his laces.

'Are you in a hurry to get somewhere?' she asked.

He looked at Keeva briefly, dropped his half-eaten apple core and said, 'Away from my parents,' and rubbed his hand on his trousers. They walked side by side along the forest pathway; birds sung in the trees, new lime buds of spring pulsed with energy and created a vibrant hue around them on the wind. Branches swam to and fro, and Keeva looked up again at Arthur's face – made for a portrait in charcoal, the way his profile curved and dovetailed together perfectly at his lips.

Walking side by side with him felt like a moment of intimacy, where she alone could hear him breathe upon the breeze.

'I wanted to see you,' he said and took her hand. He slid his warm fingers between hers as they walked.

She was glad she had listened to Rosie and Edith. She didn't want to talk about the fire or thank him for saving her life; it seemed too dramatic and yet she could smell the fire and feel the heat again now he was with her. His hand squeezed hers.

'Are you all right?' he asked, slowing down to look at her intently.

She nodded but could not reply; her mind was too fuzzy.

'I'm sorry about Gladys,' he said.

'Why does everyone keep saying that to me?'

'I know you were good friends.'

'Can I ask you a question?' she asked, removing her hand from his.

'Of course.'

'Did anyone try to save Gladys?'

He wiped his hair from his brow and looked through the trees to the view up the forest towards Symonds Yat.

'We didn't know she was there,' he said.

She stopped and looked up at him. 'What do you mean?'

'We only realised when you told us. When you ran into the fire to save her.'

'Oh, I'm so sorry, I …'

'No, you risked your life to save hers.'

'And the girls said you risked your life to save mine,' said Keeva.

'No, I didn't. I know that's what people are saying, but I didn't. You crawled out of the burning forest on your own. You tried to save Gladys, not me,' he said.

'But I can't remember anything,' she said.

'Maybe it's for the best.'

'What do you mean? Do you know what happened?'

'No—' he hesitated '—not really.'

'You do.'

'I went to see what happened. The other fellers, who work with Father, told me to stand back. It all happened so fast.'

'What happened so fast?' Keeva asked.

'You came hurtling up and they tried to stop you. I tried too. But you kept saying Gladys, you had to save Gladys, and no one would listen, and eventually I let you go.'

'What do you mean?'

'I … I let you go. I couldn't stop you, and watched you run in towards the flames. You were so strong. I couldn't hold you back any more. I realised it was a mistake.'

'What was?'

'To let you go, to hold on to you … both. I didn't know what to do. The men were cursing me. But you knew where she was, and I thought just maybe there was a chance. But it was too late. If only I had let you go at the start.'

'Did they find Gladys?' asked Keeva, as a foul acrid taste filled her mouth.

Arthur's lips trembled and he nodded. No, no she didn't want to know. Her breathing came in spasms. Arthur took her hand again and marched her on through the forest, the breeze on her hair.

'Don't tell me.'

She held her throat and chest. He put his hand in his coat pocket and pulled out a folded newspaper, *The Western Daily Press* with yesterday's date – 21st March 1940 – and pointed to an article on page four.

'We think it was one of these.'

She read the headline aloud – 'The Raid on Sylt' – and looked up at Arthur.

'By far the most important air raid executed since war broke out was made by the RAF on Tuesday night when a sustained attack was launched on the seaplane base and other objectives on the island of Sylt. Altogether it's estimated thirty bombers took part.'

'The first British air attack on Germany?' she asked. He nodded.

'Nearly a thousand incendiary and high-explosive bombs,' she continued, 'were dropped during the course of the onslaught … terrific damage was inflicted – hangars in flames after direct hits, blazing oil tanks, a jetty and light railway reduced to ruins.' What has this got to do with it?'

'Read the end,' he said.

'The attacks made on Hörnum were spread over a period of seven hours through the night. All aircraft returned safely with the exception of two, one was badly damaged the other is presumed to have been lost.

'So what?' she asked.

'They took off from RAF Madley in Herefordshire, not far from where we were felling, and the last one landed just after half past eight yesterday morning.'

'How do you know?' she asked.

'Father knows the local firemen and police. The fire destroyed five acres of forest; nearby cottages had to be evacuated. They found mangled pieces of fuel tank.'

'So, it was a British bomber. I saw the insignia. No one believed me. They said I was confused because of the fire and smoke,' she said.

'Badly damaged, losing height … we think it needed to lighten its load and discharged its fuel tanks,' he said.

'Oh, Jesus Christ. Why not discharge into the River Severn, or somewhere else? Gladys didn't need to die.'

She looked back at the newspaper article and read aloud again.

'Above all, the episode is a welcome reminder that this "strange war" is not so dead as it sometimes seems, and that Great Britain is capable of taking a powerful initiative when the occasion suits.'

'Not so dead? Is there no mention of Gladys in the paper?' She flipped through the pages of the paper, scanning page after page for a mention of Gladys, and began to tremble.

'I'm so sorry,' he said.

She told herself to breathe.

They walked towards a stone wall, a dead end. She looked along the wall, which traversed the hillside, made of flint stones and bordered by gorse bushes on either side. There was nowhere else to go, and Keeva burst into tears. He took her into his arms. He was warm when she felt cold. He was kind when she felt the cruelty of war. He was there for her when she needed someone.

'The fire damage in the forest looks dreadful right now, but in time the green shoots of spring will push through, and the forest will grow back lush and green again. Maybe you can come back and see it then?'

She nodded and he wiped the tears from her cheeks with his rough thumb. Then, carefully placing his boot where the stones were missing, he climbed up onto the wall and reached out towards her. She took his hand, and stepped up.

From the wall, there was a view of the vast sky that skimmed the tops of the trees. It was so beautiful. She paused for a moment to regain her composure. Then she set off along the top of the wall, away, as if to escape from him. The stones were uneven and narrow so she raised her arms for balance, wondering if he would follow her.

'Where are you going?'

'This way,' she said.

As Keeva heard his footsteps behind her, she walked even faster. A thrill rose inside, like she was being chased, and so she ran. Wobbling at times, he pursued her. Some distance ahead of her there was a gap in the wall, maybe five foot wide, where a gorse bush stood. She could make the leap. She rocked backwards on her heels and ran, jumped and landed on the other side. She nearly fell as she turned around to see him hurtling through the air towards her.

Keeva screamed as he landed right behind her and grabbed on to her to keep himself upright, with a musky warm smell and his rough hands holding hers. As her feet inched backwards to make room for him, she wondered what it would be like to kiss his soft lips. He toppled to the ground.

'Come on, I want to show you something,' he said.

The drop down was six foot. Seeing him disappear into the woods, she jumped down to follow. Out of breath, she caught up where a pine had fallen against the crook of a huge oak. He was climbing his way up, balancing on the fallen trunk, which lay at an angle. She climbed up behind him and slowly they weaved through the branches making their way up together.

The wind blew across her arms, through the trees, as she dared herself to go higher. Dappled leaf shadows stroked the conifer. Short of breath, she held on tight to its branches, frightened of her brogues slipping. The leaf litter on the forest floor lay far below. The great brown bough of the oak tree lay ahead. Arthur, already there, held on to the trunk and reached down towards her. Their fingertips met.

'I've got you,' he said.

Keeva breathed out, pulled herself upwards and hugged a nearby branch, now safely enclosed in the great boughs of the oak. The wind rushed across the forest to their perch. The sky dazzled her eyes and the beat of her heart felt as conspicuous as the ringing of a school bell. He stared at her with his dark-brown eyes from the other side of the branch.

'You all right?' he asked.

'I've always wanted to climb a big tree like this,' she said.

'Have you?'

He stared back at her; cheeks flushed.

'I used to love the apple tree at home in the garden with its soft pink blossom and fresh green leaves, and I climbed it when the apples were rosy and ready to pick. How I loved to dangle my legs from a branch on those carefree summer days. I used to call it "my office", and because Da was a thatcher, he said his office was on a roof.' She giggled at the memory.

She didn't tell him that the tree had fallen down this winter.

'My father would never do that. Me and my old butties like climbing on rocks, trees, sheds and telegraph poles. You name it, we've climbed it – the higher the better. One day when Father came home, he caught me sitting on the top of our chimney stack. I thought I was king of the castle, but he went mad. He said I was taking unnecessary risks and Mother and he depended on me to be fit and well, so I could help with the business. Now, I have to keep a lot of secrets from him.'

'I saw you jumping across the tree stumps that day, with your friends and doing a handstand on one of them,' said Keeva.

'Oh yeah, the lads dared me to. I'll follow you if you want to go higher.'

She reached up for the branch above. He stood so close, his warm breath on her face. She grasped firmly around the branch, pulled herself upwards and found a foothold.

'Where now?' Keeva asked, holding on tightly.

'To your right,' he said, climbing up just above her.

She squeezed by him, her body brushed against his and she climbed further up through the oak tree, hands trembling. For a moment she looked down through her legs, feet pressed firmly apart against the branches. Arthur made his way up through the boughs beneath. Now was not the time to be afraid. She held on tight to the cool bark of the slimmer branches as they swayed gently in the wind.

Arthur looked so agile as he clambered up towards her. High enough, she sat on a branch and wrapped the nook of her green woollen elbow round another tree limb. He settled himself in front of her, so close. They coupled their legs, calves touching through her socks, his trousers.

He sucked on something.

'What are you eating?' she asked.

'A cola cube.'

Keeva groaned. She hadn't eaten a sweet for months. They could never afford them. 'Where did you get that from?'

'I found it in my pocket,' he said, smiling.

'Where's mine then?'

He fumbled in his pocket and brought out another, but it rolled across his palm and fell down through the branches.

'That was my last one,' he said.

'You're joking.'

A grin appeared on his face. 'You can share this one with me.'

She giggled and then he leant towards her. His lips, colder than hers, tasted otherworldly, cola sweet. Keeva tried to take the sweet but he didn't let go. He saw her smile, and so he leant forward again, and she received the warm cola cube in her mouth in a daze.

The trees rocked and they looked out across the forest to the horizon, where the green hue of trees in the distance turned to longing blue. Arthur had smoothed the sweet's sharp corners that used to scratch the roof of her mouth. She breathed in the exotic cola flavour and the forest breeze gently caressed her skin. Arthur kissed her cheek, still bruised from the forest fire, and, for a moment, she forgot to breathe. Palms and fingers clamped onto the branches steadied her light head.

They made their way back down through the limbs of the oak tree, Keeva with more confidence. About twelve feet from the ground, Arthur grabbed a branch and swung down horizontally, as it bowed under his weight and sprung him upwards again, as if on a coiled spring. Keeva gasped.

'You're crazy,' she said. 'What if it breaks?'

He swung down and up again, each time as if he were falling out of the tree only to be pulled back upright. He took great delight in smiling each time he appeared up alongside her, like a jack-in-a-box, then leapt and swung down to the ground.

'Watch out,' he yelled as Keeva ducked to avoid the branch springing back upwards.

She took the springy branch and jumped off as it bowed under her weight.

He shouted, 'Let go', and grabbed on to her as she landed.

'Oh, my goodness, that was terrifying,' she said.

She held on to his firm body, safely on the ground and out of breath. She looked up and kissed him. His lips were full. She kissed him again. Small kisses at first. Her breath lingered upon his mouth as he squeezed her in his arms; she felt wonderful and so dizzy.

'I was so worried about you in the fire,' he said.

Intense feelings torched through her body; his fingers on her cheek made her glow with pleasure as he kissed her again. Patches of light shone through the leaves. Little holes through to the sky and freedom beyond appeared, as she shivered with excitement. She lost herself as their fingers intertwined once more.

'Oh Jesus, sorry, what time is it?' she said.

He pulled out his brass pocket watch with roman numerals. 'Nearly half past eleven.'

'I've got to be back. We've got a meeting at midday to find out our next billets.'

'Here, take my watch. Keep it, until I see you again,' he said.

'I can't.'

'Please.'

He opened her palm and lay the smooth-backed watch inside, still warm from his breast pocket, so close to his chest.

'Thank you.'

But now she had to go back to the girls to resolve some things with her friends. She pulled herself away from him, took one more look into his brown eyes, kissed him and said, 'Goodbye, Arthur.'

'Write to me,' he replied.

'I will.'

Chapter 34

Keeva turned and ran back towards Parkend, along the sandy path that burned orange in the near midday sun. She couldn't be late today. She stopped to catch her breath for a moment and looked up to the top of the hill, remembering the chalk ridge back home where the edges of the earth met the sky. She continued upwards, giddy on the pine breeze sighing in the trees. Arthur wanted her to write, to see her again. He didn't mind that she was the daughter of a conscientious objector. He liked her just the way she was.

Panting, she arrived at the top of Church Hill, opened the latch on the gate, which clunked shut behind her. She was now fond of the well-worn footpath. She passed the church, through into the graveyard. Some headstones were old and grey, covered in lichen; others too new, recently set in the soil. The sun dazzled her eyes as she looked out across the view of the forest, her heart beating loudly as she remembered dear Gladys with affection. She could see her blonde hair shining in the sun, and her smile that brightened the day.

She turned to leave and saw the arched doorframe where she had sat that wretched night, hiding from the storm, after Beatrice had read her father's letter. How unfairly she'd felt treated; she'd hated Beatrice and Rosie back then. But now they were her friends. In a strange way, she could see that some good had come of that evening, when Beatrice had exposed her painful secret. Rejected and humiliated by her friends, like a plaster being removed quickly, the disclosure had hurt; but, with everything out in the open the wound had had time to heal.

She continued through the graveyard and remembered Beatrice's money. She still kept it, like a dirty secret, in her sock at the bottom of her bag. She wanted to finally return the money to her now, but how? Out of the sun, beneath the trees, she could smell frost on the air. What if she hid the envelope? There were few hiding places in the dormitory, except under suitcases, and she didn't want anyone else to get in trouble. She imagined sliding the money under Beatrice's pillow or mattress in the hope that she would find it before she left, but there was no guarantee she would.

She could hand it back to her privately with an apology, but not if all the girls were present. She might have little time before they all said goodbye. Perhaps Missus Potter could find it. The imposing three-storey forestry school rose ahead of her, the place she had called home for the last two months. New shoots were appearing on the lacy web of creepers beside the grand pillars of the porch. She pushed the front door. Her time here had ended so abruptly, she wasn't ready to go.

'Keeva, there you are,' said Missus Potter. 'I just wanted to say farewell to you, my dear. I am really going to miss you.' Missus Potter held out her arms and embraced Keeva, holding her head into her shoulder.

'Do come back and see us, won't you?' The dear old lady looked her in the eye.

Missus Potter had always been so kind.

Keeva lay a hand on her heart. 'Of course, I will.'

She could not bear embroiling her in the rediscovery of the stolen money. Captain Blunt passed by and entered his office.

'Captain Blunt, can I have a word, please?' She followed him inside, not waiting for his reply.

'I have a special request, please.'

'What is it? Spit it out,' he replied.

'That all the girls from room two stay together on the next posting. Wherever we go, be it Scotland or Kent, we must stay together.'

'Hmm … I'm sorry,' Captain Blunt said, 'the posts have already been decided.'

She sighed as her spirits slipped, wishing she'd asked sooner; but at least she had tried.

'What are their names?'

'There's Edith Walker.' She wished she had been more generous towards her, especially on the morning of the accident.

'Rosie Worsell.' She wanted to stay with Rosie because she would be good fun.

'Lily Wingham.' Dearest Lily, who was so honest and caring.

'And Beatrice Oxley.' She couldn't leave her out; she knew what that felt like.

Captain Blunt did not say a word but seemed to listen as he made a note of each name in his book.

He paused for a moment and then looked over to his desk. 'There was a letter from Lady Gertrude Denman today.'

Whoever was this Lady Gertrude Denman he kept mentioning? Wasn't she the one who had asked for them to be sent to the Timber Trade meeting? That had been a disaster. The same lady who, according to Blunt, was meddling in war work? She didn't like the sound of this.

Captain Blunt thumbed through his in tray and then splayed the papers across his table.

'Here we are.' He pulled the letter from the envelope. 'Women's Land Army Headquarters. Balcombe Place. Yes.' He grabbed his glasses and began to read aloud:

'Dear Captain Blunt, thank you for your letter of the twentieth of March. On behalf of the Women's Land Army, we would like to express our deepest sympathy for the loss of Miss Gladys Goodheart. The accident whereby she lost her life was utterly tragic.

I hope that you are all managing to cope with the dreadful shock.'

He tilted his head, looked over his glasses and intently observed Keeva, then – to her relief – returned his gaze to the letter. 'We also confirm that Miss Hazel Hardy has been signed off on medical grounds.' His voice lowered in tone, as he said, 'Dear, oh dear.'

'I understand that there will be a certain amount of delay before you are able to place all the girls that have passed their training into forestry work.' Captain Blunt raised his eyebrows as he read on.

She wished he'd hurry up. She didn't have time to listen to him droning on, reading out every word of the letter; she had to get back upstairs to sort the stolen money out.

'Therefore, the clerk of works at Balcombe Estate office has requested six temporary volunteers to assist for two months in timber work, principally planting.'

Captain Blunt rubbed his lips, while in thought. 'I'm sorry, Keeva, but I can't see what I can do at this late stage.'

'Thank you anyway, Captain Blunt.'

Now she had a more urgent matter to address. With that she raced up the stairs, two steps at a time, remembering her beautiful morning in the forest with Arthur.

As she entered the room, Rosie yelled at her, 'I can't believe you've made it back on time. You nearly missed our transfer to the station, while scampering around the forest with Arthur. We were going to have to send a search party for you.'

'Rosie, I need to talk to you.' Keeva checked for any girls outside on the landing.

'That's a coincidence.'

'Where is everyone?' Keeva asked.

'Fetching their clothes from the laundry and drying room, returning towels,' said Rosie. 'I wanted to speak to you too. I'm thinking about going home, Keeva, and I just wanted to let you know. My mum needs me and, after Gladys, I can't let anything happen to Mum.'

'No, Rosie, you can't; I need you too.'

'No, I'm going to help my mum out. She's written again and me old man's turned worse. I can't ignore her.'

Keeva couldn't imagine carrying on without Rosie, she wanted her to stay.

'I'd rather not go back to the factory. But family comes first, right?' said Rosie.

'You can't choose your family, but you can choose what's best for you, Rosie.' Keeva shoved her hand inside her bag and scrabbled for the sock. The thick cream paper crackled as she pulled at the envelope.

'Blimey, it's Christmas come early,' Rosie said with a giggle.

Keeva showed her the envelope. 'Give it to your mother. Send it back to her like you planned.'

'I thought you'd spent the money.'

'It's all there. Take it,' Keeva whispered as she heard girls' voices come from the bottom of the stairwell, among them Beatrice's distinctive accent. She could not understand why Rosie didn't snatch the money with glee.

'Quickly, take it.' She held the money towards Rosie. 'They're coming.'

Rosie grabbed the envelope and paused for a moment. Footsteps were coming up the stairs. Rosie groaned and strutted across the room, lifted Beatrice's art deco leather suitcase from the floor and put it on the bed, flipped the catches and opened the lid. She slipped the envelope inside the green and red shot silk pleated pocket in the lid of the case. Keeva's mouth fell open and her eye darted towards the stairs.

'There. All done now,' said Rosie. She closed the lid, popped the catches shut and returned the suitcase to where she'd found it.

Beatrice reached the landing outside: '… the staff might expect a tip before we leave.' A second later she appeared through the door with Lily and Edith, bearing washed dungarees, Aertex shirts, socks and underwear over their arms. The dormitory felt warm and stuffy, so Keeva wrestled with the window to let some fresh air in. She took a deep breath and began to strip her bed of the grey blankets and sheets. Catching Edith's eye, she raised her eyebrows and gave her a wry smile.

'Well, how was it?' asked Edith, coming over.

'Wonderful, truly wonderful,' Keeva said, in a hushed tone.

'Oh, I'm so pleased. I knew he liked you.'

'I wanted to ask you something, Edith,' said Keeva, taking her hand.

'Of course.'

'If there was any chance that we could … well, if we had an opportunity to choose who we could be billeted with after the Forest of Dean …'

'Yes?'

'Well, I would like to be with you,' said Keeva.

'Oi, what about me?' said Rosie.

'And you.'

'Oh, I'm sorry, I agreed I'd be paired with Beatrice,' Edith said with a sad smile.

'Of course. Don't worry, I'm too late. Could we at least keep in touch? I just wish we could all stay together,' said Keeva.

'Me too,' Edith sighed.

'I don't believe it.' Beatrice took a sharp breath. She was sitting on her bed, her open suitcase beside her, holding a cream envelope.

Keeva was alarmed to see her pull out the green notes, which flashed in her hand. Nervously she flicked a sideways glance to

Rosie, who was busying herself with stripping her bed and folding blankets, dust flying on the air.

'Is that your tip for the staff?' asked Lily. 'I'm sure Missus Potter would be pleased.'

'No, Lily—' Beatrice fanned herself with the notes '—it's the missing money.'

'Where did you find it? Lily asked.

'In my suitcase pocket.'

'Are you sure it wasn't there all along, Beatrice?' said Lily.

'Of course I am. I would have looked in there, wouldn't I? Edith, you can vouch for me, can't you?'

Edith nodded.

'We would have seen an envelope that size. Edith, did you look in the pocket?'

'I didn't see it in the pocket.'

'There.'

The room fell silent.

Uncharacteristically, Rosie didn't try to wind up Beatrice. She said nothing. But Keeva knew Beatrice was watching them both intently. Keeva couldn't help looking up, and Beatrice caught her eye.

'Can you offer an explanation, Keeva?'

Keeva shook her head and Beatrice turned her attention to Rosie.

'You,' said Beatrice. 'I knew it was you.'

Keeva swallowed as she watched Beatrice stand up and walk slowly towards Rosie, her heels clicking on the wooden floorboards.

'You've got it back now,' said Rosie, staring at her.

'You violated me,' she said.

'I think you're jumping to conclusions,' Rosie replied.

The two women stood face to face, inches apart.

'I should have reported you to the police.'

Rosie stepped away. 'I … I'm sorry for what I did.'

'Well, you should have considered that before.'

'Look, I want to get myself a good job, put this behind me. Please don't report me.'

Beatrice walked back to her suitcase and snapped the lid shut. She struggled to find the key in her purse to secure the locks. Keeva's heart thumped; she couldn't let Rosie get into trouble.

'Rosie didn't take the money for herself. She wanted to give it to her mother. Isn't that right, Rosie? Tell her why.'

'We've got no money, Beatrice; we're bleedin' coals and coke and you arrived off the train with all this money and fancy clothes. I wanted to give Mum a new start.'

'Lay it on thick, why don't you?' Beatrice replied. 'That's no excuse.'

'You wouldn't miss a few pounds, would you?' said Rosie.

Beatrice suddenly looked across at Keeva. 'Hold on, so you knew too?'

'The money was exchanged with the letter in my bag from my father,' Keeva explained.

Lily and Edith looked worried.

'I had no idea,' said Lily.

'Why didn't you give it back to me?' asked Beatrice, turning to Keeva.

'It wasn't your place to read out her letter, Beatrice,' said Lily.

Beatrice shot Lily an angry look.

'I didn't know what you would do. You'd already accused me of taking the money. My father was in prison and I was scared, so I kept it until today when I gave it back to Rosie.'

Edith stepped forwards. 'Beatrice, she's given you the money back. Haven't we lost enough of our friends? I've stood by you throughout, but I can't on this. None of us like being judged for our mistakes. Show some understanding.'

'I know what Gladys would have done,' said Lily. 'She would have forgiven Rosie.'

Keeva had never experienced someone stick up for her before.

Beatrice was stunned to silence. After a moment, she said, cautiously, 'So, you gave the money back to me, Rosie. And how is your mother?'

'My old man is not well and when he's had a jug of wallop, he lashes out at her. I was worried he was going to kill her when I left.'

Beatrice walked back slowly towards Rosie and thrust the money in her hand.

'Keep it and send it to your mother,' she said.

'What?'

'Take it, before I change my mind.'

'I didn't expect you to do that.' Rosie rubbed her eyes, and Keeva felt a lump in her throat.

'It's yours. My mother replaced my lost money over a month ago.'

'Thank you. You may have just saved my mum.' Rosie sniffed as she wiped her cheek on her sleeve.

Missus Potter appeared at the door. 'Is everything all right dears? The rest of the group are waiting for you downstairs to find out their next billet.'

'Everything's all right, Missus Potter,' said Lily. 'Let's get down there, girls.'

Keeva threw her arm around Rosie and gave her a squeeze, as Rosie wiped her eyes. Beatrice skittered down the stairs, and Edith and Lily squealed, as they leapt round the bannisters and jumped the last four steps to the ground floor. Keeva linked arms with Edith and Rosie, and together they marched into the lime-green dining hall, where Captain Blunt and the rest of the girls waited for them. With suitcases and bags stacked up ready for the trucks to take them back to Norchard Station, they squeezed through to join the rest of the girls. Captain Blunt tapped a spoon against a glass and waited for the crowd of girls to quieten down.

He raised his hands and said, 'Settle down, girls. Much to our surprise, we have noticed that figures have shown an increase in timber production in the Forest of Dean over the last few months. The amount of timber measured and felled is up, up, up. We have high hopes for a dozen more sawmills in the Forest of Dean by the end of this year. We hope to become one of the great powerhouses of timber production in the war, so vital for victory. No doubt down to the exceptional programme, I am pleased to say you have all passed your training. You are now, officially, new members of the Forestry Section of the Women's Land Army, and ready for action out in the forests of Britain.'

The girls cheered and Rosie threw her beret high into the air. With that, the rest joined in.

'Calm down, girls, please,' Blunt said. 'Some of you have shown promise as measurers, and others as fellers, and I'm sure there will be some opportunities for you.'

Captain Blunt hesitated as he looked at Keeva.

'And, although it is against my better judgement to say such things, I know all the wishy-washy emotional stuff is important to you girls.' He inhaled, shook his head and said, 'Well done.'

Beatrice put her arm around Keeva's shoulders and smiled.

'Well done, Keeva, you made it through.'

'Thanks.'

Captain Blunt tapped a spoon against his glass once more.

'I know you are all keen to know your next billet and so I do not want to keep you waiting any longer. I do, however, want to warn you that this is where the real work begins; you've had it easy on training camp. The work will be more gruelling out in the forest, especially working amongst the timber merchants who will not offer you the same care as we have done here on camp.'

Did he really just say 'care'? Keeva raised an eyebrow.

'In that, umm … as itinerant workers you will have to move where the work goes. You will have to find your own billets on occasion, cook your own food and so forth. I have it on bon avis that merchants are not keen to employ girls. But our nation desperately needs timber, so we are sending you to the places with the highest demand first. And, without further ado, here are your billets. Some of you are in pairs, others in threes, and, before you ask, we have tried to put you with your friends.'

'The posts are as follows: Mary Broadhead, Edna Packwood and Dorothy Turner – Chartham in Kent. You will be going to one of the large sawmills there.'

'Lucky escape,' said Rosie.

Keeva hung on every word he said. The names from the list went on and on, until at last, she heard her name.

'Keeva O'Connor is to be posted with Rosie Worsell, Edith Walker, Beatrice Oxley and Lily Wingham in Sussex.'

'We're all together,' Rosie said as she lifted Keeva off her feet and spun her round.

Keeva was reeling to hear him mention Sussex. Which part of Sussex and how far from her parents would she be? Just as she had resolved to stay in the Land Army, she did not want to be billeted back at home.

'You'll be pleased to hear,' said Blunt, 'we have put you on lighter forestry duties, such as measuring, and the nice and easy stuff like burning brushwood and planting trees, clearing up after the men. There are lots of smaller woodlands in Sussex, so you'll be helping out with census work too, finding out how much timber is in each wood, and how much will be cleared. Balcombe is not far from the coast, for a little rest and recuperation. But it will be no holiday, mind.'

'What's the matter, Keeva?' asked Edith.

'Oh nothing,' she said, 'I'm so pleased.' She knew she didn't look so pleased.

'We're together, aren't we?' Edith said.

'Yes,' she said, hugging Edith.

She could almost hear the determination in her mother's voice, quoting the Roman philosopher Tacitus: 'the desire for safety stands against every great and noble enterprise. That is why we must live a life of uncertainty on the edge of society, risk our freedom in the hope of a better world.' She would go back to visit her mother when the time was right. She needed to set things straight, discover news about Dilly and her father, in time.

The girls gathered round. Keeva had spent much of her life wanting to be accepted, but looked down on the other girls as somehow inferior. Now, she realised, she was proud to be one of the girls.

'How could I leave now?' said Rosie with a wink.

'Let's pause to remember Gladys,' said Edith. They lent their heads together in the middle.

'She'll always be with us in spirit,' said Lily. Ten boots moved round in a circle: arms woven round their waists.

'Whatever we do, we'll do it for you, Gladys,' said Rosie, beginning to laugh.

'And we'll fight this war from the forests of Britain,' added Beatrice.

'We will ensure Gladys's life is not forgotten,' said Keeva.

Each one with different strengths: Beatrice with a mind for mathematics; Rosie a great sense of humour and mischief; Edith a wise and loyal friend; while Lily had the endurance and courage of a rock. In her heart, Keeva knew creativity was her closest ally. They were all different, but together they were stronger.

'Just because we're taking on a job that society said is for men, because they are the stronger sex,' Keeva said, 'it doesn't mean society is right. So, no matter what they think, we must prove them wrong. We can do this job, just as well as – if not better than – the men. Maybe one day we'll drive the lorries too, don't you think?'

'Hear, hear,' said Beatrice.

Keeva was certain the first British raid on Germany would result in many more revenge attacks against Britain. She had now witnessed the horrors of war her father spoke of, and Gladys's death showed its futility. And, like her father, Keeva realised her conscience was a precious possession. Her father stood by his conscience, not out of cowardice, but in courage, risking his own physical freedom to let his conscience be free. Like her father, Keeva had to be true to herself and listen to her own inner guide.

Captain Blunt passed amongst the girls with a cardboard tray containing some brass badges. 'Take one and pass them on,' he said. 'We thought you needed a badge and we took inspiration from the Royal Pioneer Corps combatant corps. The pair of crossed axes was an obvious choice for you girls.'

Keeva took the dainty badge in her fingers, no larger than a small pine cone. Two beautifully curved brass handles lay over one another and formed a diagonal cross with strong angular axe heads looking outwards. Keeva knew she would cherish the badge with pride as she pinned it to her chest. She was now a lumberjill.

Epilogue

Lewes Prison, Sussex
22nd March 1940

To my dearest daughter Keeva,

I hope you are safe and well, my child. As you can see, I have now arrived at Lewes Prison for my sentence. As you know, I am only allowed to send or receive one letter a month and the prison guard chose to give me yours. Thank you. Of course, I have been thinking about you ever since. And even though I am writing to you, not knowing where to send this letter or whether my words will ever reach you, I want you to know how much you are loved.

If only I knew where you were? You mentioned a forest. There are so many in our country. Where would you live in a forest and with whom? We only have a few remaining family friends in London. If only you had uncles or aunties you could have gone to stay with. Remember that in the first war, within a very short space of time, your mother lost her brother, her mother and two best friends, as I did my brothers. The shock waves that have affected our lives, now cast a shadow upon yours. I am so sorry, my dearest Keeva.

In a week you will be seventeen on March 28th and so I've been thinking about the day you were born. Do you remember how much you loved to hear this story? How your mother and I were so excited for your arrival that we couldn't sleep? We set off in the dark to walk slowly up to the top of the South Downs to see the golden sunrise above the sea. What a glorious view and beautiful moment, filled with all the expectant joy of your arrival. By the time we were home and had brewed a strong tea, your entrance into the world came so quickly. Your mother said she expected you to be a boy, the way you kicked inside. I had already delivered, washed and wrapped you in soft blankets by the time

I opened the door to the doctor.

Your mother never wanted you to know until now, but she lost two babies after Dilly was born and before you arrived. The tragic loss of those two children has weighed heavily on her and affected her nerves. And so that is why we say you were like a miracle from the gods. You were such a wanted child. I am sure your mother misses your beautiful face and comforting presence in the house every day.

You have always been strong-willed, determined to do things your own way. She never wanted to be like other parents that squashed their children's personalities and gave them a conventional outlook on life, and I agreed. Although sometimes I wondered whether I was too lenient. But I thought the sooner you started making decisions for yourself the better.

You are so independent. I always knew how brightly your spirit shone. But I realise now that I have been too wrapped up in my own troubles and I forgot that you had the call of the wild and a fire in your belly. When you feel wronged, you are quick to ignite and fast to take off on the breeze like a wildfire. You always have been. My dearest Keeva, I understand why you left. I am not cross with you. I was young once too.

The prison guard is shouting and clanging on the doors, I must go. I pray that you will write to me or your mother to let us know you are safe and that one day I may give you this letter myself.

Your loving father xxx
P.S. I love you!

Acknowledgements

My greatest admiration and thanks go to all the women I met who bravely worked in the forests and served in the Women's Timber Corps during World War II. They not only took on tough work in gruelling winters, but also coped with prejudice in doing what was thought to be 'a man's job' in the 1940s. My sincere thanks go to the original Lumberjills and their families who, over the last decade, have shared with me their wonderful stories, letters, photos and memories with incredible generosity. You are my absolute inspiration!

To my dearest writing buddy, Alice Fowler, my deepest thanks for your brilliant comments on my writing, and your dedication and support in my writing journey. Thank you to my dear friend, Sophie Artemis, for being so willing to read my book – over and over again – with such enthusiasm, from the very first draft in 2016. Thank you to Suzanne Goldring for her unwavering support and encouragement, over many years, in getting my book published.

For reading and commenting on my manuscript, I thank: Donna Hillyer – copy-editor, Catherine Brown – proofreader, Ruth Brandt, Helen Allen, Helen Dickens, Aggie Johansson-Hartley, Anne Kealey, Fiona Newcomb-Hicks, Debbie Roberts, Sara Waterfield and Philippa Young. Many thanks to Marcus Wehrle for typesetting and to my cover designer Richard Ljoenes.

A very special thanks to my daughters, Lucy and Milly; my brother, Marcus; sister, Leisa; and Mum, for all their love, support and encouragement. A final thanks to my dad for buying me an axe for Christmas, before I had ever heard of the Lumberjills.

About the author

Joanna Foat is the author of Lumberjills: Britain's Forgotten Army, the definitive history of the Women's Timber Corps in WWII, published by The History Press in 2019. With a love of nature, she is an environmental communications consultant and works for a nature charity. She writes about protecting wildlife – from birds, butterflies and bees, to recovering wild landscapes, forests, rivers and seas.

Joanna first discovered the Lumberjills in 2012 when she worked for the Forestry Commission (now Forestry England), and was surprised she'd never heard of them. With a wild and adventurous spirit, she had a heartfelt desire to tell their forgotten story. Joanna travelled the country to meet over sixty of the original women to uncover their wartime stories. In their late eighties and nineties, many of them could hardly believe anyone was interested in them after all that time.

Joanna dedicated ten years to researching the Lumberjills, giving TV and radio interviews and many public talks to raise awareness of these incredible women. Joanna first decided to write a novel about the Lumberjills in 2012 and completed her first version in 2016. However, she then decided that she must write the history of the Lumberjills, in honour of the women she had met. After The History Press published Lumberjills: Britain's Forgotten Army, Joanna went back to the novel, started again, and has written the first in a series of novels: The Lumberjills: Stronger Together.

A note from Joanna

Thank you so much for reading The Lumberjills Stronger
Together. If you enjoyed this book and would like to keep up
to date with the latest news and talks on the Lumberjills and
be the first to hear about the next book in The Lumberjills
series please sign up to my newsletter. Your email address
will never be shared and you can unsubscribe at any time.

thelumberjills.uk/signup

If you are interested in finding out more about the original
Lumberjills, you may recognise some of the stories from
this novel in my history book, Lumberjills Britain's
Forgotten Army. I was lucky enough to meet so many
of the women who served for their nation in the forests
and wrote the definitive history of the Women's Timber
Corps in WW2, which is available in bookstores.

I love hearing from my readers, so please get in touch
on my website, Instagram, Twitter or Facebook.

With best wishes, Joanna

You can connect with Joanna Foat at:

thelumberjills.uk
instagram.com/jofoat
twitter.com/jofoat
facebook.com/thelumberjills.uk

Lumberjills: Britain's Forgotten Army

When war was declared in 1939, Britain was almost completely dependent on imported timber – but only had seven months of it stockpiled. Timber was critical to the war effort: it was needed for everything from aircraft and shipbuilding to communications and coal mining.

The British timber trade was in trouble. Enter the Lumberjills. Lacking in both men and timber, reluctantly the government opened timber work for women to apply – and apply they did.

The Women's Timber Corps had thousands of members who would prove themselves as strong and smart as any man: they felled and cross-cut trees by hand, operated sawmills, and ran whole forestry sites. They fought their own battles on the home front – for respect and equality. In Lumberjills: Britain's Forgotten Army, researcher Joanna Foat tells their story for the first time, and gives them the recognition they so truly deserve.

Printed in Great Britain
by Amazon

30317829R00202